# SHARK

Cover design by David Stockman

Novels by Brian Nicholson
featuring John Gunn

GWEILO

AL SAMAK

ASHANTI GOLD

FIRE DRAGON

CALYPSO

SHARK

# SHARK

BRIAN NICHOLSON

TRAFFORD PUBLISHING

Order this book on line at www.trafford.com/
or email orders@trafford.com

Most Trafford titles are also available at major online book retailers.



ISBN: 978-1-4269-1716-5 (sc)

*Our mission is to efficiently provide the world's finest, most comprehensive book publishing service, enabling every author to experience success. To find out how to publish your book, your way, and have it available worldwide, visit us online at www.trafford.com/10510.*

Trafford rev. 10/26/2009

**TRAFFORD**
**PUBLISHING**
www.trafford.com

**North America and International**
toll-free: 1 888 232 4444 (USA & Canada)
phone: 250 363 6864 + fax: 812 355 4082

To D, Charlie and Sasha

# Acknowledgements

I am most grateful to many people who gave me advice on various aspects of SHARK, but there are those who require a special mention. Charlie who devoted months to the task of editing the final draft; Tony Hockley, a celebrated neurosurgeon, for his detailed medical advice; Sasha and all her friends who have assisted with the viral marketing of my novels; David Stockman for his front cover design and lastly, for those serving and retired members of the British and US Armed Forces who made sure that all the military detail was accurate.

# FOREWORD

In 1988, after a series of damaging leaks and defections in MI5 and MI6, the Prime Minister tasked a relatively young Major General, who had retired at the age of 48, with the complete reorganisation of the UK's Intelligence Services. After retirement he had redirected his talents into management consultancy and turned two companies from near bankruptcy to healthy, profit-making concerns.

Within eighteen months of being given the remit to set up an effective, efficient and secure intelligence service, he had created the British Intelligence Directorate. Both the espionage and counter-espionage branches were brought under the same roof which immediately resulted in improved dissemination of intelligence and operational effectiveness. Very few MI5 and MI6 personnel survived the stringent security vetting initiated by the new director. The two buildings at Millbank and Vauxhall Cross were retained, but only for a limited period during the changeover, as an overt intelligence front. In reality they had little more than a clerical role for low grade classified material.

Kingsroad House was purpose-built for BID in Cale Street to the north of the King's Road. Outwardly it claims to be the head office of Express Delivery Services (EDS). Access to EDS is by the main entrance on Cale Street while access to BID is either via the main entrance or via the 10th floor of the adjacent multi-storey NCP car park. There are two other headquarter buildings; one in Kingston-on-Thames and another in Southampton. Both have a similar layout to Kingsroad House but with subtle variations in case security were to be compromised.

Kingsroad House has 14 above-ground floors, with a helipad on the 15th floor. There are 3 basement levels, which contain BID's emergency medical centre - the main medical facility is at Maidenhead - an extensive transport department, stores, a small armoury and a shooting range. The lowest basement level also provides access to four exit routes for use by BID staff to leave the building avoiding any form of surveillance.

BID has been operational since 1990.

# PROLOGUE

**Shark** 2 ▪ n. *informal* a person who dishonestly obtains money from others. Oxford Dictionary.

The human species is infinitely more lethal than the fish. Anon.

## THE GULF WAR 1991 – OPERATION GRANBY

General Norman Schwarzkopf considered the US Special Forces to be nothing more than a bunch of prima donna gangsters who had no place in a firmly disciplined army. His entire combat experience had come from repeated tours in Vietnam, where he'd watched them balls it up again and again. As far as he was concerned, Special Forces operations rarely lived up to their exaggerated reputation, and he was convinced that the SAS wouldn't be any different. He was certain that here was nothing they could do that the main Coalition Forces couldn't do better, especially with their overwhelming air superiority.

General Sir Peter de la Billière, Commander of the British Forces and an ex-commanding officer of 22 Special Air Service Regiment, thought differently. Although too diplomatic ever to say it, he knew the SAS operated in a different league. Instead, he called on every trick in his negotiating skills to persuade General Schwarzkopf of the value of using the SAS to cause diversions ahead of the main attack on the Iraqi Forces occupying Kuwait. There was certainly plenty for them to do. Both his and General Schwarzkopf's over-riding concern was to prevent Saddam Hussein from launching his Scud missiles at both Israel and the Coalition bases in Saudi Arabia risking retaliation and escalation to nothing less than World War Three. It was vital to find them. The mission for 22 SAS - in this case, for Bravo Squadron of the Regiment - was to identify both Scud launchers and radar and communications centres and then direct A10 'tank-busters', F15 Eagles and RAF Tornadoes onto the targets. The plan was to insert three teams on the night of 22nd January, six days before the main attack on 28th January.

But the war started five days early. Just before dawn on 17th January, eight Apache attack helicopters destroyed all the Iraqi air defence radars, allowing the Coalition Air Forces unhampered access to all their targets. The A10s and Tornadoes could now seek out the Scud launchers without any risk of being shot down by air defence missiles. Although not negating the need for the SAS mission, it was less vital. But Peter de la Billière was convinced they could still be a useful diversion.

Three eight-man SAS teams were inserted by Chinook helicopters on the night of 22nd January, operating out of the northern Coalition base of Al Jawf, closest to the main supply routes (MSR) between Baghdad and Jordan. These were being used by Saddam Hussein to deploy his Scud launchers. The MSR from Baghdad to the Jordanian border - in constant use by the Iraqi forces - split into three routes

60 miles west of Baghdad, one taking a northern route to Rawah, another to Qasr al Khubbaz and the southern one to Ar Rutbah, where all three joined up for the last 50 miles to the border with Jordan. As the Iraqi radars had all been destroyed, the hastily revised mission was to monitor these three routes and identify the Scud launchers, and any other high value target, and then call in the strikes.

At the mounting base at Al Jawf, the teams carried out last minute equipment checks, rehearsed drills and, as confirmation of the mission arrived, loaded onto the Chinook helicopters which lifted off and carried them at near-zero altitude into the desolate and inhospitable Iraqi desert.

Only two men of one of the teams of Bravo Squadron would return.

*

The report dictated by Cpl Harker on completion of the mission was typically terse and brief in its content. One of the three teams, it stated blandly, had decided not to take its Landrovers and was unable to use its satcom radio because of an inexplicable military cock-up which resulted in the issue of incompatible frequencies to communicate with SAS Tactical HQ in Saudi Arabia. It continued:

*"Team 2 then bumped a company-sized Iraqi force of approximately a hundred well-armed soldiers and was unable to call for help from the remainder of Bravo Squadron, who were on standby for a rescue mission. Three of its Troopers were killed, four were captured by the Iraqi Forces and one Trooper escaped to Syria. Team 1 chose to*

*take more equipment and opted to use its Landrovers; it returned intact to the mounting base in Saudi Arabia. Team 3 decided to split into two four-man teams, each mounted in a Landrover, armed with a rear-mounted .50 calibre RAMO machine gun and twin GPMGs. They both identified Scud launchers hidden under bridges, in ravines and under camouflage netting; these were destroyed by the A10s."*

Corporal Harker states: *"I was sitting in the back of the Landrover commanded by Sergeant Quiller, manning the RAMO machine gun and was blown clear when the Landrover hit an anti-tank mine. When I regained consciousness, the Landrover was scrap and Sergeant Quiller and Corporal Miller – the driver – were dead. Their corpses were unrecognisable. Corporal Soames, the radio operator, was in the back of the Landrover with me. He survived, but was unconscious and badly injured, with bruising and lacerations. I buried the other two and contacted the other four-man team who gave me the co-ordinates for an RV. I don't know who I was talking to – there was a lot of static – but he said they couldn't come to me because they'd sighted an Iraqi company guarding a Scud site. It took me about 11 hours, carrying Corporal Soames, to get to the other Landrover, which was in a shallow wadi and covered in camouflage netting. There was no sign of the other team. I concluded that they must have hidden the Landrover and gone forward to observe the target but bumped another Iraqi company. I assumed they must have been captured or killed. I did what I could for Corporal Soames' injuries from the first aid pack on the other Landrover – I gave him some morphine* [Cpl Harker pauses to think]. *I don't know how much, I can't remember, I was trying to get a move on. But he didn't regain consciousness at all during the drive back to coalition lines at Al Jawf...........*" Report closed.

*

Harker was awarded the Queen's Gallantry Medal, left the Army and with his SAS pedigree, advanced quickly through the ranks of the commercial security services. An unsuccessful application for a job with the British Intelligence Directorate was quickly shrugged aside. His success brought him to the attention of the Head of Security Division in the Cabinet Office, to whom he became a Special Adviser. This appointment brought Harker into close contact with the Press Officer at 10 Downing Street and, in 2000, he was promoted to Security Supremo for the PM. Over the next five years, Harker became one of the most powerful unelected advisers brought in by the government. He virtually controlled his own security force and, some sections of the Media and Press reckoned, wielded more power than the Metropolitan Police Commissioner.

*

LONDON 1997

Cpl Harker wasn't the only one who knew that his report about the SAS patrol during Op Granby bore no relation to what really happened that day in the desert. Cpl Soames knew the truth, but was Harker's closest buddy and a willing partner to the dreadful crime which had been committed. The two men had spent weeks planning the crime both back in the UK and during the pre-operation training at Al Jawf in Saudi Arabia. Once Harker had reached the appointment of a senior adviser to the Head of the Cabinet Office Security Division, with access to the personal files of senior members of the Diplomatic, Civil and Intelligence Services he knew that he must use that knowledge to ensure that the secret of what lay buried in the sands of the Iraqi Desert was never discovered. He had already heard from his contact in the British Intelligence Directorate that an agent was making inquiries into the deaths of the soldiers on his patrol. That investigation had to be stopped and it was of paramount importance that he took immediate steps to ensure that his pension would be a gold-plated one.

*

ET JOSHUA AIRPORT, ST VINCENT - JUNE 2008

'What do you think will happen when the aircraft arrives?' Nina Ramone asked Gunn as they found an empty table on the terrace of St Vincent's ET Joshua Airport, overlooking the tarmac where the aircraft were parked.

'No idea.' Gunn scanned the scene outside the window. 'It pays to expect the unexpected, though.'

'Huh…' Nina half laughed at the irony.

'I think the jet'll land and then park over there somewhere, away from the commercial area. Passengers'll get off and then…ah!' he interrupted himself.

'Look over there.'

He indicated with a nod of his head a minibus with opaque windows, which had driven out airside and parked up where there were other small private aircraft.

'Bet you that's Hussein's contact here in St Vincent.'

'Yeah…' Nina studied the vehicle intently, chewing her lip.

'He'll take him to wherever the RV with the seaplane is that'll fly him to his base on Bird Island,' John mused, getting out his binoculars for a closer look.

'How's he going to avoid immigration? There's no way Hussein'll want to go through arrivals and transfers.'

'Don't know, but I guess if you have enough money, anything can be arranged. He's been doing this for some time so he must have some special arrangements to skip the usual formalities. As he's going straight out of the Island again, I suppose it doesn't really matter.' Nina's cell-phone rang. 'That's the tower, he's two or three minutes away from landing.' John reached down and checked the Glock 26 in his ankle holster to make sure that it hadn't snagged on his socks.

'There it is!' and Nina pointed out to the east.

The Learjet was coming straight in to the single runway and with a burst of blue smoke from the landing gear tyres, it touched down and headed towards them.

'Right, let's go to departures. If anything happens I want to be able to get airside as fast as possible,' and Gunn got up from the table.

In the departure area, Nina hurried over to the security staff and showed them her BID ID, then pointed at Gunn. The large security guard smiled broadly, recognising the equally large agent from several days ago. He waved both of them through into the departure lounge.

The Learjet turned off onto the taxiway and, as Gunn had guessed, headed for the park-up area for private aircraft. It was met by a ground handler who waved it into position and then signalled engine shutdown to the pilot. The whine of the twin jet engines faded, the mini-bus drove over to the port side of the Learjet, which was facing towards the terminal, and the aircraft door swung down with its integral steps. Gunn had his binoculars trained intently on the doorway. But nothing could have prepared him for what happened next.

'Shit!'

A man jumped out of the doorway, fell heavily onto the concrete, rolled over, got to his feet and ran with a heavy limp away from the Learjet. A figure appeared in the aircraft's doorway and fired three shots at the fleeing man, all of which missed by a wide margin. Gunn grabbed the larger Glock 17 from his rucksack and ran for the nearest boarding gate out onto the tarmac. He had only just reached the gate when there was a blinding flash and a huge fireball. The blast completely enveloped the Learjet and the other small private aircraft. The shockwave knocked Gunn to the ground and rattled the heavy, laminated plate glass windows of the departure lounge. The sound of breaking glass echoed elsewhere in the terminal. Terrified tourists scattered in all directions, looking for the airport's front entrance, causing chaos as they pushed past the guards at security. Deserted luggage littered the terminal.

The large security guard had reacted as quickly as Gunn and dashed out through another gate, screaming orders at the other guards over his shoulder. He jumped into an air-side staff jeep and headed off across the apron to cut off the man who had fled from the Learjet seconds before it was vaporised. The fireball rose into the sky like a mini-nuclear mushroom, leaving behind the smouldering carcasses of the Learjet and three other aircraft.

The airport fire crews were now racing across the tarmac towards the burning wreckage. Gunn also ran towards the burning plane, leaving the security guard to deal with the fleeing passenger. As he approached what was left of the jet, now being smothered with foam, there were two shots from way over to his left. The security guard had cut off the man's escape, jumped out of his jeep and had been hit by at least one of the two shots fired at him. He was down, whether dead or wounded was impossible to tell, but the man had now changed direction and was running towards the terminal. John turned and sprinted back towards the terminal to try and cut him off. But, fit as he was, he had no chance of intercepting him.

'Jesus!...' to Gunn's dismay he saw the departure gate open and Nina appeared. The man was about 80 yards from Gunn - and about the same distance from Nina. He knew he hadn't a hope in hell of hitting him at that range. His lungs burning, he forced himself to run faster, desperate to prevent what seemed horribly inevitable. Even as he considered a wild shot at the man to distract him, he saw him raise his automatic to shoot Nina. Then Gunn stopped dead. Nina had plunged her hand into her bag and pulled out a large automatic. Holding the automatic in one hand, she fired twice. The powerful muzzle velocity of Nina's Colt automatic slammed the man onto the ground, his gun skittering across the concrete to end up at Nina's feet.

'Jesus!........' Gunn said again, doubling over in relief and gulping lungfuls of air.

He removed his mobile from his pocket and pressed the speed-dial for his CIA contact, Doyle Barnes.

'Doyle....a change of plan,' he gasped.

'Hey, you sound a little out of breath buddy…'

'Well…' John caught his breath, 'Hassan Hussein's jet has just blown up killing everyone in it. The one man to escape, who I think is Abdul Hassan, is also dead; he was shot trying to escape at the airport. More a bit later…. just thought you should know if you're headed to Bird Island.'

'Thanks John, good to know. Shit, what a fucking mess. I'm on Bird Island now. It's the most amazing place. You'll have to come see it. We've also got the Captain and crew of the submersible cargo ship and that's really something else. Be in touch,' and Doyle broke the connection.

John headed to the terminal where an ambulance had departed with the wounded security guard. Nina was surrounded by airport officials and the departure lounge was now packed with faces pressed up against the glass to get a better view. A blanket covered the body of the dead man. After turning back the blanket to identify him, John found Nina and returned the Glock 17 to his rucksack.

'I didn't see that coming' he said, leading her away from the throng. Nina's body was still shaking from the adrenalin rush.

'No... that's about as unexpected as it gets,' Nina pulled her black hair into a ponytail and loosened her shirt.

'Drink?'

'Sounds good.'

Once the police had arrived and taken control of both the local press and the crowd of onlookers, Gunn and Nina headed back to their table on the terrace where they could wait to make their statements to the police. Gunn ordered two large rums and they nursed them as they assessed what had just happened. Gunn contacted the Operations Centre at BID and debriefed them. Nina put down her glass. 'What was all that about?'

'You know as much as I do. There were four people on that plane in addition to the pilot and co-pilot including Qasim - Hussein's gofer - Trevet, the security guard from Barbados and Abdul Hassan.'

'Obviously this guy Hassan knew he was for it, though...'

'Yeah... I knew Hassan Hussein wanted to get his revenge for his disfigurement and for the gassing of all those people in his village, but I didn't realise Abdul Hassan knew about Hassan Hussein. Obviously I was wrong.'

Gunn downed his rum and continued: 'From the looks of it, Hassan had a rucksack with him when he boarded that plane and that must have had the bomb and his gun inside it.'

'I s'pose we'll never know…'

'I think he knew what was in store for him and no one checked his rucksack, simple as that. If it was a time-pencil detonator, which it looks like, all he would have to do is reach into his bag as they landed, break the pencil timer, grab his gun and run for it.'

'God...........at least he wasn't hauled off to be tortured,' Nina shuddered at the image and drained the dregs of her rum.

# CHAPTER 1

'Good day, sah! Your pretty lady frien'.......jus' like you, she shoot a lot better than that Bond fella in the movies.'

Limping slowly across the coffee terrace with the aid of a stick was the old Vincentian man who had wanted to shake Gunn's hand at the airport some four days previously, when he'd shot Claude Dubois, Hassan Hussein's Haitian security guard. Gunn stood up to shake hands with him, his faded safari jacket now sporting his World War II campaign medals. The old man removed his baseball hat, proudly displaying the badge of the British West Indian Regiment, and held his hand out to Nina Ramone, St Vincent's in-country agent for the British Intelligence Directorate and senior newsreader for Radio Grenadines.

'Corporal Gabriel Jackson, ma'am; D Company, 3rd Battalion, British West Indian Regiment; I sure can't decide which is better.......your shootin' or your pretty face!' The retired Corporal had somehow circumvented the police and security cordon restraining both the Press and onlookers from swamping Gunn and Nina.

Corporal Jackson had shared a flight with Gunn from St Vincent to Grand Cayman after the shooting incident at the airport the previous week. Gunn had been sent to St Vincent during Operation Calypso – a joint BID/CIA mission - to put the arms and drug dealer, Hassan Hussein, out of business. Hussein, abandoning his property in Barbados at exclusive Sandy Lane in favour of his private island 100 miles to the west of Dominica, had dispatched his security chief, Claude Dubois – one of Papa Doc's vicious Haitian 'Tonton Macout' - back to Barbados to tie up a loose end. The loose end was another Haitian, André Trevet, who, with two other thugs who guarded Hassan Hussein's sprawling Spanish Hacienda style Bajan mansion, had failed to carry out Hussein's orders to kill Gunn while he was staying at the Barbados Hilton. Having arrived on the island in Hussein's yacht, Dubois had avoided any security checks, but had very foolishly underestimated the thoroughness of security at Joshua Airport by attempting to board an aircraft with his Model 645 Smith and Wesson .45 automatic. In a desperate bid to avoid arrest he'd tried to hijack a plane and shot a security officer and a stewardess. Gunn had been waiting to board his flight to Grand Cayman and had shot Dubois twice - first shot in the head and the second in his neck - at a range of thirty metres.

Chief Superintendent Malcolm Slater of the St Vincent Police Force arrived moments after Corporal Jackson and escorted them to a police mini-bus, which took them to Police Headquarters in Kingstown. Once they'd made their statements, they avoided the Press with the help of the police by being taken out of a back exit from the Headquarters, and then drove to Nina's white, weatherboard bungalow in the lush, green volcanic hills above Kingstown.

Gunn's assignment on Operation Calypso had

started in Barbados before moving quickly to St Vincent and then to Cuba. The British High Commission in Barbados was one of the very few Diplomatic Missions, which still retained an agent of the British Intelligence Directorate within the building. In all other countries where BID required the permanent presence of an agent, the person had no connection with the High Commission or Embassy and his or her identity was only known to the Head of Mission, his Deputy and the Defence Adviser or Attaché.

*

The American Airlines flight from Miami landed at ET Joshua Airport five minutes late at 18.45. The two Cuban passengers presented US passports at immigration and were met in the arrivals hall by a group of six Rastafarians, who had twice been given warnings by airport security staff for disturbing the peace and abusing other travellers. This ensured that anyone using the terminal would remember, when questioned, the intimidating group, but would have no recollection of the two Cubans who were lead out to a battered and psychedelically painted Volkswagen minibus with black opaque windows.

*

The massed bands of the Brigade of Guards changed direction to face the saluting dais in front of Her Majesty the Queen on her official birthday. In the third row of the VIP spectators stand behind the dais, two men were paying only scant attention to the Trooping of the Colour.

'What happened to Paul Manton?' Clive Sterling muttered to John Cornwall, seated on his right, careful to keep his eyes on the parade.

'He was taken to BID's medical facility at Maidenhead under sedation on Thursday evening.'

The Queen and all the spectators stood to honour the Grenadiers' Colour as it was lowered in salute.

'How much does that agent, Gunn, know, do you think?' Sterling asked as they resumed their seats.

'Difficult to say.......probably nothing, but with such high stakes we can't be too careful, especially since Manton's under sedation. There's no telling what he might say on the drugs.

'So....?'

'I've made the call.' Cornwall heaved his corpulent frame reluctantly to his feet again for the guns of the King's Troop.

'Thank God this is nearly over,' he added, slumping back into his seat as the last of the horse-drawn guns returned to the far side of Horse Guards Parade

A few minutes later, the Queen and Prince Philip departed in their open landau. The two men joined the throng of spectators leaving Horse Guards Parade onto Whitehall.

'So.......no change of plan?' Sterling prompted.

'None........conveniently, the agent's in St Vincent where there's only a token police force and Paul is comatose in BID's clinic...' Cornwall checked his watch.

'The text I received indicated that BID's agent will be dealt with very soon and Paul Manton will suffer a massive heart attack.......also very soon.'

He stopped, waiting to cross the road, and added with a shrug:

'At least it'll save BID from the embarrassment of Manton's trial as a paedophile. Bye Clive,' and the two men parted, one in the direction of the Underground in Parliament Square and the other in the direction of Trafalgar Square and the Travellers' Club at 106 Pall Mall.

*

It was close to 7pm by the time Gunn and Nina reached her bungalow. Gunn's jet-lag felt like lead weights dragging on his eyelids.

'Why don't you crash out for a bit while I do something about food?'

'Thanks,' and Gunn disappeared with his backpack into the small spare bedroom at the side of the bungalow.

It was nearly 9 pm when Nina roused him from a deep sleep. He had a shower and joined her on the veranda of the bungalow, where she'd laid out a spread of grilled fish and anything else she could find. The view looked down on the lights of Kingstown and the black velvet of the moonlit sea beyond. Nina sank gratefully into a chair and uncorked a bottle of chilled Pinot Grigio.

'You must have been exhausted; I couldn't wake you.'

'I was, I get terrible jetlag - this is great, by the way, thanks for cooking.'

'Pleasure. Um..' she took a large slug of wine, 'while you were asleep, that lovely old soldier, Corporal Jackson, phoned to ask if he could come over tonight to show you some photos of his war service. I'm sorry but I didn't have the heart to refuse. I hope you don't mind.'

'No,' but he did mind. 'How's he going to get here?'

'His son's driving him. Name's Robert Jackson, he's a doctor – actually a surgeon – he trained at St Mary's in London and at Bethesda Naval Hospital as a neurosurgeon - that's where Kennedy was taken after being shot in Dallas. And he runs a fantastic clinic here – it's basically for the well-heeled, but has a wing reserved for those who can't afford the treatment; so the rich pay for the poor. Good family,' she mused.

'Hope I can stay awake. I just…' Gunn hesitated, rubbing his face and then slouched back into his chair, frowning.

'What's wrong…?'

'It took me ages to get to sleep…' Gunn searched for the right words. '….I think there's something not right at the 'house' at the moment…'

'Really…?' The 'house' was Kingsroad House, the BID head office in Cale Street.

'In the last 48 hours, a hell of a lot seems to have gone wrong.'

'Like what?' Nina prompted.

Gunn sat up again: 'Well, after the shake-up of the intelligence services in '88 and the relocation of espionage and counter-espionage under one roof, the buildings at Millbank and Vauxhall were only retained for the changeover to handle the mass of low-level classified material - against Jeremy Hammond's wishes, but Thatcher insisted..........probably to appease the unions... '

'That's common knowledge isn't it?'

'Yeah, but what's not common knowledge is that a small handful of people - only eight, I think - survived that shake-up to achieve the transfer from MI5 and 6 to Kingsroad House. I knew seven of them,' Gunn toyed with the crumbs on his plate, suddenly anxious. 'Six of them are dead and one was sacked today.......well, yesterday in London,' he continued.

'Okay....'

'So – '

'Hang on, let me get some more wine,' and Nina hurried into the bungalow from the veranda to reappear with another bottle of Pinot Grigio. When their glasses were refilled, John continued.

'No one I've mentioned this to seems to know who the eighth person was, except that he was supposed to have been ex-SAS, joined MI6 in 1991, was accepted initially by BID, but then disappeared, apparently, when Sir Jeremy insisted on more stringent vetting procedures. The last anyone heard he was security adviser for a commercial engineering contractor in Baghdad. But that could be anyone ex-forces – so many have gone out there; lots of rumours, but no name.'

'Who are the ones that have died?'

'Humphrey Goldman – he was shot at the Army and Navy Club in Pall Mall by what BID now believes was a London-based assassin. Richard Anderson and

Tim Driscoll were both killed in Hong Kong. Tony Bristow was a waste-of-space SIS agent at the British High Commission in Accra who vanished on a boating trip - they never found his body. Simon Peters, the Assistant Director for South East Asia, who tragically killed himself – poor guy - when he found out his wife's careless bridge chatter had led to two attempts on my life. That leaves David Chesham of Counter-Espionage who was killed 24 hours ago and his boss, Paul Manton, who appeared to have some sort of breakdown after the death of David and was sacked by Sir Jeremy. Paul's now under heavy sedation at BID's clinic. They won't let him go 'til they've done a risk assessment on him,' John yawned in spite of himself.

'Want some coffee?' Nina got up to go to the kitchen.

'Yeah.......please - I'm going to need it if this soldier turns up.'

'Okay, I'll be back in a minute...'

Gunn's head began to pound as he tried to make sense of everything, sifting through snippets of information that had reached him from London. He sipped his wine as he looked out over the lights of Kingstown. Music from a steel band drifted lightly on the night air, competing with the rising nightly cacophony of the cicadas. Suddenly he realised that it was nearly five minutes since Nina had gone to fetch the coffee. He got up and strolled through the bungalow to the kitchen. The slatted door was ajar, but there was no sound from the kitchen.

'Nina?' Gunn called as he opened the door. But he got no further. Nina was crumpled on the tiled floor in a widening pool of blood. Her throat had been slashed from ear to ear in a grotesque grin. Gunn spun round as he sensed rather than heard movement behind him and instantly stooped to reach for the Glock in his ankle holster.......too late. He saw three men; two were holding knives and the largest of the three an automatic - pointed at him. There was a deafening explosion and bright flash followed by stygian blackness. A roaring crescendo erupted in Gunn's head.......and then........nothing.

*

'Seems quiet roun' here,' said Corporal Jackson as his son parked the car behind Nina's.

'Are you sure this is a good time to be visitin'?' Dr Robert Jackson asked wearily, eyeing the dark, silent bungalow and stifling a yawn. 'It's nearly ten and Mr Gunn must be exhausted after all that drama at the airport.'

Gabriel Jackson ignored his son and made a show of trying to get out of the car. Robert sighed and got out of the car and went round to help his 83-year-old father out of the passenger seat.

'Don' forget the album, son.'

'I won't,' Robert reached into the back of the car and retrieved the worn old album stuffed with his father's World War II photos and newspaper cuttings. He took hold of his arm and the two headed slowly to the front door. Robert rang the bell but there was no answer.

'Jus' stay here while I go roun' the back.'

'Okay, son,' and the old man leant against the wooden veranda rail that surrounded the bungalow.

Robert walked round to the back of the house. Light spilled out from the open kitchen door. He climbed the steps and pulled aside the netted anti-mosquito door. It took a split second to adjust to the light, then.........

'Oh God...!' He let out an involuntary cry and rushed into the kitchen, his heart thumping wildly. He knelt by Nina's body to feel for a pulse, knowing it was useless, and then turned to Gunn, who had a gaping head wound. Sudden terror - what if the people who did this are still close by? - Robert ran back to the driveway where his father was puffing on his old Meerschaum pipe.

'Somethin's happened!' he cried, 'somethin'.........Nina's dead.....she's been murdered and Mr Gunn's been shot in the head,' and without waiting for a response, he picked up his father as though he were a child and carried him to the car, where he put him in the front passenger seat.

'What's happenin'? Nina what - what's wrong?' the look on his son's face terrified the old man and he glanced around anxiously.

'They've been attacked - Nina's dead - just wait there...' Robert sprinted back to the kitchen, heaved Gunn's dead weight over his shoulders and staggered out to the car.

'Open the back door!'

'What, son?' Robert Jackson's rising panic had stupefied him.

'Open the damn door!' Robert cried, his knees beginning to buckle.

'Okay, okay, son - there...' the sight of Gunn's bloody body shocked him into action.

'Oh Lord! Mr Gunn,' Gabriel Jackson stared uncomprehendingly at the lifeless agent and then looked at his son, his eyes widening in terror.

'Someone's shot him in the head. Can't do anythin' for Nina,' Robert answered the question before it was asked.

'Shit!' He swore as he remembered the photo album, which his father had left at the front door. He got out of the car, ran to the front door, scooped up the album, got back in the car and reversed out of the drive onto the road. Ten minutes later they reached his clinic. Robert dashed into the clinic and reappeared with a trolley, stretcher and two nurses and between the three of them they lifted Gunn onto the stretcher and wheeled him into the clinic.

Hands trembling, Gabriel Jackson picked up his photo album and pipe and shuffled off to the family house just a short distance from the clinic.

*

'Ops, BID, Controller speaking.'

'This is Chief Superintendant Slater of the Royal St Vincent Police. If you need to verify this call my number is 001784213141. You need to authenticate..... no?'

'Thank you Chief Superintendant, got that,' Terry Holt, the Controller of BID's Operation Centre in Kingsroad House, replied as the automatic recording system was activated.

'We had a call from the Deputy Director of Radio Grenadines at 0840 hours this morning, local time, that a Miss Nina Ramone, its senior newsreader, didn't arrive for work at 7am and wasn't answerin' cell-phone or landline. When one of our patrol cars called at her house, they found her body in the kitchen. She was dead. Her throat had been cut. There was another person's blood on the tiled floor of the kitchen and my constables found a backpack in the spare bedroom with a passport in the name of John Gunn and a Glock 17 automatic - you gettin' this?'

'Yes, go on…' Holt scribbled frantically in his shorthand on a notepad.

'Er - after the incident at ET Joshua Airport yesterday - we know that you received a report about that - Mr Gunn came to our Police Headquarters to make a statement before leaving with Miss Ramone for her house where he told us he would be stayin' the night before returnin' to London today. Our scenes-of-crime officers know that there was a second body on the floor in the kitchen, which has been removed. Samples of the blood of the second body have been analysed, but we need Mr Gunn's DNA profile to make a match. Uh…' a pause and the sound of rustling paper, then the policeman continued:

'…the forensics indicate that the second person did not walk out of the kitchen, but was dragged or carried out through the back door into a vehicle. We have to believe at this early stage that that body - alive or dead - was Mr Gunn. Please call back asap with Mr Gunn's DNA. I'm sorry…..'

'Thank you, Chief Superintendent - we'll get back to you immediately,' and Terry Holt, who was wearing headphones with an integral mike, pressed the button to break the connection. He turned to Alan Paxton, the Espionage Directorate duty officer.

'Alan, John Gunn's personal file and medical records please,' and then Terry tapped out the number of Miles Thompson, Deputy Director of BID and Head of the Espionage Directorate.

'Miles Thompson.'

'Terry Holt, sir. Could you come to Ops please?'

## CHAPTER 2

'On my way.'

Miles Thompson had been head-hunted from the Civil Service; he was the youngest Principal Private Secretary and was tipped to become Head of the Civil Service. The challenge of the new appointment had appealed to him; he had abandoned the assured knighthood without a thought and had devoted all his energy to moulding the Directorate into a highly efficient, effective and secure intelligence-gathering agency for the Government. And John Gunn was one of his greatest assets.

'Terry - what is it?' Miles had picked up the urgency in Terry's voice.

'Sir; Nina Ramone has been killed. And from the report we've just received from the Chief Superintendent of Police in St Vincent, it looks like John Gunn is either dead or severely injured and missing. I have to call back to authenticate…….'

'Yes, do it.' There was usually a subdued murmur of conversation, but now there was absolute silence in the Ops Centre. The hum of cooling fans in the computers and the muted sound of the air-conditioning seemed deafening. Terry dialled the number he'd been given once it had been verified by IT.

'Chief Slater…….'

'BID Ops, Controller - authenticating you report of 1511 Zulu today.' Zulu time was Greenwich Mean Time - one hour earlier than British Summer Time - it was used during BID and all military operations to avoid confusion.

'OK. I'm sorry to bring you such bad news, Slater said again. 'We're doin' everything we can but...' he paused, '...if you can send anyone - it jus' seems completely motiveless.'

Miles Thompson had picked up an extension: 'It's Miles Thompson; we met in London at the beginning of the year.'

'Yes I remember - We'll do everythin' we can to help, Mr Thompson. But our resources.......'

'We'll be sending someone over asap,' Miles interjected. 'In the mean time, we'll await for any more news from you, especially on the missing second victim. I have to go, we need to get moving. Thanks Malcolm.' He left Ops without another word.

Miles headed straight to the Director's office. Sir Jeremy Hammond was in a meeting with Mary Probert, who had just been promoted to the rank of Assistant Director, Counter Espionage, and Head of Team 2, Counter Terrorism, to replace David Chesham, who had been killed barely 48 hours previously. The Counter Espionage Directorate, which had replaced MI5, had four departments of which CE1 (Counter Terrorism) was by far the largest, with ten teams, each with a leader and eight agents. CE2 handled drugs, CE3 immigration and CE4 covered foreign Embassies, High Commissions and political and diplomatic cases. Paul Manton, still confined in a secure wing of BID's clinic awaiting a risk assessment, had been Director of Counter Espionage.

Sir Jeremy's PA, Melanie, interrupted the meeting to announce Miles' urgent need to see him.

'Sorry Mary.' Sir Jeremy got up to see her out. 'I think we covered everything though.' Mary smiled, nodding her thanks, and left the Director's office.

'Miles?' and then the Director saw the expression on Miles' face. 'What's happened? Sit down......' and he waved him into a chair.

'Our agent in St Vincent, Nina Ramone - she's been murdered.....'

Sir Jeremy let out a long sigh and cursed under his breath.

'...and it looks like they might have got John Gunn too.'

'What?' Sir Jeremy got up furiously. 'What do you mean might have...?'

'The police found Nina's body in the kitchen with her throat cut.......'

'Oh God...'

'...but the police SOCO found a second victim's blood on the floor of the kitchen, which they've assumed is Gunn's as he was staying at Nina's. They've asked us for Gunn's DNA profile, which we've just sent them. At this stage, the police have no idea who might have done this or, if Gunn was killed or injured, where he or his body might be. They've asked us to send an agent to help with their investigation.'

'Has someone gone?' Sir Jeremy interrupted.

'I'm about to send someone. I just can't think who would do this. I mean, I know John's made enemies but all our agents have, of course they have.......' He was on his feet now too: '...but who would *need* to go this far?'

'I know, it doesn't make much sense,' Sir Jeremy acknowledged.

'Right,' Miles sighed, heading for the door. 'I'd better go and send someone to find out.'

'I want to know who you send to St Vincent. Oh... what about Claudine...?'

'She's working with the French DGSE on a drugs op in Marseille,' Miles pre-empted the question. 'I'll tell her.' That was something that he knew he would not enjoy as Gunn and Claudine had become an item since she joined BID some five years previously. As Miles walked into his office he asked his PA to call Jason Wolstenholme, the Assistant Director Espionage for the Caribbean, and Charles Gardner, the Assistant Director for the European Community, up to his office. Jason had been Gunn's controller during Operation Calypso. Miles wanted to know which agent he'd send to St Vincent. Charles would know how soon they could get Claudine back from Marseilles. Miles' intercom beeped:

'Jason's on his way, but Charles is at the French Embassy in South Ken so Marie de Fontblanque is on her way up.' Marie was Claudine's controller in the EC section.

'Thanks, show them both in together please.'

The door opened and Marie and Jason appeared in the doorway. Miles gestured to them to sit. He didn't offer any coffee, which was a bad sign; he took a deep breath:

'We've lost Nina Ramone; she was murdered last night at her home in St Vincent...' Jason swore angrily and got up, pacing the room with both hands clamped behind his head, visibly trying to hold it together; he'd never lost an agent before. 'And…' Miles turned to Marie, '…I'm afraid it looks like they might have got John Gunn too.'

'Jesus…' Marie barely whispered, leaning forward, putting her head in her hands.

'When does Claudine get back from the op?' He asked gently.

'It's finished, sir.' She addressed her reply to the floor. 'She arrives back at Heathrow tomorrow morning. Charles is at the French Embassy at the op debrief.'

'Will she be in the office on Monday?'

'Er… Yes…' She looked up at Miles. 'I think she was hoping that John might be back from St Vincent.'

'I know the two of you are good friends. Would it be better if she heard it from you first?'

'As soon as she gets home, she'll phone John. When she gets no reply, she'll phone me. I'll tell her. What should I say?'

'You can just tell her what we know…….' Miles was interrupted by the intercom.

'Call from Terry Holt in Ops, sir.'

'Thanks Angela.'

'From the police in St Vincent, sir; the DNA's a match.'

'Thanks,' he put the phone down. 'So what we know is John's injured and missing and an agent is on his way to find out what has happened. Tell her she can call me over the weekend if she wants, but I want to see her first thing Monday - whatever happens between now and then.'

'Okay'

'And obviously… tell her we're doing everything we can…' he added.

'Sir…' Marie quietly left the Deputy Director's office, exchanging looks with Jason as she passed him on the way out.'

'Jason, who do you want to send to St Vincent?'

'Er, Mike Soames, sir,' Jason replied immediately.

'Fine.........see if you can get him briefed up and on a flight tomorrow. Terry'll brief you on everything we know from the St Vincent police but otherwise over to you.' There was a pause. 'At some point you'll need to go to St Vincent to find a replacement agent for Nina. Keep me updated on that too, please. Questions…?'

'None now, sir,' and Jason nodded goodbye and left hurriedly, the door slamming with a bang behind him.

Miles stared blankly at the door for a few seconds; agents had been killed before causing the inevitable sadness, but the death of these two agents seemed particularly painful. He swore at the closed door.

'Some bastard's going to pay dearly for this.'

*

'Cornwall.'

'It's Clive; lunch, Sid's Cafe, St George Wharf, 1pm - okay?'

'I'll be there,' and the connection was broken.

Sid's was not so much a café as a fast food trailer. It was some 200 yards upstream on the south bank of the Thames from the old MI6 building at 85 Vauxhall Cross. Plastic chairs and tables littered the area around the trailer along with discarded cans, bottles, straws and polystyrene cups.

John Cornwall was Head of 85, Vauxhall Cross, an empty title now that it was nothing more than an administrative appendage to the Espionage Directorate of BID. Clive Sterling held the equivalent appointment at Thames House on the other side of the river, which had been similarly castrated, little more than a sorting office for BID's Counter Espionage Department. Both men had been appointed to the now impotent MI buildings after proving to be so incompetent in their appointments in the Cabinet Office that even their colleagues had noticed. Their new jobs were thinly veiled dismissals; and everyone knew it. They, and many others, were symptomatic of politically expedient appointments that had been made in the last few years during the tenure of the current government. But it had been a bitter pill to swallow for the two men. Now, finally, the Director of BID had been given approval by the Cabinet Office Joint Intelligence Committee to close them both down; leaking like sieves and riddled with moles, they posed too much of a security risk

It was a warm Sunday in June, London was packed with tourists, and there had been three full days of play in the England/New Zealand Test series. Sid's Café's assortment of diners included stray spectators from the Oval Cricket Ground and workers from the nearby Nine Elms industrial estate. Two middle-aged men, who'd exchanged their habitual suits for jeans, ate their lunch unnoticed.

John Cornwall was leaning against the railing with a hotdog in one hand and a coffee in the other, watching a tug making heavy weather of towing two refuse barges downstream against the tide. Clive Sterling appeared next to him, though didn't acknowledge him, focusing instead on his coffee. He reeked of whisky.

'Any news yet from St Vincent?' Sterling asked.

'Done,' spluttered Cornwall through a mouthful of hot dog.

'Do you know how much Gunn knew?' Sterling asked.

'Enough. He was overheard telling Miles Thompson that the place where Chesham's body was found was nowhere near where the terrorist was hiding. And he knew the pathologist found a Russian manufactured 7.62mm bullet. Obviously that didn't come from the 9mm Heckler and Koch sub-machine guns the terrorists were carrying.'

'Shit…'

'Yeah, well… That's what made our contact give the nod. Nina Ramone was just in the wrong place at the wrong time.'

'Who made the Chesham hit?'

'Carl Durer'

'Who's he?'

'Ex-SIS, as instructed.'

'What about him…?'

'Durer was sharing a squat with a bunch of drug addicts, so the contact said; shame, he overdosed last night. He's dead.'

'Shit, John……how many more?'

The panic in Sterling's voice irritated Cornwall.

'Look, just shut-up and sit tight. It's nearly payday and then we can get out. Retire; remember?' Cornwall drained his coffee and binned it. He continued:

'All the cut-outs have worked as planned. Whoever did Gunn and Ramone is the last link to us. Contact says he's got that sorted. A couple more days and it'll be over, so just......keep it together.'

Cornwall stole a glance at Sterling and noticed his hands were shaking. He was drinking way too much; he definitely wasn't keeping it together.

'And stop fucking drinking so much!' he spat, never raising his voice above a murmur, and calmly strolled away.

Clive Sterling stayed a few minutes longer, staring blankly at the glassy brown river; unaware he'd just become another cut-out.

*

'Matt, can you go an' see who's there mate?' the duty security guard at BID's Maidenhead clinic was eyeing his bank of CCTV monitors. He spoke into his radio again:

'There's some woman at the front who says she's Mrs Valerie Manton.'

'On my way,' the night patrol officer abandoned his eleventh sweep of the clinic's silent corridors, appearing a minute later on the CCTV monitor covering the front entrance. He returned within two minutes accompanied by a well-dressed woman in her forties who asked if she could visit her husband. She looked tearful and anxious, barely making eye contact. Not surprised, poor woman, thought the guard, he's really lost it.

'I'm sorry but I'll need proof of ID please Madam –

photo ID... yep that'll do the job,' he said, as she quickly held out a passport.

Valerie Annabel Manton, it read, born in London on 10th September 1963. The guard cross-referenced the information with what he had on file from the head office.

'Thank you Mrs Manton. Your husband's in Room 22 on the second floor. My colleague here will escort you.'

Valerie Manton left without a word and followed the patrol officer into the lift. On the second floor, he led her to the nurse's night station. The nurse had been warned by Jack that Paul Manton's wife was on her way.

'Good evening, Mrs Manton. I have to tell you your husband is heavily sedated so won't be aware that you're here. Please follow me,' and she led Valerie Manton into her husband's room. Paul Manton lay motionless in the bed on his back connected to a drip and monitors that blinked and beeped above his bed.

'We'll be here if you need us, Mrs Manton; just call – my name's Melissa' and she left the room, leaving the door open, as was policy for all visitors, even family.

Only three minutes later Valerie Manton reappeared at the door, wiping her eyes, which were red from crying.

'Oh... Mrs Manton...' surprised, Melissa leapt to her feet, ready to offer some sympathetic words, but Valerie Manton waved her away.

'I'm sorry, I just can't...' crying again, she hurried back along the corridor and down to the front entrance where she got into a chauffeur driven car which was immediately driven away. Melissa watched the retreating figure sadly, and then went to check on her comatose husband. The ECG screamed as she walked through the door...........

'What? Shit!' She punched the alarm and ran for the crash cart, where she collided with the duty doctor and two other nurses. For the next 37 minutes they desperately tried to resuscitate the patient.

But at 2342 hours Paul Manton was pronounced dead.

*

It was just after midnight when the phone in Miles Thompson's study rang. It had a secure line to BID, so when it rang it usually meant bad news. Miles was about to turn out the light when the phone rang. Careful not to wake his wife, he got out of bed and hurried down to the study.

'Miles Thompson.'

'Duty officer, sir; we've just heard from Maidenhead. Paul Manton was pronounced dead at 2342 hours...'

'What?! ........he was only under mild sedation...'

'He was murdered, sir...'

'Oh God! How? for Christ's sake... What the fuck is going on with our security?'

''His wife, Valerie, came to visit him - she had her passport as proof of ID so the guard let her through. The duty nurse took her to his room and she did leave the door open but she just couldn't see everything from where she was sitting...'

'Well why didn't she bloody move?' They both knew it was rhetorical.

'...she - whoever she was - was only in the room for about two minutes and then left in a car which had a driver.....that's what the security guard reported.'

'Number plate...?'

'We got it on the CCTV. Hire car, paid for in cash and found by the police abandoned on the Embankment by Chelsea Bridge.'

Miles' mind was racing. What the hell was going on? Why all these killings? Who else was going to die? This balls-up was escalating out of control. He rubbed his temple and tried to order his thoughts.

'Sir...?'

Finally he spoke, his voice belying his exasperation.

'Sorry... It's Marilyn Green isn't it?' Miles recognised her Scottish accent; she was an officer from Counter Terrorism Team 2, an ex-Naval Petty Officer.

'Yes sir.'

'OK Marilyn... OK, who've you spoken to?'

'I called Barry Windsor, who's standing in as Director of Counter Espionage until the new Director's appointed. He's on his way to the office now. He's going to find out who was impersonating Manton's wife - assuming it wasn't his real wife. I've not contacted the Director.'

'OK great, that's good - please tell Barry that I'll be in just after seven and that I'll talk to the Director - when we have a bit more information.'

They rang off and Miles went back to bed, though he didn't get any sleep. Lying awake in the dark, he went over and over the events and crises of the last 48 hours trying to tease out a thread that might make some sense.

# CHAPTER 3

'Everythin' ready?' Robert Jackson asked his theatre sister.

'Yes, they're ready for you.'

'Have you told the others about him?'

'Yes, I said…'

'They know they can't say anythin' to anyone? If whoever did this finds out he's not dead, we'll all be in danger. We have to keep this quiet,' Robert was frantically scrubbing his arms with disinfectant.

'Don't worry, sir; we're goin' to put him in the detox ward – no-one would wanna look there.'

'Good idea – thanks,' Robert said, as the sister helped him into his scrubs and opened the doors to the theatre. Gunn's large form lay lifeless on the operating table, a nurse shaving off his dark, matted hair. Robert walked over to six large x-rays and CT scans mounted on a backlit stand.

'OK everyone,' he began, seconds later, 'the gunman must have been standin' to the front left of the patient.....as the patient faced him and higher.....or maybe the patient was bendin' down when he – I'm assumin' it was a he – fired. This could be a very lucky man.....it looks like the bullet may not have penetrated the frontal bone – it's too tough - but glanced roun' it at an angle, and travelled roun' the left side of the parietal bone to lodge down here – see? - in the region of the lambdoid suture. There's jus' a chance that once we've removed the bullet and debrided the wound, the patient could recover consciousness with nothin' more than a headache.' Robert looked around at his staff: 'Are we ready?'

The operation lasted two hours, and Robert found no sign of any injuries that could indicate permanent brain damage. As he carefully stitched Gunn's head closed, all the life signs of his patient were steady. In the recovery room minutes later, he began to show the first signs of returning to consciousness, so Robert stood aside as two nurses arrived to wheel the patient to his room.

*

'Hello.'

'Hi Marie, it's Claudine; I'm at Heathrow.....thought I'd check with you first before I go home.'

'Good to hear from you,' Marie avoided injecting the news about Gunn. 'Actually, it would be quite useful if you could come to the office, there are a couple of things we need to discuss,' Marie squirmed inwardly; she could hear herself trying to sound casual, which meant Claudine probably could too.

'OK... fine, I'll see you in about an hour. Is John back from the Caribbean?' Both women chose their words carefully as personal mobiles were not secure.

'Not yet,' Marie said evenly, offering no elaboration.

'I wondered why he wasn't answering my calls. OK, see you soon.'

'Bye,' Marie ended the call and dialled another number.

'Miles Thompson.'

'It's Marie sir; Claudine's on her way to the office from Heathrow - she'll be here in about an hour. Do you want to see her as soon as I've broken the news?'

'Yes......thanks.'

To Marie it seemed only minutes before she heard Claudine's voice in the outer office. She appeared at the door, tanned but thinner and drawn, whether from travelling or the French op Marie couldn't guess.

'What's happened to John?' Claudine fired at Marie, studying her face intently. She hadn't missed a trick, but Marie was grateful to be able to come straight out with it.

'Er…' Marie took a deep breath, 'in the early hours of today, St Vincent time, the police were asked to call at Nina's house as she didn't turn up for the early schedule at Radio Grenadines. They found Nina on the kitchen floor. She was dead and her throat had been cut. There was another person's blood on the kitchen floor and after John's DNA profile was sent to the St Vincent police, the blood was confirmed as his. There was evidence that John had been carried out of the house and placed in a vehicle.' Marie tactfully avoided saying 'John's body'. 'The St Vincent police are doing everything they can to find John - Mike Soames was sent out to find out what's happened.'

Claudine hadn't moved a muscle while Marie was talking. Her eyes were fixed on Marie's face as if to judge whether something was being kept from her.

'Miles Thompson's asked if you could go and see him. I'm so...' Marie began, but Claudine held up her hand.

'I knew something was wrong when John didn't answer my texts and calls. And I could tell from your voice on the phone it was bad news…' Claudine ran her fingers through her slightly messy blonde crop and re-tied it in a pony tail, processing everything, avoiding eye contact with Marie.

'I didn't think I was very convincing either,' Marie said eventually, apologetic.

'Don't worry,' Claudine put a hand on her friend's shoulder and squeezed it. Then she inhaled sharply: 'Right, I'd better go and see Miles. You've had my report, so I don't think there's anything that can't wait for a few days. I'm going to take some leave so I'll catch up with you and Charlie shortly,' and with that Claudine left Marie's office and climbed the stairs to the 12th floor. Marie stared after her friend, chewing her lip distractedly.

The door to Miles Thompson's office was open so Claudine went in. The Deputy Director was standing by the window, which had a view over the rooftops out to Albert Bridge on the Thames. He turned as Claudine entered. The two sat down at opposite sides of Miles' desk without saying anything. Miles was eyeing her dry eyes and taught expression, detecting the challenge. Before she could say anything, he jumped in first.

'You want some leave and you're going to use it to go straight out to St. Vincent - am I right?' he asked.

Claudine opened her mouth and closed it again, then grinned broadly in spite of herself.

'You could have written my script, sir. I was ready for a fight.'

'No point,' said Miles, 'I would have done the same, so would John.'

'I assure you, I won't get in Mike Soames' way…'

'I know you won't. When you get down to Jason's office you'll find that your flight is booked for this evening from Heathrow on BA, This is an official assignment on full BID expenses, but as yet Mike Soames doesn't know that you'll be joining him. Now, is there anything………' but Claudia's tears flowed freely, the wind taken out of her sails by Miles' empathy.

'Sorry,' she sniffed, shielding her reddening face. Miles passed her a handful of tissues.

'I have only one instruction for you, of which Jason is fully aware. You are to deal only with me, not with Mike Soames and not even the duty officer, unless it's a matter of such urgency that it can't wait. And there's something you need to be aware of… somebody or some bodies, who have access to this building or BID's classified information, are involved in some…….plot, for very high stakes, I believe. What the goal is I don't know yet, as all of this has happened coincident with your return from France. I think that John was on to it though – he was asking questions - I'm sure that's why someone tried to kill him. Before he left for St Vincent, John told me he thought there was something very odd about David Chesham's death. Paul Manton, who Sir Jeremy removed from his job on Friday, was either a part of, or aware of this plot, I'm sure, which is why he was murdered last night…' Claudine gasped, '…yes, I'm sorry to say, murdered in his bed in the clinic by someone claiming to be his wife.'

'Oh God…'

'Yes…..look, I sent John to search for an SIS agent who'd disappeared in Ghana once…..just watch yourself. These people have shown us they're totally ruthless and will kill without hesitating. Got that?'

'Yes, sir.'

'Go on,' Miles opened the office door, '…and bring John back with you - BID needs you both.'

*

After a harrowing visit to Paul Manton's mother in Islington to break the news of her son's death, Pat Scarsdale from CE1 flagged down a taxi and gave directions to Sloane Avenue where Paul Manton's wife had an apartment in Nell Gwyn House.

'Can I help you Madam?' asked the uniformed receptionist in Nell Gwyn House.

'I'm visiting a Mrs Manton in Apartment 73,' Pat Scarsdale replied.

'Are you expected?'

'No, perhaps you could see if she's in?'

'Of course, who do I say is here?'

'Pat Scarsdale - she does know me.' The receptionist dialled the apartment and Pat was pointed towards the lifts. Immediately she rang the bell, the door to 73 was opened by Valerie Manton, whom Pat remembered from the infrequent and slightly starchy social functions while her former husband had been the Director of Counter-Espionage at BID.

'Hello Pat, come in. Did you draw the short straw?' she asked pointedly.

'Pardon…?'

'Well what brings you here? What else have the police discovered about Paul that I would rather not know?' Valerie led Pat from the minute hall into a reasonable sized sitting room and indicated an armchair.

'No, thank you… Er, no, nothing like that. I have to tell you that Paul was murdered last night in the clinic.' Valerie sat down abruptly.

'How…? I mean isn't it... doesn't the clinic have guards, CCTV and things like that?'

'A woman got past the security guards with either your passport or an expert forgery. We're not sure why yet.' Valerie was staring at the floor, probably wondering how she was going to tell their two children, thought Pat sadly. 'Do you have your passport?'

'Yes I do,' and she got up, wiping the corners of her eyes, and went to a desk, opened the drawers under the fold down flap and produced a file.

'Here we are. This is the file...' but there she stopped. 'My passport's gone. I know it was here three weeks ago because the children and I went to Disney World in Paris,' she looked at Pat anxiously. 'I clearly remember putting all three passports back in the file before the children went back to school,' she tapped it with her finger as if to emphasise her point.

'Yes, I thought that might be the case. I expect a different photo was substituted, but all the correct information was there when the security guard passed the ID page under the scanner so he had no cause to question the identity of the visitor. You'll need to report the loss of your passport, Valerie. Is there anything else that you can tell us about Paul that might help us find who did this?' Pat didn't hold out much hope.

'Pat, I moved out of the house over nine months ago and our decree became absolute three months ago. I've had no contact with Paul, not since........well, you know what happened,' Valerie was agitated, but Pat indicated that she continue.

'It was about three weeks ago that I found the items missing - some quite valuable jewellery - which I reported to the police. It was the police who decided to search his mother's house in Mildend Park where they found that paedophile material on his computer. I suppose the theft of the jewellery must have been to mask the removal of my passport. I wasn't aware of Paul's interest in...' Valerie broke off, crying '...they always say that the wife is the last person to find out. Paul was an insufferable bastard to live with, but I would never have suspected him of anything like that,' she finished quietly.

'If anything else comes to mind, Valerie, can you please phone me personally.......here, take my card and phone me, however trivial you think it may be....OK?'

'Yes, of course I will....what about the funeral?' she looked up at Pat, wide-eyed.

'We'll take care of all that and keep you informed if you'd like to be involved.'

'Thank you......and I will get in touch if I remember anything,' Valerie assured Pat as she showed her out of the apartment.

*

'Christ, Miles, the plot bloody thickens,' sighed Barry Windsor, who'd barely had any sleep in the last 48 hours. 'Pat's just debriefed me on her visits to Paul's mother and Valerie. The two men were sitting, both exhausted, in what had been Paul Manton's office, now occupied by Barry until a new appointment of Director Counter-Espionage could be made.

'Did she turn up anything useful for us?' Miles asked, more in hope than expectation.

'Three starters.....the first, from his Mum at the house in Islington. We knew that the divorce settlement had bled Paul white; his own fault really, but his mother told Pat that there would be no financial worries for the two of them. So where was this sudden windfall of cash coming from? Secondly, Pat discovered that Valerie's passport had been stolen.....and probably went at the same time as the jewellery that was stolen three weeks ago. It could well be that the jewellery theft was a cover for taking the passport. Third, uh...' he consulted a notebook, 'yes, Valerie told Pat that although Paul was an unmitigated bastard to live with – her words of course - she had no idea about the paedophilia - it wouldn't be the first time that a wife has had to find out about it the hard way,' Barry paused to let everything sink in. Miles was nodding slowly.

'So what do you think?' he prompted Barry.

'Well, I have no proof – yet - but I believe that Paul Manton was involved in a high-powered conspiracy; by high-powered, I mean that the people he's involved with are not only very senior, but also very powerful. I mean, Christ, they have the ability to direct a professional hit team From Miami to St Vincent at a moment's notice and expert thieves who can break into houses without leaving a trace and a woman who was able to impersonate Valerie Manton and murder a patient in what was supposed to be a maximum security location at our clinic. But whatever this is, these people know so much that the tentacles of whatever conspiracy Paul was a part of have to lead right back into this building.'

'I agree. Look, Barry, I know your teams are working flat out and I know you've barely had an hour's sleep these last two days, but we have to unravel this conspiracy as our top priority.

'Absolutely.'

'OK, I'd better go and brief Jeremy and let him know how compromised BID is until this cancer is rooted out. Thanks for all that,' and Miles Thompson left hastily, mentally rehearsing how he would break the news to the Director.

*

Claudine had only just caught her flight out of Heathrow. During her pre-assignment briefing from Jason Wolstenholme he had repeated Miles Thompson's warning to act on her own and only to communicate with the Deputy Director. From Jason's office she had paid a quick visit to Tony Taylor, BID's armourer, to have her .45 calibre Colt Combat Elite automatic checked out. It was a powerful weapon, but years of helping her father in Guernsey haul in nets on his trawler had given her wrists of steel. He made her fire off a magazine of seven rounds to check the weapon after he'd stripped, cleaned and oiled it. All the rounds punctured an orange-sized hole in the middle of the Figure 11's chest. Claudia's philosophy was that on ninety per cent of the occasions when she had to use the Colt she was up against men who, despite her skill at self-defence were bigger, heavier and stronger than her. When she hit them with a .45 calibre bullet, they stayed down, so great was the shock of the impact. Tony Taylor and Gunn were long-standing friends and the latter's subdued mood reflected that of many of Gunn's colleagues in BID on what, perversely, was a gorgeous, bright, sunny Monday in the middle of June.

Claudine had just enough time to dash back to her flat in Fulham – she had sold the small house in Richmond having found the mortgage left her very little from her salary - threw a whole mass of washing into the machine, repacked her rucksack, scribbled a note to the cleaner she shared with Gunn and jumped into the BID car waiting outside for her. She had no hold baggage, only her rucksack and as a business class passenger, she was rushed through check-in, where she handed over a plastic bag with her Colt, spare magazine and ammunition, and reached the gate just minutes before it closed.

Kingstown and its airport lie at the foot of the Soufrière Volcano which forms the main feature of the island and provides it with the lush, green slopes on which the main export crop of bananas is grown. The airport runway runs along the grain of the land and therefore has one end pointing inland at the volcano and the other pointing out to sea along the line of the valley where the Island's capital has grown up. For some supposedly entirely logical meteorological reason, the prevailing wind is offshore which means that both landing and taking-off aircraft do so directly towards the slopes of Soufrière. Claudine had spent two or three sailing holidays in the Caribbean, one of those with Gunn, which had been interrupted by him being summoned back to London prior to an assignment in Indonesia. This was her first visit to St Vincent and thus the first time she had experienced her Airbus 340's 250 mph approach over the sea to a runway which seemed far too short and the mountain slopes beyond, far too close.

The 'Bee Wee' Airbus which had connected with her BA flight to Barbados landed with at least another 200 yards of runway to spare as it turned off and taxied back to the terminal, which was painted in whimsical pastel shades of green, blue and yellow. Claudine passed quickly through immigration and customs, and then in the arrivals hall met up with the Captain of her flight, who was unable to hide his surprise at handing over the plastic bag containing the firearm, which had been in his care, to this slightly rangy blonde who, to him, looked more like a gap year student than a spy.

Both Claudine and Gunn were totally unsuited to their roles as BID agents. An ideal agent would never have made such an impression on the Captain, and the face would have been instantly forgettable - unnoticeable in a crowd. Both tall, Gunn's height of 6'3" put him about twelve inches taller than the average male in his specialist area - South East Asia - and Claudine's 5'9" frame set her apart from the majority of women. It was not an asset for either of them, so both had found other ways to blend in.

Looking as though she was on her 'year out' always worked well for Claudine, who dressed her slender frame to look more youthful than her years. She pocketed the weapon, put the ammunition in her rucksack, and headed off into the crowd, messing her hair up as she went.

# CHAPTER 4

In contrast to John Gunn, Mike Soames was ideally suited to the role of an intelligence agent. His slim build, unremarkable looks and moderate height of 5'10" masked a fetish-like obsession with fitness. He was a Second Dan black belt in karate and, since joining BID from the SAS in 1991, had become fluent in Spanish and had qualified as a pilot of both rotary and fixed wing. His ordinary appearance meant that he could adapt to disappear in a crowd in almost any country other than sub-Sahara Africa.

Soames had arrived via the Virgin Atlantic flight from Gatwick, which had landed some seven hours before the arrival of Claudine's connecting British West Indian Airways 'Bee Wee' flight. He had been met at the airport by Malcolm Slater and the two of them had gone directly to the Police Headquarters in Bay Street. Soames' presence wasn't high profile, but was similar to the presence of intelligence agents from every country in embassies and high commissions around the world. In countries where it was deemed necessary to have an intelligence presence, an embassy would declare to the host nation the name of its intelligence agent. More often than not, there would be at least one, if not two or three other agents masquerading as cultural, commercial or consular attachés. So it was with Mike Soames and Claudine. Mike, for the most part, was required to keep the St Vincent Police informed of his movements; but neither the St Vincent Government nor the Police were aware of Claudine's presence other than she was just one of the many thousands of tourists at that time of year.

Mike Soames was in Slater's office after being shown briefly around Police HQ, which included a formal meeting with the St Vincent's Commissioner of Police, Sir Leo Hugues. The meeting had been brief; the Commissioner had made it abundantly clear that he neither wanted nor saw the necessity of BID's assistance to his Police Force. Back in his office, Malcolm Slater apologised for the cold reception.

'I don't know how much you know of the history of our Islands,' Slater mistook Soames' expression of utter indifference for residual irritation, 'but our Commissioner is descended from the radical French politician Victor Hugues, who, in 1796, rebelled against the terms of the 1783 Treaty of Versailles which had ceded St Vincent and the Grenadines to the British. His rebellion was soun'ly defeated by Sir Ralph Abercromby, but the Commissioner finds it difficult to hide his resentment of all things British. He's been 'on the mat' in front of our Prime Minister more than once for it. He should've done five years in this job, but rumour has it he'll be replaced at the end of this year after jus' three.....' Slater stopped when he realised Mike Soames had stopped listening, and switched abruptly to running through the case details.

'Unfortunately, we didn't get to the scene of the crime 'til some eight or more hours after the killer or killers had gone. However, we did do a thorough check of the passenger lists of all arrivin' and departin' aircraft on Saturday. Other than transit passengers, that threw up six possible suspects. We think we can reduce those six to two after the Miami Police confirmed that two Cubans travellin' on US passports under the names of Carlos Ocampo and Romero Garcia matched the identities of Fidel Carillo and Ernesto Diaz, both wanted for pretty much every crime in the book - an' a few that aren't,' he raised his eyebrows knowingly at Mike. 'These two beauties arrived on the American Airlines flight from Miami at 1845 hours and departed on the 2245 hours flight back to Miami - they would have got there long before we'd even been called to the scene of crime. We're pretty sure these are the two who murdered Miss Ramone and Mr Gunn, but they're just hired gunmen. We're sure someone in London hired them an', I regret to say, a local Rastafarian gang provided them with the weapons. We know the various haunts of this gang and the Miami Police will let us know the instant it has a lead on the Cubans. So,' and he gestured to Mike in an over-to-you motion, 'that's where we are right now.' He added: 'We have no idea why Gunn's body - and it's almos' certain he was dead - was removed. The tyre marks on the drive at Miss Ramone's house would fit every utility truck on the Island. Of course there were shoeprints, but where do you start to look for a match? You have a free hand, Mike, as far as I'm concerned. Miles Thompson told me that you've been here before so I guess you know your way aroun', but I've allocated you Sergeant Toby Charbonnier who can accompany you whenever you want. I strongly recommend that you use him as much as possible if you're goin' after the Rasta gang - he's had a lot of dealings with them. OK… well I guess you'd like to go to your hotel room?'

'Thanks, but I'd like to meet Sergeant Charbonnier first,' Mike said, rising from his chair.

'OK - of course, I'll call him; good luck, Mike, and please keep me informed,' and the two men shook hands, Malcolm Slater wincing at Mike's bone-crunching grasp.

*

Gunn slowly became aware of sound - voices, footsteps, the clink of metal on metal and a muffled, busy clattering of objects; sensation began to return to his body and limbs, which felt weighted to the bed by what he would soon realise was the vestiges of the anaesthetic. Gunn wondered if he could speak and the first attempt sounded like a frog's croak. He cleared his throat and tried again.

'Nurse…?'

A nurse nearby looked up from some paperwork and hurried over, smiling broadly.

'Good mornin', Mr Gunn, how are you feeling?' She picked up his chart and began checking the monitors and drips crowded around his bedside.

'My head hur… uh' he gasped at a sudden searing pain across his temple.

'You were shot in the head, Mr Gunn, do you remember anything?

'Er…..' he frowned, the effort of trying to think back to what had happened at Nina's house causing the throbbing pain to intensify. He remembered sitting on her balcony having dinner...........

'Nevermin'.....jus' rest. I'll go get you some more drugs for the pain. The operation was very successful,' she added, shaking her head in disbelief, 'they got that bullet outta your head an' it looks like you won' be havin' any real problems. You're a lucky man, mister, lucky our Dr Jackson found you when he did, eh?' and she bustled off, drawing a curtain after her.

The next person to appear from the other side of the curtain had to be a doctor.

'Hello Mr Gunn, I'm Robert Jackson,' he said, leaning over the railings around Gunn's hospital bed.

'You must be Doctor Jackson. I hear I owe you my life,' said Gunn, offering a weakened handshake.

'I got a real shock when I foun' you Mr Gunn. I'm not usually the first one at the scene of crime. The first I see of a shootin' is in the theatre. My father, ex-Corporal Gabriel Jackson, is a great fan of yours. It's because he was so keen to show you his photo album that we found you in time. What is extraordinary,' he continued, gingerly examining the dressings on John's head, 'is that you seem to be recoverin' so well from what was very nearly a fatal gunshot wound.' Robert decided to leave Nina Ramone out of the conversation for now, wondering if Gunn could even remember what had happened to her.

'Nina....? Gunn started, answering the unspoken question.

'No....I'm real sorry Mr Gunn....'

'John.....please call me John.'

'Okay, John,' Robert sighed heavily, the slightly practised sigh of someone who's had to break such news many, many times, 'Nina was dead when we found you. The police have her body in the morgue for a post-mortem.' The two men had been talking in low tones anyway, but Gunn now dropped his voice to a whisper.

'Does anyone know that I'm here?'

'No; no one saw us at Nina's house. Every member of my staff has been sworn to secrecy, but with the best will in the world, one of them may let somethin' slip, so it would be better if we move you so that you can recuperate in safety. I will take your stitches out in five days time, but I'm goin' to make arrangements to move you immediately now that you're awake. I don't need to know what this is all about to guess you're in real trouble if anyone finds out you're still alive.'

'Thank you…' Gunn was grateful not to have to bat away curious questions. Robert Jackson was obviously no fool, and knew that the less said, the better; he already knew more than was safe for him.

'One last word of advice - as your surgeon; if you don't rest for at least ten days before you go off chasin' Nina's killers, I will be attendin' your funeral as well as her's. It should be more like a month, but I know that would be impossible,' Robert smiled warmly, then made to leave, saying, 'I'm goin' to go and organise a transfer for you now.' The wisdom of Robert Jackson's advice was evident within minutes of the surgeon's departure as Gunn drifted back into a deep sleep.

Robert waited until 4 am the next morning and then with the help of just one other male nurse they gently heaved the sleeping Gunn into the back of a Toyota Landcruiser in which all the rear seats had been folded flat. It would have been much easier to have used one of the clinic's ambulances, but people notice ambulances and Robert intended to make Gunn's move as inconspicuous as possible. The destination was a small holiday cottage owned by the Jacksons in a sheltered cove in Layou Bay, to the west of Kingstown. The cottage had been built on piles driven into the seabed and was used only by Robert and his father when they wanted to fish and escape the tourist haunts. The small weatherboard cottage had two bedrooms, a kitchen/dinette, a lounge which extended out to the veranda and the luxury of two bathrooms. The drive from Plantation Road to Layou Bay only took twenty minutes and they passed not a single car on the journey. The male nurse, Jacob Robin, had the task of both caring for and guarding his patient while he recovered from the operation. Once Gunn was comfortably settled in a bed, which had been moved out of the bedroom into the lounge so that there was a view out to sea, and Robert had checked that all the medication and drugs which had been loaded into the Landcruiser in a cold box had been carefully transferred to the cottage's refrigerator, he drove back to the clinic taking a different route.

*

After Malcolm Slater had introduced Mike Soames to Sergeant Toby Charbonnier, he left the two men together and returned to his office to deal with the pile of paperwork which had stacked up during the 24 hours since the destruction of Hassan Hussein's aircraft - and three other private aircraft - and the deaths of John Gunn and Nina Ramone. Toby Charbonnier was a sharp and highly motivated policeman who had just completed a two year attachment to the New York Police Department and whose talents were largely wasted on the relatively few drug-related muggings and crimes in Kingstown. He spent some ten minutes explaining the routine of the Headquarters and the Royal St Vincent Police Force, but was mildly irritated to note that Mike Soames barely had the good grace to even feign interest in what he was being told.

'Right, that's the touris' crap out the way,' Toby snapped abruptly, cutting short any niceties. 'Where d'you wanna start lookin' for your Mr Gunn?'

'Any suggestions.....Toby?' Mike asked, with an almost imperceptible sneer - almost, but not quite. It was enough that Toby knew where he stood. He wasn't required, but Soames would humour him as the course of least resistance. But Toby didn't take the bait; he imagined this is what most spooks must be like, and decided not to kick against it, instead jovially offering that they start with the haunts of the Rasta gang on the north side of the city.

Kingstown is the capital city of St Vincent, but because of the geology of the Island, with its steep-sided, conical shape, inherited from its volcanic origin, there was very little level space for the capital, its docks and the airport, much of which were built on landfill reclaimed from the sea. The city consists of three parallel streets charmingly named Bay Street - nearest to the shore line of the bay, Middle Street and Back Street; the latter being the last reasonably level road before the ground rose steeply to the hills which formed the city's backdrop. Both the Island's Administration building and the Police HQ were on Bay Street, together with the market and docks, whereas the Parliament building and the Island's Courthouse were relegated to Back Street. The Rasta gang's hangouts varied from one cafe or bar to another, hidden away in narrow, cobbled Hill Street, which wound up the steep foothills of the Soufrière volcano. Toby explained all this to Mike as the two of them set off from Police HQ into the winding streets which crossed Middle Street and Back Street and led to Hill Street. The latter was not a tourist haunt because there were no fast-food restaurants and the gradient usually proved too much of a strain for the Island's habitual cruise line passengers, who stuck to the low lying areas near the bay. Toby had no idea whether Mike was listening or not, but continued anyway, more to assuage the awkwardness of his sullen companionship.

Toby knew his patch well and tracked down the Rastas in the Black Patch Bar. It took a few seconds for both him and Mike Soames to get used to the smoky, stygian darkness of the bar after the bright afternoon sunlight on the street. The air was thick with the stench of skunk cannabis. Toby was clearly well known to the gang, as remarks of, "here come the pigs", loud snorting and other slurs, to which Toby was totally inured, erupted from the group of six men he'd indicated seated around a table at the back of the bar.

'An' who's the honkie, pig? You got yo'self...' but the mockery stopped dead, almost as though some silent signal had passed between the dreadlocked

Rastas. Toby glanced over his shoulder at Mike, but there was no indication of any expression on his face other than the somewhat resigned expression that had been there ever since they'd first met. Toby had expected considerably more harassment, but it was almost as though the men were frightened, which was a first in his experience.

Toby didn't recognise the man sitting nearest to him and assumed that he was a new recruit to the gang, but he didn't miss the silent warnings being urgently sent him by the others; signals which he failed to heed because he had now turned, with his back to the other men, coughed up a gob of phlegm and spat it at Mike's feet. Mike's reaction was so quick that even Toby and his two years of experience of New York policing had never seen anything so slick, clinical and brutal. Mike lifted the man out of his chair as though he weighed no more than a child. A blur of chops and side-hand hammer blows followed - so fast it seemed to Toby as if someone had pressed a fast-forward button; he reeled backwards, out of the way. Blood burst from the man's mouth and nose and the snap of his collar bone sounded like a chair leg breaking. A customer screamed in horror somewhere, but all were afraid to flee for fear of being caught up in the violence. Mike threw the man's lifeless body into a corner of the bar like a piece of rubbish then lent over the bar and pulled the cloth off the terrified barman's shoulder. He calmly wiped the blood and snot off his hands, barely out of breath and turned to the remaining five men.

'Anyone else want to spit?' Toby had bent down to the unconscious Rastafarian and felt for a pulse; he was barely alive, so he hurriedly called for an ambulance. Toby glanced at the five men; abject terror paralysed them, but one dared to stammer a protest.

'Hey man, police ain't allowed to do that.' The man on his left was digging him in the ribs in an attempt to quieten him.

'Who said anything about the police, dogshit?' Mike purred menacingly, almost seeming to enjoy himself, as he turned towards the man. The latter looked around for support from his gang, but he realised that the bar was now empty and his four colleagues had purposely shuffled away from him.

'You's with that pi.........policeman,' he quickly amended pig to policeman.

'Get out of here,' Mike spat, 'and take that filthy piece of shit with you,' he jerked his head at the crumpled heap in the corner as the sound of an ambulances two-tone siren reached the bar.

'Hey, you can't...' but those were the last words he blurted before a blindingly fast snap-kick caught the man in the groin and sent him writhing and screaming across the tiled floor of the bar. With a rush to escape, the remaining four Rastafarians grabbed him and dragged him out of the bar, leaving Toby and Mike to greet the paramedics.

Toby was puzzled by a number of things that had occurred in the very few minutes since they had entered the bar. Some of the six Rastafarians had recognised Mike Soames; of that there was no doubt. They'd barely disguised their reaction at seeing him and Mike's over-reaction by half-killing one man and emasculating another might well have been to smother any impression of either recognition or collusion.

'Do you think that will help with your search for Gunn, Mike?' Toby asked calmly.

'Might well do; in my experience, the only thing that bunch of little shits understands is violence - they deal it out often enough. The next time I meet with that lot, I might get some information out of them,' Mike replied, as he ordered a Coca-Cola from the barman.

'Well, each to his own. Er, we're pretty close to your hotel - the Montrose, right? I'll leave you there,' Toby was eager to get back to the station and away from Mike Soames.

'Thanks. Sorry if that upset you, but I think it might produce results.' Toby knew that would be the limit of Mike's explanation for the rough-house in the Black Patch Bar. Toby left him outside the Montrose Hotel and returned to Police HQ. It was now just after 5pm, but as Toby walked past Malcolm Slater's office, he saw that the Chief Superintendent was still at his desk. On impulse, he knocked on the door.

'Come in,' and Malcolm looked up over his reading glasses as Toby entered. 'Hi Toby, everythin' okay with our visitor?'

'Have you got five minutes, sir?' Toby asked.

'Of course, take a seat,' Malcolm said, despite his piled in-tray. 'Somethin' botherin' you?' he added, noting his Sergeant's worried expression immediately.

'Just as you suggested, sir, I took Mike to Hill Street an' we foun' the Rastas immediately in the Black Patch Bar. You know their usual jive - calling us pigs and an' such like, well they started off with all that, but as we came further into the bar that all stopped suddenly. I'm convinced they recognised Soames - not only recognised him, but were petrified of him - all of them except the new guy, who obviously didn' know any better. He turns away from his gang so couldn' see what I saw. They were tryin' to warn him, but without makin' it obvious to us. This guy spits at Mike an' got the most brutal kickin' I ever seen in my time as a policeman. Another of the gang got the same handout. One of them is in hospital and the other is unlikely to be visitin' ladies any time soon. I think,' and Toby measured what he was saying carefully, 'that beating he gave those two was to cover the mistake of letting me see that he was recognised - an' partly as a warnin' if somethin' similar happened again.'

'You're sure about all this?'

'More than sure; Mike Soames is not here to fin' this guy Gunn - or if he is, it's a pretty low priority for him. Mike has his own agenda - an' I don't think it has much to do with BID's. He knows Kingstown - really well. I think he knew that bar as well. I think this guy's dangerous - very dangerous,' Toby concluded, shifting uneasily at the certainty of his accusation, but excited in spite of himself at what he may have uncovered. Malcolm slowly took off his glasses and rubbed his eyes.

'I know for certain Soames has been here before - his boss in London admitted that when the visit was set up. After my visit to the scene of the shooting in Nina's house, I'm pretty certain that Gunn is dead and those who shot him have removed the body and thrown it into the sea, so no one is going to find it as the sharks will have dealt with it by now. Poor Nina was collateral damage. You say he's at his hotel now? Okay, look now......he's under no compulsion to be escorted by you, but see if you can set up a roster of three or four constables - really experienced ones - to keep an eye on him. Make sure they're fully aware of how dangerous he is and they are not, under any circumstances, to get involved - alright?'

'Yes, sir, thank you,' and Toby hurried out of the office.

*

After getting back her plastic bag of 'duty-free', Claudine walked round the arrivals hall re-enacting in her mind's eye what Jason had told her of both events at the airport which had involved Gunn and Nina the previous week. She found the coffee terrace where they had been sitting when Hassan's private jet was blown up. She then went back into the main entrance hall, ticketing area and check-in. Before leaving the airport to check in to her hotel, Claudine judged that just one or two enquiries might bear fruit. There were two security guards evident, and on the pretext of being a travel journalist, she approached one of them, standing by the entrance to the departure lounge where the baggage and passenger scanners were in operation. As it was nearly 9 pm on a Monday evening, there were relatively few passengers around.

'Good evening officer,' Claudine started, 'I'm a journalist for Caribtravel Magazine. I just...,' she stuttered sweetly, 'I wondered if you could help me with some information?'

'Sure, Miss; what was it you wanted?' he smiled helpfully.

'One of my colleagues was here on Saturday and told me that you had a bit of excitement. She said that an aircraft caught fire and there was some shooting or something,' Claudine adopted an expression of innocent enquiry.

'We sure did, but I wasn' on duty when it all happened. My colleague, Daniel, was on the late shift. He was here when we had all that trouble. Don' do us any good that sorta thing Miss, makes folks nervous to travel.'

'Yes I'm sure. That's one of the reasons I'm here. The people who read our magazine are mostly older people and it's my job to reassure them that St Vincent is a great - and peaceful - place to go on holiday.'

'Well it is, for sure – this kinda thing never usually happens here. Oh,' he touched Claudine's shoulder and pointed, 'that's Daniel over there by the car rentals. You come with me an' I'll make sure he helps you out.' and the guard led Claudine to where Daniel was chatting with the girl at the Budget Car Rental desk.

'Daniel, this is Miss...' and he turned to Claudine with raised eyebrows.

'Carter,' she offered.

'Miss Carter; she's a journalist and she wanna know what happened here on Saturday. She's doing a piece that tells folks this is safe place to come for a holiday.'

'That right?' Daniel finished his conversation and gave Claudine his full attention. 'Yes, jus' like a movie. Horace - our senior officer - he was on duty with me an' he took a bullet in his shoulder. He's still on sick leave.'

'God, poor man! Are you able to tell me what happened from start to finish?' Claudine asked hopefully, producing a small notebook to authenticate her role.

'Well, lotsa people saw it,' Daniel shrugged. 'This plane lands - private one - an' as it stops a man jumps out an' runs away from it with someone shootin' at him. Then....woof!.....plane goes up in smoke – like a bomb. Horace, he jumps into his jeep and drives to cut off this guy, but gets shot. 'Nother man – we don' know who he was - but he could shoot! Must've been nearly fifty or sixty yards last week when he put...' Daniel stopped, aware that he was probably saying more than he should to someone in the tourism business.

'Oh – no, this can be off the record!' Claudine laughed, then added conspiratorially, 'there's no way I can let any of our readers see all of this!'

'Okay,' Daniel relented. 'Well he ran out to help Horace, but the guy runs towards the terminal an' Miss Ramone - she works on our Radio Grenadines - she goes out an' jus' as cool as that fella, pulls out a gun from her bag an' shoots the man. All jus' like the movies....an' then the police an' photograph guys all come.'

'Wow. But this is a total one-off right? You sure you don't know who these people were?'

'No, the police wouldn' let the Press bother them, so all we know is they must have been the good guys. I'd guess…'

But Claudine cut him off before he could guess: 'Did you happen to see anyone else talking to Miss Ramone and this man........you know, people that you know who perhaps I could interview?'

'Er, well...' and Daniel cocked his head, thinking back. 'Walter,' Daniel turned suddenly to his fellow security guard, 'who's that ole guy we meet at the bar of the ole soldiers' club?'

'Which one? There's always lots of ole men there.'

'No, the one who has a doctor son who drives him to the club - gave us a lift once... you remember.'

'Oh him! that's ole Gabriel... you'd think he was the only one to fight in that war!'

'Yes Miss, that's Gabriel Jackson. I saw him talking to Miss Ramone and that man before the police arrived.'

'You don't know where he lives do you, Walter?' Claudine asked, chancing her luck.

'Sure do; his son, Robert - real clever fella - studied to be a doctor in England an' 'merica. He has a clinic jus' outa town on Plantation Road. You turn off left, right by Saint Joseph's church.'

'Thanks so much, both of you. That's been really helpful and I'm sure that we'll get lots more tourists to come to this lovely island,' Claudine cringed inwardly at having to deceive two such helpful men, but 'maybe, just maybe,' she thought, as she made her way out to the line of taxis, she might have something to start her search. She got into a taxi and asked for the Sunset Inn in Villa Bay - a small guest house on the beach in a secluded bay, selected for that very reason by Jason's PA.

# CHAPTER 5

Ever since his arrival in the office at a leisurely 9.45, when the majority of the staff at 85, Vauxhall Cross had been there since 8.30, John Cornwall had been unable to concentrate on his work. Twice, his PA had had to repeat the calls she'd received before he arrived. She was unaware that his mind was occupied, not with the tedious business of managing what was little more than a repository for routine classified material, but with the potential threat which Clive Sterling posed to the embezzled pension fund.

John Cornwall and Clive Sterling were chameleons; they lacked the ambition and ability to reach the dizzying heights of the Civil Service and so had quickly learned to compensate by adjusting the colour of their political skin to find favour with whichever party was in power. But even a chameleon's luck runs out. The bright civil servants in the Cabinet Office achieved the key appointments at Private Secretary and Director, but those who failed quickly found that they were unwanted anywhere else in the Service; their careers hit a brick wall. Cornwall and Sterling had found themselves languishing in this pool of surplus manpower, and it was from within this pool that five others, from both the Cabinet Office and Intelligence Services, had been contacted by letter. All had one thing in common; they had something to hide, something that could be used as blackmail.

Those who received this letter were Paul Manton and David Chesham in BID, John Cornwall in MI6, Clive Sterling in MI5 and, finally, Venetia Akehurst, Andrew Barton and George Paterson in the Cabinet Office. Their individual vulnerability to blackmail spanned a comprehensive range of depravities: Paul Manton's preoccupation with downloading child porn; David Chesham's gambling debts; Cornwall's hit-and-run accident, which had killed a child, but was still unsolved by the police; Sterling's flirtations with rent boys; Andrew Barton's and George Paterson's joint embezzlement of the Millennium Dome's contingency fund; and Venetia's dubious liaisons with under-age girls. The letter listed all seven names and their departments in government offices; and it revealed that the writer possessed a detailed knowledge of their secrets. It instructed each of them to slice £20 million from the budgets for which they were responsible and credit the sum to a specific account in the Security and Intelligence Agencies' provision for the Civil Service Pension Scheme. The audit of the budget for the Security and Intelligence Agencies was never published or made public, so an influx of £140 million in a budget of £1.5 billion was hardly likely to arouse interest, the letter assured them. Their co-operation would result in a generous pension payout running into millions; failure to comply would be a fatal mistake. The letter had concluded by encouraging each of the now co-conspirators to get to know each other and to report any suspicion of betrayal or lack of resolve via a speed-dial number on a Nokia mobile phone enclosed with each letter.

David Chesham's and Paul Manton's deaths had reduced the original seven people involved to five. And John Cornwall now resolved that Clive Sterling, too, would have to go. His mind made up, the Director of 85 Vauxhall Cross told his PA he would be out until after lunch, left the building and took a taxi to Whitehall. He asked the driver to drop him at the southern end, at the arched entrance to King Charles Street. He paused outside the entrance to the Foreign Office, scrolled to a contact on his mobile and pressed the connect button.

'Akehurst!' snapped from the minute microphone on his mobile.

Venetia Akehurst had a volatile temper and a tongue that could slice through seasoned oak. She was, however, a very capable administrator and would have risen to be Director of her Cabinet Office department, which advised the Minister for Women, had it not been for her temper and a voracious interest in girls young enough to be her daughter. Her affairs had nudged her on to the Met's radar more than once, requiring a lot of string pulling higher up the Civil Service chain, and resulted in her being passed over no less than twice by much younger colleagues.

'It's John, Venetia. We need to talk - urgently.'

'McDonalds in ten minutes?'

'I'll be there,' and he rang off. Venetia made one more phone call and then left her office. She arrived ten minutes later to the second and they both walked to Gordon's Wine Bar in Villiers Street, which could have been purpose built for conspirators. It was almost pitch dark amongst the ancient curved arches of the old cellar and impossible to see anyone in its nether regions. Cornwall spotted a table and ordered a bottle of St Emilion and the cheese platter. They were early for lunch and the area around them was deserted.

'How much longer have we got to go on with this?' Venetia asked.

'Six months at the outside. The last letter said the share out would be before the end of this year. Vauxhall Cross closes at the end of August and I retire in September, but we have a problem - very similar to Paul. Clive's losing it - he's drinking..... become a bit of a loose cannon. I think he's going to try and look for an exit; he could blow the whistle. If we don't take steps the remaining four of us - and whoever's controlling this pension fund - will be spending the rest of our lives in prison rather than comfortable retirement.'

'Two people have been killed already. Are you saying Clive's got to go too?'

'Shhh...' Cornwall hushed her.

'Sod off John!' she retorted, though in a whisper.

'Venetia, we are collectively guilty of two murders. You yourself gave Paul his lethal injection. If we suddenly get squeamish, that £140 million that's been earning interest for the last eight years in the Cayman Islands will never see the light of day. Of the original seven there are five of us left. If Clive met with an accident, that'd leave four of us, plus the unknown party, to share a pot which must be fast approaching £200 million. That's £40 million each,' Clive jabbed the table urgently with his finger.

'You greedy bastard,' she seethed. 'Should you get greedy for my share, you need to know that I've deposited a letter with my solicitor, which she is to open only on my death. That letter explains everything. Call it my life insurance policy or whatever you want, but you'd better make sure I live to see that money. She took great pleasure in seeing Cornwall's already puce face flush with anger.

'Jesus Christ!...' he started angrily, then checked himself, changing tack with about as much subtlety as a charging rhino. 'Look, I've never doubted your commitment, but Clive...'he sighed heavily.

'Clive's made the mistake of having a conscience,' Venetia finished sarcastically, sneering into her wine glass as she downed the remains of her St Emilion.

'It's too bloody late for that,' he said coldly, dropping some notes on the table to cover the bill. 'I'll talk to Andrew and George tonight and let you know what we decide.' Cornwall drained his glass of wine, heaved himself to his feet and left. He didn't see Andrew Barton and George Peterson get up from their table in an even darker corner of the cellar and join Venetia.

Once back on Villiers Street, Cornwall turned right for the Strand, but after some ten yards stopped, turned and retraced his steps, passing the Embankment Underground Station and turning right into Northumberland Avenue. He stopped at the Sherlock Holmes Pub, where punters were spilling out on to the pavement, and pulled out a mobile phone from his jacket pocket. The message had to be sent by voice and the response would always come back by text. Cornwall had used this phone only once before, to express his concern that David Chesham had aroused the suspicions of BID's agent John Gunn. David had been killed in an anti-terrorist operation less than a week later. Who had contacted the unknown source about Paul Manton he had no idea, but Venetia had then received detailed instructions of what she must do. He also had no idea what number he was dialling as speed dial had been set up on the '5' button when he received it and the number never registered on the screen. He pressed '5' now as he stood amongst the crowd of smokers outside the pub.

'Please speak after the tone,' a recorded message instructed him.

*

Claudine was awake shortly after sunrise thanks to jetlag, but she considered this a plus and busied herself showering and dressing, impatient to get on with her search. She knew, however, that she would have to reign herself in, her bullish competence at odds with the laid back lifestyle of the Caribs; she'd get nowhere by offending them. Even so, at 7am precisely she was down on the breakfast veranda, which overlooked the serene blue of Villa Bay, and helped herself to scalding hot coffee and fresh fruit. On her late arrival the previous evening, Claudine had been welcomed to the Sunset Inn by its owner, Madam Divine Twintoe, who would have regaled her with the delights and attractions of the Island all night if she hadn't pleaded jet-lag to escape. This morning a much younger woman appeared.

'Good mornin', Miss Carteret, I'm Suzy Twintoe. Is

there anythin' I can do to help with your visit?'

'Hi; er, yes, thanks. I need to hire a car as soon as possible – or a scooter would do. Can you arrange that?' Claudine carried her coffee over to a table by the front of the veranda with an uninterrupted view over the lapis-blue sea, the brilliant green of the small islands and the yachts anchored in the sheltered bay.

'No arrangement necessary,' Suzy smiled sweetly. 'We have three small cars here for hire – a Toyota Yaris, a Renault Clio and a Mini. Would any of those do?'

'Great – I'll take the Toyota. I'd like to leave as soon as I've finished breakfast. Will that be possible?' Claudine cracked a wide grin, hoping it might compensate for her edginess, and to her relief, Suzy responded in kind.

'That's no problem Miss Carteret; the tank is full of gas and I'll get you the keys and the forms to sign at reception as soon as you're done. Enjoy your breakfast,' and Suzy disappeared into the kitchen. True to her word, the form and the keys were at reception together with a road map of the Island on which Claudine quickly found Plantation Road and St Joseph's Church. She returned to her room, removed the .45 Colt automatic from under the mattress and put it and its silencer into her beach bag. She waved a deliberately breezy goodbye to Suzy, who cheerfully reminded her to drive on the left, and then headed inland, round the outskirts of Kingstown, before picking up Plantation Road. The directions she had received from the security guards at the airport were easy enough to follow and she had no difficulty finding St Joseph's Church and the turn-off opposite.

The clinic was just over a mile down the turn-off, and Claudia drove into the car park, found a visitor's slot, grabbed her beach bag and headed for the main entrance.

As she approached the glass door leading into the clinic's reception, an old man wearing a safari shirt with a single row of faded medal ribbons came out, placing an ancient slouch hat, with a West Indian Brigade insignia on one side, back on his thinning white hair. When he saw Claudia, he courteously touched the brim of his hat before shuffling on, holding a paper bag in his other hand in which she assumed he had just collected a prescription. He had already passed Claudine and she had one hand on the door handle when, on a hunch, she turned and said: 'Good morning, Gabriel.' The old man stopped, turned around and removed his slouch hat.

'Good mornin' Miss,' he squinted at her as she walked towards him, trying hard to place her. 'Can't say I remember who you are, but then I'm nearly 84 so ma' memory's not so good. I'm sorry.'

'My name's Claudine de Carteret and there's nothing wrong with your memory; we've never met before, but I've heard a lot about you from your friends at the old soldiers' club. You are Corporal Gabriel Jackson?'

'Yes Miss, I am,' he replaced his hat, 'an' what brings you here?' he eyed her nervously.

'I'm looking for my friend - and colleague........I work with him. His name's John; you met him at the airport when there was all that shooting and a plane was blown up. I was hoping that you might be able to help me as I've lost touch with John. Your friends at the club gave me this address.'

'John?' Gabriel murmured, frowning as though he was trying to remember the encounter.

'Yes, John; he was with Nina Ramone from Radio Grenadines. Please help me if you can,' Claudine pleaded, trying hard not to be impatient with the old soldier.

'Perhaps I can help?' The voice came from behind Claudine, and she spun round to see a tall, good-looking man.....middle-aged, she guessed.

'Doctor Robert Jackson; I'm sorry, I din' mean to scare you. That's my father.' He studied her a moment, then said: 'You're right, he did meet your friend. It's all right Dad, you go on home and tell Mum I'll be out for lunch,' and his father shuffled on his way, gratefully.

'OK, Miss…?'

'de Carteret - Claudine.'

'Claudine; well this is my clinic so why don't you come to my office and I'll see what, if anythin', we can do to help you find John.' Claudine followed Robert wordlessly inside, where he paused at reception to speak to the girl behind the desk.

'Can you wait here for a couple of minutes, Claudine? I need to take a call.' Claudine nodded, reluctantly, and Robert disappeared through a door with his name on it. She sat down in the reception area and wondered if she was about to be given a polite, "sorry, but we can't help you", when the door opened again and Robert invited her in.

'I think I might have some good news for you,' he began, as he closed the door behind her.

'Good news?' Claudine said in surprise, not allowing herself to get her hopes up.

'I'm sorry for makin' you wait in reception, but while you were waitin', Tina behind the desk took your picture on her cell-phone and sent it to one of my nurses, Jacob. Jacob is caring for a patient by the name of John Gunn. Not here at the clinic - somewhere else. That's the John you mean isn' it?' he said with a half smile. Claudine stared at him in wide-eyed disbelief.

'He's alive?' she said finally.

'Yes, an' he's goin' to be fine.'

'He was shot?'

'Yes, in the head. He's very lucky we foun' him when we did.'

'Shot in the head... Jesus. I'm sorry,' she said, blinking back tears. 'I'd prepared myself for the worst.' But she wouldn't believe anything yet, not until she'd seen Gunn for herself. She still didn't know if this doctor was trustworthy. She quickly regained her composure.

'Why didn't he get word back to the UK?'

'John asked us to tell no one, not even someone claimin' to be from British Intelligence in London, that he had survived the attempt to kill him. You can ask him yourself why that is; he don' want to say too much to me and honestly, I don' want to know.'

'Right. Will he...?'

But Robert pre-empted her: 'He's had minor concussion, but he don' appear to have any memory loss. As far as I can tell, he won' have any lastin' damage beyond some scarrin' provided he rests for a week or so.

'How was it that you were in the right place at the right time to help John?'

'That's because of my father,' Robert said with a

broad grin. 'He became a fan of John's after an incident a week or so ago when he shot some Haitian thug at the airport and then, purely by coincidence, he was at the airport again the other evenin' when the plane was blown up. Dad spends quite a lot of time, especially this time of year, flyin' aroun' the islands visitin' his ol' wartime comrades. He wanted to show John his photos of his wartime service and asked me to drive him up to Nina Ramone's house the other night. We must have arrived about five or ten minutes after the shootin'.........probably passed the gunmen on our way to Nina's house. There was nothin' I could do for Nina; but we got John back here to the clinic and I operated that night. He's recoverin' at my beach house - we thought it would be the safest place because it's remote. Shall we go and see him?'

*

'Oh Mr Sterling, one last thing; you asked me to remind you that you are taking your sister and her children to the 'Lion King' at the Lyceum this evening. You're meeting them at Burger King in the strand at 6.30. Will you be going back to your apartment first or straight there?' Clive Sterling's PA wound up their daily catch-up, eager to get everything out of the way so she could leave early.

'I'll take a shower here and then get a taxi to the Strand - no need for you to stay late. Thanks.' Sterling barely looked up from the paperwork on his desk.

When she had left his office, Sterling abandoned his pretence of working, slumping back in his chair then getting up and walking to the long windows overlooking the Thames.

'What a bloody mess I've made of my life,' he thought. 'Implicated in two murders and what for? A lot of money I don't really need and the prospect of spending the rest of my life in prison.'

It was also becoming abundantly clear to him that Cornwall was not to be trusted. Sterling pondered, as he took at the London skyline, how he could protect himself, in case Cornwall decided that a fifth share wasn't enough for him. He made a mental note to ring his solicitor, then went back to his desk and worked through until 5.30. He showered and shaved in his en-suite washroom and picked up a taxi on the Embankment, which dropped him at Burger King in the Strand.

He immediately spotted his sister, Veronica, and his nephew and niece - now aged 12 and 14 - who were making light work of some burgers and chips. He settled for a coffee, his appetite non-existent. The children's excitement and his sister's banal yet strangely comforting banter about their life in Godalming, where her husband was a school headmaster, temporarily banished Sterling's depression. They reminded him of how simple life could be - simple desires, simple pleasures - and it convinced him more than ever that he must get himself out of the conspiracy. Owning up to his sordid exploits now seemed like the softer option.

The musical was approaching its climax, when all the animals appeared from the back of the theatre and processed through the audience to the stage. There was a slight commotion in the row behind Veronica and she was surprised to see someone leaving. Her children were entranced with the music, dancing and the costumed actors advancing on the stage. She glanced to her left, where her brother was sitting on the other side of the children and noticed that he had nodded off. 'Never mind,' she thought; 'long day in the office.'

The musical ended and after three curtain calls the lights came up and everyone started to leave. Veronica turned to her daughter, who was sitting next to her uncle.

'Mary, wake your uncle.' Mary did as bidden and shook Clive's shoulder, but he slumped forward over the back of the row in front. Mary jumped back in fright, close to tears.

'Mum, I can't wake Uncle Clive. I think he's ill or something.'

*

'Is he really not going to suffer any after-effects? Really? A gunshot wound to the head?' Claudine asked as she got into the front seat of Robert's Toyota Landcruiser.

'Well, I'm not a psychiatrist, so I can't really comment on that side of things, but I've examined him thoroughly and I can't see any sign of anythin' to worry about. You'll see for yourself in a few minutes,' Robert explained, as he drove the Toyota down the winding mountain road to Layou Bay. He turned off the metalled road and continued on a laterite track, which ended in a gravelled clearing by the sea. A short, sturdy bridge jutted out into the pristine water, leading to a small timber cottage out on stilts.

'What a magic place!' Claudine exclaimed.

'Yes, an' no tourists,' Robert grinned. 'Now, go over the bridge and roun' the balcony to the side facin' the sea - that's where John likes to be. I'll catch up with you in a moment - I've got to fetch some more drugs,' Robert excused himself to allow them some privacy.

Claudine was slightly nervous of what she might find - had they just been kind to her about John's condition? A surgeon's idea of a good recovery was very different to her own. She tried to imagine how she'd feel about him if he was in any way changed; perhaps not able to do as much as before. She was honest enough with herself to know that their physicality played a big part in the mutual attraction She took a deep breath and crossed the bridge, then followed the veranda around the house, peering in at the windows. She immediately saw the empty bed being tidied by Gunn's nurse, Jacob, who started as he heard her footfall on the wooden-planking.

'Oh Miss! You scared me. Miss Claudine?' Jacob smiled. He stopped making the bed and pointed to the door leading to the veranda that faced out to sea. She continued walking, faster now, anxious to know.

Suddenly he was there, and she hesitated in surprise. A little thinner, but otherwise looking normal apart from a heavily bandaged head and some bruising around one eye, he was sitting on a makeshift bed, a sun lounger padded with cushions and towels. He was re-hooking bait on a fishing rod propped up on a chair beside him.

'Hi!' Claudine half laughed, half gasped, unable to

believe that 48 hours ago he'd been as good as dead. Gunn looked up.

'Claudy!' He let the rod clatter to the floor and attempted to get up. Claudine dropped her things and ran to him, halting within inches to slow her momentum lest she cause any more damage, before collapsing into his arms.

'Thank God,' she said, through tears. 'It's going to be okay, he's okay,' she thought.

Gunn held her tightly, the most certain thing in his fractured life.

'How in God's name are you still alive?' Claudine smiled through her tears. 'Robert said he doesn't think you'll suffer any major after affects. It's just... incredible.'

'It was just blind luck that Robert found me when he did. Well, that and Gabriel - it's down to him really.'

'How are you doing? Really?'

'I've only been for a short walk each day, but I feel stronger almost by the hour. Not surprisingly, my head hurts like hell, but the drugs take care of that mostly. Seeing you has helped too,' he added, stroking hair off Claudine's face. 'I knew you'd come straight out here and I thought you'd find me. I hated you thinking I was dead. I would have...'

'I'm so sorry about Nina, John.'

He suddenly looked furious: 'She was murdered because I was in her house. I feel so bloody useless. I want to be out there now, finding them.' He threw the newly baited fishing line out into the sea angrily.

'I know.'

John was silent for a few moments, then changed

the subject entirely. 'So what's been happening back at Kingsroad House? We've...'

But Robert appeared at that moment and suggested he go back to the clinic, return Claudine's car to the Sunset Inn, settle her bill and bring her bag down to the bungalow, where she was welcome to stay as long as she wanted.

'Thank you Robert; but please don't bother. I'll come back and do that. No really, you've done so much for us - if you can just take me back to the clinic, I'll take it from there. I'd love to stay here if that's okay. Please let's do it like that.' Claudine, like Gunn, was anxious not to involve the Jacksons any more than they already were. She looked at Gunn.

'Go, it makes sense. I'm not going anywhere,' he added, smiling weakly. Claudine kissed him once more then jogged back to the Landcruiser.

'We'll pick this up as soon as I get back!' she called over her shoulder.

It was barely two hours later that she returned with Robert, who had followed her to the Sunset Inn and then driven back to the bungalow. She had suggested a taxi, but Robert told her that Gunn had insisted that there couldn't be any clues for anyone investigating his death. He wouldn't go as far as the Sunset Inn, instead parked out of sight of the Inn.

Robert stayed to have a drink then left, promising to call back the next day to check on his patient. Alone with Gunn, Claudine stripped off her clothes, the warm tropical air soft on her skin, and just lay with him on the veranda, listening to the waves and holding on to him tightly. Gunn, full of strong painkillers and sedatives, could do little else, but Claudine's warmth, her familiar smell and her unspoken affection did more for his recovery than any of Robert Jackson's drugs ever could.

# CHAPTER 6

Toby Charbonnier finished his breakfast, shouted up to his two children to get out of bed and kissed his wife goodbye.

'Baby, why don't you bring this guy you're mindin' to the house? He might enjoy a meal with a local family. What d'you say?' Toby paused at the front door.

'Er, I'll see how it goes today and give you a call later; bye.' After what he'd seen the day before, inviting Mike Soames into his house was the very last thing Toby wanted, but he also didn't want to have to tell his wife the reason why and wanted to avoid an argument. He drove into Kingstown, but once he reached the city, on impulse, he turned north and headed for the Montrose Hotel. It wasn't quite eight o'clock and there was only one young girl behind the reception counter.

'Mornin,' Miss,' Toby greeted her, flipping his warrant card. 'Detective Sergeant Charbonnier. I jus' wanted to check on a frien' of mine who arrived yesterday.'

'Mornin' Sergeant, what's the name?' she raised an eyebrow.

'Michael Soames.' Then he added, 'I don' have time for any fancy women,' smiling at the assumption.

'That's a pity, Sergeant,' she giggled, as she tapped

the name into the computer. 'Michael Soames, you said,' and she scrolled through the names of all the guests in the hotel's 36 rooms, frowning. 'No, there mus' be a mistake. We have no 'Soames' in this hotel. You sure you got the name right?'

Up to that moment, stopping off at the hotel had been a spur-of-the-moment gesture of hospitality, but now warning bells tinkled. All Toby's thoughts of courtesy evaporated.

'Are you sure? I made arrangements for his bag to be delivered here yesterday and then I dropped him off - it would have been about five yesterday afternoon.'

'Were you with him when he checked in?'

'No... but I saw him walk into the hotel. Were you on duty at the time?'

'No, Sergeant, that would've been Bella, but the duty manager, Mr Quinton, he'd know - I'll get him for you. Won' be a minute,' and she disappeared into the office behind the reception desk. The door reopened almost immediately.

'Sergeant? Jolie tells me that you're lookin' for a Mr Soames you think checked in yesterday evenin'. I was on duty; I'm afraid no one of that name checked in.'

'But his bag was delivered here by a police car, aroun' lunch time.'

'No, Sergeant; no bag was delivered to this hotel - not for a Mr Soames anyway. I'm sorry,' Mr Quinton hovered anxiously.

'No worries, I've probably got that name wrong. Thank you.' Toby returned to his bike, but dialled the office before starting it.

'Police HQ, CID, Constable Smith.'

'Ashling, it's Toby.'

'Hi Toby, the Chief's been askin' for you.'

'OK, I'm on my way. I need you do somethin' for me. Can you run a search of all the hotel registers on the Island for the name 'Michael Soames, that's S-O-A-M-E-S.'

'Okay; anythin' else?'

'No, I'll be in the office in about ten minutes.' The traffic was particularly heavy that morning and it was nearer 15 minutes before Toby got back to the office. Chief Superintendent Slater was sitting on the edge of Constable Ashling Smith's desk.

'Problem, Toby?' he asked.

'Yes, sir; Ashling?'

'There is no Michael Soames registered in any hotel on this Island. If he is here then he's stayin' privately... or he's sleepin' rough. Or he's usin' a different name.'

'Thanks; just one minute, sir,' and Toby quickly dialled the front desk Sergeant. 'Was that bag belonging to Mr Soames delivered to the Montrose Hotel yesterday afternoon?'

'No... You gave me a message to cancel the delivery.'

'Thanks Wilf, that's okay, I'll explain later, bye. OK, sir,' Toby turned to his mystified boss, 'I arranged for Soames' bag to be delivered to the Montrose Hotel and dropped him off at that hotel yesterday evenin', but no one at the hotel knows anythin' about him and he was never checked in. An' he must've cancelled my order to Wilf on the front desk to have his bag delivered to the hotel.'

'Why?'

'I don't know yet, sir. I know we're s'posed to let this guy have his head and only help if he asks, but I think somethin's goin' on. I'd like to make a few enquiries to see what I turn up......with your permission.'

'OK, do it, but you report only to me, no one else. Ashling, this conversation didn't happen.'

'No, sir........ I mean, yes sir.'

*

Gunn and Claudine had just finished a dinner of fresh fish, caught by Gunn earlier in the day and prepared by Jacob. Once they'd cleared it away, they returned to the veranda, where Gunn was sitting at the now empty table with pen and paper, which he handed to her.

'Creative writing?'

'In a way..... Calypso ended in such a frenetic scramble that I didn't have a chance to.....figure out what's going on at Kingsroad House,' Gunn began as Claudine sat opposite him, his finger to his lips to indicate they should keep their voices down.

'What do you mean?'

'Well, for starters there've been a lot of deaths recently. Too many. And I don't think they're all legit.'

'No death is legit,' said Claudine pointedly.

'No, I mean... I don't think all the reports into their deaths came to the right conclusions,' Gunn chose his words more carefully. 'And it's possible the deaths could be linked. Something's not right, anyway. I tried to talk it through with Nina but didn't get far...' fury coloured his face for a moment. 'Another mind to help make sense of things might help.'

'Sure. What's first?'

'Okay, I'm going to start with those people in BID who've been killed since the time I joined it and eliminate all those whose deaths are leg... er, explicable. So....I was at university with Humphrey Goldman, who recruited me in 1997 for the Hong Kong job. He was one of the few agents who passed Jeremy Hammond's vetting and transferred from MI6 to BID. He was shot at the Army and Navy Club in Pall Mall while in the process of recruiting me. We never found his killer; he's the first name.'

'Richard Anderson, Tony Bristow and Tim Driscoll were all killed during an assignment and we know who killed them, so no need to consider them any further. So on to more recent events.'

'Simon Peters?' Claudine suggested.

'Christ, poor Simon; you're right we have to include everyone. He took his own life and we know who was involved, so....we don't need to consider him any further,' John winced at the memory of his former controller's macabre suicide on a live rail. 'Now I want to focus on the people who moved across to BID from MI6. All of those I've just mentioned make five. Add to that David Chesham...'

'And Paul Manton.'

'He's under sedation in the clinic.'

'No, John... he's dead. He was murdered on the same night that you were shot.......a real pro job - a woman. She got past all the BID security at the clinic and injected him with a huge dose of insulin, which caused a massive heart attack.' Gunn was silent.

'Sorry, it completely slipped my mind that you didn't know,' Claudine apologised.

'No, no....it's not that; I was just thinking that makes total sense – it proves there's some sort of conspiracy in BID.' Gunn was suddenly animated, his bulk engulfing the small table as he leaned across it, eyes widened, his voice little more than a whisper. 'All the other five deaths could be attributed to a combat situation – killed on the job – but I heard from the Major who commands Alpha Squadron of 22 SAS.......he was on the same selection course as me......that David was shot in the back. Sure, it's possible that the terrorist shot him in the back, but all the terrorists guarding that airfield were armed with 9mm Heckler and Koch sub-machine guns. The autopsy on David Chesham removed a 7.62mm bullet fired by an AK47. The case for David being murdered was always pretty dubious but the whole thing got sidelined by Paul's breakdown. Everyone was so focused on preventing the terrorist attack in London that the circumstances of David's death were never properly investigated. Paul's murder is the first time that this assassin has left us in no doubt that he - or she – exists and is targeting the ex-MIs.........someone with access to BID or within it and who knows.....or might know the identity of the person who is behind this conspiracy. Don't you agree?'

'Yes, I see – and that would explain a lot. Miles and Barry Windsor – he's the acting Head of CE at the moment – are both convinced that there are moles in BID and possibly in the Cabinet Office. I was told I mustn't contact Mike Soames or anyone else except Miles with whatever I find here in St Vincent. And he's been leaving the building to take my calls.'

'Shit!.........what a bloody mess.'

'I know.'

'OK. We've accounted for seven of the eight who moved from the MIs to BID. So who's the eighth man - or woman?'

'Presumably there must be records,' Claudine said.

'Yeah, unless this person either destroyed those records or altered them to hide his or her identity. '

At that moment Jacob appeared at the veranda door carrying a medical tray, and Claudine discreetly pocketed her notes.

'Time for that dressin' to be changed.' He led Gunn to the bed and ordered him to sit still while he changed the dressing. As the last bandage fell away, it revealed both the entry wound in Gunn's forehead and the surgical scar at the back of his head where the bullet had been removed. The wound at the front, now a red, zip-like scar, was healing fast and Jacob pronounced that there wouldn't be too big a mark.

'Stitches out in three days, John,' he said finally as he fastened the new bandage and removed the old ones, disappearing into the cottage. Gunn and Claudine hurried back out to the veranda, making sure the door and all the windows were closed on that side of the cottage before resuming their talk.

'Do you want to keep going? We can carry on tomorrow if your head's…'

'No it's fine.' It hurt like hell, but John simply downed some more painkillers. 'Okay, this is what I think we have to do. I'm going to use Malcolm and his contacts - not ideal to get him involved, I know - to spread a rumour that two men were seen loading something like a body wrapped in plastic sheeting into a boat on the day of the shooting. You'll go back to London and tell HQ that everything indicates that I'm dead. Actually, I want you to phone Miles before you go and tell him that...'

'But I...'

'Just hear me out; I'm pretty sure that the mole, whoever it is, has bugged our comms, so I want him to hear that information. When you get back to BID, talk normally to Miles in his office about your assignment here, but put a note on his desk asking him to leave the office and have lunch with you or something. Once you're outside BID tell him the real situation. You'd better go to my parents and tell them, too. Unfortunately it's not the first time they've thought I'm dead,' Gunn sighed, before adding, 'sorry to wish that task on you as they'll probably throw you out.'

Claudine shrugged, 'understandable.'

'I know. Thank you,' he squeezed her leg under the table.

'What else?'

'Make arrangements for a memorial service for me. Get Miles to buy a new mobile and you too and let me have the numbers. Tell Miles to speak only to me on the new mobile and only outside the BID building. Tell him that when I need to speak to him I'll send him a text, which will mean that I want him to leave the building. The text will read something like "Vodaphone's new call rates are on its website." Hopefully that won't attract any bugging interest.'

'When do you want me to go back to London?'

'The day after tomorrow; that'll mean you've been here for three days. Having found out about the body being dumped in the sea,' Claudine winced at the image, 'there would be little point in staying any longer. Before you go you should go and see Malcolm Slater at Police HQ tomorrow and get an update from him on their investigation.

'What are you going to do? Don't do too much until you are properly fit, or you'll just be out of action even longer.'

'I'm not going anywhere. I'm going to contact Doyle Barnes once you've reported back to me on the police investigation. I might need a complete outsider like him to get to the root of this.'

'Good idea. He's completely removed so they won't be expecting him,' she surveyed John across the table, noticing for the first time how haggard he looked. 'Bed?'

'Bed.'

*

The Moorings was a twelve-storey, new-build apartment block in a re-developed area overlooking the Grand Union Canal in Brentford. Venetia Akehurst owned a two-bedroom apartment on the tenth floor, which had a balcony overlooking the canal. It had been a very long day at the office, with all the Ministers eager to clear their in-trays before the summer recess. It was nearly eight-thirty before her train pulled into the station. She walked wearily down the steps from the station and headed south along Manor Road and then Somerset Road to her apartment block.

Once inside her apartment, Venetia switched on

the TV, which was always tuned to the BBC News channel, kicked off her shoes and started running a bath. She then headed for the drinks cabinet in the lounge, craving a scotch, but stopped with her hand on the cabinet door as the newsreader's words suddenly registered.

"A devastating fire broke out in south-west London this afternoon. The Chief Fire Officer at the scene believes it was started by a gas explosion in the kitchenette of a solicitors' office..." Venetia's heart started lurching in her chest as she walked towards the TV. "…the offices of Holmes, Wilson and Fairweather, local solicitors in Brentford, were razed to the ground by the intense heat of the fire. All of the law firm's staff was out to lunch except the senior partner, Georgina Holmes, whom the police and firemen were unable to save. Apart from the tragedy of Ms Holmes' death, this will cause considerable difficulties for the law firm and their clients as it is thought not a single document survived the fire..."

But Venetia was no longer listening. She'd seen Georgina less than 48 hours ago to hand her the letter. The letter that explained everything.....her life insurance. There was no doubt in her mind that it was Cornwall. Panic rising, sweat prickling her skin, Venetia walked out onto the balcony, where the sun was setting over the flight-path, silhouetting a 747-400 on its finals into Heathrow, and steadied herself on the railings, gulping deep breaths of air. The roar of the jet's four, throttled-back engines masked the sound of footsteps on the carpet in the lounge behind her.

The police responded quickly to the hysterical emergency call from an apartment at The Moorings but it took them nearly an hour to find the body in the murky canal. A family had been in the throes of a barbeque on their ground floor balcony when the body of a woman crashed on to the canal wall in front of them, almost snapping in half, before flopping limply into the water.

*

Toby Charbonnier's first stop was the airport. He parked his 600cc Honda bike outside the entrance to the terminal and, after checking with one of the security guards, was shown to the airport's management offices. Toby was fairly certain that there would be little point in asking if a passenger by the name of Mr Michael Soames had bought a ticket the previous evening, so he had asked Ashling to download a photo of Soames from the digital record of Police HQ's CCTV system. He now showed the photo to the Customer Relations Manager, who, armed with the photo, led Toby around the ticketing counters. Fortunately, ET Joshua Airport was not equipped with automatic ticketing machines, which would have made things more difficult. They struck lucky at the United Airlines ticket counter, where a young check-in clerk recognised the otherwise unremarkable passenger as a Mr Frank Dawson, because he'd paid his entire fare in cash and had caught the 19.40 flight to Miami.

Toby hurried back to Police HQ, found an empty interview room and put a call through to Sergeant Tom Jones of the Miami-Dade Police Department. After the establishment of the US Homeland Security Department in the wake of 9/11, Toby had been sent on a briefing session hosted by the MDPD, where he'd struck up a friendship with the affable detective.

'Hi Tom, it's Toby from St Vincent.'

'Toby! How the hell are you? What can I do for you? I'm guessing this isn't just a social call.'

'I'm good, I'm good. But I'm afraid you're right; we've had a double murder here and we're pretty sure that two men from your jurisdiction - two Cubans - could help us with our enquiries; I think they're the killers.'

'I'm sorry to hear that - must be pretty unusual on your island.'

'It is; it's shaken everyone up.'

'Well, what are the names?'

'Fidel Carillo - alias Carlos Ocampo and probably many others and Ernesto Diaz - a.k.a. Romero Garcia; they're both wanted by the MDPD for a whole lot, includin' murder one. Anythin' you can find on them would help me a lot.'

'Sure.'

'But there's another thing; one of the two victims was an agent with the British Intelligence Directorate.'

'Oh man. What was he doing there? I'm assuming it was a he?'

'Yeah; he was here keepin' an eye on that arms dealer, Hassan Hussein, who was blown up in his private jet a couple of days ago.'

'Yeah, I read about that.'

'At our request, BID sent out another agent to assist with the investigation into the murders. They sent a guy called Mike Soames, but I've just discovered that he never even stayed the night in Kingstown. He caught a United Airlines flight - UA 520 - straight out to Miami at 19.40 last night usin' the name Frank Dawson.'

'Yeah, got all that; what do you want me to do?'

'I have to warn you, Tom, this guy is seriously dangerous. I've seen him in action and he doesn' need a weapon' to kill. He's workin' to his own agenda and I'm pretty sure it's got nothin' to do with BID. I took him to see a local Rasta gang who we're sure armed the Cubans and they recognised him. Didn't say anythin' but they didn' need to, they jus' looked shit scared. Two guys who were obviously new to the gang and din' know better tried to stir it up an' he damn near killed them in as many seconds as it's taken me to tell you that.'

'And this guy's now in Miami?'

'Yeah, and if you can find him or get any leads I'll owe you.'

'You won't owe me anything. I already owe you for those Guyanian drug mules. I'll get in touch as soon as I have something.'

'Thanks, Tom,' and Toby rang off, just as Ashling stuck her head around the door.

'Toby, the Chief would like to see you in his office. He's got someone he wants you to meet.'

'Couldn' you say I was out or somethin'?'

'Could've, but havin' seen the lady in question I thought you'd probably wan' to meet her.'

'Lady?'

'Yeah, about the best lookin' girl I've ever seen in this buildin'.'

'For real?'

'Go on, the boss is waitin' - and don't forget you're a married man,' Ashling called after him. Toby knocked on the Chief Superintendent's door and was called in. Ashling had not exaggerated. Even in battered beige cut-offs, trainers and T-shirt, her thick sand-blonde hair tied back in a pony-tail under a baseball hat, Claudia's lithe frame was unmistakable. Pretty striking, Toby thought impatiently, but she looks like some student; what did she have to do with him?

'Sergeant Charbonnier, I'd like you to meet Claudine de Carteret; Claudine, Toby Charbonnier,' Malcolm introduced them.

'Toby,' Claudine held out a hand, which Toby noted was slightly rough-skinned. 'I work for BID with John Gunn. I was sent here at the same time as Mike Soames to help search for John.'

'Claudine.'

'It's your lucky day,' Malcolm smiled. 'Claudine, please tell Toby what you've just told me.'

'John Gunn is alive and well.'

'What? Are you sure?'

'Let her tell you the whole bit,' Malcolm suggested.

'By a stroke of luck,' Claudine began, 'Robert Jackson and his father, Gabriel, arrived at Nina Ramone's house within minutes of the shooting. Gabriel wanted to show John his war album. They found the two bodies in the kitchen. Nina was dead but John was alive – just. Robert operated on him that evening. It's hard to believe, but the bullet missed everything vital and Dr Jackson was able to remove it without there being any lasting damage......John's fine and recovering somewhere safe.'

Toby looked at his chief incredulously and back at Claudine, 'how did you find him?' he asked, shaking his head.

'That doesn't matter now. I'm here to ask for your help. BID has been penetrated by a mole or moles. Communication both to and from the building in London is no longer secure. John and I want you, the St Vincent Police, to put out a statement to the effect that two men were seen carrying what looked like a body into a boat on the evening of the shooting. We want the moles to hear that. Then I'm going back to London tomorrow to brief Miles Thompson, the Deputy Director, which I'll have to do outside HQ - Kingsroad House - and I'll also set up a secure system of communication which will be free of any bugging. There will also be a statement from BID about John's death. I know you've been tasked by HQ to help Mike Soames, but nothing of what I have just told you must reach him...'

'Fine by me,' Toby interrupted. 'I've been doin' some checkin' up on Mr Soames an' none of it looks good. Sorry, sir,' he turned to Malcolm, 'but I didn' have time to tell you. Soames never stayed at his hotel last night, but caught another flight straight out to Miami, an' I can guess why. We think we know who did the shootin'.'

It was Claudine's turn to be on the back foot.

'Two Cuban men - real goons - arrived from Miami on Saturday, got weapons from a local Rasta gang, shot John and knifed Nina and then caught the flight back to Miami that evenin'. These guys are wanted for close to every crime in the book, includin' murder one, but this wasn' anythin' to do with them - they're real crackheads, jus' hired hands from one of the Miami drug cartels. But I reckon Soames has gone to Miami to silence them.'

'Shit…' Claudine was already making to leave.

'Yeah, you got it.'

# CHAPTER 7

'What was the result of the post mortem on Clive?' Miles asked Sir Jeremy Hammond as soon as their waiter at the Institute of Directors Club in Pall Mall was safely out of earshot. They were lunching at the IOD so they could talk without fear of being bugged. Terry Holt, the Head of Communications and Security at Kingsroad House, had swept each floor of the building at night during the last 48 hours but found no bugs. "Whoever they are, they know what they're doing," he'd said; the only way to be sure was to get out of the building until he'd figured it out. The opulence of the IOD, with its marble-effect pillars, gold-leaf linen wall-covering and prevailing whiff of old boy self-assuredness was wasted on them, but the tables were widely spaced and the thick carpet absorbed all sound, so private conversations remained private.

'Well, the pathologist initially said it was some 'unidentified' toxin, but then she called in an expert on animal toxins. The substance injected into the back of Clive's neck turned out to be tetrodotoxin, which is peculiar to only two creatures: the blue ringed octopus and the fugu or puffer fish. Apparently, if you eat incorrectly prepared fugu, you will gradually become paralysed and be unable to do anything about it; death takes about a week. However, the blue-ringed octopus injects its venom, which kills within sixty seconds. That's what killed Clive in the theatre.' They stopped talking while the waiter served their food, and then continued.

'Sixty seconds? Jesus.'

'Terrifying.......the funeral's on Friday at Mortlake Crematorium. Barry Windsor's teams are baffled by this, as are the police. Gunn was right to be worried. You know he confided in me before he left for St Vincent that he thought there might be some sort of internal conspiracy?' said Miles.

'Yes I did, he spoke to me too. Have you heard any news from Soames or Claudine?'

'Nothing, but I wasn't expecting anything just yet.'

'Why do you think Gunn's body was removed from the scene of crime?' Sir Jeremy asked.

'I'm sure you've thought of as many reasons as I have but...' Miles was interrupted by his mobile vibrating in his pocket. He checked the screen. 'It's my PA - could be Claudine - hang on; won't be long,' and he went out to the hall to take the call.

'It's Angela; I've got some really bad news,' he heard her take a shaky breath on the other end of the phone. 'I've just had a call from Claudine in St Vincent. John is dead. His body was taken and dumped in the sea on the night of the murder. Claudine's coming back to London tomorrow to brief you. I'm really sorry, Miles…'

'Thank you, Angela; I'll be back soon.' Miles stood for a few moments, feeling as though he'd been kicked hard in the guts. So he really was dead. He returned to the restaurant.

*

It was overcast with a light drizzle, which made Venetia Akehurst's funeral, with its pitifully small gathering of mourners, even more depressing, John Cornwall mused, as he laid his wreath along with four or five others outside the chapel. He spotted Andrew Barton and George Peterson standing separately from another group, which he assumed must be Venetia's family, and walked over to them. Andrew, a non-smoker, was drawing heavily on a cigarette, his eyes everywhere but the funeral. He glared angrily at John as he approached.

'We're all buggered, John,' he said in a harsh whisper; 'completely fucked. We're never going to see this money - never were. It's stupid to think otherwise. We're all being picked off - one by one - by whoever's on the end of the phone. He's the only bastard who'll benefit; David, Paul, Clive and now Venetia, but not me. George and I are out.' Andrew pulled the mobile phone out of his pocket, pulled off the back and took out the SIM card, which he dropped on the tarmac and ground under the heel of his shoe. George followed suit.

'We've both resigned as of the end of this week. I'm leaving the country with my family and George… I don't know what George is doing and that's how it should be,' Andrew stopped, glancing around nervously, and took out another cigarette.

'We don't want our share of that fund or any association with all the killings...' George's tone was accusing, but utterly defeated. 'Unless you know a hell of a lot more about who's doing this, I suggest you disappear too.'

It was John's turn to look anxious: 'Aren't you even staying for the funeral?' he asked.

'No; time's not really on our side,' and both men picked up the destroyed SIM cards to dispose of elsewhere and disappeared down the yew-lined path to the car park.

John hesitated and then caught sight of Venetia's casket being lowered into the sodden ground. Not me either, he thought, and hurried after the other two men, all thoughts of paying his respects to the woman he'd just had murdered driven from his mind in favour of his own salvation.

*

'How'd you get here?' Toby asked Claudine.

'I got a bus.'

'Can I give you a lift?'

'Thanks,' Claudine instinctively trusted Toby, with his obvious dislike for Mike Soames and his impressive resourcefulness. 'I think John would like to hear what you've found out about Soames.'

'Yeah, sure. Oh wait,' Toby suddenly remembered Gunn's rucksack which the police had retrieved from Nina's house, and ran back into the building to get it. Claudine put her small rucksack inside Gunn's, slipped her arms through the straps, climbed onto the back of the bike and they headed off to Layou Bay. Gunn walked out onto the veranda as they crossed the bridge.

'John, this is Sergeant Toby Charbonnier; he's got

Malcolm's personal vetting,' she added quickly. 'He has some interesting information about Mike Soames. Toby,' Claudia turned to him, 'John Gunn.'

'Toby,' they shook hands.

'How's the head?'

'Not in a pine box, thanks to Robert Jackson.' The three of them went and sat on the veranda overlooking the bay.

'So what's this about Mike Soames?'

Toby repeated his account of the incident at Hill Street and Mike's disappearance on the flight to Miami the night before. Gunn was silent for a few moments when Toby had finished.

'Have you told him what's going on at BID?' he asked Claudine finally.

'No, not yet; thought I'd let you meet first.'

'We believe there's some sort of....conspiracy,' John looked Toby steadily in the eye, 'coming from within the UK Government; BID's been completely compromised......it's crippling us. Someone's been listening to everything; a lot of our people have died.'

'Is Mike Soames involved?'

'Looks like it from what you've discovered. Mike's been on at least five assignments that I know of in the Caribbean. He's usually BID's first choice for anything in this part of the world because of his fluent Spanish, unless it involves sailing or boats, and then if they can't find anyone else it's given to me. That's why I'm here; my assignment effectively ended when Hassan Hussein's jet exploded and killed Abdul Hassan al Tikriti - he was the cousin of Chemical Ali, the Iraqi who gassed all the Kurds in northern Iraq back in the eighties.'

'Here's to that then,' Toby took a sip of the beer Claudine had found in the fridge.

'Nina Ramone was a BID agent, and has been for seven or eight years; she was working with me and I stayed at her cottage, that's why she's dead. Before I left London, I spoke to some people I trusted - still trust - in BID of my suspicions about the death of one of our counter-espionage agents and that I thought there might be a mole. I think someone must have bugged their phones; or they in turn mentioned it to someone else they thought they could trust. Anyway, I had those conversations on Thursday and Friday of last week. On Saturday I flew here. Then that evening someone shot me in the head and murdered Nina. That's how much power this person has. Someone in London was able to hire two gunmen in Miami, alert that Rasta gang to provide their weapons and then get the gunmen back to Miami before the police here had even heard of the shooting. Had Gabriel not insisted on coming to see me, I *would* be dead and the police here would have had bugger all to go on.'

'Now you know as much as we do,' said Claudine.

'But I'm hoping Malcolm will let you help us find out what the hell's going on.' Like Claudine, Gunn had taken to Toby more-or-less instantly, his easy affability belying a razor sharp mind.

'I hope so too. What are you planin' to do?' Toby asked.

'Well, this is the plan for now: Claudine goes back to London tomorrow to confirm that I'm dead and brief our Deputy Director - who's Head of BID's Espionage Department - on the true situation. She'll have to do this outside BID. She will also set up a secure means of communication so I can talk to BID without any risk of being overheard,' Gunn explained. 'You...'

'Wait,' Claudine interjected, shooting John an angry look. 'Slow down a second. Toby, you need to know that if you work with BID you will be putting yourself deliberately in harm's way. You've already seen how dangerous Mike Soames can be. Are you married?' she eyed a gold band on his right hand.

'Yeah, I'm married. But if it hadn' been for my attachment to the NYPD and the bust up with the Rastas yesterday, I'd probably want to emigrate because it's so quiet here,' he laughed, but without any mirth. 'Look, my wife's a lawyer - she loves her job; she understands. I've got somewhere I can send her and the kids if need be.'

'If you're absolutely sure.' said Claudine.

'If it looks like it could get dangerous for them, I'll get out,' Toby said. 'But this is what I joined the police for; I want to help.'

'Good,' John cut back in. 'Claudine, why don't you go back with Toby and talk to Malcolm? Then let's all meet back here tomorrow morning before you fly back - just to run through everything again.'

'Fine.' Claudine ushered Toby out, furious with John. After what had happened to Nina - a trained agent - she had hoped he'd be a bit more cautious about getting anyone else too involved.

Gunn went to bed early, determined to speed up the healing process.

*

United Airlines flight UA520 landed at Miami International Airport at 21.10 hrs. Despite only having hand luggage, it was nearly ten before Mike Soames - now Frank Dawson - emerged from Homeland Security's immigration controls and headed for the taxi rank. The queue diminished quickly and he got into a silver-painted Diamond Taxi.

'Where to, Señor?' the driver asked.

'Comfort Suites Motel at the junction of 27th Avenue and 103rd Street.'

'Why you wanna stay there, Señor? There're many, many better places in Miami I can take you.'

'No thanks, just take me to that motel.'

The junction of 27th and 103rd was in the Opa-locka suburb of Miami-Dade County, just east of Opa-locka airport. It was a seedy area of industrial sites and low-cost housing in the northwest of Miami, a world away from the luxury hotels, beaches and clubs of South Beach. It had the highest crime rate, not only for Miami but the whole of Florida.

'You from Australia, Señor?' the driver asked.

'St Vincent. I have some calls to make so just drive and save the small talk for another fare.' Soames took out his phone and dialled a number. 'Yes it's me,' there was a short pause while he listened. 'Okay. Leave that and the information I need at the motel for me to pick up when I get there,' he hung up. He made another call to the motel to tell them to expect the package.

'What name was the reservation in, sir?' the receptionist asked.

'Peter Hobbs.'

'Thank you, Mr Hobbs, you're in suite 1030. That's

on the ground floor as you requested. The package will be in your suite.' After a very silent drive, the taxi pulled into the forecourt of the Comfort Suites Motel. Mike got out of the taxi, handed the driver a twenty dollar note and walked away without a word.

'Hobbs, room 1030.'

'Oh yeah, Mr Hobbs. There's a gentleman waiting for you outside your suite. He said that he wanted to make sure you received the package - said it needs to be signed for by you. Here're your keys. Can I just have your passport, please?' He handed over a passport in the name of Peter Geoffrey Hobbs; the receptionist copied the ID page and returned it. 'Anything else we can do for you?'

'Yes, I'll need a hire car; four doors, compact saloon. Could you arrange that for me?'

'Certainly - I'll just need... perfect,' Mike handed over Geoffrey Hobbs' driver's license too. 'How long will you be staying, Mr Hobbs?'

'Two days at most. If you could call me when the car's delivered?' she nodded brightly, and Mike walked outside to suite 1030, tucked around the back of the motel as he'd requested. The door of the suite was ajar; the 'gentleman' had obviously broken in without too much trouble. Mike pushed it open and walked in. The TV was on and a fat man in a sweat-stained vest, with a handful of greasy black hair combed over his bald head, was sitting on one of the twin beds. Beside him on the bed was a paper bag. He glanced at Mike as he came into the room and, in an instant, made the mistake many others had made. Seeing a man of slight build and medium height with a receding hairline, he languidly returned his gaze to the

TV cartoon he'd been chuckling at.

'You have the package and the information?' Mike asked, as he dropped his bag on the floor. The man belched and drank from the beer in his hand.

'This comes expensive,' he indicated with the beer bottle the package beside him on the bed.

'That's already been paid for.'

'Yeah, well the cost of livin's gone up so you owe me another hundred if you wan' it,' he took another pull at his beer.

'That's not a problem. But I need to see the package and information first. Then I'll pay you an extra five hundred dollars.' The man opened the bag immediately without a word, revealing a Beretta .38 with a 13 round magazine, a box of .38 ammunition, a silencer and a single sheet of paper. Soames glanced at the piece of paper; it contained all the information he needed.

'Okay; here's your payment.' The man made his second mistake by greedily watching Mike pull out his wallet. His brain never registered the whip-like kick, which snapped his neck as cleanly as a rotten tree branch. He was dead before his body fell back on the bed. The phone by the bed rang.

'Your hire car's here, Mr Hobbs. I'll have them park it outside your suite.' Two minutes later the doorbell rang; he took the keys from the driver and signed for the car. His Toyota Corolla was conveniently parked with the rear hatchback towards his suite. Soames checked for CCTV cameras and other guests, opened the tailgate, lifted the man off the bed and pushed him into the boot, locking it after him. He then opened the bonnet and removed the king lead from the distributor to ensure that no one stole the car. Then he switched off the TV, emptied the mini-bar of snacks and went to bed - fully clothed, gun under the pillow next to him, where there was still an indentation of the fat man's head.

*

Sergeant Tom Jones of the Miami-Dade Police Homicide Department knocked on the office door of Lieutenant Jack Halliday, his immediate boss.

'Is this going to be quick, Tom? I've got a report to finish for the Captain.'

'Yes, sir; I've just had a call from a Sergeant Charbonnier down at St Vincent Police - he's a friend of mine - asking for a favour. He wants me to trace two suspects for a double murder on the Island last week.'

'Why a favour and not an official request?'

'Because the two people they knocked off were BID.'

'Oh........what's he want you to do?'

'Find these assholes and report back.'

'His Chief know about this?'

'Malcolm Slater; yeah, he gave the nod. I'll take a couple of days leave...'

'No, it's OK, you can do this officially with my authority. But before you go, look in on the DEA over there,' and Jack indicated with a nod of his head to another building adjacent to the main MDPD Headquarters. 'In there you'll find a Company guy by name of Doyle Barnes. He's up to his neck in their op against that spic shit coke baron in Venezuela. He's also the CIA's liaison man with BID. Right, it's

Tuesday; I don't want to see you 'til next Monday, but if you get into trouble we'll come running. Got that?'

'Got that; thank you, sir.'

'Go!'

Sergeant Jones backed out of the office and returned to his desk, raising eyebrows from his colleagues.

'What was all that about? You sneaking off when we've got all this paperwork?'

'Sorry guys, I'll do my share next week,' and, dodging demands for an explanation he grabbed his shoulder holster and Colt 9mm automatic off the back of his desk chair, left the office and took the stairs to the ground floor, where he went into the Homeland Security office. The duty officer, a voluptuous black policewoman who struck terror into the hearts of new recruits, looked over the top of her reading glasses at Tom.

'What can I do for you, young man?'

'Oh, if only…' he chuckled.

'Sergeant Jones, you couldn't handle me,' she winked. 'Now really?'

'Trace this guy on the airport CCTV tapes of arrivals at Miami International please? He came off United Airlines UA 520 last night,' and Tom handed over the photo of Mike Soames.

'What's he done?' she asked as she fed the photo into a scanner, which would, in seconds, compare it with all the photos taken at the immigration channels until a match was found.

'Murder one.'

'You going after him?'

'Looks like it.'

'You take care, Tom Jones......there you are. He's travelling under the name of Frank Dawson. From immigration he went to the taxi rank where he took a Diamond cab, registration TFO 526 and his cab licence is... wait... 1300568.'

'Thanks a million, Tish...'

'Wait young man, you'll need the driver's cell-phone number. There you go,' she wrote it down and handed it to Tom, who hurried over to DEA Headquarters. As he walked, he dialled the Diamond Cab cell-phone number.

'Diamond Cabs.'

'Police inquiry, Sergeant Jones, Number 848; you took a fare at twenty minutes past ten last night from the taxi rank at Miami International. That man is wanted for murder one. Where'd you take him?'

'I remember; he was very rude, Seňor... Sergeant. I try to speak to him, but he tell me to shut up.'

'Okay, where'd you drop him off?'

'Comfort Suites Motel at the junction of 27th and 103rd - just east of the Opa-locka airport. Ugly place, I don't know why he stays there.'

'Thanks.'

'Also Sergeant?'

'What?

'He make a phone call and told the person to leave a package at the motel.'

'That's very helpful - thanks,' Tom hung up as he walked into the DEA building. He checked at the front desk and was asked to wait. It was only a few minutes before a man appeared who looked like Genghis Khan's double, but bigger. He was over six foot tall with long black hair, moustache and goatee, high cheekbones and an oriental slant to his eyes. He went over to the front desk and the young woman pointed at Tom.

'Sergeant Jones MDPD?'

'Yeah, that's me,' Tom's hand was engulfed by the large man's.

'Doyle Barnes; got a message that you wanted to see me. Come on up,' Doyle led the way to the first floor and into an open-plan office with desks and people seemingly scattered haphazardly around the room. Doyle's office was at the far end of this room in a glass-partitioned area. 'Coffee?' Doyle offered as he shut the door behind them.

'Thanks, black no sugar.'

'What can I do for you? Jack called me while you were on your way over and said this had something to do with BID?'

'It's about the explosion of that aircraft at St Vincent's airport last week and a double murder of two BID agents afterwards...' Tom paused when he saw the look on Doyle's face. 'Is this news to you?'

'The explosion isn't news, but the murders are. Who was it?' Doyle was oddly still.

'I wasn't given the names. I was just told that both of the BID agents were involved in an operation against the arms dealer whose jet was blown sky high and they were murdered soon afterwards by two scumbags from Miami. I've been asked, sort of unofficially, to find them. They're both wanted by the MDPD for every crime from murder one down.'

'Wait here a minute, I'll be back,' Doyle went into an empty office from where he put a call through to BID. He got the duty officer in Kingsroad House and asked to go to 'secure'. In answer to his question, he was told that Nina Ramone and John Gunn had been murdered on the Saturday night by two professional gunmen from Miami. Doyle returned to his office, slamming the door, and stood staring out of the window, head bowed, the muscles in his temples working frenetically. Tom waited.

'The agents' names were John Gunn and Nina Ramone,' he said at last, his tone flat. 'I've known John for more than ten years. We've been on at least four assignments together and he's saved my life more than once. We'd just finished another one, down in the Caribbean, that's why he was there - fuck!' Doyle slammed his palms on the windowsill.

'I'm sorry, I...'

'Let's have the names of those gunmen,' Doyle cut him off.

'Fidel Carillo and Ernesto Diaz, but both have a number of aliases, of which Carlos Ocampo and Romero Garcia are the most common. They're into the crack business - and into crack, by all accounts. But there's a complication,' Tom added hastily as Doyle grabbed his jacket.

'And that is?'

'BID sent an agent to St Vincent to look for Gunn, because his body was removed from the scene of the shooting. His name's Mike Soames.'

'I've heard that name before...'

'Well, it's looking like this Soames might also be one of the bad guys. I've been warned that he's real dangerous - lethal with or without a weapon.'

'Okay, so why does that affect us?'

'Cos he's now here in Miami, looking for those two

gunmen - we think to find out what happened to the body - and to clean up, you know?'

'Yeah, I know.'

'I've just come from Homeland Security and we now know that he booked into the Comfort Suites Motel up by Opa-locka airport last night just before eleven under the name of Peter Hobbs, having entered the USA with a passport under the name of Frank Dawson.'

'In that case, we've wasted enough time talking already,' and Doyle picked up his shoulder holster with its Sig-Sauer 9mm automatic and his jacket and the two of them left his office and headed for the stairs to the ground floor. 'Do you have any leads on the places these two crack-heads hang out?' he asked as they climbed into his Dodge Challenger.

'Yeah, they both hang out in the clubs and pool bars in an area to the north of Opa-locka Airport and south of Interstate 95. Here,' and Tom handed across two photos of the men. 'It's a rough area; I'm pretty glad to have a guy of your size with me.'

'So Mike Soames got here last night,' Doyle swung north onto Interstate 95, and activated the light and siren to clear his way through the dense traffic. 'That means that he's got a head start on us so we have to find the gunmen before he does. If that piece of shit's had anything to do with John's death, I'll personally emasculate him before I kill him.'

'We'll need him alive...'

'Well, he won't want to be then.'

# CHAPTER 8

Andrew Barton and George Peterson said their goodbyes in the cemetery car park, got into their cars and drove out onto the A3 Kingston bypass, George to his house in Kingston and Andrew to his house in Cobham. As Andrew pulled into his driveway, there was a police car parked outside the house. He stamped on the breaks in panic, fumbling to get the gear stick into reverse. Suddenly, he felt as though a steel hoop had tightened around his chest. The shock and crippling pain nearly caused him to crash into the back of the police car. Winded, he fumbled to get his seatbelt off, gasping for air. His left hand started to curl into a claw. He got the car door open with his right and took two steps towards his horrified wife and the two policemen standing by his front door. Then his legs buckled beneath him and he collapsed on the gravel, scattering stones in all directions.

'Andrew!' Jenny Barton ran to her writhing husband and tried to cradle his head off the ground.

'Shit! Call an ambulance!' One constable barked at the other as he knelt to feel a pulse. 'Hurry!'

The constable kneeling by Andrew's crumpled body loosened his clothing and started CPR in a desperate attempt to keep him alive long enough for the paramedics to take over. Within minutes, a siren heralded the arrival of the ambulance and the paramedics spilled out. The policemen moved away and helped Jenny to get her keys and lock the house while Andrew was loaded onto a stretcher and into the back of the ambulance. Jenny climbed in after them, white and shaking. The ambulance reversed back to the main road, turned and then disappeared, its siren blaring.

'Wonder what caused that?' the younger of the two constables commented, catching his breath, as they continued with their neighbourhood beat.

'Probably a guilty conscience when he saw two coppers outside his house. Bloody nearly gave me a heart attack too!'

'Poor sod, I hope he's alright.'

As they walked up the path to the front door of the house opposite, number 16, Blundell Lane, an innocuous black Ford Mondeo, which had been parked in the road outside number 12, did a three point turn in the lane, drove back to the A3 and turned left towards London.

*

George Peterson and his wife Ellen had finally taken the plunge two years previously and bought themselves a two-bedroom apartment in Portugal on the Quinta da Beloura golf resort, ten miles north of Estoril. With both their children married, it was time to spend time and money on their own enjoyment. George had never breathed a word about his and Andrew's embezzlement of the £40 million of Lottery funds. He had fondly believed that retiring with a pension fund of some £20 million, in addition to his

Civil Service pension, would have allowed them to retire permanently to Portugal, possibly buy a larger property and live very comfortably. If Ellen asked where the money came from, he'd think of something to tell her. But the sudden deaths, one after the other, of his co-conspirators had been a brutal reality check.

Now, George's only thought was for the safety of his wife and himself and to put as much distance between them and the shadowy controller of the pension fund. With the country's economy sliding into recession, he had managed to persuade Ellen that now was an ideal time to let their house in Kingston and re-locate to Portugal.

Even before meeting with Andrew at Venetia's funeral, George and Ellen had put their house in the hands of a letting agent, packed their bags and booked a one-way flight with Iberia to Lisbon. After leaving the cemetery, George returned his hire car, took the company's minibus to his house in Kingston's King's Road and loaded their luggage into the back. After he'd finished doing the last checks around the house, he threw the pension fund mobile into the dustbin on his way out. He was so preoccupied he didn't notice the mud-spattered grey Vauxhall Astra, which had been parked in the road opposite their house. Once they were out of sight, the driver of the Vauxhall retrieved the phone from the dustbin, where its GPS circuitry, like an emergency beacon, had been transmitting a warning signal to the master station. The signal had been activated the instant George and Andrew had removed the SIM cards from their phones.

George and Ellen had phoned their friends in the

golf resort and the husband and wife who owned the adjacent apartment were at the airport to meet them. It took just over forty minutes to reach the golf resort. As their neighbours dropped them by the entrance to their apartment, they announced they had organised a small welcome party for them at 8.30 pm. It had been a long day for them both so they decided to take a couple of hours' siesta before showering and getting ready for the party.

It was nearly 9.15 before the Peterson's neighbours began to wonder about the absence of their guests of honour from the party. A woman volunteered to go round to the apartment. She burst back through the door two minutes later, screaming. Terrified and barely coherent, they managed to get out of her that George and Ellen had been murdered. The police later confirmed they had both been shot in the head while they slept. Their apartment had been turned up-side-down, drawers upended and upholstery shredded pointing to a burglary, but hardly justified the double murder of two British expats.

*

'Okay, where to first?' Doyle asked Tom as he turned onto the ramp leading off Interstate 95 and headed west towards the Opa-locka airport district.

'Reckon we start with Rancho Romero – that's on 28th Avenue. Take the next right and then first left on 26th. Nothing special about this place, 'cept that Carillo and Diaz use it 'cos it has Cuban and Mexican hookers. Most are illegal immigrants so I guess they don't make a fuss if they get knocked around. Owner of the place is Salvador; he owes me a few favours so even if they aren't there, he might know where they are.'

'That it over there?' Doyle asked, as he turned into 28th Avenue.

'That's it.' Doyle parked the Dodge and the two men entered the bar. After the bright sunlight, the interior was like a cave, but once their eyes adjusted to the smoky gloom they were able to see their way to the bar, through pool tables, slot machines and tables filled mostly by Hispanic punters.

'A lot of these guys are baggage handlers from the airport,' Tom muttered to Doyle as they finally reached the bar. Their arrival had obviously been flagged up to management, as he was waiting for the two men by the time they reached the bar. Salvador nodded a greeting to Tom.

'Can I get you anything?' he sniffed. It wasn't really an offer.

'Not this time, Salvador,' Tom produced the photos of Carillo and Diaz. 'These two been in lately?' Salvador's eyes flicked briefly across the photos, and there was a slight pause before he answered, as though he was weighing up the pros and cons of co-operating. He looked agitated, and furtively glanced around the room and out of the windows before answering.

'These two men have not been here for two days, Sergeant Jones, but a little while ago another man - foreign accent, maybe English - he was asking for them too.' Tom put a photo of Mike Soames on the bar.

'That him?'

'That's the one. He asks just like you, but there were three men at the bar - right there where you stand. They all drink a lot and tell this man they don' like people – especially foreigners - asking about their friends. This man, he then turns round and beats the shit out of them. I think one of them may die. Then he walks out of the bar and I call an ambulance. I guess he's not a cop?'

'No, he's not. So do you know where we'll find Carillo and Diaz? We want to try and get to them before he does.'

'Sergeant Jones, if I knew I'd tell you. Perhaps you should try the Pink Flamingo, Ruby's Place on 27th or the Gator Bar over on the Lakes side.'

'Is that what you told this guy with the English accent?' Tom asked.

'Yes,' his fingers were drumming the top of the bar.

'C'mon, let's go' Tom led the way out. 'I wondered why all those guys were so quiet. Soames must've scared the shit out of them,' he added as they reached the Dodge.

'Which one first?' Doyle asked.

'The Gator Bar,' Tom replied, checking his Colt automatic. He pulled back the slide, caught the ejected round, replaced it in the magazine and clicked on the safety catch before putting it back in the holster.

'It's that sort of bar?' Doyle asked, glancing to his right, as they drove along the north side of the airport towards the Miami Lakes district.

'It's that sort of bar. Take a right at the next intersection and then park when you find a gap.'

'So what makes this bar so special?'

'The guy who fronts up as the owner is an ex-con called George Tyson – no relation, but he might as well be as he's the same size and shape and just as vicious.

He's there to frighten any difficult customers. The place is really run by Carlos Amerigo; we know it has Mob connections and it's a favourite haunt of the Cuban drug barons. It's been raided by MDPD at least five times, but never any convictions. Carillo and Diaz are small time thugs - small fry for The Gator - but I guess maybe it does their image good. The last time...' but Tom stopped suddenly as they both saw thick black smoke ahead of them and were overtaken by a fire truck with siren wailing. 'Well that was the Gator Bar until someone torched it.'

Doyle pulled over and parked and the two men ran to what was now a raging inferno. The whole area was cordoned off and the police were doing their best to keep the crowd of spectators out of the way of the fire fighters and paramedics. Tom recognised the police Lieutenant who was coordinating the activities of the emergency services and walked over to him holding out his badge.

'Sergeant Jones, sir, from Police HQ and this is Agent Barnes of the CIA. Can you spare a couple of minutes to tell us how this fire got started?'

'What's your interest in this?' the Lieutenant asked, addressing Doyle.

'We're interested in two guys for murder one and a third guy who's looking for them. We've just come from the Rancho Romero where we were told that we might find them here,' Doyle explained, knowing the Police Department's dislike of interference by Federal Agencies in local crime. 'There's a connection to British Intelligence, which is why I'm here.'

'That figures; the eyewitnesses we rescued from the Gator said the man who did this had a European accent. Those that weren't taken to hospital are over there,' and the Lieutenant nodded to a blackened huddle of men and women being questioned by his officers. 'Seems that this guy came into the bar asking for two men – Carillo and Diaz - he had photographs. The barman told him to fuck off and pressed this warning pedal they've got under the bar which brings the muscle out from the back – a gorilla by name of Tyson...'

'I know the one,' said Tom.

'Then no need to tell you that you don't mess about with him unless you're looking for a hospital vacation. But this guy, your British guy, apparently took a swipe at the barman – some sort of kung fu type blow the witnesses say - which damn near decapitated him. So Tyson got hold of him – this is what they've all told us,' and the Lieutenant again nodded in the direction of the witnesses, 'but had the shit kicked out of him. And apparently this guy's pretty small, but he was smashing chairs and tables in the fight – total psycho. Right here some of the witness accounts don't agree, but it seems that these two – Carillo and Diaz - either join in the fight to try and get the guy or one of them takes a shot at him. Whatever happened, both Carillo and Diaz were shot – probably by your guy, but by this stage the whole place was a rough-house of people fighting and screaming. The Fire Chief and his guys will tell us what really set this place on fire, but it seems that some form of incendiary device must've been used because the witnesses say the whole place exploded.'

'Carillo and Diaz, both dead?' Tom asked.

'Carillo dead and Diaz taken to ER at the Lakes

Hospital,' the Lieutenant replied.

'The British man?' Doyle asked.

'Vanished... I'm sorry, I've got to go, but if you want to talk to Diaz, you need to get to the hospital fast 'cos he probably isn't going to be around very much longer,' and the Lieutenant headed for the growing crowd of press and TV journalists. Tom and Doyle quickly showed their photo of Mike to the witnesses, who confirmed that he was the man who'd started the fighting.

'No point in staying here any longer,' said Tom, 'but there's just a chance we might get something from Diaz if we're quick. Hospital's only two blocks away from here.'

'Call your HQ and get a description of Soames and his aliases to all airports, particularly any private airfields, ports and marinas and the road cops,' Doyle had his foot almost flat on the accelerator. 'Don't let anyone approach him, just tail him. He's too dangerous - only your SWAT guys should tackle him.'

The hospital's ER was chaos, filled with survivors with minor injuries, police, nurses and doctors trying to isolate the more pressing cases. Doyle and Tom finally got to the reception desk and as soon as Tom showed his badge, they were escorted by a hospital porter to a triage booth where a young doctor and two nurses were trying to stabilise a patient ready for surgery; he had a gunshot wound to the chest.

'Is he conscious?' Doyle asked, holding out his CIA badge.

'This patient is dying. What is it you want?' asked the doctor angrily, her arms bloodied up to her elbows as she fought to stem the bleeding.

'Doctor, the man you're trying to save is a professional assassin wanted for murder. If you could let me have thirty seconds it might prevent more killings,' Doyle said calmly. After a moment's tight-lipped hesitation, she nodded to the nurses, who disappeared through the curtains. He's done this before, thought Tom.

'Go on then; he's conscious, but only just so I doubt if you'll get any sense out of him. Thirty seconds and I'll be back – no more.'

'Thank you Doctor,' and Doyle bent down so that he was close to Diaz's head. 'Diaz, who shot you and Carillo?' There was no response. 'Who told you to kill the man in St Vincent?' Diaz's eyes flickered opened and stared back vacantly at Doyle, who switched to Spanish. 'The man and woman you shot in St Vincent; who paid you to do that?'

'Gun...' he mouthed feebly using the Spanish word 'pistola''

'That's right, his name was Gunn. Who told you to kill him?' Doyle felt the doctor's arm on his shoulder. 'C'mon, tell me who gave you the order,' Doyle urged in desperation as the doctor attempted to pull him back from the patient. 'Whoever it was ordered your death too.'

'Tib... ti...' the dying Diaz gasped, but the bleep of the cardiac monitor dropped to a single tone, and the two men were shoved out of the way by the nurses wheeling in a crash cart. They listened to them trying to resuscitate him from the other side of the curtains, but a few minutes later the doctor pronounced the time of death. Diaz was dead.

'Did you get anything' Tom asked as they made

their way back to the car.

'He was trying to tell me something... my Spanish is pretty fluent. Yours?'

'Only adequate.'

'He was trying to say something which started with 'ti' or 'tib', but he didn't get any further. There must be hundreds of Spanish words that begin with 'ti' - flowerpot, corkscrew - it doesn't help us very much. Shit!'

*

It was only a few minutes after eight the next morning, and Gunn and Claudine were finishing breakfast, when they heard the now familiar sound of Toby's bike approaching fast.

'This sounds like news,' Gunn remarked as he went to meet Toby at the bridge. The bike came to skidding halt on the gravel at the far end of the bridge.

'Mornin'; I've heard back from Miami.'

'Come and sit down; coffee?' Claudine offered.

'Thanks. My contact called – a guy called Tom Jones, he's a sergeant with the Miami PD - he's had some help from a CIA guy workin' at the DEA – says he has some connection with BID…?' Toby looked at them quizzically.

'Doyle Barnes,' said Gunn.

'Yeah, d'you know him?'

'We know him well. He's the CIA liaison officer for BID.'

Toby told them everything that had happened at the Gator Bar and what Diaz had tried to tell Doyle before he died.

'They put out a call to all the agencies and ports to stop Soames, but the police foun' his hire car at Opa-locka airport - and a dead man in the boot. When they checked with the motel where he stayed last night, the receptionist said a man fittin' the description of the dead guy had delivered a package to Soames' room.' Toby paused and gulped down some of his coffee.

'And Soames?' Gunn asked

'He'd arranged to charter a helicopter from Opa-locka Airport. The pilot of the helicopter is missin' and Soames has vanished. But he's now wanted for the murder of the man who delivered the package, the murder of the owner of the Gator Bar, who died from the beatin' Soames gave him and the murders of Carillo and Diaz. And he's wanted in connection with the disappearance of the chopper pilot. And…' Toby caught his breath, 'Mr Barnes told Tom that he was flying to St Vincent,' Toby checked his watch, 'today. He thinks you're dead and he wants to speak to my boss.'

'Do you have a flight time?' Gunn asked.

'Yes, United Airlines - arrivin' at Joshua in just over an hour. I'm goin' to meet him.'

'Can you bring him straight here?'

'Okay, I'll do that; I should go. What time's your flight, Claudine?'

'11.50.'

'Are you packed? Do you want to come to the airport with me?' Toby offered.

'Yeah, great, thanks; I'll just get my backpack.'

Gunn turned to Toby: 'your investigation showed that these two Cuban gunmen flew into St Vincent on the Saturday, killed Nina and shot me and then caught a flight the same night back to Miami,' Gunn checked with Toby.

'That's right, somethin' wrong there?' Toby asked, on the defensive.

'No, just one fact that has been bothering me since I regained consciousness. I know I'm lucky to be alive and to have a really clear recollection of those split seconds before the gunman shot me. In fact, I keep getting flashbacks to that ghastly scene in the kitchen with poor Nina on the floor in a pool of blood.'

'So what's botherin' you?' Toby asked, getting ready to leave with Claudine.

'There were three men.'

'Could be that one of the Rastas wen' into the house with the gunmen,' Toby suggested.

'Yes....quite possible, but it was this third man who was holding the automatic. Neither of the other two men - Carillo and Diaz - had a weapon - anyway not one that I saw in those few seconds - and my impression was that the man who shot me was stocky and bald.'

'You took a hell of a blow to your head and your memory might be playin' tricks on you.'

'Sure - that'd explain it and anyway my memory may well be playing tricks on me,' and Gunn got up to see the two of them off to the airport.

'Okay I'll wait out front.'

'Do you need to go through anything again? Gunn asked Claudine, gathering her around the waist and pulling her to him.

'No, I know what to do.'

*

Miles Thompson arrived at his office to find his PA waiting in the corridor outside.

'Everything okay, Angela?' he asked.

'Terry Holt's in there but said he'd be finished shortly,' and in the same moment the door opened and Terry appeared.

'Sorry about that, sir,' he said, holding a finger to his lips. He looked around and, seeing no one, switched on a small radio he was holding and lowered his voice. 'There's definitely some kind of listening device in this building. Our equipment's detecting some sort of alien power drain, but I can't find what's causing it and neither can the specialist team from GCHQ. Until we do, turn on the radio or the TV - with the volume up - so it scrambles any sensitive conversation you're having.'

'OK, but how long do you think it'll take to trace the device? I need to know whether I should advise Sir Jeremy to move ops to our alternative HQ in Kingston.' Miles went into his office followed by Terry, who was looking haggard.

'I'll get back to you before midday today, sir; I've got the technicians from GCHQ arriving any moment to have another go. I also need to check with Mary Panter whether there's been any maintenance work that could've provided an opportunity to breach the building's secure comms.' Miles nodded his agreement and Terry hurried off as Angela came in.

'Claudine's back from St Vincent; she wants to see you. She's in my office right now.'

'Thank you, tell her to come in,' Claudine walked through the door as Miles picked up the remote on his desk and turned on the TV.'

'Miles.'

'Claudine! How are you doing?' Miles asked, writing quickly on a memo pad and holding it up for Claudine to read. "Sorry - room bugged."

'Not good, sir,' and she wrote on the memo pad, "TV off – want bug to hear this". Miles nodded, more than a little confused.

'Sorry, er, I wanted to catch the news. Sit down.' Claudine hastily scribbled another note on the pad: "When I finish, need to leave building and will tell you what's really going on. John alive and well! But pretend dead - ask what happened." Miles stared at her, and then mustered a sympathetic tone.

'What happened to John?' he asked gently.

'As you know, he really is dead,' Claudine stifled a sob and sniffed, allowing a few moments of silence. Then she took a deep, convincingly shaky breath: 'both John and Nina were killed at Nina's house by two men brought in from Miami. They shot John in the head...' she sobbed again. 'They took John's body from the scene and threw it into the sea. There are witnesses. Then they left the island that same evening and returned to Miami. The St Vincent Police know who they are; they've asked Miami PD for help. Mike's still working with them, but as you directed I didn't make contact with him. That's it, sir. That's all. I confirm... John's dead.' She allowed a few more moments of silence and sniffing.

'I'm so sor...' Miles began quietly, but Claudine interjected.

'I need to go and see John's parents. I expect there'll be a memorial service to organise.'

'I understand. Thank you, Claudine. I know there's nothing I can say that will be of any comfort. His death is a huge loss to us all. Take as much leave as you need. I'll go and let Sir Jeremy know; and I'll take care of the report.' As they went out through Angela's office, Miles beckoned to her and once they were in the corridor, briefed her in a whisper.

'Claudine and I will be out for about an hour. I've left my mobile on my desk in case that's bugged as well. Don't say anything to me in my office that is sensitive unless the TV or radio is on - the same if you're speaking on the phone or to anyone in your office. I'll explain later.'

# CHAPTER 9

Miles didn't say anything until he and Claudine had settled into a quiet corner of Starbucks in Cale Street.

'Now what the hell *is* going on? You say John's alive? How come?'

'Okay, this comes in three parts; first the conspiracy. Eight people transferred from MI5 and 6 between 1988 and 1990 when BID was set up. Of those eight men, seven are now dead; Anderson, Bristow and Driscoll were all killed on operational service; Simon Peters committed suicide; and Goldman was shot in 1997 by an unknown killer. David Chesham was supposedly shot by a terrorist sentry at that airfield in Kent, but John found out from the Commander of Alpha Squadron of 22 SAS that he was shot in the back with a 7.62mm bullet. All of the terrorists were armed with 9mm Heckler and Koch sub-machine guns. That leaves just Paul Manton who was murdered in his hospital bed in a professional hit.'

'That's seven...'

'Yes, that only accounts for seven of the eight. John is convinced that three of that seven were murdered because, possibly without realising it, they knew the identity of the eighth person. He's convinced this eighth person is at the root of all of this, and is probably highly placed in the Intelligence Service, the

Government or the Cabinet Office. He - or she - has had some eighteen years in which to destroy or bury his or her identity and now with the death of Paul Manton we've lost the last witness who might have known the identity of this person. So, first off I'm going to go back through all our records of those people who joined BID when it was created, particularly those who were accepted by Sir Jeremy from the Military Intelligence offices,' she paused for breath.

'Questions?'

'No, go on,' Miles said numbly, his voice hollow. He gratefully noticed a group of mothers with pushchairs and several screaming kids settle on a table near them, which would completely obscure anything they were saying if anyone was trying to listen.

'John,' Claudine flinched, 'was shot – in the head. He admits he should have been more cautious about discussing his suspicions about the conspiracy before he left for St Vincent. He's certain this eighth person got to hear of that and gave orders for him to be killed while he was in St Vincent. Two Cuban illegal immigrants in Miami were brought over to do the job on the Saturday – the same day that Hassan Hussein's aircraft was blown up.'

'That quickly…' Miles murmured, almost to himself.

'Yes…..we're sure these two men – Fidel Carillo and Ernesto Diaz – got their weapons from a Rastafarian gang in Kingstown then broke into Nina's house, where they waited in the kitchen until Nina went in there and then cut her throat. A couple of minutes later John went into the kitchen and they shot him in the head. The gunmen left the house with the two bodies on the kitchen floor. They went straight to the airport where they caught a United Airlines flight back to Miami.'

'Jesus. How...?

'At the airport John had met this old World War Two veteran called Gabriel Jackson, who'd seen him shoot that Haitian security guard from Hassan Hussein's property in Barbados. He was also at the airport when Hussein's jet blew up. Gabriel - I don't know, I suppose he felt some kind of soldierly kinship with John - anyway he wanted to show John his war photo album and got his son to drive him to Nina's house - they knew her. His son, Robert, is a surgeon, thank God - a neurosurgeon - and runs his own clinic. They found John, took him to the clinic, and Robert operated immediately. John must have a concrete skull because the bullet never penetrated, but went round it and lodged at the back, where Robert removed it. He should be fit again in a week or so and his memory seems to be okay too. He's convalescing at a seaside holiday cottage owned by the Jacksons. But he wants it broadcast that he's dead to get whoever it is off his back so he can go after them - with your approval....'

'I'll need to run it past Sir Jeremy, but I don't think we have any choice. What else?'

'The next part concerns Mike Soames. Malcolm Slater allocated one of his sergeants, Toby Charbonnier, to assist Soames. Toby took him to a bar where he knew the Rastafarian gang often go and he's convinced some of them recognised Soames - he said when they saw him they looked terrified. He nearly killed two of them - Toby thinks to distract his attention from the way they were acting.'

'Oh, for Christ's sake,' Miles sighed.

'Toby then dropped him off at his hotel and went home. The next morning he called at the hotel, only to discover that they knew nothing about him. Soames went straight to the airport after leaving Toby the previous evening and took a flight to Miami under the name of Frank Dawson, then booked into a motel under yet another alias, Peter Hobbs. We guessed he was going after the Cubans. At the motel he was met by a contact who – we think - provided him with a gun. Whatever the meeting was about, Soames then killed this man too and shoved his body into the back of a hire car.'

'How d'you know all this?'

'Toby has a contact in the Miami-Dade Police Department, a Sergeant Jones. He got him to do some digging on both the Cubans and Soames for us. By chance his captain told him to go and join up with a CIA contact at the DEA because he knew they have links with us and…

'Doyle Barnes... of course, he's in Miami on that DEA op,' Miles interrupted.

'Yes, exactly.......... Doyle and Jones decided to try and find the two gunmen rather than look for Soames, because they assumed, rightly as it turned out, that if they found the gunmen they would probably find Soames.'

'They got some tip-offs on bars where these guys hang out but by the time they got to one of them, a place called The Gator Bar, it had gone up in flames. Soames had been there. Carillo had been shot dead and Diaz critically wounded; he died in hospital. It seems that Soames then set the place on fire with some form of incendiary device as all the witnesses say they saw an explosion.'

'Did..'

'Doyle and Tom got to Diaz before he died, but all they could get out of him, when they tried to find out who ordered the hit on John, was a part of something in Spanish - a word which started with, 'ti' or 'tib' - not much use.'

'And Soames?'

'They put out an all points bulletin immediately to arrest and, if necessary, shoot Soames on sight, but by then it was too late; he'd chartered a helicopter from Opa-locka airport, got rid of its pilot - who's now missing - and vanished. The helicopter charter company confirmed that it was fully fuelled and had a reserve tank which would give it a maximum range of 350 miles, if lucky with a following wind, but nearer 300 miles if not. That range puts Daytona and St Petersburg airports within reach to the north, Nassau to the south-east and Matanzas in Cuba to the south.'

'Shit! This is our agent and he's killing innocent people.'

Claudine let Miles digest everything for a moment, then reached into her bag and took out a new mobile phone.

'This is for you. I have one too; I've put John's number in it for you. Remember we can only use these outside Kingsroad House. When John wants to speak to you he'll send you a text message that says something like, "Vodaphone's new rates are on its website". That's the signal to leave the building and call him.'

'The name 'Mark' on the mobile means that he's using a covert BID alias?'

'John has a number of leads and wants to operate on his own. He won't use his BID credit card, but will take out a new card in the name of Mark Knight - an alias he's used before -- because he already has a passport, driving licence and everything else he needs in that name.'

'Got you.'

'John also wants to base himself at the BID safe-house - the flat in Drayton Gardens - and asked if an account could be opened for him in that name at the bank on Brompton Road. It's essential that the funding for that account doesn't come from BID's finance branch...'

'Fine.'

Also he has a housekeeper - a Mrs Charlesworth - he believes she is likely to be one of the first people who would be targeted for questioning, so I'm going to go and see her and tell her he's missing in action.'

'That's good; it's important that you lay a false trail, especially by going down to John's parents and making a show of arranging a memorial service. Make it sometime in September, the excuse being that people take their holidays in July and August and, of course, the Olympics in Beijing will be on us in no time. I'll brief Sir Jeremy, overtly in his office after I've had a chance to get him out of the building and passed on everything you've just told me. I'll take everything else from here and sort out the bank account. I only have one question; is John really fit enough to take this on?'

'Yes; I'm as amazed as you, I really am, but he is. He seems very strong mentally too, but of course we won't know for sure for some time...'

'Then we'll just have to give him as much support as he needs.' They drained their coffees and parted outside Starbucks.

*

The gauges for both port and starboard fuel tanks on the Bell Longranger 206 indicated that the thirsty Alison turboshaft engine had nearly sucked them dry. Soames reached across to the central instrument console and switched to reserve. Throughout the hurricane season from June to October, the prevailing wind was south-east, south or south-west which meant that the helicopter had faced a head wind on its course to Matanzas Airport on the northern coast of Cuba. The Cuban coastline was now in sight on the horizon and the GPS indicated that it was 53 miles to the beacon at Matanzas Airport. He brought the helicopter down to 50 feet above the calm seas of the Florida Straits in order to avoid detection by both the Cuban coastal and airport radars.

Mike allowed himself the luxury of a few moments of self-congratulation as he approached the Cuban coast. Everything they'd been working towards since he'd joined BID from the SAS in 1991 had finally come together. He smiled as he recalled how childishly simple it had been to blackmail gullible civil servants into embezzling the government funds over which they had control. John Gunn's undue interest in David Chesham's death and the pending police investigation of Paul Manton had forced them into getting rid of the remaining contributors in more of a hurry than he would have liked. It gave them no time to be elaborate and frame the circumstances. But in retrospect, he was pleased they were out of the way now, albeit prematurely. Killing Gunn had also been much simpler than he had dared hope. But that was all in the past; his future was waiting in a bank in the Cayman Islands.

A glance at the reserve gauge indicated that the Alison turbine was very close to running only on fumes. The Longranger skimmed low over the deserted shoreline as he looked for a suitable landing site. The airport of Matanzas was now about two miles to the east and to the west was the town of Matanzas on the edge of a bay. All around that area was rough scrub and stunted trees.

Soames chose a spot that was clear of trees and landed the helicopter, quickly closed down the engine and repositioned the dead pilot from the co-pilot's seat to the pilot's. He then removed any ID from the pilot's pockets and replaced it with the passport in the name of Michael Soames. Fluent in Spanish, Soames was now Carlos Martinez, a Cuban National, his passport and paperwork all in place. He took an explosive device from his rucksack, placed it in the pilot's lap and set the timer. Then Carlos Martinez walked away through the scrub towards the airport, flinching slightly as the explosion shattered the silence.

*

It wasn't difficult for Toby to spot Doyle Barnes as he came through into the arrivals hall. Gunn's graphic description left him in no doubt he had the right man.

'Agent Barnes?' The towering, piratical figure sauntered towards him.

'You must be Sergeant Charbonnier, pleased to meet you; Tom said lots of good things.' The two men shook hands.

'Toby, please.'

'Hell of a shit storm this has turned into. Is Malcolm able to meet with me now? I want to find out exactly what happened to John.'

'Of course, but before we go to Police HQ I'd like to take you to meet someone - it's important,' he added quickly, when Doyle looked impatient.

'Uh, sure... Do I know this person?' Doyle asked as he cautiously hunkered down on the back of Toby's bike. But Toby's answer was drowned by the roar of the Honda's 600 cc engine. Twenty-five minutes later they arrived at Layou Bay and Toby stopped the bike just short of the wooden bridge.

'This is a nice spot...' but Doyle stopped dead as he saw John Gunn standing on the bridge. 'What the fuck...?' Doyle leapt off the bike with more agility than Toby would have given him credit for and strode across the bridge to embrace his old friend.

'Oh God, buddy... Aren't you dead?' he laughed warmly and felt the tension draining out of him.

'I thought I was dead - I should be.'

'Hey, Toby, you might have warned me!'

'Couldn' be too careful; we need everyone to think he's dead. I'm goin' back to HQ to check in. I'll be back later,' and Toby sped off up the track to the metalled road.

'Wow, this changes everything. I think I'm owed an explanation.'

'You definitely are.' Gunn led the way into the cottage.

'What the hell happened? Are you okay?' Doyle was eyeing Gunn's bandages and the bruising on his forehead and around his eye; now in the late stages of healing it had turned a deep yellowish colour, making Gunn appear slightly jaundiced.

'I'm really okay, but it was a close one this time,' and for the next hour Gunn took Doyle through the events of the last few days, the conspiracy crippling BID and why he planned to stay 'dead.'

'Provided Miles gives me the go-ahead, there's an obvious start point to all this and that's the BID and MI personal records of all the employees taken on since the creation of the Directorate. Claudine's getting to work on that as we speak. I can't believe that we'll be lucky enough to dig up evidence of the eighth person as they've had ample opportunity to get rid of it, but the lack of certain records that have vanished might point us in the right direction. It looks like Soames is a part of this conspiracy and that in itself may also give us clues about this person. I'm hoping Langley will let you help me on this but...'

'What do you want me to do?'

'What about your work with the DEA?'

'That's pretty much all wrapped up, so I see no obstacle there. Come on, what can I do?'

'Well; although I've had barely a dozen words of conversation with Mike Soames since I joined BID in '97, I know he was in the SAS - Jason Wolstenholme, the Assistant Director for the Caribbean, mentioned it once. Mike's fluency in Spanish has meant that most of his assignments were either in Spain, South America or the Caribbean. Anyway, if he was in the SAS then there is a possibility that the eighth man - I'm assuming it was a man - was too. Mike joined BID shortly after the '91 Gulf War. Can you get access to all the classified documents, maps and war diaries from the war?'

'Sure, no problem, but you must have access to the UK's classified documents on Op Granby?'

'Right, but my worry is that Soames and this unknown guy have had nearly 18 years to alter, destroy and bury the information which I may need. They couldn't possibly have had access to the documents held at either Langley or the Pentagon.'

'Got it, consider it done.'

'Okay, that's a good start. Can you get yourself a new phone and then text me with the new number?'

'Again, no problem; when do you expect to hear from Miles?'

'Tomorrow, I hope.'

'Okay, well I'd better call in on the Chief Superintendent so that anyone watching my movements isn't disappointed and then I'll catch the return flight to Miami. Do you have any transport here?'

'Jacob does.' They said warm farewells, and Doyle squeezed himself into Jacob's diminutive Citroen 2CV, which lurched and spluttered its way up the track to the road.

*

Claudine turned off the M23 at Junction 10 and joined the road to East Grinstead. The Gunns' house was up a small side road leading off the A264. She turned into the gated entrance and stopped the car in front of the house. She saw John's mother, Vanessa, look out of the window. When the news of the shooting had reached BID, Sir Jeremy Hammond had driven down to Sussex to speak personally to them – a duty he fulfilled with the death of any of BID's agents. It wasn't the first time she'd paid a visit to the Gunns. Claudine couldn't imagine what it must be like to think your son is dead, to come to terms with that, only discover that he's not after all - and several times over. She steeled herself, walked up to the front door and knocked. Seconds later the door was snatched open.

'Hello Vanessa.'

'Claudine; what do you want?'

'Do you mind if we talk outside for a moment? It's possible that you might have some form of bug in your house.'

'What?' Vanessa looked stupefied and livid at the same time. She didn't move for a few moments, clearly debating whether to just slam the door. Eventually she relented, came out and closed the door behind her. She looked exhausted.

'What do you want?' she said again.

'I'm going to tell you the truth while we're standing out here away from any bugs and then when we go into the house I'll tell you a lie for the benefit of any device. If you could react…'

'Just get on with it.'

'John is alive and well.' Claudine stopped to let the news sink in. Vanessa looked away, hiding her face; she was visibly shaking, though whether she was crying Claudine couldn't tell. If anyone was watching, this would work in our favour, she thought; Gunn's mother looked distraught.

'What happened?' She asked eventually, in barely a whisper.

'John was shot in the head, but the bullet never penetrated his skull. By a miracle, there was a surgeon on hand and John is now convalescing in a safe location. He of course sends all his love and he's desperately sorry for the unhappiness...'

'Oh please...' Vanessa interjected sharply. 'Enough.'

'I'm sorry.'

'Ness? Who is it? David Gunn called from inside the house.

'No-one dear, I'll be back in a minute.'

'I have to ask if we could go into the house for the other version.'

'No, you can just go.'

'Please – '

'Just leave.'

OK. But please just don't talk about this in the house unless it's a conversation that supports the untrue version. I'm going to organise a memorial service in September...' Vanessa was closing the door, but Claudine jammed her foot in the gap.

'Please, Vanessa, listen; if you could mention the memorial service in the house; if someone's listening they'll believe John's dead and that will keep him safe. You can call me...' But Vanessa had slammed the door on her. Claudine took out a notebook, wrote down hers and Miles' numbers and posted it through the letterbox with a note saying, "If you need anything please call."

*

Mike Soames checked the departure screens for the next flight to Caracas. Matanzas Airport wasn't busy; in fact, there were hardly any travellers on the main concourse. The next flight to Caracas was a Cubana flight leaving in an hour and a quarter's time. He went to the ticketing counter where the girl behind it was almost asleep and bought himself a single economy ticket to Caracas.

His exit from the USA, after tying off all the loose ends, had been but a part of the careful planning that had taken place in London, as soon as the decision had been taken to kill John Gunn. Soames had had plenty of time to close down his affairs in London, transfer his bank account to Rio de Janeiro where he owned a two-bedroom apartment with a view of Copacabana Beach. The Flight to Caracas took a few minutes short of five hours; the next morning he bought a ticket on Varig Airlines to Rio under the name of Jesus Garcia where he arrived in the late afternoon. He hailed a taxi in the rank outside the airport and gave directions to his apartment - and a new life.

# CHAPTER 10

Robert Jackson arrived at the cottage shortly before ten in the morning to find that Gunn was out jogging on the beach. He went out on to the veranda, from where he could see the entire length of the beach, joining Jacob, who was keeping an eye on his ward. Gunn jogged towards them.

'Time for the stitches to come out?'

'Let's take a look an' see how it's healin'.'

Gunn sat down and Jacob removed the small dressings that protected both the wound on his forehead and the surgical scar at the back of his head. It was two days now since Jacob had taken off the bandages and padded dressings. Robert examined his patient and, happy with his handiwork, carefully began to remove the stitches.

'Despite the humidity, John, you've healed real well,' Robert muttered, adding as he snipped the last stitch, 'these need to be left open to the air now. If you can stay put jus' a few more days, I'd say you'd make a full recovery. Do what you appear to be doin' already; get yourself fit and if you can do your business for a while from a phone, you won' regret it.'

'I'm not going anywhere.'

'As soon as you have time back in the UK, you should go an' see a specialist - you need to be scanned and have a psychological ex....'

But Gunn's new mobile vibrated into life, clattering noisily on the glass tabletop.

'Sorry, Robert, I need to take this.'

'Of course.' Robert closed his medical bag and walked out to his car with Jacob

'Yes?'

'Is this Mark Knight?' Gunn recognised Miles' voice.

'Yes, Miles, it's me.'

'I'm calling from the garden at the back of my house. It's good to hear your voice, John. For the record, I don't know what we'd have done if we'd lost you. Claudine briefed me on everything; you've got the go-ahead from the boss and me. The bank account's ready and the card's on its way out to you now.

'Great, thanks.'

'John, Claudine went to see your parents; they more or less slammed the door on her. I'm sorry.'

'I thought it might be like that. Did…'

'She managed to get your mother outside for a few seconds to tell her that you're alive, and that they might be bugged, but they wouldn't let her in to feed the news of your death to anyone who might be listening. But she says your mo… uh, well if anyone was watching them, they would have seen an angry, grief-stricken mother.' He added: 'they won't jeopardise anything, John, you're their son.'

'Barely,' John sighed. 'Memorial service?'

'Claudine's setting it up for September.'

'Okay; let's hope this is all over by then so we don't have to go through with it. I don't know how much longer my parents will play along.'

'I agree. Claudine's also spoken to your cleaner, in case anyone gets to her. We've told her you're MIA and asked her to call in once a week to your house to keep it clean until a decision is made whether to sell it or pass it on to your sisters.'

'Are they okay?

'Your sisters? As far as can be expected. Not as angry as your parents.'

There was a silence; family - always the loser in this game - was often an awkward subject. Eventually Miles spoke.

'Please take the time you need to get really fit. With the terrorist attacks in London and Operation Calypso, I think we've taken our eye off the ball, which is why we've been caught off guard with this thing. We could do with taking a step back.'

'Don't worry. As you know, the gunmen who killed Nina and shot me are both dead and Soames has vanished, so that side of things can go on a back-burner - I've got Doyle using his CIA resources to trace Soames.'

'Good; there's something else though that you won't have heard yet. Clive Sterling, our Assistant Director at Thames House, was murdered a few days ago - very professionally using a rare toxin injected into the back of his neck while he was at the theatre. We're checking whether there have been any other sudden or suspicious deaths, not only in the Intelligence Community, but also in the Cabinet Office, Civil Service and Diplomatic Service.'

'Jesus; how far has this thing spread?'

'Claudine's already going through the personal files of all BID's employees, particularly at the time of its creation 18 years ago, to see if that will shed any light on the identity of the eighth man. I think finding that person will be the only way to stop the killings. Look, I have to go. Is there anything else I can do for you?' Miles asked.

'One thing.........could you speak to Mike Harris, the CO of 22 SAS, and arrange for me to visit him under the name of Mark Knight - say in about a week's time?'

'Done; be in touch,' and Miles ended the call.

*

For the rest of the week, Gunn concentrated on getting fit. Robert had brought him weights from the clinic's physiotherapy department to help build up strength and Toby volunteered to act as personal trainer. He had also stopped shaving and had grown a moustache and beard, which changed his features completely.

On the last morning that they would train together before Gunn's departure, Toby arrived at his usual time - shortly after seven, before it got too hot. Gunn couldn't fail to notice that Toby looked exhausted as he collapsed into one of the chairs on the veranda.

'I think we should scrub the morning session; you look absolutely knackered. What's been going on at Police HQ?' Gunn asked, taking the seat opposite Toby.

'Pretty sure I'd be of no use to you this mornin'; I've been up all night with Malcolm trying to unscramble a major crisis of confidence between the PM and our Commissioner.'

'If it has a bearing on the murder of Nina and our search for Soames then I would like to know what this is all about. If not, then I won't pry into matters which don't concern me.'

'Oh, it concerns you alright, John,' and Toby paused to drink the black coffee which Jacob had unobtrusively placed on the table in front of him. 'Aaaah, that's good coffee and should help me stay awake for a little longer.......now, let me make proper sense of this.'

'OK.......John, this all started about a week ago when Malcolm Slater called me into his office after I got back from a trainin' session with you. For some time now, it's been public knowledge that the Prime Minister and the Police Commissioner were no soul mates - in fact the PM is supposed to have done everythin' he could to prevent Leo Hugues' appointment. The Commissioner comes from an old Vincentian French family and makes no attempt to conceal his dislike of the British and the Island's membership of the Commonwealth. Since Leo Hugues was promoted to Commissioner and Knighted he has been responsible for a number of embarrassin' incidents - both for the police and the Government.'

'Without the Commissioner's knowledge, our financial controller brought in PricewaterhouseCoopers to do last year's audit. Previously this had been undertaken by Holt, Pankhurst and Samson, a Barbados-based audit company. The follow-up action to that audit is still in progress as it uncovered a number of contracts that had been awarded to French companies whose directors had close connections with the Police

Commissioner, in spite of cheaper tenders from other companies. The Commissioner's efforts to silence the auditors were blocked by the Prime Minister who ordered a full investigation into the contracts and a number of other incidents by a select committee of the Island's Parliament. That investigation is nearly finished and there have been one or two intended leaks, both to the media and to senior police officers, like Malcolm.'

'I think I can guess where this is leading.......go on,' Gunn encouraged.

'Anyway, the investigation got hold of all the telephone records and when certain numbers were checked it was discovered that there had been five calls made by the Commissioner to a number which only appeared in St Vincent on the day that Mike Soames arrived here. Further checks tied that number to previous visits by Soames to this Island. The gardener at the Commissioner's house was questioned by our CID and when shown a photo of Soames, he confirmed that he had visited the Commissioner's house the same evenin' that I left him at the hotel and before he went to the airport. I'm not sure how much longer we'll be able to keep your presence on this Island confidential because of this investigation so it's just as well you're returnin' to London. Gossip in our Headquarters is that the Commissioner will be sacked, probably before the end of this year, and Malcolm will be promoted into his appointment.'

'Many thanks for that, Toby. You're right, this will give me the ammunition to silence any suggestion from London that I might not be fit enough to return. I'll speak to my boss now and plan to leave tomorrow after saying my farewells to the Jackson family.'

'Right John, I'll see you off tomorrow and I'll make sure that the Glocks are passed to your flight crew.'

Gunn sent the Vodaphone text to Miles Thompson who returned his call within twenty minutes. Gunn explained briefly the political hiatus on the Island and his intention to return to London the following day. He ended the call and turned to Toby.

'Are you okay to train today?'

'Yeah, come on, let's get started.' But training never started. At that moment, John's phone buzzed; it was Miles again.

'John, we've hit pay dirt. When I started looking for any other suspicious deaths, well, Christ, it's a massacre. Within the last month, Venetia Akehurst, who was a senior Cabinet Office Civil Servant, fell, jumped or was pushed to her death from the tenth floor of her apartment block in Brentford. Andrew Barton, a Civil Servant in another government department, died from a heart attack - uncertain whether that was going to happen anyway, but it was triggered when he came home to find two policemen on his doorstep; and then, by coincidence - or not - a George Peterson, in the same government department as Barton, was shot dead in his apartment in Portugal – his wife too.'

'Jesus - it's like the final act of a sodding Shakespearean tragedy!'

'It gets worse; I've had to get help with this from Mary Panter, the Head of Finance and Admin. I asked her to do an audit on the budget controlled by Paul Manton to see if there were any significant sums that defy a convincing explanation. I also spoke with the

Head of Economic and Domestic Policy in the Cabinet Office and he agreed to do an immediate audit too on any current and previous budgets which came under the control of those three civil servants.'

'And?'

'Both George Peterson and Andrew Barton were in the Cabinet Office Special Projects Department responsible for both the construction of the Dome and Millennium celebrations. The audit unearthed a sum of £40 million that was earmarked for Public Relations and Media facilities, but somehow got transferred into another Cabinet Office fund - supposedly set aside for 'pension contingencies' - from where it vanished.'

'I don't believe this.'

'Oh, it could get worse, and we may be as guilty as the Cabinet Office for negligence. I expect to have a lot more detail from Mary before too long.'

'So let's just re-cap for a second here. Seven people have been murdered because they could identify this eighth person. Of those seven, two - the two in BID - may have been involved in embezzling huge sums of money from budgets over which they had total control...'

'And I fully expect to hear that Venetia Akehurst had control of a significant budget and that a similar sum of money has gone missing.'

'I expect you're right. So in addition to those seven, four civil servants have been murdered - all of them linked by suspected embezzled sums of money - probably amounting to some £80 million...'

'Has Claudine found anything in the personal files yet?'

'Nothing yet, but I'll brief you on that when you

get back; you'll need it for your visit to 22 SAS. Call me when you're back and we'll meet.'

John hung up and looked at Toby, who saw the urgency in his face.

'What's happened?

'Can you get me on an earlier flight?'

'How early?'

'Today?'

*

'Cornwall.'

'It's Alice, sir; just a reminder of your weekly appointment at Thames House.'

'Thanks, Alice; I shan't be back after that appointment, so feel free to wrap up as soon as you want.'

'Thank you, sir,' Alice switched off the intercom and winked at the other two PAs in her office. Their colleagues in Thames House had told them months ago that although there was a security conference every Wednesday afternoon, it had never been attended by their Assistant Director. Instead, John headed straight for 'Pinks.' The club billed itself as an exclusive fine-dining private members' club and hotel, and from the outside there was no reason to suspect otherwise. It was, in reality, nothing more than a brothel, and an expensive one, where virtually anything could be bought.

'Good afternoon, Mr Adams,' the receptionist greeted Cornwall as he entered the maroon wallpapered lobby with its gilt mirrors. The door only opened when his image on the CCTV camera had been matched with the one stored on the club's database. The management of Pinks made it their rule that every detail of a prospective client must be known before he, or she, would be allowed to benefit from the services it provided. Although the face of management was a wealthy Russian property developer, the club was in reality owned by a drug cartel, which made almost as much from feeding tit-bits of information on their clients to scoop-hungry tabloid hacks. The club's Madame kept a close watch on the arrival of all her clientele and as soon as she saw John, she left her private office to one side of the lobby.

'Mr Adams, always a pleasure to see you.' Her voice had a heavy Eastern European accent. 'Please come into my office, we've had to make adjustment to your programme.' John followed her, fidgeting nervously; he was usually shown straight up to a room on the second floor, where a very young Filipino girl would screw him senseless.

'Is there a problem?' he asked.

'It's just a staffing problem, but we've lost Susannah. So for today I have for you another girl - little older than usual but I think you will like her.' She buzzed an intercom on her desk. The door opened; a striking Asian girl glided into the room, her curves poured into scraps of midnight lace, and draped herself over her now sweating client.

'This is Vivienne. She'll take care of you.' Vivienne took John's hand and led him from the room. As soon as the door closed, the Madame picked up the phone.

'Yes?'

'He's here.'

In his usual room on the second floor, Vivienne

slowly removed all John's clothes and pushed him down on to the chaise langue, gyrating over him teasingly. Then she stepped back towards the bed, letting him remove what few clothes she was wearing. She lowered herself on to the end of the bed and John groaned with excitement as he sank to his knees in front of her. As his head dipped between her thighs, she reached behind her, grasping at the sheets in feigned ecstasy before slipping her hands under the pillow and pulling on a pair of surgical gloves. She pulled out a condom, its packaging already removed, and, holding it in her left hand, urging him on, she used her right hand to pick up a small syringe from under the other pillow and injected a minute quantity of clear fluid into the open condom. Still holding the condom in her left hand, she hid the syringe again then bent down and fitted it over his penis, blocking any view of her gloved hands with her long black hair. When the condom was in place, she carefully removed the gloves behind his back, kissing him hard on the mouth as she did.

Then, abruptly Vivienne jumped back as John started to heave and choke. The toxin she'd planted in the condom was paralysing the muscles of his lungs and his heart. John was dead in less than two minutes, contorted grotesquely on the carpet. Vivienne dressed, then took a second pair of gloves from her purse on the dressing table and put them on to remove the condom from the dead body; she dropped it and the other gloves into a medical disposal bag. She grabbed her negligee without bothering to put it on and turned to leave the room, but stopped, hands flying to her throat, when she suddenly couldn't get her breath. Then a searing hot pain shot through her left side, as though she'd been branded from the inside; unable to scream, she doubled up in agony. She collapsed before she could reach the door, her dead eyes wide with terror.

Three minutes later, the Madame entered the room, having watched everything on CCTV. She was completely clad in sterile overalls as she removed the gloves from Vivienne's hands, wiped them clean and then washed and dried John's genitals. She put the medical disposal bag, gloves and all the cleaning materials into a larger plastic sack, followed by the bed linen, which she stripped off the bed and replaced with clean sheets. Then she took everything down a back stairwell, reserved only for staff, and out to an incinerator in the yard behind the club.

*

Gunn collected his two Glocks, spare magazines and holsters from the First Officer of his flight and walked out into the arrivals hall at Heathrow's Terminal 5. As he headed for the Underground, he switched on his phone to check for messages; there was one. Miles wanted to meet as soon as possible.

He got off the Piccadilly Line at Gloucester Road and walked to Drayton Gardens. The flat was on the second floor and accessed by its own metal staircase. Claudine had texted to say she'd buried the keys in the soil of one of the potted plants by the front door, second from the right. Gunn unholstered his Glock 17 as he unlocked the door. He was familiar with the layout of the flat as he had visited it on several occasions when BID's 'guests' had been staying there.

These guests were agents from other nations' secret services who preferred the anonymity of the flat to a hotel room. Gunn sent the Vodaphone text to Miles. His mobile rang almost immediately.

'Can you make the Coffee Republic on Fulham Road in half-an-hour's time?' Miles asked.

'No problem.'

Gunn glanced at his watch - 8.45. It was only a five-minute walk at the most, so he stripped off his travel-weary clothes and showered. After towelling himself dry he glanced in the mirror above the basin and only then realised how much the combination of a slightly greying beard, moustache, his uncut hair and a month of Caribbean sun had altered his appearance; he looked about five years older. He dressed in the jeans, linen shirt and trainers he'd bought at the airport, checked the smaller Glock 26 and clipped it into his ankle holster. Five minutes later he slipped into the shady interior of the café from the bright, sun-dappled street.

Miles was already waiting for him at a table in a corner. He looked straight through Gunn before realising who it was.

'Christ, I would never have recognised you. Good to see you,' they shook hands warmly. Miles didn't wait for John to get a drink. 'Your visit to Mike Harris is cleared; he knows all the background. He's been doing some checking of his own on personnel in the Regiment from 1988 to 1995. He's expecting you as Mark Knight and one phone call to that number...' Miles handed over a page from his diary with a number written on it '...will set up your visit.

'Thanks.' Miles seemed to have shrunk in size

since Gunn last saw him, his eyes ringed by dark circles and his clothes hanging off him; his hand shook slightly as he lifted his coffee mug.

'And John; the death toll's just gone up by one. John Cornwall, our AD at Vauxhall Cross, has been murdered.'

'Jesus, this is turning into a slaughter. What happened?'

'I told you Clive had been murdered, but not how; he was poisoned by an incredibly powerful tetrodotoxin injection in the base of the neck. That toxin is only found in the blue-ringed octopus. It's a neurotoxin which paralyses the muscles and the victim dies of respiratory failure. There is no known antidote and the only way of saving a victim who has been bitten by the octopus is to provide respiratory support for at least 24 hours. In Clive's case, it was over half-an-hour before the paramedics got to him, by which time he was long dead. The blue ringed octopus is only found in small tidal pools in the southern Pacific – not a poison therefore, that is easily bought over the counter at your local pharmacy!'

'So what exotic method was used to murder John Cornwall?'

'You might well ask,' Miles continued. Cornwall used to pay a regular weekly visit to a brothel called Pinks – it's just.....'

'Yeah, I know the one.'

'The receptionist is on a BID retainer to keep us informed of everyone who makes use of the club's services. It's used by a significant number of VIPs – minor Royals, politicians, senior military officers, Civil and Diplomatic Service and Cabinet Office, which is why we keep an eye on it. Cornwall went there yesterday afternoon, but his usual girl wasn't there so they gave him another girl - one the receptionist had never seen before. Both Cornwall and the girl were found dead in a room on the second floor. She's certain that the Madame - who calls herself Ava Buck…' Gunn raised a smile in spite of himself, '… no, really; her real name is Irena Novotnya, an illegal immigrant from Romania who used to entertain Ceauçescu.'

'So what killed them?'

'Cause of death was another very rare, highly poisonous toxin. It took the pathologist some time to identify it. He traced the point of entry into both bodies - it only takes skin contact. In Cornwall's case it entered through his penis, so it was probably in a condom, though there was no trace of one at the scene. In the girl's case it entered through her hands so was probably in some form of glove she used to handle the condom - we don't know for sure because someone cleaned up after they died.'

'What was it?'

'A batrachotoxin… It's secreted by 'Phyllobates terribilis' - the Golden Poison Frog, which only lives in the Columbian rainforest. It's not only very rare, but probably the most deadly of any alkaloid poison produced by a vertebrate. It can be passed to another creature, or a human, just by touching the frog's skin where the toxin is secreted from glands. After contact, the effect is almost instantaneous, preventing any impulses from reaching the muscles, leaving them in a state of contraction that stops the heart from beating. Less than one milligram of the toxin is enough to kill as many as twenty people.'

# CHAPTER 11

The hard-copies of BID employees' personal files were kept separately from all other BID files in a concrete-walled, steel-lined, fire-proof vault. It was protected by a half-ton steel door, CCTV, time locks and combination locks requiring two people to open them simultaneously. All records were backed up on computer discs stored in another safe in BID's Finance and Administration Department. There were only five people who were allowed access to BID's records: Mary Panter and her deputy, Martin King – 'Luther;' the Director, the Deputy Director and the Deputy Director of Counter Espionage. If Mary or her deputy weren't available, the security system would accept the palm prints of the Director and his, or her, deputy, who also held copies of the combinations to open the door.

Claudine arrived in Finance and Admin on the 10th floor shortly after 9am and was escorted through the department by both Mary and Luther to the safe door. Mary first, followed by Luther, placed their palms on a screen and then tapped in the code. There was a slight hiss of escaping air, as the room beyond was maintained at an over-pressure of 10 psi to prevent contamination. Claudine, the only person entering the room, was wearing white overalls to protect its contents. She stepped forward, eager to get started, but Mary quickly pulled her back as the door swung outwards under its own power. She explained the fail-safe system to prevent the safe door from being closed while someone was still inside the room and gave Claudine what looked like a mobile phone; in fact it was a small remote control for the safe door. The door could not be closed until someone pressed the 'clear' button from outside the records room. Mary then searched her for any cameras but Claudine had already left her official mobile and new mobile with Miles. She sensed that Mary was unhappy about letting her in as she brusquely patted down her clothes, avoiding eye contact.

Miles had told her during one of their now regular meetings in Starbucks that Mary had asked if any personal files could be removed before Claudine was given free rein, inferring that perhaps the Director's file and Miles' ought to be removed, but Miles got the distinct impression that Mary didn't want Claudine to see her file. Miles had had to show her the signed memo from the Director specifying that all files were to be made available.

Moreover, everyone in BID was aware of Gunn's 'death.' The death of any agent in either department of BID caused a ripple of unease and alert levels were heightened for weeks. There had been three deaths in the last five weeks, which, to say the least, was unusual, but knowledge of the bugging of the building was limited to the Director and his deputy, Claudine and, of course, to Terry Holt, who was doing everything in his power to trace it, physical or electronic. Nevertheless, there was a nervous frisson throughout the building.

In the centre of the room was a workstation with two desks, each with a computer. The stations faced the door, so that anyone working at the desks would see any other person entering or leaving the records room. On either side of the workstation the steel file racks went from floor to ceiling, but left a passageway at either end. Each rack had a sliding ladder attached to it so that the top shelves could be reached without having to move a ladder around. The racks were marked alphabetically from the right of the entrance - A to M to the right of the workstation and N to Z on the left. In each alphabetical area, the files were divided into two sections; the first section contained the files of all employees who joined after the creation of the Secret Service Bureau in 1909 - which was subsequently divided into the two Military Intelligence Branches - up to the creation of BID in 1988. The second section contained the files of all those employees who joined BID after 1988 up to the present date. At the end of the room, beyond the 'Z' rack, was a small washroom. The whole room was air-conditioned and humidity controlled to preserve the longevity of the older files, which still contained information that would probably never be released under the Freedom of Information Act.

Claudine had worked out a search plan, which she hoped might save her some time. First of all would be the files of the seven men who had transferred from MI5 and MI6; Goldman, Peters, Bristow, Anderson, Driscoll, Manton and Chesham. Next on her list would be Sterling and Cornwall. Then would be the bulk of the search as she checked the files of all those agents recruited to BID between 1988 and 2000, with particular emphasis on 1988 to 1992 - the period during which Mike Soames had joined BID.

It didn't take her long to trawl through the seven files of the agents who had transferred from the MIs. There was absolutely nothing to indicate a connection to, or knowledge of, an 'eighth person.' Likewise the files on Sterling and Cornwall revealed nothing. Claudine moved on to the files of agents recruited between 1988 and 1992, starting with Mike Soames.

The file contained every detail of Soames' military record in addition to his annual BID assessment report. While serving with the SAS, he had had no less than three citations for gallantry awards for operations in Northern Ireland, but they had all been downgraded by the Second Superior Reporting Officer (SRO) to Mentions in Dispatches. Why? She wondered, having noted that the Second SRO was the Director of Special Forces. Claudine wondered what had happened to make both the SRO and the Second SRO less than enthusiastic about the citation. Then she came to Soames' service in Bravo Squadron of 22 SAS. They'd been deployed with the Coalition Forces in Saudi Arabia at the end of 1990 during Operation Desert Shield through to the Gulf War in 1991.

There was a detailed account of Soames' action as one of an eight-man team inserted into Iraq on the night of 22nd January 1991. His Landrover had been destroyed by an anti-tank mine, killing the driver and patrol commander, Sergeant Quiller, and seriously wounding Soames himself. The fourth member of the patrol, a Corporal Harker, had been blown clear of the vehicle. After burying the bodies of the two men who had been killed, the report went into some detail about how Cpl Harker had carried Soames for 11 hours through freezing desert nights followed by scorching heat as soon as the sun rose; through deep, rocky wadis and featureless sand plains back to the Landrover of the other four-man patrol, only to discover that all of them had been killed. Cpl Harker had driven back to the Saudi border with Soames, certainly saving his life - the report recorded - and was subsequently awarded the Queen's Gallantry Medal, which he had collected after leaving the Army. Soames had recovered from his injuries and left the Army at the same time as Cpl Harker, according to his file.

Claudine re-read the report twice. Both men had applied to join BID the report recorded. Soames had been accepted whereas Cpl Harker had not, in spite of his exemplary record and apparent bravery. She dug through the pile of files by her desk to see if there was one for Harker. Even if he had been rejected there'd still be a file on him containing all the vetting forms and interview documents detailing the reasons for his rejection. But there was no file for anyone called Harker; if he had applied to join BID then his file had been removed from BID's records.

Claudine yawned, stretched and glanced at her watch; 4.45. Only 15 minutes before they'd come and throw her out. Had she missed a file? She went back to the 'H' rack to check and was just climbing down the ladder when the main lights went out, plunging her into pitch darkness.

'Shit!'

Unable to see even an inch in front of her, heart thumping audibly, she started groping her way back to the workstation. Moments later, the dim emergency lighting flickered on. As her eyes adjusted to the weak red light, she saw that the safe door was closed. The safety remote was nowhere to be seen. She knew she'd left it on the desk. She double-checked by up-ending her handbag onto the desk, in case she had left it there, but it was gone. She was sealed into an airtight vault.

*

'Adjutant.'

'Could I speak to the Commanding Officer, please?' Gunn asked.

'Who's speaking?'

'My name's Mark Knight; your CO's expecting a call from me.'

'I'll put you through, Mr Knight,' and the phone went silent until he heard Mike Harris' voice, the Commanding Officer of 22 SAS.

'Mark, hi; I understand you want to visit us here in Hereford?'

'Yes, as soon as possible if I can.'

'You in London?'

'Yes.'

'Think you could make it to Credenhill by 11.30? That's marginally closer to you than the old Stirling Lines at Hoarwithy.'

'Should be able to.'

'Good, I'll let the guys on the gate know – see you then.'

Gunn was grateful for his efficiency. He ran out of the flat and into his hire car. Fortunately, the M4 was clear and as soon as he had got past the Heathrow traffic it was reasonably roadwork-free up to Junction 15, where he left the motorway and made for Gloucester. He glanced at his watch as he left Gloucester and took the A49 to Hereford; 10.55. He pulled up at the guarded gates of Stirling Lines at 11.20. Access to the barracks was controlled by armed MOD police, who asked him for his ID. Gunn showed them his passport. The policemen went into the guardroom, made a phone call and then came back out to the car with another policeman.

'My colleague will come with you, sir. There are visitors' parking spaces in front of the building.'

All of this was new to Gunn, who'd done his selection testing for the SAS at Stirling Lines in Hoarwithy before 22 SAS and its supporting units moved to an ex-RAF barracks at Credenhill in 1998. Gunn was shown into the CO's office as soon as his escort had handed him over to the Adjutant.

'Come in, Mark; sit down.' As Gunn settled, he glanced around the room, taking it in.

'This room is completely secure and bug-free, we've just had it swept,' Mike second-guessed him, 'which I gather from Miles Thompson is more than can be said for Kingsroad House.'

'Yes; we still haven't found anything.'

'Well I was sorry to hear about what happened in St Vincent. I'm really glad to see you're okay - and you look surprisingly well.'

'Thanks; sorry for the cloak and dagger stuff but after what happened I've got a better shot at finding out what's going on if everyone involved thinks I'm dead,' Gunn replied.

'I'm sure you're right about that. I've been busy myself since Miles called a week ago and have turned up some pretty strange leads - might mean a lot of legwork on your part.

'Yes?'

'Well, Miles gave me some pointers about where to look. I dug out everything I could find from the Gulf War - just before, during and after: war diaries, regimental historical records, photo albums and operational log sheets - you name it. Mike Soames was a Corporal at the time and had been with the Regiment for eighteen months. His parent unit was the Worcesters and Forresters, now the Mercian Regiment - the same unit as a Sergeant Quiller, who was in the Landrover with him when it was blown up by a mine. Soames owes his life to a Corporal Harker, whose parent unit was the King's Regiment, now part of the Duke of Lancaster's Regiment who carried him on his back for 11 hours through the desert to safety in the most extreme conditions. Now I didn't join the Regiment until '95 for my first tour - which was a Troop Commander in Bravo Squadron - but even four years after the Gulf my guys used to tell me of everyone's surprise that Harker had nearly lost his own life in his efforts to save Soames. Apparently the two hated each other - why? God knows, but they never missed a chance to make it very obvious.'

'In contrast - and it was this, apparently, which kept the feud in check - Quiller and Soames were inseparable. But look at this,' Mike reached into a brown envelope and pulled out some photographs. 'Okay, look carefully at that photo,' and he handed over a postcard sized photo of an SAS Trooper leaning against a Landrover, smiling for the camera and holding a 203 - a 5.56mm Armalite with a 40mm grenade launcher under the barrel. 'And now look at this one, taken at the same time as the other photo. You can see the Trooper's in the same pose, same Landrover, but now he's holding a Minimi - a 5.56mm machine gun with integral bipod.' Gunn held the two photos side by side.

'Same guy, but different weapons,' he commented.

'Wrong, but you'd be forgiven for making that mistake. Turn the photos over.' On the back of one was the name 'Sgt Quiller' and on the back of the other it said 'Cpl Harker.' Gunn turned them over again and studied them closely.

'That's extraordinary; they could be identical twins. Are you sure it's different guys in each photo?'

'Absolutely; apparently it was quite a joke in the regiment at the time. As was the apathy between Soames and Harker. They had remarkably similar backgrounds, too. Both were orphans, both were fostered and both sets of foster parents have long since died. There are no records of any other relatives.'

'That's pretty strange.'

'Yeah, but here's the rub........Sgt Quiller had been the Sgt's Mess Secretary for the six months prior to the Regiment's move to Saudi Arabia. During the audit of the Mess account for that period, a sum of £3,465 was unaccounted for in the container account. Quiller was undoubtedly facing a court martial as soon as he returned from the Gulf War and would probably have gone to prison and been dishonourably discharged from the Army. He was killed when the Landrover hit that mine, which meant that he, at least, died with an unblemished military record. Yes?'

'Seems so…'

'Think about this Jo........Mark. If you were Quiller, standing beside the burnt wreck of the Landrover and holding the dog tags of the unrecognisable burnt remnants of a man who was your doppelganger and you knew you were facing a court martial for embezzlement on return to UK, what would you do?'

'But the medical records.......'

'Have disappeared from both Quilller's and Harker's files.'

'But surely on discharge there must have been a check on Harker's medical documents? There must be records kept in medical centres or at the MOD?'

'Yes, you're right to think that. Unfortunately the MOD, perhaps not to be outdone in incompetence by the Home Office, has lost tens of thousands of personnel records from all three services. Everywhere that we've checked has drawn a blank, whether that was due to the destruction of those records or MOD incompetence, who knows? There are no medical records of those two soldiers anywhere.'

'Jesus; nothing?'

'Nothing. Whoever it was that returned from that mission was a hero, invested by the Queen at Buckingham Palace.'

'There must be *something.*'

'This was seventeen years ago, John. I've spoken with the CO at that time; he certainly remembers the characters, but has no knowledge of the missing medical records. You have to remember that in 1991 computers were still novelties, as were CDs, floppy discs and hard discs. All records were on hard copy only and if someone needed to destroy those records, Harker or Quiller, whoever it was, had plenty of time to do it,' Mike Harris concluded with a quick glance at his watch.

'Did Soames apply to join BID as soon as he was discharged?' Gunn asked.

'From what I gather, both Soames and Harker applied to join MI6 - that was during the transition period to BID. I would hope that that would show on your BID records. Whoever it was that left the Army in March 1991 with Soames, he did a thorough job of destroying any evidence of his real identity, and if he breached every level of our security in the Regiment to do that, why not the security in Kingsroad House, particularly if he had an accomplice? He even altered the exact location of where he buried the two bodies with their weapons.'

'Shit; I was going to ask...'

'Well you're in luck; he overlooked two things. Firstly, the log sheets of the comms between the patrols and Regimental Tactical HQ in Saudi Arabia; these were kept in a safe at the Special Forces Directorate in Duke of York Barracks in London. Secondly, Harker had a motorbike accident on the A438 over Christmas 1990 and was taken to the Hereford County Hospital, where we found a record of his treatment. He has a fairly rare blood group - B negative. Our MO says less than 2% of the population of this country have that blood group. DNA science was still pretty new back then but they kept a record of his DNA because of his rare blood type. If you were able to get something from this man Harker - blood, a hair - well, then you'd know what happened.'

'Harker... It must be pretty common but isn't that the name of the PM's Head of Security? I mean we're looking for someone pretty powerful...' Mike smiled and threw a copy of The Daily Telegraph down on the desk in front of Gunn.

'That's a copy of last Thursday's edition of the DT, which you wouldn't have seen. Look at that picture of the PM leaving Number 10. Look at the man behind him, on his left.'

'That's him! Harker...or Quiller! Christ...'

'I know; there might well be an impostor holding one of the most powerful appointments in Government.'

'I'll need to borrow these,' Gunn got up to leave, gathering the photos.

'Sure; take these too,' Mike handed him a copy of the Daily Mirror, 'as soon as I spotted that last week I got hold of all the papers that had similar photos. That one in the Mirror's a bit grainy, but shows him even better.'

'Great, thanks.'

'You need to find that corpse, Mark. Here.......this didn't come from Harker.....very unlikely that you'll find anything at the location he gave of the mined Landrover.......this was the automatically recorded GPS location of his call using a satcom radio to the other four-man team,' and Mike handed Gunn a small white card on which was written:

Wadi Hawran Lat 33° 27.25' Long 41°46.85'

'It's a hundred miles to the east of the border with Saudi Arabia in a wadi overlooking the northern MSR between Baghdad and the border with Jordan - our guys called it 'Scud Alley'.'

'This is where...?'

'Yes.'

'I see what you mean by legwork. Do you have any documents signed by Harker and Quiller?'

'That we do have; on the travel claims both men submitted,' Mike said, sifting through another pile of documents, placing two AFB 1771 Claim Forms in front of Gunn. 'Harker's first name was Steven and that's how he signed himself, hence his nickname.' Gunn looked closely at the signature where the 'S' joined the first four letters of 'Hark' and the 'er' disappeared into a straight line.

'He was called 'Shark?''

## CHAPTER 12

'Shit, shit, shit!' Claudine cursed her stupidity at leaving the remote on the desk.

Mary Panter had come into the secure records room four times while she'd been sitting at the desk facing the door. Each time the gadget had been on the desk in front of her. She picked up the phone on the desk, but it was dead. She hadn't expected anything else. If this was an attempt to get rid of her, they'd hardly leave her with a means of calling for help. Even if she'd had a mobile it would have been useless as the steel-lined room blocked any signals. At least there was the emergency lighting, for now anyway.

Claudine went straight to the 'P' racks on her right and found Mary's file. It showed that she had joined BID in 2000, replacing the retiring Head of Finance and Administration. She had passed all the relevant accountancy exams and was a member of the Institute of Chartered Accountants of England and Wales. There was proof of her accountancy qualifications, but Claudine was surprised to discover that she had then gone to Imperial College in London and got a good 2:1 in electrical engineering; slightly unusual, perhaps. Her first job had been with a City fund manager, after which came a move to the Civil Service where she'd worked in the Treasury before moving to the Cabinet Office, where she was appointed Deputy Head of Economic Affairs. That job had lasted three years and then she made the move to BID.

All the papers detailing her interview for the appointment were in their own folder within the main file. Claudine flicked straight to the page that showed the decision made by the interview panel of five senior BID executives. Sir Jeremy had chaired the panel with Miles Thompson, James Rayner from Espionage and Paul Manton and David Chesham from Counter Espionage. During the voting, Manton, Chesham and Rayner had voted for Mary and Miles and Sir Jeremy had voted against. That was interesting, but not especially significant taken alone - hardly a reason to believe it may have been Mary who closed the safe door on her.

She was about to close the file when two loose sheets of paper fell out. On the top of each was a hand-written note saying that the original document was kept by the Director of BID. Even if Mary had wanted to destroy these documents she couldn't because the originals were in Sir Jeremy's safe. Both were personal letters addressed to Sir Jeremy; the first was from Sir Benjamin Markham, Secretary to the Cabinet Office and Head of the Civil Service. The letter endorsed Mary's application for the appointment, but hardly in glowing terms. It flagged the fact that during the time that she had been in the Cabinet Office, an unspecified sum from the budget had gone missing. It was not an accusation of complicity, but she'd been tasked with tracing it and had failed.

The second letter was from the Dean of Imperial College, which in 2000 was still part of the University of London. Sir Robert Menzies had written to Sir Jeremy, most likely after they'd spoken on the phone, Claudine reasoned, saying that he was surprised that a graduate of such extreme political views wanted to join the Intelligence Service unless there was a sinister motive. That explained why Sir Jeremy had voted against Mary's appointment, but not why Miles had voted against her.

Claudine then searched for the paperwork dealing with Mary's positive vetting – a process Sir Jeremy had tightened up considerably. She glanced at each of the reports by the three referees submitted by the vetting officer – a retired Assistant Commissioner from the Metropolitan Police - who had interviewed each one. Two of the reports merely confirmed that she was a very capable accountant, enjoyed her life as a single person and, as far as the referees were aware, indulged in no deviant sexual behaviour. The third referee gave Mary a particularly strong recommendation, eulogising about her outstanding intelligence, ability, loyalty and integrity. The referee was a Mr Steven Harker. Claudine thumped the table with her fist.

'Gotcha!'

She was convinced that the same name could not be a coincidence. Almost everyone in Government circles and certainly every branch of the media knew of Steven Harker as the controversial Head of Security at Number 10. The tabloids had christened him the 'Shark,' partly because of his signature but also for some of the more outrageous 'incidents' in which he'd been involved. These varied from inexplicable accidents to those who had crossed him or the PM to the disappearance of at least two journalists who had dared to write articles which both investigated the 'accidents' and questioned Harker's suitability for the appointment. This had to be the same man who was a soul mate of Soames, had saved his life, left the Army at the same time and possibly tried to get a job with BID.

But what had put him off? Anyway, he'd done really well for himself ending up in such an influential appointment in Number 10. Perhaps it was that which helped Mary get the job. Claudine returned the file to the 'P' rack; as she went back to the desk she realised that she was a little short of breath. She was more angry than frightened when she discovered that the door had been closed on her, because she knew that the over-pressure was maintained 24/7 by a pump that sucked in filtered air. So if air was sucked into the room then all she had to do was wait until 9am the next morning and the door would be reopened - she hoped.

Claudine went to the vents, which were at either end of the room. She could hear the subdued whirr of the pumps. She went back to her desk, picked up a piece of paper and went back to the vent, which was set in the wall where it met the ceiling. She climbed up the metal rack nearest the vent and held the piece of paper up to it. It should have been blown away from the protecting grid; it stuck to it. The pumps were sucking all the air out of the room.

Someone had reversed the pumps - maybe someone with a degree in electronic engineering? Claudine looked at her watch: 7.45. She'd agreed to meet up with Gunn at the Bistro Angelique in the Brompton Road at 8pm. He probably wouldn't start worrying until she was ten minutes or so late and didn't pick up her phone when he called. She sat down on the floor and tried to slow her breathing wondering whether she would survive another half hour.

*

Gunn arrived at the Bistro Angelique shortly after 8pm and was shown to a table for two.

'Apéritif, Mr Knight?'

'No thanks, I'm waiting for someone.' At 8.15, Gunn dialled Claudine's new mobile. He had agreed with Miles and Claudine that their new phones would be with them at all times, even if they were in the shower. A lack of response would be an automatic alert that something was wrong. There was no response. Gunn dialled Miles' number; he answered immediately.

'Yes?'

'It's Mark. Claudine should have met me here at the bistro at 8. It's now almost 8.20 and no response from her mobile.'

'She was in Mary's department all today. I'll get back to you asap,' and Miles broke the connection. He dialled both Mary's mobile and her landline. There was no answer from either. He tried Martin King's number; he picked up on the fourth ring.

'Martin King.'

'Martin, it's Miles. Was Claudine with you today?'

'Yes, through lunch and as far as I know until five,' Martin replied.

'What do you mean, "as far as you know"?'

'Mary said it would be alright to go at 4.30 as I was taking my children on the London Eye. I mean I didn't need to but.......'

'Go back to Kingsroad House now and I'll meet you there. There's a police car on its way to collect you; it should be with you in a couple of minutes. Got that?'

'Yes of course; what...' but Miles had rung off. Next he dialled the 24-hour emergency number for the manufacturer of the safe door to the records vault. The duty technician was told that a police car would pick him up in five minutes.

Like Gunn, Miles owned a house in Chelsea and flagged down a taxi, which got him to Kingsroad House inside ten minutes. Marilyn Green, the duty officer in BID's Operations Centre, had been alerted and met Miles as he arrived on the 10th floor. The two of them went into the Finance and Administration office and Miles went straight to the switchgear cupboard; it was locked.

'Get the axe from the fire hose box - quickly!' he barked at the duty officer.

A few sharp blows with the axe broke the padlock, hasp and most of the cupboard door. Miles studied the wiring diagram pasted to the inside.

'May I, sir?' Marilyn asked briskly.

'Of course, Marilyn.....are you an electrical whizz-kid?' Miles asked stepping back from the switch gear.

'My Weapons and Electrical training in the Royal Navy, sir; what are we looking for?'

'I think Claudine may have been locked inside by accident. I want to make sure there's air being pumped in.'

'The terminals have been reversed.........the pumps will be sucking the air out of the room.'

'Shit!' Miles was furious. 'Hurry up, we don't know how long she's been trapped.' He called BID's emergency medical treatment room in the basement and told the duty nurse to bring up some oxygen.

'Just a second...' Marilyn disengaged one of the breakers, undid both terminals, swapped them over, tightened the nuts and then re-engaged the breaker. 'There,' she said at last. 'Whoever did this, it was deliberate.'

The safe technician opened a small safe to one side of the door and made an adjustment, which disengaged the time lock. He turned to Miles and raised his thumb.

'Martin!' Martin placed his hand on the scanning screen and tapped in the code, followed by Miles. There was an agonising pause and then the huge steel door clunked open a crack, but without swinging. The two of them heaved it the rest of the way open. Claudine was curled up on the floor, her ribcage rising and falling in quick, shallow breaths.

The nurse rushed in and quickly placed the breathing mask over her nose and mouth and turned on the flow of oxygen. After a couple of minutes, she helped Claudine to sit up; still breathing the oxygen, she weakly raised a thumb to show Miles that she was OK.

Miles texted Gunn: "Locked in safe. Now out - she's OK".

*

Gunn had only just read Miles' text when his phone rang.

'Mark Knight.'

'Mark, it's Mike Harris; can you talk?

'Yes, go on.'

'I've been doing more investigation of our records.'

'What've you found?'

'We've all been concentrating on three of the soldiers in that Landrover; Harker, Quiller and Soames. Just to make sure that we left no stone unturned, I looked up the records on the fourth trooper, Corporal David Miller, who was the driver. There's nothing particularly remarkable about him except his family background. His mother married again after the death of her first husband, Joseph Goldman...' Gunn's stomach suddenly lurched; he could guess what was coming.

'You still there Mark?'

'Yes; sorry, go on.'

'That marriage produced a son by the name of Humphrey who must have been bright - he went to Nottingham University and then into MI6 - you should, therefore, have records on him. Our records aren't that specific, but it seems that the elder half brother was killed in an accident in 1997; hope that's of some help.'

'I was at Nottingham University with Humphrey; it was he who recruited me into BID in 1997. We met in the Army and Navy Club in Pall Mall; he was killed by a shot from outside the Club. We've never found out who did it – we just couldn't find a motive. But it looks like you might have found it,' John's voice was flat, his mouth suddenly dry. He cleared his throat: 'My controller at that time was a guy called Simon Peters; he told me Humphrey had been digging into the circumstances of his younger half-brother's death in the Gulf War. It looks like the Iraqi desert may hold the answer to that too. There's someone at the door..... I've got to go, thanks, Mike.'

'Mark?' It was Claudine. Gunn let her in. He kissed her for a few long minutes.

'Are you okay? What happened?'

'I'm fine; and I'm starving. I brought a takeaway, so let's eat and I'll tell you.' Gunn upended the food on to plates and Claudine wolfed most of hers before saying anything. Then she told him of her ordeal.

'I wasn't absolutely sure about Mary Panter until I found out who had recommended her so strongly for the job. Having read the account of the SAS patrol in Soames' file which revealed the Quiller/ Harker/Soames connection, Harker's report pretty much nailed it. But I only read Mary Panter's file after the safe door had been closed on me. My stupid fault - I'd left the safety control on the desk instead of carrying it with me. Mary was probably waiting for me to do that; she'd checked four times to see what I was doing. I had gone to the 'H' rack on my left, well out of sight of the workstation, and she must have slipped in. I wasn't too worried as I knew air was being pumped in but then I discovered it'd been reversed - the air was being sucked out. You know the rest.'

'We're getting too close for them. You're going to have to be more careful now.'

'What did you find at 22 SAS?'

Gunn told her of the suspected Quiller/Harker switch and the destruction of all documents relating to the two soldiers.

'But after I'd gone, Mike did more digging and he found something else - something we've been trying to find for a long time. He rang a little while ago; the driver of that Landrover in Iraq was a Corporal Miller. He was the younger half-brother of a BID agent called Humphrey Goldman who was at Nottingham University with me. He was shot by a gunman through a ground floor window of the Army and Navy Club in Pall Mall – while trying to convince me to join BID instead of going to work for Euro-Pacific Construction in Hong Kong. He was a good friend,' Gunn paused, looking away as the painful memory of that day collided with the present. 'At the time of his murder he'd been investigating the circumstances of his brother's death and must have discovered something because someone - and that someone would seem to be Harker - reckoned he was getting too close to what really happened in the desert.'

'Shit; this guy's all over everything.'

'Judging by what's just happened to you, Mary Panter's shown her hand too so I'm pretty sure BID, for the moment, has seen the last of her. Miles asked her to do an audit of the various accounts in BID's budget over which certain heads of departments have total control. He said she'd been dragging her feet – this explains why; she's part of it.'

'Bitch; I can't believe they hired her in the first place.'

'If we're right, and it transpires that all this was conceived as long ago as the early nineties by Harker and Soames, possibly with Mary as an accomplice, then BID has really got to have cast iron proof of Harker's guilt before any move is made. But it'll be up to the Boss to decide if he needs to warn the PM. There's potential for a major disaster if Harker is cornered. Worst case… he could kidnap the PM as a hostage for his safe passage somewhere…'

'We can't let that happen,' Claudine cleared their plates and made coffee. 'Let's plan the next move. I'll go after Mary.'

'The only way we can prove Harker's guilt beyond any doubt is for me to get the DNA samples. I don't see any great problem getting that from Harker - I'm guessing he has a room he uses at Number 10.'

'We're seeing Miles at 10 tomorrow, he'll know.'

'Good. Then after I've done that I need to be on the next flight out to Iraq.'

*

'Are we any closer to tracing the source of the bugging, sir?' Marilyn Green asked Miles. They were both in the office early supervising the re-setting of the records room.

'No, moving to Kingston seems inevitable while this building is pulled apart; why?'

'I've just been on a course on electronic surveillance; I'd like to help if I can. I have some ideas, which I'm sure Terry has covered, but…'

'We need all the help we can get. Why don't you go and see him now?'

'Thank you, sir,' and Marilyn went to the Operations centre while Miles briefed Martin King on the audit he'd originally given to Mary. Martin had been promoted with immediate effect to acting Head of Finance and Administration.

*

'Hello.'

'It's Mary.

'What's happened?'

'I did everything I could to prevent that fucking woman from seeing my file, but there are copies held elsewhere and if I'd removed them she would have known. So I locked her in and reversed the air pumps. It wouldn't take much more than an hour for her to suffocate. But when they find her they'll know it was deliberate so I can't go back. Other than that they're still getting nowhere - and with her gone they should get there faster now.'

'Alright; the bugged phones are still providing us with adequate warning anyway, but the moment they're discovered we'll have to switch to Plan B; agreed?'

'Agreed; I've moved to the boat in Chelsea Wharf. They'll probably be searching my flat soon, but they won't find anything. With Gunn and, hopefully, de Carteret out of the way, there's very little chance of anyone else making the link back to the SAS. Has Mike bought the apartment for us in Rio?'

'Yes; the funds have been transferred from Grand Cayman to the Banco do Brasil on Rua Joana Angelica. Look, I'm going to be off the radar for a little while; the close protection team is off to Beijing to make preparations for the PM's visit to the Olympics. I need you to take care of everything while I'm gone. And make sure de Carteret's dead.'

'No problem; will I see you tonight?'

'I'll be there at about ten.' Steven Harker broke the connection as he walked back along the Embankment to his Dolphin Square apartment. He consoled himself with the thought that he only needed to keep it up – literally – with Mary until he got back from China.

*

'Right, I'm going home to my wife. She's hardly set eyes on me over the last month,' said Terry. 'Is Claudine OK?'

'Yes she's fine.' Marilyn turned up the volume on Terry's transistor while they talked. 'Just before you go; I asked Miles if I could help you with your 'sweep' of this building as you've been so busy. I hope that's alright?'

'Delighted.....of course, you've just done that course. Well, you're probably more up-to-date than any of us,' Terry added.

'Does anyone, like you or Admin, have access to our official mobiles for any reason?'

'Not until recently; a few weeks ago Martin in Admin asked if he could implement a programme of mobile phone servicing to make sure they were all working properly.'

'Was that his initiative?'

'I think he said that it was one of Mary's efficiency drives.'

'Thought so; can I have a look at your mobile?'

'Sure,' Terry removed it from a small pouch on his

belt and handed it to Marilyn. She took it to her console, got a magnifying glass out of her toolkit and, lifting out the SIM card, pulled the light on her console close to the card to study it. Then she got her own mobile out and studied it too. Both SIM cards came from the same service provider. She handed the glass to Terry and asked him to look at both cards. After careful scrutiny, he turned to Marilyn.

'There's an extra dot on the official SIM card.'

'Exactly; this magnifying glass isn't powerful enough, but if you put your SIM card under a really powerful microscope, I think you'll find it's a micro-dot chip receiving its power from the mobile and transmitting to an amplifier and booster transmitter - probably down in the Admin Department.'

'Shit! I can't believe we missed this. You're a genius!'

'Not really; I've just spent several days with some of the wierdest computer geeks in this country. And remember that Mary Panter has a degree in electronic engineering. But we should think very carefully how we debug ourselves; we don't want them to know we're on to them. We may be able to input some disinformation to confuse them. Let's talk to Miles tomorrow.'

## CHAPTER 13

Both Terry and Marilyn were waiting outside Miles' office when he arrived at 8.25.

'Come in both of you,' Miles indicated for them to sit and switched on the small transistor Terry had given him. Terry held up a notebook on which he'd scribbled "PLEASE GIVE ME YOUR MOBILE." Miles handed over his official mobile. Marilyn made some small talk about the weather while they watched Terry remove the back cover, lift out the SIM card and replace it with another one. Then, using the nib of a biro he destroyed the minute quad-band dot. Then he turned off the transistor.

'You're now bug-free, sir.'

'You've found them! God, they're almost invisible. How…?'

'Marilyn's the one we all need to thank. But we need you to decide whether we leave a decoy bugged phone somewhere so as not to alert these people that we now have a clean building. The amplifier and boost transmitter were in the secure records vault, shielded by the steel lining, which I should have suspected,' Terry admitted.

'Well thank you both. Thank God we don't have to move HQ now. If you could make arrangements to clean up all the rest of the phones and then let's meet again later today to discuss how to play the decoy game. It seems like a good idea - it'll buy us some time, anyway, especially now that Soames and Panter, our moles, are long gone.' Miles pressed the button on his intercom. 'Would you ask Don Hastings and Alan Paxton to come and see me as soon as possible please.'

Don was the Assistant Director for the Middle East and Alan was his controller for the agents currently deployed in Saudi Arabia, Iraq, Afghanistan, Israel and Syria. The two men appeared in Miles' office within five minutes. They were slightly startled when Miles held up a sheet of paper asking them to leave their mobile phones with his PA.

'Terry will be calling in all the mobiles today to check for bugs, but as what I'm about to tell you is particularly sensitive, better to be on the safe side. John Gunn is not dead.'

Both men started in shock.

'He's alive and well and living in our Drayton Gardens safe house under the name of Mark Knight.'

Miles explained the background to the conspiracy, ending with the attempt on Claudine's life the previous evening.

'So we have two priorities: one is to find Mary Panter and the other is to obtain cast iron proof of the identity of the man responsible for the security of the PM at Number 10.'

'Clearly someone's got to go to the Iraqi desert to try and find the bodies,' said Don at last.

'Exactly; Gunn wants to go. Over the last two weeks he's grown a beard and is as tanned as any Iraqi. He speaks Arabic - not totally fluent yet, but enough to get by and he's able to read some of the Arabic script. Don, I need to know if you're comfortable with Gunn being deployed on this operation?'

'It's not ideal as far as I'm concerned, but Alan knows him better than me; I'd defer to him first.'

'Alan?'

'It's some time since I looked at Gunn's file, sir, but I think I'm right in saying he was involved in the '91 Gulf War. And was awarded a Military Cross…?' Gunn's file was open on the desk in front of Miles Thompson.

'Yes, that's right; he rescued the crew of a Challenger tank which had thrown a track. He shot five Iraqis who were attempting to set fire to it.' They both looked at Don.

'That's very impressive,' he said, 'and I would never have doubted his courage, but the desert to the north-west of Baghdad where those SAS patrols were is very different from the terrain in which Gunn would have fought in the south-east. It is, I think, one of the bleakest and most hostile areas on this planet. We call it the 'empty quarter'. Everything west of the 42° Longitude is a barren inhospitable wasteland; there's nothing there except dried-up riverbeds, weathered rock outcrops, deep ravines, surfaces as hard as concrete in the summer and like glutinous mud in winter. Even at this time of year you fry in a daytime temperature of nearly 46°C and freeze at night when the temperature falls below zero…'

'He's right; even the Bedouin survive with difficulty,' agreed Alan.

'In comparison, the terrain east of Longitude 42° is

like paradise - hence the hanging gardens of Babylon. That half of Iraq is irrigated by the Al Furat and Nahr Dijlah rivers - the Euphrates and Tigris. If we're considering inserting Gunn, and hopefully at least one other person with him, I just want to put down a marker that it'll be an incredibly tough assignment. Gunn's just been shot in the head. I know he's one of our best but are *you* satisfied that he's fit enough to take this on?' Don asked Miles.

'If I hadn't seen him, no, I wouldn't be, but even so, I take your point. However, our medical team at Maidenhead say that he is fit enough. And General Hayden at Langley has given his blessing for Doyle Barnes to go with Gunn. Barnes also fought in the '91 Gulf War, with 101st Airborne. His knowledge of Arabic is on a par with Gunn's.'

'Well, that's a bonus,' admitted Don.

'Look, here's how we'll do it,' Miles said finally. 'You need to brief him for the assignment as soon as you've decided on both a method of insertion and recovery; that is bound to involve some pretty nimble diplomatic dealings - we've got to move fast. For obvious reasons, Gunn can't come to this building so I want you to do the pre-op brief at the flat in Drayton Gardens. If you have any doubt then, after seeing him, as to his fitness, then we'll have a rethink. Agreed?'

Don agreed and the two men left Miles' office. Miles picked up his brief case, took the lift to basement level three and entered tunnel two, which had its exit in Baxter's Estate Agents on the Kings Road. The office was in fact owned by BID and handled all its safe house rentals as well as its overall property portfolio. From there he took a taxi to the Coffee Republic on the

Fulham Road, where he arrived four minutes late for a 10 am appointment with Gunn and Claudine, who'd arrived separately.

'Sorry I'm late; your official mobile please, Claudine.' The buzz of conversation all around them would have made the bug useless. Miles removed the SIM card and destroyed the micro-dot chip. 'We can thank Marilyn Green for that. Martin King will give you a new SIM card.'

'Everything okay?' asked Gunn.

'I was meeting with Don Hastings, who'll be overseeing your assignment in Iraq, John. He was very concerned about your health, as we all are. Are you absolutely sure that you are physically and mentally ready for this? It could be the toughest assignment of your time in BID. I said you were ready, but I don't...'

'I'm sure, Miles,' Gunn interrupted, losing patience. 'Is the assignment a go or not?'

'John, Miles is right to ask, ease off; we nearly lost you and Christ knows, we need you; we can't go through that again...' Claudine held his gaze for a moment.

'I know, okay; I understand. But I know I'm ready and this time I've got my eyes open - I know who's involved.'

'Then it's a go,' said Miles, 'and last night General Hayden signed off on my request for Doyle Barnes. Don's doing all the background as we speak. He'll contact you and then come and brief you in the flat. In the meantime he's made arrangements for Mohammed Abbas Beg of Jack Ford's CE1 team to be available to you for Arabic conversation.'

'That's good; in that case I'm going to go now -

there're a lot of gaps that need filling in. Speak later.' Gunn slipped on a pair of sunglasses, grabbed a newspaper off a table, which he tucked under his arm and sauntered casually out into the crowded street. Miles and Claudine exchanged looks, but let it drop. Miles was the first to speak.

'Okay, you're joining Mary Probert's team in CE1 and will be working with Marilyn to find Mary Panter. Mary'll brief the two of you at 2 p.m. in her office today.'

*

Gunn met Doyle off the United Airlines redeye flight two days later and took him to the flat in Drayton Gardens. Alan Paxton had contacted Gunn and told him that Don Hastings hoped to be ready to brief both of them by the following Monday, but he had gone on to explain that the closure of US airfields in Saudi Arabia had made the choice of selecting a mounting base very limited. The moving of US forces from the huge Prince Sultan Air Base, south of Riyadh, and the further closure of the King Khalid and the Khamis Mushayat Air Bases, now only left Al Udeid Air Base in Qatar to which the US Central Air Command had moved after leaving Saudi Arabia.

That had left BID with various options: mount the operation to insert Gunn and Barnes from Qatar, which was 750 miles from the target area; mount it from the Gulf - either from a Royal Navy or US Navy aircraft carrier, which reduced the distance to 450 miles; or, mount it from the British air base at Akrotiri in Cyprus - a distance of 500 miles if the aircraft flew direct. Each of these had advantages and disadvantages: mount from either Qatar or the Gulf and there was no requirement to overfly any country other than Iraq. Mount it from Cyprus and the aircraft would have to overfly Israel, Jordan and Saudi Arabia to reach the target area, and this was causing some pretty complicated diplomatic bargaining. It was this that was taking all the time. The gulf option was certainly feasible, as both HMS Ark Royal and USS Ronald Reagan were deployed in those waters.

There was really nothing to choose between the two aircraft carriers, Alan had continued, except that one was 22,000 tons displacement and the other 88,000 tons. Ark Royal was equipped with the Mark 4 version of the Sea King helicopter and Ronald Reagan had both Sea Kings and Chinooks. Neither the Sea King nor the Chinook had the operating range to complete a round flight of 1,000 miles, so if they went with that option then both would have to refuel - at least once and possibly twice. If they went with the Cyprus option, then they'd be inserted by a Hercules C130 and a HALO parachute descent, but that immediately begged the question of how to recover them on completion of the mission.

While the diplomatic wrangling continued, Gunn and Doyle spoke nothing but Arabic under the strict tutelage of Abbas Beg. They also practised dressing in the clothing that the Bedouin would wear. During the hot weather, white robes, called 'dishdasha,' were worn together with loose white trousers - 'sirwal'. 'Keffiyah' was the cloth used to cover the head and was held in place underneath by a small tight-fitting white cap called a 'taqiyah' and a corded band on top called an 'igal'. The colours of these robes and fittings varied with national customs and during the winter months, instead of cotton, the robes would be made of wool for warmth. Having explained in detail the various forms of national dress, Abbas then admitted that the Bedouin took no notice of any customs and dressed how they wished. The style was similar, but the cloth would usually be died in shades of brown, beige and sometimes black, and was worn day after day for months, if not years, without ever being washed. For the Bedouin, water was for drinking, not washing.

There were advantages and disadvantages to wearing military uniforms or Arabic clothing. The chances of them meeting anyone in the area to which they were going were remote, but if they did bump the Bedouin, then, dressed similarly, they might stand a better chance of survival. The Bedouin took objection to any uniform whether Iraqi, British or American, because it represented officialdom, which was abhorrent to them and their way of life; they would be just as likely to rob and kill an Iraqi soldier as a British soldier.

Negotiations by the CIA on behalf of BID for this very low profile operation, well clear of any on-going US or Iraqi military operations in Iraq, met with stiff opposition from the Pentagon because of its ongoing provision of billions of dollars worth of US arms to Iraq. This included F16s, helicopters, Hercules C130s, tanks, guns and a raft of other equipment. The discovery of any US involvement in a Special Forces operation in Iraq - undeclared to the Iraqi Government - could finish the current lucrative arms deal.

Moreover the US experience of clandestine Special Forces operations in the Middle East - or anywhere else, for that matter - was not a happy one.

On 24th April 1980, an operation mounted from the aircraft carrier USS Nimitz to rescue 53 hostages from the US Embassy in Tehran ended in disaster, when a violent sandstorm caused one of the six Sea Stallion helicopters to crash into a Hercules C130. Five US Airmen and three Marines were killed and, in addition to the loss of equipment worth tens of millions of dollars, the credibility of the US Special Forces was severely dented. What wounded US pride even more was the success, only six days later on 30th April, of an SAS operation to free hostages being held by a separatist group in the Iranian Embassy in London.

The ideal aircraft for this operation was the Boeing Vertol Chinook helicopter, but all the British Chinooks were committed to the war in Afghanistan so, as ever in both military and diplomatic negotiations, a compromise was reached; a long way from being ideal, but marginally better than a blunt refusal. Through the good offices of the CIA, it was agreed that the US would provide both the Chinook and the refuelling aircraft, but the operation would be mounted from HMS Ark Royal so that no accusation could be levelled at the USA if the operation ended in a 1980s type Iranian disaster.

*

Mary Probert had only recently been promoted to the appointment of Team Leader of Team 1 of CE1, the Counter Terrorist Section of BID's Counter Espionage

Directorate, replacing the previous Team Leader, Barry Windsor. There had been a lot of learning on the job going on at BID in recent weeks. Looking as though she'd been living solely on black coffee for a week, she waved Claudine and Marilyn into her office.

'How are you feeling, Claudine?'

'I'm fine thanks, no lasting damage. How about you?' Claudine noticed the dark shadows under Mary's eyes.

'Oh, you know........glad not to have to switch on a bloody radio every time I want to open my mouth,' she nodded her thanks to Marilyn. 'Okay, your assignment. Mary Panter has a flat at 89, Crescent Grove in Clapham. That's where your search will have to start, but if, as seems pretty obvious, she has been a part of this conspiracy with Harker and Soames for some time, it's highly unlikely you'll find anything. There's always that outside chance she's been careless; but I doubt it,' she sighed, massaging her temples. 'I want you both to be fully aware of what you are up against here. Claudine, sloppiness nearly cost you your life; Mary Panter is collectively guilty with Harker and Soames for the murder of Nina Ramone in St Vincent, the attempted murder of John Gunn, the murders of both David Chesham and Paul Manton, the murders of Clive Sterling and John Cornwall and, as yet, an unknown number of other murders. She, or they, won't hesitate to add the two of you to that list and neither of you will get a second chance. Have I made myself clear?' The steel in Mary's voice left neither of them in any doubt about the angst Claudine's carelessness had caused BID management. 'Marilyn?'

'Yes,' Marilyn answered.

'Claudine?'

'Yes.'

'Good, let's move on. The last we heard from Doyle Barnes was that Soames had headed south for Cuba in the chopper he hijacked in Miami. I can't imagine that Cuba was his destination; it's far more likely he was headed for South America - somewhere like Brazil that has no extradition treaty with the UK. Clear with me first if the search takes you away from the UK. On no account are you to conduct the search for Panter anywhere near Downing Street, until we have absolutely cast iron proof of the identity of this man Harker and his part in all this. We're unlikely to have that until John Gunn returns from Iraq.'

'When we find Mary?' Claudine asked.

'It would be useful if you could bring her in for questioning, but failing that, a body will do fine. Also you need to be aware that Jack Ford's team has been tasked with getting a DNA sample from Steven Harker's apartment in Keyes House at Dolphin Square. Anna Kingsbury's been dressed up as one of the cleaning staff who look after the apartments; I'm sure she'll enjoy that. Do you have any questions?'

There were no questions. The two agents continued their preparation with appointments with Terry Holt's Communications Department on the 14th floor and with the Armourer in the basement.

*

Chief Superintendent Bruce Lochart of the Metropolitan Police's Special Operations Section

(SO14) showed his pass to the police guarding the gated entrance to Downing Street and headed for the front door. The main purpose of the Special Operations Section (SO14) was to provide close protection for the Royal Family in its various UK residences and when travelling abroad. It also had the task of providing the same protection for visiting royal families and Heads of State to the UK and last, but certainly not least in the opinion of Steven Harker, close protection for the Prime Minister and his family, both in the UK and when travelling abroad.

Bruce Lochart was met in the black-and-white tiled hallway by a uniformed member of the house staff and taken to Steven Harker's office, which adjoined, and had direct access, to the cabinet room through the pillared ante-room area. The office door was open and the Chief Superintendent was shown straight in.

'Morning, Bruce; sit down.'

'Thanks.'

'So what's your protection plan for the PM at the Closing Ceremony?' There was no offer of coffee or even a glass of water on the hot July afternoon.

Harker's appointment had caused considerable resentment at the Met, because although it was a new one created by the present PM, it should traditionally have gone to someone in the Met with experience in close protection. Although Bruce Lochart was well aware of Harker's military record, what he had done between leaving the Army and being selected for the appointment of Head of Security at Number 10 appeared to be a well-kept secret. There were rumours, which Lochart had disregarded, that Harker had been involved in some very suspect deals with private security firms in Baghdad after both the '91 and 2003 Gulf Wars, from which he had made a personal fortune. But that was just rumour in Scotland Yard and Lochart had no time for that form of gossip.

'My recommendations are contained in this brief; I know you're busy, I didn't want to take up too much of your time,' Lochart handed over a folder. 'As I understand it, you want to leave the day after tomorrow, with the advance party to do the inspection of the Ambassador's Residence in Beijing and the other venues on his schedule?' Lochart ended on an interrogative note.

'That's right. I'm aware that the Ambassador has sent assurances to the PM that his residence has had nothing changed since it was last inspected, but my experience tells me that that's the very best reason to do it again.'

'How many of my staff do you want to take? They weren't expecting to go until next week so I'll need to prepare them asap.' Lochart managed to exclude even a hint of his frustration at these last minute changes to what was usually a pretty straightforward task.

'None; I intend to go on my own and will meet up with your four officers on 31st July.' It was clear the decision was not open for discussion.

'And the PM's close protection while he's on holiday during the Parliamentary recess prior to the Games?'

'Over to you and your boys and girls. I have a meeting to get to now. Thank you for your briefing paper,' and Harker stood up and just stopped short of pushing the Chief Superintendent out of his office. Bruce Lochart left Number 10 seething and more than a little anxious about the security of the PM.

# CHAPTER 14

Claudine and Marilyn left Clapham Common Underground station, crossed over the busy intersection on the A3 and followed Mary Probert's directions to 89 Crescent Grove. The properties in the cul-de-sac were all Grade II listed Georgian townhouses. They ranged from six bedroom semi-detached houses on sale for £3.5 million to those that had been converted into flats, where a two-bedroom version was on sale for £450k. Number 89 had been converted into five flats; basement, ground, first, second and third floor. Mary Panter's flat was on the third floor. Access to the flat was by the main front door of the property and then either the staircase or a claustrophobic lift, which more closely resembled a vertical coffin.

The landlord of the property lived in the ground floor flat and opened the front door when they rang the bell. When Marilyn showed her police warrant card, he handed over a spare key to 89C with a grunt of surprise, though mercifully no questions. The two women took one look at the lift and opted for the stairs. After getting no response to the bell, they entered the flat. It was a nice London flat, in a good state of repair and tidy; nothing stood out. They edged quietly from room to room. They were both armed and Marilyn had her Glock 17 concealed under a scarf draped over her arm. Behind her, Claudine had removed her Colt automatic from her bag. Within a few minutes it was clear no-one was there.

'If she's done a flit' Marilyn said finally, opening a drawer half full of neatly folded clothes, 'then it wasn't done in a hurry.' There were some empty hangers in the bedroom wardrobe and the bathroom shelves were empty of cosmetics, toothbrush and toothpaste. There were no signs of frenzied flight, just methodical packing, as though she had gone on a holiday that'd been booked for months.

Claudine checked all the obvious places first - cupboards, drawers, behind pictures and radiators, under mats and carpets, water cisterns, hollow curtain rails and so on, bearing in mind that she was searching the property of a fellow BID employee who would have been on many of the same courses she had - one of which was the technique of searching a property. She then stripped the bed and checked the hems of the sheets and pillowslips, detachable filials on the metal bedstead and curtain rails, anything glued to the back of drawers, mirrors or pictures, the waste paper basket, which was empty - they'd have to go through the plastic bin bags they'd seen stacked outside the property - and under the fitted carpet; but the room had been stripped of anything that could give the slightest clue to its occupant's current whereabouts.

Marilyn was still busy with the living room, so Claudine went across the short corridor to the second bedroom, and gave it the same treatment. The airing cupboard in the corridor, which contained the hot water tank and pressurized central heating system, likewise yielded nothing. They re-convened in the living room.

'Anything?' Marilyn asked.

'Nada.'

'Yeah, same here; okay, I'll start on the kitchen, can you do the bathrooms?' Because the assignment was a Counter Espionage led operation, Mary Probert had been very clear that Marilyn was to lead the search.

'Sure,' and Claudine headed for the bathroom. A really thorough search of that and the next-door toilet produced nothing. Once again, the two women met in the living room.

'If we've missed something then it's so bloody well hidden that it would take an entire search team at least a week to pull this place apart and find it,' Marilyn sighed. 'Okay, that's it. Let's go and check the bin bags. If there's nothing there, we'll need to have a rethink,' she locked the door and followed Claudine down the stairs. The landlord was waiting for them.

'Are you able to tell me when Miss Panter might be coming back?'

'I'm afraid not Mr...?'

'David Jamieson.'

'Mr Jamieson... but if she does return, please get in touch with us,' and Marilyn handed him her card and opened the front door.

'I will, thanks; er, Miss Green?' Jamieson called after her, reading her name off the card.

'I'll get started on the bin bags,' Claudine offered, heading down the short flight of steps to the large pile of refuse sacks out the front.

'I only wondered,' Jamieson continued, 'because I have a business suit belonging to her that the dry cleaners delivered just before you arrived.'

'Oh, I'll take that - I'll put it back in her flat.' He handed over what looked like a dark jacket-and-skirt suit. It was just possible that Mary Panter had forgotten that she had a suit at the dry cleaners; it could be the oversight they needed – that Mary Probert had warned them not to miss. Back up in Mary's flat, Marilyn laid the suit on the bed and removed it from its plastic cover. It was expensive; it looked tailor made, possibly Savile Row. The pockets on the outside of the jacket were dummy ones, but inside there were two more; one purposely designed for a mobile phone and the other, perhaps, for a slim pen and diary. Marilyn checked the phone pocket; it was empty. She checked the other pocket; her fingers touched a slip of paper. Heart thumping, she held it up to the light. It was a receipt from Westminster Council for a resident's parking ticket dated 15th January 2008. At the top of the receipt was a number; a number that would indicate the location of the resident's parking area.

'You've cocked up, Mary,' Marilyn muttered as she hurried back downstairs.

*

'Hello.'

'Mark, Don Hastings. We're ready to brief you on your next assignment. Sorry it's taken so long, but we seem to be in something of a political vacuum - neither our own government nor the US want to know. I regret that you'll have to forget most of what Alan told you – both governments want deniability. We've come up with a compromise - far from ideal and it'll be bloody hard for you two, but that's what we've got. Alan's on his way to your flat now. I apologise for not coming with him, but I've got to catch a flight to Kandahar.'

'Don...'

'Sorry I've really got to go – good luck.' There was a click; Don had put the phone down.

The doorbell rang a couple of minutes later. Alan Paxton walked in carrying a large brief case. Gunn and Doyle had been drinking coffee and chatting, in Arabic, with Abbas who got up, wished both men luck and let himself out. The conversation switched to English and Gunn introduced Doyle to Alan.

'Okay, here we go,' Alan began. 'I need to do this in two stages, the first here, which will take about an hour, then a car will come and take you both to Northolt. Malcolm'll be waiting for you with a Gazelle to fly you to RAF Lyneham for the rest,' he paused, unfolding a map. 'Terry Holt's already there; he'll deal with comms and code words and Tony Taylor will check your weapons and show you some of the specialist equipment you'll be taking. You leave Lyneham at 0600 hrs tomorrow on the first leg of your insertion, in a Charlie 130 from 97 Squadron. The aircraft will refuel at RAF Akrotiri in Cyprus and then take you to the target area in the Iraqi desert – here,' he tapped a blank yellow space on a map of Iraq. That's the general outline of the operation, which will be known from here on in as OP RAPTOR. Any questions before I give you the detail?'

'No, go on,' Gunn said.

'OP RAPTOR will be conducted in three phases: Phase One will be the insertion, Phase Two the search for the two bodies of the SAS patrol and Phase Three the recovery of you two back to the UK. So, Phase One; because of the diplomatic shitstorm, you'll be dropped into Akrotiri from the Charlie 130 by parachute from an altitude of 25,000ft. After your aircraft has refuelled, you'll fly south, entering Israeli airspace over Tel Aviv and leaving it at Eilat into the Gulf of Aqaba, where you'll turn northeast, imitating the flight path of passenger aircraft flying from Tabuk in Saudi Arabia to Baghdad. You'll cross the border between Saudi Arabia and Iraq in one of the bleakest areas of the Al Hamad desert and from there to Wadi Harwan is 150 miles. The total distance of that flight is exactly 1,000 miles. The Charlie 130 has a range on full load of 2,500 miles, so with a minimal load of you two and your equipment there'll be no need to deploy refuelling tankers. You and your equipment will exit the aircraft at 25,000 feet and open your chutes at 2,000 feet. It's called a H...'

'HALO - high altitude low opening - yeah, we've done one of those before,' Doyle interrupted, raising his eyebrows at Gunn.

'Okay, good; on to Phase Two. You'll both have Magellan GPS navigators, highly sensitive metal detectors and SAS-modified Suzuki 250cc, four stroke scrambler motorbikes with pannier-mounted additional fuel tanks, which will give each bike a range of 550 miles. You'll also be carrying two gallons of water apiece and freeze-dried rations. You'll be in Bedouin clothing and neither of you will be carrying any papers, because they don't. You'll both be carrying Armalite 5.56 assault rifles fitted with 40mm grenade launchers, pre-made Semtex charges with timers, satcom radios and folding spades to dig for the bodies. All of that equipment will be packed in a lightweight graphite container whose parachute will automatically open at 2,000 feet. Your mission is to find the burial site of the two troopers, which should be right beside the burnt carcass of the Landrover. That Magellan GPS is accurate to less than two feet so hopefully it won't take you too long to find the bodies, which were buried with their weapons. You have the exact position of the bodies - no thanks to Harker who did his best to conceal it. You also have the exact location of the other four-man patrol, where Harker found the Landrover in which he drove back to Saudi with Soames. You may well need to visit that location to examine it for evidence. With me?' Gunn nodded but Doyle asked:

'How'd you get hold of the right coordinates?'

'Harker purposely gave false coordinates, but forgot that the use of the satcom radio automatically gave Tac HQ in Saudi Arabia the coordinates of the radio making the transmission.'

'Hell of a thing to miss,' Doyle mused.

'Anyway, that brings us to your recovery. I'll be controlling you from the British military base at Basrah airport, which has the necessary comms to keep in touch with you. You have a satcom radio and Terry will deal with call signs and code words, but I can tell you this now: both the US Forces and the British Forces know that this operation is taking place, but have no idea what it entails. What they do know is that if they bump into two Bedouin who speak English and give them the codeword 'RAPTOR,' to treat them as friendly forces. Now....'

'We have to get from Wadi Harwan to the British Base in Basrah on our bikes, yes?' Gunn interrupted with a broad grin.

'In a word - yes,' Alan replied.

'Always wanted to do a bit of scrambler biking so now's my chance,' Doyle chuckled.

'It won't be easy,' Alan frowned at them. 'As the crow flies, it's about 400 miles over the roughest terrain imaginable, which is why Don is so anxious about your fitness.' Alan glanced at his watch and started putting everything back in his brief case. 'Okay, there should be a car waiting for you now. I'll see you both again at RAF Lyneham. You won't be in the Officers' Mess, you'll be in an empty RAF married quarter; I'll also be staying the night.'

*

Claudine and Marilyn crossed over the busy A3 intersection at the southeast corner of Clapham Common and headed for the row of shops and cafés on either side of the entrance to the Underground. Once they were both seated with coffees, Marilyn dialled the office. The phone was answered by Mary Probert's PA.

'Julie, Marilyn here, could you find the contact number at Westminster Council for whoever it is that deals with resident's parking permits? I have a receipt for a permit dated 15th January 2008 with a reference number of SWT 4506. Could you find out the location of that resident's parking and, if possible, who it belongs to?'

'Sure; I'll call you back asap.'

'Let's hope she comes up with the goods.' They had both barely taken a sip of their coffees when Marilyn's mobile rang.

'That was easy; the location is Lots Road by Chelsea Wharf, where all the houseboats are and the receipt was made out to an 'ML Panter,' whose address was given as 'Riverbelle' - that's all one word and double 'l' - Pontoon 2, Berth 11, Lots Road.'

'Brilliant, thanks,' Marilyn scribbled everything down and hung up, adding, 'I think we've got her!'

'So Mary either owns or rents a houseboat,' Claudine murmured, reading the address and taking a big gulp of her coffee before abandoning it.

'Looks like it,' Marilyn dropped some cash on the table and they headed for the Underground.

They got off at Fulham Broadway and headed south through oblivious shoppers on busy streets filled with small businesses, bistros and cafés, skirted round a gas works and then joined Lots Road as it bordered Chelsea Creek, on which the boats were moored. The houseboats were grouped onto two pontoons. Pontoon 2 was the furthest away and had the greater number of houseboats; they were moored in two rows with a central floating walkway. Claudine delved in her bag and produced a baseball hat to cover her hair, which she tied back into a bun.

'Okay, how do we play this one?'

'We need to get inside that houseboat, but I know someone who lives on a houseboat in St Katherine's Dock and if security here is anything like there, there'll be a gate onto the central pontoon which has to be opened with a combination. Let's just walk along the Embankment and do a recce first.' As it was sunny, there were a number of pedestrians walking along the pavement beside the river; people walking dogs, young children in pushchairs and tourists taking photographs. Both in jeans and trainers, they wouldn't warrant a second glance if Mary were keeping a lookout.

'Maybe we should come back after dark. What do you think?' Claudine asked.

'We may have to... look! There's the Riverbelle,' Marilyn nodded imperceptibly in its direction, 'that bright red one with the sundeck on top.' Even as she spoke, Mary came out of the deckhouse door, locked it, walked over the gangplank to the pontoon and headed for the exit gate.

'I'd never have recognised her. She's done a peroxide job on her hair and cut it all off.'

'Both of us follow her, or one of us follows her and the other searches the boat?' Marilyn asked.

'I'll search the boat, you follow her,' Claudine said without hesitation.

'Good hunting.'

'Keep in touch.' They separated, Marilyn following Mary, who had turned right onto the Embankment and Claudine heading for the wharf security gate. She waited until a couple of workmen opened it to come out and slipped in, clutching her keys so she looked like a boat resident.

*

Gunn and Doyle got out of the car at Northolt Airfield and each collected a small carrier bag from the boot, which contained their personal weapons. They climbed into the rear bench seat of the Gazelle for the flight to RAF Lyneham, which took just over 40 minutes. When they arrived, the Gazelle put down right outside a giant hangar in which a hulking Hercules C130 was being prepared for the early morning flight. Terry Holt and Tony Taylor were both waiting for them. They started with Terry, who checked that they both knew how to operate the satcom radio; he then handed over to Tony, who had laid out all their equipment for inspection.

He told them to try out the Suzuki scrambler bikes, which they did, riding around inside the hangar like a couple of 12-year-olds. Then came all the rest of the equipment - weapons, ammunition, explosives, oxygen for the 25,000 foot leg of the flight and the freefall; backpacks, water, rations, metal detectors, sleeping bags, their Bedouin clothing and lastly their thermal suits and parachutes for the descent. By the time they'd finished it was nearly 9pm. An RAF Regiment driver and Landrover took them to one of the married quarters where they found Alan Paxton and a hot supper waiting for them, cooked by the wife of the Wing Commander piloting the mission.

'I'm Pam, John's wife. John told me that he was going to cook you a decent meal and the thought of his cooking being inflicted on anyone was more than I could bear, so after a lot of wrangling I was allowed to come and do the honours. I have no idea what the two of you are doing or who you are and John tells me that it will have to stay that way. Supper's roast chicken followed by apple pie. It's all ready so I'll now disappear so that you can talk freely. John told me that I'm not allowed to wish you good luck – rather like the theatre I suppose - but I insist on asking you both to come home safely. There! I've said my bit and I'll leave you to your supper,' and Pam hurried out of the house. Neither Gunn nor Doyle had had a chance to say anything, but were grateful for the meal, which they knew was the last decent one they'd eat for some time. They were up shortly after 4.30 the next morning and, once they'd eaten a hasty breakfast, were driven to the hangar, where Wing Commander John Brake met them.

'Hope you guys survived Pam's cooking last night,' John greeted them cheerily, having to shout over the roar of the Hercules' turbo-prop engines. 'We're only stopping at Akrotiri to refuel and will take off immediately that's completed. I'm told you won't be using the facilities at RAF Akrotiri during the refuelling so we've installed toilets at the rear of the plane. Most of the flight will be at 12,000 feet, but as we turn northeast over Saudi Arabia after the Gulf of Aqaba we'll be climbing to 25,000 feet for your HALO descent. My Loadmaster, Warrant Officer Harding, will keep you briefed and will despatch you over the target area. I think that's about it; perhaps we'll have a chance to meet when you get back,' he shook hands with them and climbed the steps at the front of the plane, followed by Gunn and Doyle.

The eight-hour flight to Cyprus seemed interminable, made bearable only by the frequent cups of scalding hot coffee supplied by their Loadmaster. It was also bitterly cold in the Hercules' fuselage, so the combination of the coffee and the cold meant frequent visits to the chemical toilet screened off at the rear end of the fuselage by the hydraulic tailgate. Gunn and

Doyle would not get dressed in their thermal suits for the drop until the aircraft started its climb to 25,000 feet, so Alan had given them military sleeping bags to ward off the bitter cold until then.

By the time they reached Akrotiri it was nearly 1700 hours - taking into account the two-hour time difference. The Drop Zone at Wadi Harwan was another hour-and–a-half ahead of Cyprus. The jump wouldn't take place until 2200 hours – local Iraq time - when it was dark. Wing Commander Brake told them that the flight time from Akrotiri to Wadi Harwan would be three-and-a-half hours, leaving exactly one hour to complete the refuelling of the Charlie 130 before taking off on the final leg. Alan had cleverly avoided all this discomfort by rostering himself on the air-trooping routine flight between RAF Brize Norton and the British military base at Basrah Airport.

At Akrotiri they had a chance to stretch their legs, since the Charlie 130 was parked well away from the routine park-up area for the military air-trooping flights to and from the RAF airfield. The fuel tankers came out to the aircraft and it was ready to leave again at 1800 hours. The first leg of the flight was nearly 500 miles, cutting across the southwest corner of Israel before reaching the turning point over the Gulf of Aqaba. It was almost with a sense of relief that they were told by the Loadmaster that it was time for them to change into their thermal suits as the aircraft started to gain altitude. The suits would protect them from both the rush of icy air when the ramp went down and the lack of breathable air at that altitude.

After what seemed another eternity, the red light came on. The Loadmaster, attached to the fuselage by a long safety strap, positioned himself by the release catch of the pannier on which the graphite equipment container would run to the end of the ramp, before continuing on its own impetus out into the black void. The ramp opened, letting in a roaring blast of freezing air. The light turned to green, the catch released and the pannier trundled noisily to the end of its rails and then disappeared, followed by the two men. There were no navigation lights on the Hercules as it banked steeply and headed on a reciprocal course back to Cyprus.

Doyle had jumped from the ramp ahead of Gunn, but now both of them were no more than 25 metres apart and level as they followed the equipment container. The last time that the two of them had done a HALO jump together it was over the South China Sea some years previously. Their parachutes had been sabotaged and failed to open and they'd had to descend on the equipment container chute. As Gunn gratefully breathed in the oxygen, he prayed nothing would go wrong this time. The large circular face of the altimeter on his chest, with its dial only inches from his face, unwound relentlessly - 10,000...5,000...2,500.....and then Gunn saw the drogue chute on the container deploy, dragging out the main canopy.

He pulled the ripcord and felt the gentle tug as his drogue deployed, then came the reassuring jerk as the parawing of his main canopy slowed his descent. Over on his left, in the clear moonlit night, he saw Doyle doing the same. Below them there wasn't a single visible light, but gradually the ground took form and shape as the moonlight revealed deep shadows cast by ravines, riverbeds and wadis. There appeared to be little or no cross wind, so Gunn steered his chute towards an area clear of wadis. Fifty feet from the ground he turned into the gentle night breeze, almost stalling the chute, to land comfortably on his feet. Doyle came in some 50 yards away and landed right next to the container.

Both men quickly removed their parachute harnesses and rolled up the canopies into a tight bundle. They did the same with the container chute, then opened the container and quickly got out their weapons, which had been packed on top of everything else. Crouching by the container, they looked around and listened for any indication that they'd been seen. There was no sound; nothing moved.

Next out were the two spades and their Bedouin clothing. They stripped off their thermal suits and dressed in the clothes, which they had been wearing 24/7 during the past week to ensure that they were well worn in - and smelled like it. The landing site had been fortuitous because it was an area of deep sand rather than solid rock. Once they'd buried the parachutes and thermal suits they unpacked the other items. When the container was empty, Gunn and Doyle dragged it to a small gully where they covered it with rocks and then shovelled sand over it. They divided the various items between them and loaded up the scrambler bikes. Altogether it had taken them nearly half-an-hour. Gunn switched on his Magellan GPS, waited while it picked up the satellites and then checked the reading.

'Remind me to put in a formal complaint when we get back,' Gunn said in a whisper.

'Why?' Doyle asked, switching on his GPS.

'My GPS indicates that we're 100 metres from the burial site. These RAF guys could be a little more accurate with their navigation.'

Doyle smiled grimly: 'Thank God for those RAF guys.'

# CHAPTER 15

The short walk from Downing Street to New Scotland Yard gave Chief Superintendent Lochart a few minutes to calm down. Ever since Steven Harker's appointment some 18 months previously, rumours in the Met were rife about the power he wielded and his apparent lack of accountability to anyone. On several occasions, persistent members of the Press, and indeed Parliament itself, had very suddenly ceased being a nuisance; they hadn't been killed - nothing as crude as that, Lochart recalled, as he turned into the Yard's forecourt, but unfortunate accidents had happened to them or their families or both.

A particularly aggressive photo-journalist, whose calling card was a knack of taking unflattering shots of the PM, had had a serious accident on his motorbike and been left partially paralysed. Then there was one of the PM's own ministers; he'd resigned from the government and 'crossed the house' to the opposition. After a series of mishaps and accidents to him, his wife and his two children, he'd suffered a serious stroke and had to retire, which forced a bi-election in his Scottish constituency.

Lochart sat down at his desk for a few moments, contemplating the towering paperwork on his desk, then picked up the phone.

'Hi, Pete, got a minute for a chat?' Commander

Peter Stancombe was the Head of SO15 - the Met's Counter Terrorist organisation, who worked closely with Lochart's SO14. Lochart got up from his desk and went down the corridor to Stancombe's office.

'Come in, Bruce; how was your meeting with the idiot at Number 10?' One look at Lochart's face was enough of an answer. 'Like that. Here, take a pew and let off steam. I was there last week to brief him on various counter terrorist ops - what a piece of work.'

'Thanks,' Lochart sighed, sinking into an armchair. 'But apart from 'im being a rude shit, which we're all used to, I'm actually starting to think there's something really wrong.' He paused, choosing his words carefully.

'Go on...'

'For some reason that's beyond me, 'arker's leaving here tomorrow to go to Beijing.'

'But the advance security party doesn't leave 'til next week - Tuesday or Wednesday at the earliest.'

'Wednesday; so what's 'e going to do for five or six days on 'is own in Beijing, apart from 'ave an all-expenses-paid 'oliday in a five star 'otel, courtesy of the British tax-payer?'

'Have you mentioned this to the Commissioner?' Peter asked.

'No, only you, right now; I think 'is nibs has enough problems without me off-loading this one onto 'im.'

'Probably...' Stancombe drummed his fingers thoughtfully. 'Look here's an idea; why don't we both go and have a chat with BID?'

'Are you sure?'

'We both work closely with their CE Directorate

and I've had quite a bit to do with the Deputy Head…'

'Miles Thompson?'

'That's the man. The CE guys are pretty savvy about what's happening in the higher - and lower - echelons of government and Miles has never been anything but helpful. I'll give him a call,' Peter checked the card index on his desk and dialled a number. Luckily Miles was in his office, and his PA patched the call through straight away.

'Miles? It's Peter Stancombe at SO15.'

'How are you?'

'Oh you know; look, I've got Bruce Lochart in my office...'

'SO14 Close Protection?'

'That's right; look, both of us would like to come and see you if you can spare the time. Something odd's come up and we'd like your advice.'

'Yes of course; now?' Miles suggested.

'Er,' Peter mouthed 'now' to Bruce, who nodded; 'great; we could be with you in about ten minutes.'

'My PA will meet you in the car park.'

*

Looking around her, Claudine stepped on to Riverbelle's gangplank, which was secured to the blunt bow of the houseboat, and then went directly to the door from which Mary Panter had emerged. Boat hatches and deckhouse doors aren't noted for their impregnability and houseboats are no different. It took only seconds with her lockpick to get the door open. There was no intruder alarm, so she closed the door behind her and went down the short companionway steps into the saloon.

The interior was clean and tidy, much like the flat had been, which made her search much easier. She did a quick check over the whole boat. It had no engine, so if it needed to be moved it would have to be towed to its new destination. At the stern, such as it was - in reality the houseboat was the same shape at both ends and constructed on a flat-bottomed steel pontoon - was a comfortable cabin with double bed and en-suite bathroom. Despite the tidiness everywhere else, the bed was unmade and imprints on both pillows indicated that two people had slept in it.

For'ard of the saloon, there were two single cabins, a shared bathroom and storage space. The only heating seemed to come from a small, pot-bellied, wood-burning stove in the saloon. Hot water was supplied by a tank and electric immersion heater in an airing cupboard for'ard of the two single cabins. The kitchen - or galley - was in the deckhouse, where it could supply food and drink either to the saloon below or the sundeck above. Claudine was just about to tackle a built-in desk and its paperwork when the boat gave a slight lurch. She reached for the Colt automatic in her bag, backing into the stern cabin, then froze, listening intently. No footsteps across the deck. Then the boat gave another slight lurch, and she realised it was the flooding tide drunkenly attempting to lift the boat off the glutinous Thames mud.

The paperwork on the desk revealed nothing, nor did a laptop computer, which wasn't even password protected. Frustrated now, Claudine returned to the deckhouse-cum-galley, which seemed to be the focal space in the houseboat. She opened all the cupboards;

nothing except food. Then she ripped all the upholstery off its Velcro fastenings, piling it in the middle of the saloon below, looking for more storage space. There was plenty; she fumbled inside every compartment, finding spare warps; extension pieces for the table; bin liners and spare jay cloths and even spare parts for an outboard motor. Then she reached into a sliding cabinet, tucked behind the table in the cramped eating area, which looked like little more than a backrest; there was a brief case inside. Claudine almost yelped with relief. It had a combination lock; she revisited a cupboard which had contained a toolkit and removed a screwdriver. With the blade of this inserted under the hasp of each combination lock, she turned the combination slowly with her ear close to the lock. The pressure applied by the screwdriver resulted in a very faint 'click' as the combination reached the preset code opening slot. With a satisfying final click, the locks flipped open. Inside there were papers; Claudine skimmed them as quickly as she could. They referred to a three-bedroom penthouse apartment overlooking Copacabana Beach at 35, Rua Berata Ribeiro in Rio de Janeiro and a bank deposit account at the Banco de Brazil in the names of Senor y Senora Jesus Garcia - with a credit of R$ 600 million.

'Jesus…' she didn't know the exchange rate for the Brazilian Real, but it still sounded like a hell of a lot of money. She hurried back to the laptop in the saloon and with relief saw that it was connected to a modem, its blinking lights indicating it was online. She logged onto Google, found a currency converter site and fed in the amount, asking it to translate it into Sterling.

'Uh!' she gasped, '£200 million pounds!'

Hands shaking now from the adrenalin, she rifled through the other contents which revealed a flexible, first class, one-way e-ticket with British Airways to Rio de Janeiro.

*

At Battersea Bridge, Mary Panter crossed over Cheyne Walk at the traffic lights and headed north towards the King's Road. Unfortunately for her, her urchin-cut peroxide hair made it much easier for Marilyn to follow her. Both Mary and Marilyn had been on the same Counter Surveillance course, run in London by BID's training team. The course instructed trainees in the techniques of both following someone and avoiding being followed. The latter skill was impressed on all the BID employees, whether agents or on the administrative staff of the Directorate. To Marilyn, as an agent in CE, applying the techniques of identifying a 'tail' had become second nature, but she wondered how often Mary had put the skills into practice since completing her course several years previously.

As Mary turned right into the King's Road, Marilyn's mobile rang.

'Yes,' she answered.

'It's me,' Claudine sounded breathless, 'I've just found a first class, one-way ticket to Rio, the address of an apartment overlooking Copacabana Beach and a bank deposit account for more than £200 million.'

'Jesus Christ!'

'I know; I'll stay here until I hear from you.'

'Okay; tell Mary Probert straight away. I'll try and

contact you with a text every…' Marilyn glanced at her watch, '…five minutes. If you don't hear from me for ten minutes, get off that boat and get back to the 'house' asap.' As Marilyn hung up, she saw Mary dodge off the pavement and into a bookshop.

'Shit, shit, shit!' She'd been spotted; now it was even more vital that she didn't let Mary out of her sight. She followed her into the cool, dim interior, picking up a book as she passed the nearest stand. The shop was arranged over three floors, with a broad staircase leading up to each floor directly in front of the entrance.

There was no sign of Mary, but she hadn't been far behind; she would have seen her if she'd gone upstairs - even if she'd been running. Marilyn scanned the shop floor over the edge of her book. Something caught her eye over in a corner. A young female shop assistant came out from a door at the back of the shop looking agitated and talked to a male assistant at the counter; he dropped what he was doing and disappeared with the girl back through the door. Marilyn ran back out onto the pavement just in time to see Mary reappear from the next side road, glance back in her direction and then she ran towards some traffic lights at a junction further down King's Road, dodging startled shoppers. As Marilyn gave chase, she could see that Mary was looking intently at the cars coming towards her. 'She's looking to hijack', Marilyn muttered, picking up pace.

'Shit!' she swore aloud, as a black Porsche 911 pulled up at the lights alongside a Yamaha motorbike. In the same instant, Mary took off across the road and ran round to the driver's door, wrenched it open, dragged the terrified driver out onto the road and, while the lights were still red, slammed it into gear and shot past Marilyn in the opposite direction.

*

Peter Stancombe and Bruce Lochart got out of their car at the NCP car park and walked over to what looked like a maintenance lift, where Miles' PA was waiting for them. She tapped a code out on the lift's buttons, a code that changed daily, and what had been the back wall of the lift compartment slid open behind them, revealing a short corridor. Then she placed her hand on what looked like a black glassy panel set into the wall, again typing the daily code into a keypad. Something beeped and a steel panel ahead of them parted in the centre with a low hum, the top half receding into the ceiling and the bottom half into the floor. The policemen followed silently, Bruce, who'd never been in this entrance, wondering what was next.

'Mind how you go, gentlemen, or you'll trip the poisoned arrows,' their guide winked over her shoulder.

'Come in and take a seat,' Miles welcomed them minutes later. 'How can I be of assistance?'

'Uh, well let me kick off,' Peter began and outlined their concerns about Harker and his off-schedule jaunt. When he had finished, Miles studied them both quietly for a few moments, then, seeming to have made up his mind, leant forward conspiratorially.

'You're right to be concerned,' he said finally, and calmly explained what might really have happened during that SAS patrol in the Iraqi desert seventeen years ago. 'As we speak, two of our agents are on their way to the desert to exhume what's left of those two SAS troopers so that we have undeniable proof that Steven Harker is not, as we believe, Steven Harker at all.' Peter was silent, digesting everything, but Bruce was incandescent.

'Bloody 'ell!....that piece of shit... Uh, sorry, but he's been putting noses out of joints our end for a long time – mine especially. Can't say I'm...'

There was a tap on the door.

'Sorry to interrupt,' said Miles' PA, 'but you're wanted immediately in the Ops Centre. Barry Windsor is there with Mary Probert.'

'On my way,' Miles turned to the two policemen. 'You may as well join me.'

*

A couple of pedestrians, the biker and the driver of the car that had been behind the Porsche, were helping its female driver, who was more shocked than physically hurt. The Yamaha motorbike was resting on its stand with the engine still running. Marilyn chose her moment and jumped on the bike; she flicked up the stand, toed first gear and disappeared after Mary, with a stream of blue smoke from her spinning rear tyre and the furious shouts of its owner trailing behind her.

Her bag was still on its long strap round her neck, so, taking her left hand off the combined clutch and front wheel brake, she pulled it round in front of her, got out her mobile and pressed the speed dial for Claudine. She answered immediately.

'Mary's in a black Porsche heading north on Warwick Road. I'm on a motorbike following. Get help from BID, then make it look like you were never there and get out.'

Claudine dialled Mary Probert's number and relayed the message. Within minutes, Barry Windsor, as acting Head of CE, Miles, Peter Stancombe and Bruce Lochart met up with Mary in the Operations Centre. Terry Holt had just finished briefing Malcolm Springfield, who was about to lift off in the Gazelle from the small heliport on the building's 15th floor to assist in the hunt for Mary Panter. Marilyn explained what Claudine had discovered at the houseboat. Peter immediately offered police support, which Miles gratefully accepted, but not before he'd told Terry to hold Malcolm on the heliport.

'But Miles...'

'Look, before we all rush around, what do we hope to achieve by chasing Mary Panter? We now know from Chief Superintendent Lochart and Commander Stancombe here that Harker is leaving for Beijing tomorrow. I'd guess this is the first leg of a disappearing act. It also looks as though he and Mary Panter plan to meet up in Rio, possibly with Soames, but, uh, three's always a crowd, and knowing what Soames is like.......who knows what'll happen there. I'm inclined to let Mary go and hope she'll lead us to both Harker and Soames - she doesn't know that we've found her houseboat or what's in it; Claudine'll put everything back the way she found it. We'll make her think she's given us the slip and then keep a watch on her round the clock. Anyone not happy with that?'

'No, that's a good idea.'

'I go with that, call it off.'

'Right,' Miles turned to address everyone, 'Terry, please stand down Malcolm, but ask him to keep the chopper on the helipad and come down to the Ops Centre. Get on to Marilyn asap and tell her to abandon the chase and get back here with Claudine. Make sure Claudine's left no sign that she was on Mary's boat. Lastly, Peter, Bruce - thank you for your offer of help; we may well need it in the next few days. Now we wait until we have more information on Mr Harker, and from your guys, Barry, before we make a move on Mary Panter - even if that means following them to Beijing or Rio. We just can't afford to screw this up and if that means waiting, so be it.'

*

Having buried all signs of their parachute descent into the Iraqi desert, Gunn and Doyle set off, pushing their motorbikes in the direction indicated by the 'go to' feature on the Magellan GPS – the patch of sand where, almost two decades ago, the Landrover was blown up by an anti-tank mine. There was scarcely any breeze and any alien noise, like the exhaust of a motorbike, would carry a considerable distance. The exhausts on the bikes had been modified with additional silencers that reduced their performance making them less noisy, but still noisy enough to alert anyone within two or three hundred yards.

Once they'd reached the spot, they stopped and surveyed their position. The area was open for at least a hundred yards in every direction before it sloped away into a wadi to the west and to a high ridge to the east. There was no sign of the burnt-out carcass of a Landrover.

'We should wait 'til its light,' said Doyle. 'That'll be in about five hours? And then we can see what the hell we're doing. This was never going to be easy, but it'll be a darn side quicker done in daylight.'

'Makes sense,' Gunn conceded reluctantly.

'Look, I'm still jet-lagged so let me take the first couple of hours stag and then I'll wake you to take us through to dawn.'

They pushed their bikes down into a shallow depression where there was some shelter from the chill night breeze. The temperature had dropped dramatically, even in the hour that they had been in the desert. Gunn wrapped his 'dishdasha' and woollen 'bisht' tightly around him, pulled his keffiyah over his face and burrowed into the sand, resting his head on his pack. It seemed only seconds had passed before Doyle was shaking him awake again.

'Your turn on stag, John,' Doyle murmured. 'It's just a couple of hours 'til dawn.'

Gunn exchanged places with Doyle and waited until he had regained his night vision before he moved up to the lip of the shallow depression in which they were completely hidden. Gunn dragged his backpack up beside him and removed a small, folding metal stand and hexamine tablets, water and sachets of coffee and powdered milk. He lit the tablet, which burned with an almost invisible flame, and boiled the water in his metal mug, which fitted onto the base of the water bottle.

Dawn and dusk in the UK at 51° north of the equator is a gradual process, but the closer to the equator the more rapid is the transition from dark to light, and vice versa in the evening. Gunn's location was only some 20° closer to the equator, but enough to make a noticeable difference to the speed of sunrise. A thin grey line peeped over the horizon and then, barely minutes later, physical features around Gunn came to life with form, shape and muted colour. Soon after, the orb of the sun appeared, flooding the bleak landscape, spreading in a liquid glow. Gunn pulled his watch out from his pocket in his 'sirwal,' the baggy trousers worn under the disdasha; it was just a few minutes before five. He heated up another mug of coffee and woke Doyle.

Once Doyle was awake and sipping the scalding coffee, Gunn trudged off towards the ridge about a hundred yards to the east of their position with his binoculars and his Armalite assault rifle. Ten yards short of the crest, he dropped to the ground and crawled forward, cradling the Armalite. When he reached the crest, it was immediately obvious why the SAS patrol had been in this location; there was an uninterrupted view to a road some five miles distant running east/west, which had to have been one of the main supply routes between Baghdad and Jordan in the 1991 conflict. It was along this road and two others similar to it that Saddam Hussein had played cat and mouse with his Scud launchers. Gunn scanned every inch of the ground east and west along the deserted road, then turned to study the wadis and rock outcrops to the west of his position. With the exception of the road, he might just as well have been on the surface of Mars; nothing moved but a restless, lonely breeze and sporadic little dust devils chasing across the bleak desert.

Gunn wriggled backwards from the crest of the ridge and then walked back to the depression, which he nearly missed.

'Thanks, that coffee was a life saver. See anything?'

'There's a good view of the MSR, which the patrol from Bravo Squadron was probably monitoring, but nothing else. This would have been a good place to hole up with their Landrover, especially if they'd hidden it over there,' Gunn pointed to the west, where the sand turned to hard, rocky boulder-strewn ground and dipped down into a wadi.

'But we're standing, just about, on the spot where Harker claimed that the vehicle was blown up on a mine. Why on earth would the Iraqis want to place anti-tank mines here? Unless they just got bored carrying them around and buried them.'

'Hmm…' Doyle shrugged

'Are you ready?'

'Yeah, let's do this.'

They unpacked the spades, unfolded the metal detectors, walked to the exact location recorded by the patrol's Magellan GPS and then marked out a grid extending ten metres north, south, east and west from that centre point. The GPS was accurate to within less than one metre so their search area was more than adequate – if they were in the right location. They then donned earphones, switched on the detectors, checked them against the metal spades, which both squealed indicating a maximum deflection, and started their search.

Dividing the search area in half, one of them

concentrated on the search, the other acted as sentry. Gunn searched first, placing his Armalite beside Doyle. The search pattern was simple: the area had been drawn off with lines in the sand marking lanes and Gunn walked slowly up and down these lanes, swinging the head of the detector from side to side. It wasn't long before the sun made its presence felt and he was grateful for the protection afforded by the keffiyah over his head. When he'd completed two lanes, which had revealed nothing more than chunks of magnetite rock, he exchanged places with Doyle. As he turned onto the second lane, Doyle's detector suddenly wailed, giving a maximum reading. While Gunn kept a lookout, Doyle started to dig. Less than a foot down, the spade hit something solid; within a couple of minutes' frantic work, Doyle had unearthed one of the patrol's Armalites.

It took them nearly two hours to uncover the second assault rifle and the remains of the two SAS Troopers. Fortunately the bodies had been buried about three feet down in the sand, which had kept them out of the reach of desert scavengers. In Harker's report, he claimed they were 'burnt to a crisp', but there was no sign of any burning. The disruptive pattern combat clothing was in a remarkably good state of preservation and both skulls still retained parchment-like scraps of skin with hair attached, which Gunn removed and placed in sealed plastic bags.

'So the mine story was a load of bullshit,' Doyle said, resting on his spade after using his keffiyah to wipe away some of the sweat.

'Much as we suspected, Doyle,' Gunn was down

on his knees, carefully removing first one and then the other skull from the two corpses. He turned them over, revealing the neat holes in the back of the skulls.

'And both of these poor bastards were executed with a bullet in the back of the head.'

# CHAPTER 16

After they'd photographed the SAS Troopers' grave, the bullet holes in the skulls, taken wider angle shots of the burial site in relation to the features around it and recorded the longitude and latitude coordinates on the GPS, Doyle and Gunn replaced the Armalites in the grave and refilled it. As neither knew the words of the burial service, both of them stood in silence for two minutes and then re-packed their equipment.

'Okay, what's the next move?' Doyle asked.

'We need to find the location where Harker claimed to have met up with the other four-man patrol. If his Landrover wasn't blown up by a mine, he must've driven with Soames to the other location while they came up with a convincing story to tell the other patrol,' said Gunn, entering the co-ordinates of the next location. 'Direction is 278° and it's 8.5 miles. Assuming he was driving the Landrover, let's take the route he's most likely have taken. You select the route and I'll ride shotgun and watch your back.' They both started their bikes and rode out of the soft sand onto the firm surface leading down into the wadi.

It was impossible to take anything like a direct route on the 278° bearing, as their way was blocked by gullies, wadis and great pillars of rock, weathered by aeons of sandstorms, blistering hot days and frigid nights into contorted shapes, like grotesque sentries.

They had covered four miles, according to Gunn's GPS, when Doyle stopped his bike and waited for him to catch up. In front of them was a fifty-foot high escarpment with an almost sheer side.

'Left or right?' Doyle unwound the keffiyah from his face gulped down some water. 'Christ it's hot...'

'Could be either; I'll take a look up there to the left. Why don't you go right. Don't go further than a couple of hundred yards, we can't afford to lose each other in this,' Gunn's clothes were soaked through and clinging to his skin uncomfortably. He rode his bike over the rough ground into what developed into a narrow canyon, completely shielding him from the sun. He found the Landrover barely 150 yards along it. It was tucked close into the side of the overhanging wall, even hiding it from someone standing on the lip of the canyon above. Gunn picked up his hand-held radio and called Doyle over. The Landrover was in remarkably good condition, despite having been parked there for 17 years. The tyres had rotted, but the .50 Browning machine gun would probably work if cleaned and oiled. There were jerrycans of petrol, which hadn't been used; ammunition and even the ignition keys were still in the steering lock.

'So what do we think happened here?' Doyle lifted the bonnet, propped it up with the rod support and examined the engine.

'Well let's think this through as they must have done. Remember, this is Quiller and Soames and at this stage they are expecting to meet the other four SAS soldiers. I believe that Quiller had already decided that he was going to murder those four soldiers in order to save his own hide. They were close buddies, but it wouldn't surprise me to discover that Quiller had some sort of hold over Soames which meant that he had to go along with the plan to take on Harker's identity. Soames is now wanted for his implication in a generous handful of murders. He's a very competent and ruthless killer; he's always been within a whisker of facing homicide charges. So it's more than likely that Quiller knew of something that compelled Soames to go along with his plan whether he liked it or not. They have to think up a plausible story for the death of Harker and the driver, Corporal Miller, so they invent the destruction of the Landrover by an anti-tank mine, which killed both men. Now's the tricky bit...'

'Yeah, even more tricky than murdering his pals to save his own ass,' Doyle muttered in contempt. 'What do we think about Soames' injuries?'

'Uh, well, when Quiller - by then Harker - reached Coalition lines in Saudi Arabia, according to the medical reports Soames' injuries consisted mostly of bruising and concussion from the non-existent mine - no broken or missing limbs, burns or open wounds or anything like that. So...' Gunn fell silent and punched his right fist into his left palm.

'You're saying Harker deliberately beat the shit out of Soames, in cold blood?' Doyle asked, reappearing from under the Landrover's bonnet and slamming it shut.

'How else would Soames have got those injuries?'

'Yeah, but...shit, this guy, Harker - Quiller...,' Doyle shook his head incredulously. 'Okay, so however it's done, Soames gets the shit beaten out of him and then Quiller sets off with him to the other patrol location where they've got to convince the other SAS guys of their mine story. Then they get there only to find that all their buddies in the other patrol have either been killed or captured and so there was no need to have gone through with all this anti-tank mine bullshit in the first place,' Doyle kicked the rotting front tyre in disgust.

'I don't know; the more we find out about Quiller, the less I believe those four soldiers were killed by the Iraqis. I think he murdered them too. They knew Quiller and Harker too well - only way that he could've got away with assuming Harker's identity. His report states that when he reached the other patrol, he found the Landrover, but no sign of the four soldiers. He testified that they didn't respond to frequent calls on the radio and therefore he had to assume they'd either been killed or captured by the Iraqis. Those four SAS soldiers never reappeared, even when other SAS prisoners of war were released, and so were recorded as MIA. You and I both fought in that war and I'm no expert, but I'm pretty sure Saddam never deployed anything in this sector, except the re-supply traffic on the MSR's, the Scud launchers and the soldiers protecting those launchers.'

'No, he didn't.'

'Of course, that four-man patrol could have identified a launcher and gone down from their observation position, but why? If they did spot a launcher moving along the MSR, all they had to do was send the coordinates back over the satcom, illuminate the target and then the F15 Eagles, A10s or Tornadoes, which were airborne constantly during daylight hours, did the rest with precision laser-guided bombs.'

'Right.'

'We need to find that other patrol location, see if we're right - if they were executed too. I'll lead this time and you ride shotgun.'

They photographed the Landrover and recorded its exact location, then set off back into the furnace. It took them another hour to find the other patrol position, but they knew they were in the right place, apart from the GPS reading, because Doyle discovered the camouflage net which had covered the patrol's Landrover. It had been pushed into a crevice amongst the rocks and as he pulled it out, he narrowly avoided being stung by an angry scorpion, which came out with it.

'Shit!' Doyle cursed as the scorpion scuttled away. 'That I do not need right now.'

*

Mary Panter couldn't see the motorbike in her rear-view mirror anymore, so she slowed down and took the turning off Warwick Road onto Cromwell Road and the A4/M4 towards Heathrow Airport. She felt mildly elated at having given Marilyn the slip, and patted the Porsche's dashboard appreciatively. She turned off the M4 to the airport and parked the Porsche in the multi-storey car park at Terminal 3, threw the parking ticket into the waste bin by the lift and went down to the Underground, where she caught the next train back into London. She changed from the Piccadilly Line to the District Line at Earl's Court and left the train at Fulham Broadway. Nevertheless, the chase had spooked her; it was time to go. She'd bring her departure forward, she resolved, as she reached Chelsea Wharf and the gated entrance to Pontoon 2.

Pat Scarsdale and David Dewbury of CE1 had had very little difficulty in persuading the middle-aged couple that owned 'Salad Days', a houseboat four berths further along the pontoon, to allow them to use the deckhouse to watch MaryPanter. Having received a detailed description of her new peroxide bob from Marilyn, they spotted her as soon she arrived at the security gate. The contact was reported immediately to the Operations Centre at BID, where Marilyn, Claudine and Mary Probert had set up camp.

'Are you ready to leave for Rio, Claudine? I reckon Mary's about to make a run for it.'

'Yeah, I'm ready, but I'll need to go to my flat to collect a few things.'

'Okay; in the meantime I'll get Miles down here, as it looks like this op is moving back into his Directorate, and I'll tell the Assistant Director for South America, Damien Arturo, and his Controller, Peter Stone, to get ready to brief you.'

*

The position the SAS patrol had chosen was a good one. The Landrover would have been well hidden down in the deep-sided wadi under its cam net. They would have taken it in turns to walk up to the ridge, where there were a number of large crevices in the weathered sandstone in which an observer would be completely hidden, protected from the sun and with a panoramic view down onto the MSR. Gunn crawled into the crevice that he was certain the SAS observer would have used and focused his binoculars on the road some two miles distant. There was nothing; no wonder Don called it the Empty Quarter, he thought as he wriggled backwards again, away from the skyline. When he got back to the wadi, Doyle was unpacking the metal detectors and spades. It was now just after midday and the sun was at its fiercest, but fortunately down in the wadi there was some protection from its white hot glare.

The ground up by the observation position was as hard as concrete so there was no point in searching there. If anything had been buried it would have been in the soft, deep sand to one side of the wadi. Once again, Doyle carefully marked off the search area and divided it into lanes. They searched until it started to get dark, but found nothing - not even magnetite rocks. Doyle checked that the detectors were working properly; they were. Had Quiller been telling the truth? As the short dusk quickly turned to night, they called a halt to the search and prepared to spend another night in the desert.

'I know that bastard murdered those guys,' Doyle sighed wearily, as they prepared their evening meal.

'I think so too. How d'you think they did it? I mean....ambush four men?'

'Well, there'd always have been one man up at the OP, watching the MSR. In order to take them by surprise, Quiller would have to have gone up to the OP, on the pretence of taking an interest in the mission, then murdered the guy there. He would then have come back here and shot the other three. Or, if Soames wasn't as badly injured as we thought, he might well have helped dispatch the rest of the soldiers on a signal from Quiller.'

'Hmmm... Sounds likely. We'll find something tomorrow,' Gunn said, clapping Doyle's shoulder. 'I'll take the first stag,' he offered, as they finished up.

The moon rose shortly after Doyle had wrapped himself in his bisht and the cam' net. Also wrapped snugly in his bisht, Gunn grabbed his Armalite and night vision binoculars and explored the wadi, partly to keep warm but he also wanted to try and put himself in Quiller's shoes. They now had hard evidence that Quiller and Soames had murdered Harker and Miller. As far as the other patrol was concerned, Gunn mused, all the teams were under instructions not to engage the Iraqi forces, but simply to identify the Scud launchers that posed a threat to Israel and the Coalition bases in Saudi Arabia. So the report Quiller had submitted on return to the Regiment made no sense whatsoever, though it was, perhaps, corroborated by what happened to other patrols that had bumped the Iraqi Army, resulting in troopers being captured and killed.

Gunn stopped; if he had just murdered four fellow soldiers, though, there was no way he'd hide the evidence at the scene of the crime. Quiller knew that the location of that patrol position would be known back at Tactical HQ in Saudi Arabia and it was quite possible that after the war, the Commonwealth War Graves Commission might well visit sites where British Soldiers had been killed. Doyle had explored to the left along the wadi and said it would have been impassable for a mountain goat, let alone a Landrover, so that left the route to the right, where he was now standing. Gunn pulled out his watch and checked the time; nearly midnight. He decided to give Doyle another hour while he explored a little further along the wadi.

After another fifty yards the wadi opened out into a depression, with narrow, deep gullies running off it on his left, the southern side. These run-offs would have carried away the heavy rain that fell during the winter months. Gunn decided to go back, he'd strayed far enough from their campsite; they could come back in the morning. He turned to retrace his steps, but spotted a large twig sticking out of the sand, casting a long shadow by the light of the full moon that had risen. It was the first sign that he'd seen of any flora in this God-forsaken desert and he bent down to examine it more closely.

'Ugh!' Gunn suddenly recoiled.

Reaching out of the sand were the slender ulna and carpus bones of a human wrist.

*

Steven Harker abandoned the rest of his full English breakfast in first class on British Airways Flight 039 to Beijing and gulped down three refills-worth of coffee instead. He'd barely slept on the 10-hour flight, his mind frantically dotting the 'i's and crossing the 't's of the days ahead, and he was exhausted. It was 9.45 am local time and they'd begun their descent. An hour-and-a-half later, he emerged into the arrival hall and was met by a uniformed Chinese driver from the British Embassy.

'Thank Christ for that,' Harker muttered, as he

handed over his suitcase and followed his driver. A brand new, gleaming black Jaguar XKF was parked in the privileged position reserved for dignitaries and Heads of States, guarded by two airport security police. Harker climbed into the back seat, which smelt comfortingly of new leather. It was sixteen miles to the Forbidden City in the centre of Beijing, which would normally take anything from one to two hours, but as the Chinese Government had cleared the capital of traffic for the Olympics, it only took 45 minutes. The Jaguar pulled up under the portico of the St Regis Hotel in the Chaoyang diplomatic enclave, the automatic choice because of preferential rates for diplomats.

Harker got out of the car, watched as his suitcase was whisked away by the hotel concierge and then went to check in. At that moment his mobile phone rang, and he paused to answer it.

'Harker.'

'It's Mary; I'm bringing forward my departure for Rio.'

'What's happened?'

'I was followed by one of CE's spooks.'

'What happened?'

'We were in the King's Road so I hi-jacked a car and got away from her although she tried to follow me on a motor bike,' Mary said, her tone defiant.

'Are you sure you lost her?' Harker gritted his teeth, furious; she was drawing too much attention to herself.

'Yes.'

'Good; where are you now?'

'On the boat.'

'Were you anywhere near the boat when they followed you?'

'No; they don't know about the boat.'

'Is it time for Plan B?'

'Definitely; when are you off to Beijing?' Mary asked.

'I'm there – I'm in the hotel now.'

'I thought you were leaving next week with the SO14 team?'

'That was the idea, but your business with Claudine de Carteret and the safe have forced a change of plan on us.'

'Oh... I ha...'

'It's okay, I know she was getting too close,' Harker spoke calmly, trying not to spook Mary any more than he could tell she already was; they couldn't afford any more cock-ups. 'Right, we're moving to Plan B. You leave asap for Rio and I'll meet up with you and Mike there. I've got to go.'

'See you in Rio,' Mary smiled, allowing herself a moment of excitement.

'Stupid fucking bitch', Steve simmered, wincing as his stomach began to throb from the stress. He made a mental note to buy more antacids as he silently followed the bellboy carrying his suitcase to the bank of lifts.

Libby Stewart, on the night shift at GCHQ Sigint Centre in Cheltenham, removed the tape with the recording she'd just made and took it to her supervisor.

'I think BID might be interested in this phone call.'

*

Gunn hurried back to where Doyle was still fast asleep, any tiredness he may have felt long since evaporated in the chill night breeze. He crawled up to the OP again and used his night-vision binoculars to do a thorough sweep of the desert to the north of their position and then did the same from the top of the wadi to the south. Nothing moved; it was as still as the grave and Gunn shuddered at the thought. He collected his spade and returned to the narrow gully where he'd found the bones protruding from the sand. The gully had offered a ready-made trench to bury the bodies, but the winter rain must have washed much of the sand away, partially revealing the gruesome burial site. Whether Harker and Soames had considered that, he would probably never know, but in their haste to hide the evidence, they'd opted for the easiest solution. Working during the bitter cold of the night was infinitely easier than toiling under the relentless heat of the sun, especially as the gully was out in the open.

Gunn worked with both the spade and his hands, scooping away the sand carefully as archaeologists do when taking great care to avoid damaging an ancient relic. As the full moon set, it was replaced by the muted grey glow of the first dawn light. Gunn stopped, covering the grave with his bisht, and went back to their camp, brewing coffee to wake up Doyle.

'Jesus, why'd you let me oversleep?' Doyle asked, rubbing his eyes. 'And coffee? This really is service. What've you been up to? You look like shit.'

'I've found the bodies!' Gunn announced, collapsing on the sand beside Doyle.

'You devious bastard! Where?'

Gunn told him of his night time walk and the eerie hand beckoning from the sand.

'Should've guessed they moved the bodies,' said Doyle when he'd finished, and quickly began to clear away breakfast. 'Let's see what you've found, before it gets too hot.'

Minutes later they stood staring down into the pit Gunn had dug and its sad, grisly contents.

'Over there, on the other side of the depression,' Gunn pointed, 'there's a patch of deep sand, which looks like it isn't affected by the seasonal rain running down from the wadi. I thought we'd get all four skeletons out of the gully, lay them out here for examination and photos and then re-inter them in that deep sand there.'

'Any clues yet as to what happened?' Doyle asked.

'Yes,' John sighed, 'like we thought, they were all murdered; at least this one was – the one whose hand I saw last night - look,' Gunn lifted the skull and turned it slightly, revealing two bullet holes.

'Poor bastards, they never knew what hit 'em.'

It took them two days to gather the four skeletons - their uniforms, their weapons and four sets of dog tags - and lay them out on the even surface of the depression. The first soldier, whom Gunn had found, had been shot through the head; another had no signs of gunshot wounds, which suggested that he might have been stabbed to death. The other two had clear signs of a multitude of bullet holes in the remains of their desert combat clothing, which indicated that they had probably been killed with an Armalite - set to 'automatic'.

Gunn and Doyle carefully photographed

everything, took two samples of hair and skin from each skeleton - Doyle carrying one set and Gunn the other, in case one of them shouldn't make it back - and recorded the exact location of the grave. Then they set about burying each soldier in his own grave.

'What d'ya reckon they'll tell the families of these guys?' Doyle asked, as he paused for breath.

'That's up to the Commanding Officer of the Regiment to decide. At least they won't be MIA anymore. Is it true the Americans never stop looking until every MIA is accounted for? That you still have people searching for World War 2 MIAs?'

'We do, and for hundreds of MIAs in Vietnam, Cambodia and Laos – mostly pilots shot down.'

'If it were me,' Gunn continued, 'I'd tell the families they were ambushed by an Iraqi patrol. The less said about this the better. The futility of their deaths…' he trailed off.

'Guess it depends how all this ends…'

As dusk turned to night again, the last of the graves was filled in and, once again, they stood in silence for two minutes with heads bowed, as they thought of the four young soldiers who'd been so cruelly slaughtered. That night they set up a satcom dish and sent a full report to Alan Paxton on the British Base at Basrah Airport.

## CHAPTER 17

What's the update on Mary, Barry?' Miles asked as he hurried into the Operations Centre.

'About to flee the Country for Rio; you might like to listen to this; Sigint recorded it at GCHQ a little while ago. Can you run it again, Terry?' Mary Panter's and Steve Harker's voices carried around the room, discussing the car chase and the move to Plan B.

'He sounds pissed off,' Terry concluded. 'Not surprised; she's a bit of a loose cannon!'

'Luckily for us. What time is the flight to Rio?' Miles asked.

'21.30 tonight from Terminal 3,' answered Mary Probert. Miles turned to Claudine.

'And your pre-op briefing?'

'All done by Peter Stone, and I'm booked on the TAM Linhas Aéreas flight, which leaves just after the BA flight but calls in at Sao Paulo first.'

'Do you speak any Portugese?' Miles asked.

'Only a little; my Spanish is pretty good though.'

'Peter's made it quite clear that you're only to watch from a distance and report on Soames' and Mary's movements – if he's there - yes?'

'Yes, sir.'

'Good; now we just have to wait and see what Gunn's turned up in the desert.' The informal meeting broke up and Claudine alone remained to listen to the updates from Pat Scarsdale and David Dewbury on the houseboat. Miles returned to his office and sent an encrypted email to Wu Hong Bo, BID's in-country agent in Beijing, briefing him on the taped conversation between Harker and Panter and telling him to watch Harker's movements. Next he put a call in to Sir Marcus Lord, the Governor of the Bank of England, who he hoped could offer advice on how to retrieve embezzled funds from Brazilian bank accounts.

*

Sir Leo Hugues, Commissioner of the Royal St Vincent Police, was sitting in his office discussing with his lawyers how best to answer the charges being brought against him by the St Vincent Parliament's Independent Commission Against Corruption. It was a windless day; the fan was broken, the air in his office hanging closely about them, and he was sweating profusely, beads trickling down his bald head. His private mobile rang.

'This is Hugues.'

'It's Jesus Garcia.'

'Uh, please excuse me, gentlemen - a personal call from my wife.' Sir Leo dabbed pointlessly at his forehead with a drenched handkerchief. The two lawyers picked up their briefcases and left the office.

'Go on, Jesus.'

'I need to know if you've opened that bank account for me. Also I need your account number so I can make arrangements for the transfer of funds.'

'Jus' wait... I have the information you want in my briefcase,' Sir Leo delved amongst the papers in his case. 'Here we are; it's the Eastern Caribbean Central Bank on Bay Street. It's in the name of Señor Jesus Garcia; the account number is 876325004 and the sort code is 563-40-21. My bank is the Grenadines National Bank on Market Street; the account is 16547832 and the sort code is 15-09-43.'

'..43; OK, got all that.'

'So, what's happening? Is everythin' movin' forward as planned?'

'Everything's fine; we expect the Shark to join us within the next week. My previous employer has no idea of the connection between us. You'll soon be able to resign with dignity and an assured pension; it's all in sight.'

'That's good news. How…' but the line was dead before Sir Leo could finish.

At GCHQ, the duty Sigint officer rewound what he'd just heard and played the call back to the Operations Centre in Kingsroad House.

*

Gunn and Doyle were ready to leave the wadi an hour before sunrise on their fourth day in the desert. 'What does your GPS show?' Gunn asked Doyle before they set off.

'135° and a distance of.......er...... 418 miles.'

'Me too; okay let's go,' they set off, taking it in turns to lead and select a route. They soon discovered that the grain of the desert appeared to run from east to west. Their course to Basrah in southern Iraq was directly across the grain, causing them to divert around deep wadis and canyons as steep as fortresses.

For every five miles they travelled in the right direction, they covered a further five diverting around impassable obstacles. After eight hours of dust-choking, bone-shaking travel across the Martian terrain, they'd barely covered 50 miles; they had over 350 to go. At their current rate, they would run out of fuel before they'd covered little more than 200 miles in the right direction. The only alternative was to ride to the east until they hit one of the roads and head right into the Iraqi heartland. It was the only way they could see of making better progress, and offered the possibility of buying or stealing more fuel for their bikes. It was midday; they rode down into a deep wadi to find some shade.

'If this map is accurate, we should hit a road of some sort in about another ten miles. It heads roughly south, good enough for us anyway, ending up at some place called Ash Shabakah,' Gunn said, wiping his sweat off the map casing. He pulled off his keffiyah, which was so wet it was beginning to rub the flesh around his face.

'Just where I always wanted to go,' Doyle joked dryly.

'Oh, shit!'

'What's wrong?'

'I'm burning on my face - badly.'

'Where's your factor 40?'

'Coming out through my pores.'

After a pause to check over the bikes, refill the tanks from the cans in the side panniers and take a frugal sip of water, they set off again, with Gunn leading. They reached the road in less than seven miles; they left the bikes in a shallow depression and went to recce it from the crest of a sand dune. It appeared completely deserted.

'What do we do if we see a vehicle?'

'Not sure yet,' Gunn murmured, squinting through his binoculars. 'Hide, I reckon.'

'Suits me; shall I take the lead?'

'Sure,' they started the bikes and drove down onto the tarmac road. Fortunately, there was a southerly breeze, so their first encounter after nearly half-an-hour's unimpeded progress in the approximately right direction was preceded by a dust cloud, giving them ample time to take cover behind a fold in the ground. The vehicle was a truck towing a trailer tanker behind it.

'Bet it's loaded with petrol,' Gunn remarked glumly, as they watched it disappear.

Later, as the light started to fade, Gunn estimated that they were only some 20 miles from Ash Shabakah. They'd left the road six more times to avoid trucks, all of them driving south to north. As yet nothing had approached them from behind. They turned off the road and headed into the desert to find a place to stop for the night. There was no shortage of wadis in which to conceal themselves. The GPS showed that they had another 265 miles to go to Basrah.

'I'll be lucky if I get another 200 miles out of my bike. What about you?' Gunn asked, shrugging off his back-pack.

'Same; Jesus, what I'd give for a cold beer!' Doyle sighed, reluctantly opening his freeze-dried high-protein rations. 'Er, just to be devil's advocate, what do we do if we're jumped by Iraqi soldiers or…hostile Bedouin?'

'Well, that's impossible to predict, but the important thing is to get these photos and samples back to BID. If we're captured, they'll take everything off us so we'll have failed.'

'So we separate.'

'Yeah; if we get enough warning of a confrontation, I want you to hide and I'll try and cause a diversion and lead them away from you. Then just make sure you get to Basrah and hand over those samples.'

'It's a BID job; I'm the hired help - why don't I do the…'

'No; that's why it's my job.'

'OK, buddy...' Doyle knew it was pointless arguing. 'But if it pans out differently, and you get the chance to run, you go, right?'

'Right.'

It was pitch dark by 6.45 pm; by the time they'd eaten and discussed plans for the following day, it was almost ten. Once again, they wrapped themselves in their bishts, oblivious now to their own stench, and took turns on watch while the other slept. It was fitful sleep. The constant wild fluctuations in temperature, combined with the clammy cloth clasping their bodies for hours on end, had left their skin cracked, sore and itchy; and they were both badly burnt on their faces, their skin hot and taught. They set off again at three in the morning and reached the outskirts of Ash Shabakah forty minutes later.

Although the town was marked on the map, it was little more than a scattering of stalls, huts and mud-brick buildings clustered around a mosque. The streets were deserted and even the sleeping pye-dogs didn't lift their heads as the bikes, with their silenced engines, eased past. The road they were on was the town's main street and in less than five minutes they had left the last of the shacks and lean-to huts behind them. They struck back out into empty desert again, the road their only company. Within only five miles, that was leaving them too; the tarmac turned into a track and then finally petered out altogether amongst the dunes.

It was possibly the utter desolation all around them that made them careless. Whilst heading due east to get round a particularly steep-sided wadi, Gunn rode at speed over the crest of a wadi - and into full view of a group of six or seven military trucks and jeeps. The vehicles were surrounded by a ragged collection of men - some in Bedouin clothing and others in varying forms of military combat dress. The group were about 400 yards away; the men were all armed and they'd seen Gunn, but not Doyle, travelling behind, who had responded instantly to Gunn's urgent signal to stop.

Gunn quickly scrambled back over the crest, where Doyle was crouched beside his bike. During their briefing by Alan Paxton, he had warned them that the Three Gulf Wars - the Iraqis had always counted the Iraq/Iran war, which lasted almost ten years, as the First Gulf War, 1991 as the Second and 2003 the Third - had resulted in bands of soldiers forming, men who'd never been paid or discharged from military service, left to fend for themselves. Various areas of Iraq's deserted western sector were awash with abandoned military vehicles, guns, tanks and piles of AK47s, which had been thrown away as starving Iraqi soldiers eagerly surrendered to Coalition Forces during the Second and Third Gulf Wars. Alan had warned them that some of these lost soldiers had joined forces with the Bedouin to roam the 'empty quarter,' arming themselves from this discarded weaponry, preying on Bedouin caravans or any worthwhile vehicle and its cargo making use of the few roads that crossed the desert.

'Shit! Fucking stupid, careless…' Gunn panted, falling down beside Doyle. 'We only have a few more seconds. I saw about seven vehicles and 20 men - some dressed like us, others in uniform - all armed. You back-track, go to the west and then continue to Basrah. You have the satcom radio. I'll see you in Basrah… Go! Now!'

'You be there, John!' Without hesitating, Doyle floored the accelerator down the reverse side of the crest and vanished into a wadi.

Gunn rode back to the crest into full view of the bandits, then turned east and rode along it. Although vehicle engines had been started, the gang had been caught by surprise just like Gunn, but that didn't stop some of them taking a couple of shots at him, one of which whined past like an angry mosquito.

Gunn chose his route with even more care than previously, realising that if he lost his bike he would be at the mercy of the motorised Iraqis. The crest led down into a depression and then the terrain appeared to offer a less corrugated southerly route. Just before he dipped down out of sight of the gang, he stopped and looked back. Three of the jeeps were following him, the three trucks were still stationary, and one 4WD vehicle was heading towards the spot where he and Doyle had been spotted. Gunn pulled his Armalite out of a sheath he'd fashioned from some of the webbing of his parachute before burying it. Another shot zipped close by him, fanning his face with the warmth of its trajectory; he dipped below the crest-line and headed for the plain that opened out in front of him. The soft sand of the ridge he'd been on gave way to a rock-hard surface, which made the going easier, but the advantage also applied to the jeeps following him. Just as he thought that they might abandon their pursuit, the rear tyre of the bike burst.

'Fuck!' Gunn screamed at the desert. He scoured the desert around him frantically; to his right was another wadi, which might just reduce the odds against him. He thumped down into it on the flat tyre. The base of the wadi was about 40 yards wide and the sides rose up at a gentle gradient, offering little cover in the wadi itself, but ideal for what was quickly taking shape in Gunn's mind. The jeeps were still about half a mile to his rear as he entered the wadi.

Once down in the bottom of the wadi, Gunn jumped off the bike and removed all the essential equipment from it. He opened his back-pack and removed a pre-prepared half-pound Semtex charge, detonator and timer, which he wedged under the saddle between the twin exhaust pipes. He set the timer for five minutes and then jogged quickly down the wadi leaving obvious footprints in the sand leading away from the bike. He walked back on a different tack, sweeping away the footprints he made with his bisht. Then he shouldered his back-pack, picked up his Armalite and the other equipment and hurried up the other side of the wadi on hard ground, leaving no footprints. The direction he'd chosen would place the sun behind him and in the eyes of anyone down by the scrambler bike.

The ridge of the wadi was littered with boulders, which offered both a hiding place and protection from small arms fire, but little, if any, from the throbbing midday heat. Gunn opened his back-pack again and removed two spare magazines of 5.56mm ammunition and another Semtex charge, into which he jabbed a timer pencil and detonator. He pulled out his watch from the loose-fitting thob and replaced it on his wrist; a five minute timer on the charge......too long, or too short? The first of the three jeeps breached the ridge and descended into the wadi; two men in the front and one in the back, armed with an AK47.

The second jeep appeared; they spotted the bike and accelerated towards it to be the first on the scene for any plundering. Three minutes gone; every breath Gunn took scorched the inside of his mouth. The jeep had now stopped right beside the bike and two men got out. The second jeep came forward more cautiously and pulled up behind the first one. The third jeep appeared over the ridge, drove a further 50 yards into the wadi and stopped. One minute to go; the first two men out of the jeep were bending over the bike, examining it. A shout marked the discovery of one of the spare water containers, which was held aloft; 30 seconds to detonation... the men picked the bike up and carried it to the back of their jeep, where a third man helped them load it onto the back; 10 seconds... Gunn steadied the blade of the Armalite front sight on the head of the driver of the third jeep some 70 yards away, ensuring that the change lever was set to single shot; zero!

Gunn's shot was smothered by the explosion of the Semtex charge, which tore through the stillness. The area below Gunn, around what had been his bike and two jeeps, had disappeared under a black cloud of smoke and flames. The driver of the third jeep had fallen forward over the wheel and the man beside him was standing up, trying to drag him out of the seat. It made him an easy target and Gunn dropped him with his second shot. A third man in the jeep jumped out, leaving his weapon behind, and ran, with difficulty in the soft sand, up the slope of the wadi. Gunn's third shot hit him just as he reached the crest. A pitiable breeze, cowed by the livid sun, slowly ushered the smoke away from what was left of the two jeeps and Gunn's bike. There were five bodies - recognisable as such; the other two or three were reduced to smouldering body parts. The jeeps were blackened wrecks and of the bike there was nothing left.

Gunn got up from his position on the rim of the wadi and, cradling his Armalite, walked back down to the scene of the explosion. After a cursory examination of the human and metal remains, he walked to the third jeep. His first shot had gone through the windscreen and then through the driver's neck; a second man had been hit in the right side as he tried to drag the driver out of his seat. He walked up the slope to the third occupant; his spine had been severed by Gunn's last shot. Back at the jeep, Gunn checked the fuel gauge; it was smashed. Then he discovered two jerrycans strapped to the back of the jeep, one of which was still full.

Gunn pulled the bodies out of the jeep and climbed in, pressing the starter; the engine responded immediately. He drove down past the burnt out wreckage and up the other side of the wadi, collected his back-pack and water container and loaded it all into the jeep. Then he drove back up onto higher ground and tried Doyle on his short range radio; no success. He drove for a further five miles or so - the odometer was also broken - until he reached a deeper wadi, which offered some shelter. It was time for a reappraisal; his full second container held 8 litres of water, he had an adequate supply of ammunition for his Armalite and the smaller Glock 26, four, half-pound Semtex charges with detonators and timers, rations for four days, a jeep with an unknown quantity of fuel in its tank and a spare jerrycan with four gallons. Gunn opened the bonnet; he guessed that the four cylinder engine had a capacity of either 1.8 or 2 litres. In four wheel drive across country that would give him 15 miles to the gallon. That gave him 60 miles from the spare jerrycan and - with a bit of luck - another 30 or so from whatever was in the tank; the best case scenario was 100 miles. He checked the GPS; 215 miles to Basrah on a bearing of 95°.

Gunn shut the jeep's bonnet and pulled the map out of his back-pack, which he spread out on the hot metal. Fifty miles to the south-east, the map showed a conurbation called As Salman. Between him and As Salman, the map marked what appeared to be a fairly substantial tributary of the Euphrates. From As Salman, there was a road which headed east on a bearing of 65° to a place called As Samawah, which lay on the main road between Baghdad and Basrah.

He had enough fuel to get him to As Salman - provided he was able to cross the river. As it was the non-rainy season, he hoped it would either be a dried-up riverbed or diminished enough to cross in the jeep. Even if his fuel projections were on the pessimistic side, he didn't have enough fuel to drive across-country to As Samawah. In As Salman he would have to steal or buy fuel; he had £100 in Iraqi Dinar notes, which should be more than enough. Gunn folded up the map, pulled on his goggles and headed east on a bearing of 95° towards As Salman.

*

After a substantial breakfast from the buffet, Harker left his hotel and walked the short distance from Jianguomen to the British Embassy at 11, Guang Hua Lu. As he turned into Guang Hua Lu, he immediately spotted the pink-painted facade of the Embassy with its steel-gated entrance and Peoples' Liberation Army sentry on duty. At the side gate into the Embassy courtyard, Harker showed his government pass to the duty officer in the small kiosk, who released the lock on the gate. In reception he was met by a uniformed security officer to whom he once again showed his government pass.

'Who do you have an appointment to see, sir?' the officer asked politely.

'The Ambassador,' Harker replied abruptly, unused to not being recognised.

'Sir Martin Bannerman left the Embassy ten minutes ago on his way to the Chinese Ministry for Foreign Affairs. He is not expected back here for the rest of the day. Are you sure you had an appointment, sir?'

'I'm the British Prime Minister's Head of Security and I'm here to examine the arrangements made by this Embassy for his visit. Now I'd like to know who is in charge of those arrangements and I'd like to see them now.'

'Of course, sir,' the officer answered calmly. He managed to insert just the perfect level of inflection into the word 'sir' to indicate a total lack of respect. 'But we understood your visit was next week... sir.'

'Change of plan. Who do I need to speak to?' Harker growled, increasingly agitated.

'The Defence Attaché, sir. Let me see if he's in his office.' Unperturbed, the officer unclipped a mobile phone from a brace on his left breast pocket and pressed a speed dial number. 'Bill Maynard, General; I have a Mr Harker from 10 Downing Street in reception. He wishes to see you about the PM's visit.'

While he waited, Harker seethed with anger at the guard's frustrating lack of urgency. To make things worse, two locally employed Chinese girls at the reception desk were having a subdued snigger, which he felt sure was at his expense.

'The Defence Attaché is on his way down, sir,' Bill Maynard announced in a purposely pompous fashion. 'Do make yourself comfortable in the waiting area over there,' he indicated some extremely uncomfortable looking, overstuffed armchairs.

Harker paced back and forth fitfully, incensed at the lack of VIP treatment. He'd give this clapped-out Defence Attaché a piece of his mind that would shake this fucking bunch of Diplomatic Service cretins out of their self-satisfied torpor, Harker thought to himself, just as the double doors from the secure area of the Embassy opened and a youthful DA, wearing SAS wings on the right shoulder of his open-necked shirt, strode out.

'Good heavens! It's Quiller, isn't it? What on earth are you doing here? Where's this man Harker who wants to see me?'

Harker was left speechless; it felt as though someone had punched him very hard in the gut and for a moment he was unable to get his breath; standing in front of him was Major General David Pennyfeather, his first Troop Commander in Bravo Squadron of 22 SAS; a man who knew him as well as, if not better than anyone else.

'No, I'm, uh, Steve Harker, sir,' he managed to stammer, suddenly feeling wretchedly chastened - and utterly cornered.

'You're joking, Quiller; I'd recognise you and your voice anywhere after the number of times you were marched in front of me on disciplinary matters. You don't even walk like Trooper Harker; he had a slight limp from an IRA bullet he stopped in Armagh. So what's all this guff about the PM's visit? We're expecting the advance party next week, but that's being headed up by Chief Superintendent Bruce Lochart of SO14. Why are you here, a week early, calling yourself Harker?

Two or three other people in the reception area were now listening to what was going on and the security officer, Bill Maynard, walked over.

'Is there a problem, sir?'

'Not sure, Bill,' the DA answered, studying

Harker's now puce face, 'but I think this man's an imposter. I was his Troop Commander for three years back in the late eighties; he isn't Steven Harker.'

'Very well, sir,' replied the delighted security officer, 'then we'll ask Mr Harker or whoever he thinks he is to wait while we do some thorough checking with London.'

In the space of a couple of minutes, Harker's whole fabricated world had collapsed around him. He had to get out of there. The main door had just opened to let in a young Chinese girl. Harker threw off Bill Maynard's grasp and dashed for the door, grabbing the girl as he fled through it and across the courtyard to the gate.

'Open the fucking gate or I'll break this girl's neck,' he screamed at the guard in the kiosk. The guard did as he was bidden, as the sobbing girl was dragged across the tarmac by the neck like a refuse sack. The gate opened, Harker threw her to one side and ran. The confused PLA sentry had no idea what to do and had no ammunition in his rifle anyway. The DA was the first to get to the girl, who was rigid with shock; he carried her back inside to Bill Maynard and ran upstairs to contact London.

## CHAPTER 18

It was just after 3am when the phone in the BID Operations Centre rang.

'Operations Centre, duty officer.'

'It's David Pennyfeather, Defence Attaché Beijing. I'm on secure speech; could you patch me through to Miles Thompson? Or Sir Jeremy Hammond, if he's unavailable – it's urgent.'

'Just a moment, sir.' The operator quickly transferred the call through to Miles' home in Chelsea.

'Hello…? Thompson.' Miles' voice was heavy with sleep. He dragged himself out of bed to take the call.

'Miles, it's David Pennyfeather in Beijing. Really sorry to wake you but this is urgent. We've just had a man walk into the Embassy masquerading as Steven Harker, the PM's Security boss.'

'How do you know it's not Harker?' Miles was wide awake now. How the hell did this guy know about the plot?

'His real name's Quiller; he was a Sergeant in my troop in B Squadron of 22 SAS. Granted, he and Harker looked very similar but the two were like chalk and cheese in character. Apart from that they had different accents; Quiller comes from Nottingham; Harker was a scouser. And Harker had a noticeable limp from a bullet wound in his left leg. This man had no limp at all and still retained traces of his Nottingham accent - though he's tried to bury it under some sort of pseudo-southern accent. What's going on?'

'Did you confront him with his real identity?' Miles asked, pacing up and down his kitchen.

'Yes; I recognised him as Quiller as soon as I saw him. I'm sorry, in hindsight that was probably stupid.'

'Possibly, but how the hell were you to know. Has Wu Hong Bo been in touch with you?'

'I'm told he's just arrived in reception.'

'Shit! Just a few minutes too late; look, he'll explain what this is all about. Where's Quiller now?'

'He's done a runner. I've alerted the Chinese that he's dangerous and to be stopped at all costs. They've assured me that all airports, rail stations and ports are on the lookout; shouldn't be too hard to spot a tall white man, even with the all the tourists out for the Olympics. I'll do everything I can, Miles.'

*

Having no idea of the reliability of the jeep he'd acquired, Gunn drove it at a cautious pace over the rugged terrain. It was nearly 5pm when he reached the wadi through which the tributary flowed, but at his current position the sides were far too steep to drive down. Gunn turned east along the course of the wadi, as the sun set behind him, searching for a less precipitous approach to a fordable point on the river, which looked as though it was no more than a foot deep.

His caution paid off, though for a different reason. The wadi suddenly curved sharply to the south, revealing a route down to the river and, parked up in a hollow square by the bank of the river, were the same trucks he'd spotted earlier with the bandits. Gunn backed the jeep out of sight and went forward on foot to get a closer look. He crouched down on the hard, rock-strewn ground and focused his binoculars on the vehicles. It looked as though they'd made camp for the night, as it was now getting darker by the minute.

Gunn was just about to wriggle back out of view when his binoculars steadied on the nearest truck, which had its back towards him. Two men were inside, moving something towards the truck's drop-down back. One of them jumped down, released the pins on either side of the back and lowered it. The man still inside then pushed the load towards the man on the ground. Gunn's stomach muscles tightened involuntarily. Emerging from the back of the truck was a scrambler bike. Doyle was either dead or very soon would be.

Gunn hurried back to his jeep, emptied his back-pack and then selected two, half-pound Semtex charges, which he cut in half. He put these in his pack with detonators and pencil timers. He then taped two magazines together for the Armalite, threw in the First Aid kit, his torch and a spare magazine for the Glock, then pushed his bayonet into a sheath on his right ankle by the Glock. He cut off a two foot length of nylon parachute cord; at each end of it he tied a 5.56 mm round of ammunition, creating a garrotte. He grabbed the Armalite, slung the pack over his shoulder, scrambled down the bank of the wadi onto the flatter river course and jogged on the rock-hard earth towards the vehicles, now lit in silhouette by a fire in the centre of the square.

When he was no more than 100 yards away, Gunn slowed to a walk and, keeping the nearest truck between himself and whatever was going on inside the square, he worked his way forward until he could see what was happening. Seated round the fire, Gunn counted eleven men, their light banter punctuated by outbursts of laughter. About ten yards away from the fire was a metal stake driven into the ground, with a hunched figure bound to its base; it was Doyle. Around his feet and legs they'd piled firewood; for after-dinner entertainment, they would burn him alive - if he was still alive. White hot fury started thumping in Gunn's temples. He peered more closely at his friend; he was either unconscious or dead already, as he hung limply from his bindings.

Gunn stood upright, flicked the change lever on the Armalite from 'repeat' to 'auto' and squeezed the trigger, swinging from right to left across the huddle of men. The first magazine emptied; he switched to the second, cocked the rifle and squeezed the trigger again. Two men on the left of the group reached for their weapons, but were almost ripped in half by the scimitar of fire.

And then there was silence, a thick, oozing quietness that Gunn felt as if he could reach out and touch; only the cooking fire cackled defiantly. Gunn moved in closer.

'Aaaeeee!!!'

A man who'd played dead suddenly leapt to his feet, drawing a pistol, but a burst from the Armalite threw him backwards onto the fire. Silence again. There was no movement from any of the vehicles. Before going to Doyle, Gunn quickly went from vehicle to vehicle, firing into the back of them, in case there was anyone else hiding inside. Satisfied they were alone, he went to Doyle and cut away the leather thongs lashing him to the stake. He gently laid him on the ground, hardly daring to examine him for fear of what he would find. He'd been beaten into unconsciousness across his back and on the soles of his feet - a traditional form of Arabic torture, usually followed, in due course, by the removal of the genitals. Luckily they hadn't gone that far. Gunn's First Aid kit was woefully inadequate but it did have a tube of antiseptic salve and four ampoules of morphine, one of which he injected into Doyle.

Gunn made his friend as comfortable as possible, prayed that the fire wouldn't attract any other desert marauders and then ran back to his jeep, which he drove along the wadi edge until he reached the track down to the river and parked up beside the other vehicles. A quick search of the trucks turned up some blankets and items of clothing. With those, and having stripped the clothing off the dead men, Gunn made a mattress of sorts onto which he lifted Doyle and then covered him with the blankets. He then rebuilt Doyle's intended pyre beside him, carrying burning embers over from the other fire to light it.

When he'd done all he could, Gunn boiled some water on the fire and made very strong coffee to help him stay awake through the night.

*

After calling at Sao Paulo, Claudine's flight landed in Rio at 3am, but in a city that rarely slept, there appeared to be no less traffic on the streets or pedestrians, as they teemed between nightclubs, bars and all-night shops. Before leaving London, Peter Stone, her controller, had sent her to a hairdresser, where she'd had her distinctive, stripped pine-blonde hair dyed a dark, mahogany brown so she looked more like the Brazilian women. As she hurried through the airport, she barely drew a second glance. Exhausted after the flight, Claudine gratefully sunk into the back of her taxi, directing the driver in Spanish, which he understood well enough, to the Hotel Ipanema Plaza. She checked in, hurried to her room, set her alarm and then collapsed into a dreamless sleep.

*

'Oh, come in Miles,' Sir Jeremy Hammond emerged from his private washroom, drying his face with a towel. He'd attended an overlong lunch at the Travellers' Club in Pall Mall, where he'd been asked to make a farewell speech for its departing Chairman. 'My old liver can't take these lunches anymore. How some of the members manage to eat there every day I really don't know. Now, are we in position to yet to alert the PM?'

'Yes, I believe so; we're at that stage where we'll be damned if we do and damned if we don't, frankly,' Miles admitted, taking off his glasses and rubbing the red indents they'd made either side of his nose.

'Wasn't it ever thus when dealing with politicians? OK,' Sir Jeremy continued, joining Miles in an armchair around the coffee table, 'bring me up to date and then I'll go and see the PM.'

'This goes back to the Gulf War in 91; Sgt Quiller of 22 SAS was facing a court martial for embezzlement of mess funds. To avoid this he hatched a plan with his close friend Corporal Soames...'

'That's our Soames?'

'It is; Quiller planned to take on the identity of Cpl Harker, in the same Squadron, who was a dead ringer, it seems. He submitted a totally false report on return from their mission, in which he claimed that their Landrover had been blown up by a mine, killing Quiller and the driver, Miller, and injuring Soames. He also claimed that the four men in the other Landrover had been killed by the Iraqis. He returned to the Coalition Base in Saudi Arabia with Soames, was awarded the Queen's Gallantry Medal and left the Army.'

'Umm-hmm...'

'The rest you know about; his success in the security business and appointment at Number 10. We believe that it was during his time as a security adviser in the Cabinet Office, with access to the personal files of civil servants, that he, Soames and Mary Panter decided to blackmail seven people, all with something to hide, into siphoning off funds into a bank account – this included Paul Manton, David Chesham, John Cornwall and Clive Sterling.'

'And the other three?'

'Venetia Akehurst, Andrew Barton and George Peterson.'

'Hm. And so what did happen out in Iraqi?'

'Quiller executed Harker and Miller – shot them in the back of the head. Gunn and Barnes found Quiller's

Landrover some distance away in near perfect condition. Quiller, and Soames, I expect, then executed the other four SAS soldiers. Again, Gunn found the bodies and evidence that they'd been shot. They think one of them had had his throat cut...'

'Bloody monsters!' Sir Jeremy grimaced, radiating revulsion.

'Yes...' Miles paused and there was a moment of silence, an unspoken mark of respect for the murdered soldiers.

'Go on…'

'Gunn and Barnes have collected samples from all six bodies for DNA matching on their return. As we speak they're making their way to Basrah across the arse end of nowhere - a hellhole desert even the Iraqis won't live in - to meet up with Alan Paxton at the British Base. Once they hand over the evidence it'll be flown back here immediately for analysis. We're certain it'll confirm that Harker is in fact Quiller, though it has also just been confirmed by the Defence Attaché in Beijing...'

'What's the connection there?'

'David Pennyfeather - the DA - was Quiller's Troop Commander in 22 SAS.'

'Ah, good. That's vital if I'm to convince the PM before we have those DNA samples.'

'Well if he doesn't believe you, tell him his security chief has done a runner and is on the loose in Beijing.'

'What's happening about that?'

'David Pennyfeather's alerted the Chinese and Wu Hong Bo's on the case, but Wu's no action man; the best person to find him is John Gunn, who's also fluent in Mandarin. I'd like to brief the Middle East AD,

Mike Dimmock, and have his controller, David Morris, fly out to Basrah to brief Gunn for an op in Beijing to find Quiller. And I want to go too, to make a judgement on Gunn's fitness to go straight onto another assignment.'

'Soames and Panter; where are they at the moment?

'In Rio, being watched by Claudine.'

'Alright; you go to Basrah, if that's what you feel is necessary...'

'I do.'

'...and I'll make an appointment to visit Number 10.'

*

Claudine awoke to a day of torrential rain which, the waitress at breakfast told her, was normal for that time of winter in Rio. At her briefing with Peter Stone, he'd told her that the BID in-country agent, Esmeralda Sanchez, would call on her at the hotel and provide her with her personal choice of weapon. She was just finishing her breakfast when she was paged by the hotel PA system. Claudine went to reception, where she was presented with a package that had been left by a Señora Sanchez. She returned to her room and opened it. It was a Colt .45 automatic with one spare full magazine. Wanting to come across as a young professional, she dressed in a fitted skirt suit, low-cut blouse and heels, dropping her Colt into a large, expensive-looking handbag. Then she waited for a hiatus in the rain; when it came, she walked from the hotel to the Rua Berata Ribeiro. She stopped outside number 35, a smart, 12-storey apartment block. In the reception area, off to one side, there was a marketing agent's office, which stated that it was the sole agent for the remaining apartments. Claudine went in, greeted the female receptionist in passable Portuguese and then asked if she might speak in Spanish.

'Of course, Señora.'

'I see you have three, two-bedroom apartments remaining. Would it be possible to look at one of them please?'

'Yes, Señora. Our manager will be free in a few minutes. Take a seat in the reception area; he will be with you shortly.'

'Thank you,' Claudine went back out to the reception, where she struck up a conversation with the male concierge. 'I have friends who've bought an apartment here by the name of Garcia. I'm hoping to buy an apartment too; I would be most grateful if you could tell me the number of their apartment, so that I can call on them a little later.' With practised nonchalance, she twiddled a small gold pendant that dangled invitingly down her cleavage, and met his gaze with wide-eyed innocence. Leaning on the counter, she could see that the man had a list of all the apartments and their occupants under a sheet of Perspex, but his arm rested across the page.

'I'm not really allowed to give you that information, but for this one time... why not,' he smiled broadly; so did Claudine. The Garcias owned apartment 54 on the fifth floor.

'Thank you so much,' Claudine winked at him, then turned to the manager of the marketing office as he joined them. 'Señor...?'

'Almera, Senora; Roberto Almera.' They shook hands.

'I believe some friends of mine, Señor and Señora Garcia have just moved into their new apartment.'

'Yes, you're right,' he purred, guiding her to the lifts. 'Señor Garcia has been here now for about two or three weeks and Señora Garcia arrived last night.'

'Apartment 54, they told me; they're so pleased with it.'

'That's right; this way,' Señor Almera led the way out of the lift and opened the door to apartment 71. It was a really attractive apartment and Claudine enjoyed looking round it. She cooed with enthusiasm over the features he pointed out and had it not been for the price tag of £450,000, might have shown more genuine interest. Instead, she thanked him graciously and made sure to get a business card; it would be pushing it to ask for the Garcia's phone number but she could call the building's concierge and ask to be put through.

Back out on the street, she took out her mobile phone and did just that; no answer. She gave it five minutes, then rang again; still no answer. She walked back towards the apartment block and leaned against a wall outside, from where she could keep an eye on the concierge through its glass entrance, pretending to talk on the phone. After a few minutes, the concierge moved away from his position behind the counter and four people had just come out of one of the three lifts. Claudine ducked inside and made quickly for the lift, jamming her foot between the doors to stop it closing. She pressed the five button. A few muted moments later, the lift doors opened and she walked along the corridor towards number 54, removing her lock-pick from her bag as she went. Outside the apartment, she dialled the number once more and heard the phone ringing inside the apartment. There was no response. It was reasonable to suppose, she thought, that the apartment was empty.

The door to the apartment only had one five lever lock, the development relying mostly on pricey street level security, which Claudine picked within a few minutes, glancing nervously around her as she did. She gave the door a push, waiting silently for any reaction; there was no sound of any movement inside. She put her hand into her bag and eased off the safety on the automatic.

It was another three-bedroom apartment, though considerably larger than the one she'd seen on the seventh floor. The front door opened onto a long hallway, at the end of which was a door, standing ajar. The floor of the hall was tiled; Claudine quietly slipped off her heeled pumps and put them in her bag, taking out her Colt at the same time. She nudged the far door. It opened onto a large lounge-cum-dining area, with floor-to-ceiling plate glass windows overlooking the beach. On her right, the dining area was open to the kitchen, which also had access from a door in the hallway. There was a door on her left, which presumably led to a bedroom; Claudine pushed it open. The double bed was unmade but there was nothing else remarkable.

She went back into the hall and checked the other doors; two more bedrooms, a bathroom and a small toilet by the front door. Neither of the beds in the other two rooms had been used. There was one more room to check, the en-suite bathroom to the main bedroom; she retraced her steps. The door to the bathroom was open a crack. Claudine pushed it open with her elbow, holding the Colt firmly in both hands, her heart pounding so hard she felt as though it was being piped through a sound system into all the rooms. She stopped abruptly. Mary Panter was lying in a bath of bloody water. Claudine lowered the gun, releasing her breath slowly. And then she clearly heard the front door being unlocked, opened and shut. She was no longer alone in the apartment.

*

Running through the streets of Beijing back to his hotel, Quiller had lost all the confidence and bravado of the Head of Security at Downing Street. The game was up, and although he had planned that this trip to Beijing would be the first step in his eventual disappearance, he had not expected to do it as a criminal on the run, but in the comforting cocoon of five star hotels and first class flight compartments. Luckily, he had a small head start; he hadn't told anyone where he intended to stay in Beijing.

In the hotel foyer, no one took any notice of him as he hurried across to the lifts. In his room, he opened his suitcase and removed the backpack and the clothes he had purposely packed for his disappearance. The airline ticket to Hong Kong was now useless, as the airports would be closely watched. He discarded his suit and changed into slacks, polo shirt and trainers. He tore up Harker's passport together with the airline ticket and dropped the pieces, along with his alias' driver's license and credit cards, into the plastic laundry bag provided by the hotel. His new passport was in the name of David Morgan, a name he'd carefully selected on a visit to Wales with the PM the previous year, where he'd had access, during the preparation for the visit, to the records of orphaned children who had died in childhood. David Morgan had been born in 1961, his own birth year, and when no one was looking, Quiller had removed the birth certificate, which he'd then used to apply for a new passport.

He made a thorough check of his room, slung his small backpack over his shoulder and made for the fire exit at the end of the corridor. On arrival at the hotel, he'd noticed that the stairs were fairly close to the hotel entrance, much closer than the bank of lifts, which were on the other side of the foyer. On reaching the foot of the stairs, he went into the hotel's travel agent, where he bought both a map of the city and another of China.

Quiller needed time to think and plan. He walked out of the hotel, dumped the plastic laundry bag in a litter bin and turned north along Chaoyangmen Nan Dajie until he found a coffee shop, settling himself in a corner table at the back of the room. He dug out his mobile phone and wallet. He'd made sure that he had plenty of Chinese yuan before leaving London. He counted out the notes; a little over 6,000 yuan. That was about £500; it should be enough for bribes to get him to Hong Kong, he reasoned, as he dialled Mary Panter's number. He looked at his watch; it would be about midnight in Rio so he'd probably wake her, but that didn't matter. The phone rang, but there was no answer.

'Shit!' he banged his phone down on the table, instantly regretting it as he drew looks from some of the other punters. He unfolded his map of China and scoured it for an escape route. Motorway 107 went all the way from Beijing to Hong Kong, 1,200 miles to the south. Quiller finished his coffee, paid and set off to catch a bus to the south of the city, where he intended to bribe a truck driver to take him to Hong Kong, or at least as far as possible in that direction.

*

Sir Jeremy Hammond's car was waved through the gates into Downing Street and pulled up outside Number 10. The PM was leaving shortly for his summer holiday, but had agreed to the visit when he'd been informed that it concerned the safety of both him and his family. Sir Jeremy was shown straight into the PM's private office.

'I know that you're keen to be on your way Prime Minister, but I need to inform you of an ongoing investigation that concerns your Head of Security, Steven Harker.'

'Why do you need to investigate Steven?' the PM shot back irritably.

'Because he isn't Steven Harker. He's an impostor by the name of Quiller. We believe he murdered Harker, who was his doppelganger, by all accounts, during an SAS mission in the '91 Gulf War and assumed his identity to avoid a court martial for embezzlement.'

'Oh, come on, Jeremy; am I supposed to take this seriously?' Sir Jeremy had expected this reaction, and continued without acknowledging it.

'We will have proof positive within 48 hours, when DNA samples gathered by BID agents in Iraq from the bodies of the murdered SAS soldiers have been brought back to London for analysis. Mr Harker, who is currently in Beijing, made the mistake of calling at the British Embassy without checking the identity of the Defence Attaché, Major General David Pennyfeather, who was his Troop Commander in 22 SAS. David recognised him immediately, mainly because of his accent - Harker came from Liverpool and whereas Quiller comes from Nottingham.'

'So all you have at the moment in the way of proof is the word of one Defence Attaché who probably hasn't seen Harker or Quiller for twenty years. Do you not think that's a little insubstantial?' The PM was incredulous.

'No Prime Minister, I don't, as we place your safety and that of your family above all else. And unfortunately when David confronted him he made a run for it, grabbing a young Chinese girl as hostage and breaking her arm. The Chinese Minister for Foreign Affairs, Wan Fah Seng, has demanded an explanation for the assault from our Ambassador, Sir Martin Bannerman.

'Jesus… Steven? Uh, I mean…'

'Quiller. The report that Quiller submitted on return from his mission in Iraq stated that a mine blew up his Landrover, killing two of their four-man crew. Our agents found that Landrover in perfect condition and the two soldiers that Quiller buried both have bullet holes in the back of their skulls. The photographic evidence is already on its way over to us. Quiller also stated in his report that when he'd sought out one of the other four-man SAS teams for assistance, he found they'd been killed by the Iraqis…'

'Yes, I know all of this, it's in his, uh, personnel file.'

'Well they weren't killed by the Iraqis. They were all murdered by Quiller.'

'So you're telling me that the man I've relied on for my security and the security of my family is a serial killer? And…and BID agents in Iraq? Was this cleared by me?' The PM looked as though he'd aged ten years in the space of two minutes; he was holding on to the edge of his desk with a white-knuckled grip.

'Well let me answer your second question first. There are two agents in Iraq dealing with this mission, one of ours and one from the CIA. The mission was negotiated with the US Government and the Pentagon and cleared by your Foreign Secretary and Defence Secretary. As I said, we all have your safety uppermost in our minds.'

'My Head of Security is a serial killer?' the PM repeated, pulling off his tie and opening his top shirt button, small beads of sweat dappling his upper lip.

'I'm afraid so, and there's a great deal worse to come, but I'd prefer to leave that until we have cast iron evidence. However, I took the gamble and the responsibility of coming to you before we have that because, as I have said already…'

'My safety is your top priority, yes… Why wasn't all this discovered by BID when…he was appointed as my Head of Security?'

'You may remember, Prime Minister, that your Chief of Staff informed us that BID verification was not required as he personally had checked the veracity of Harker's military record and CV. That refusal is on record.'

'I see; so what happens now?'

'We find him and bring him to justice.'

'His trial will cause considerable embarrassment to the Government…..........and the SAS and families of the dead soldiers, of course.'

'Of course; unfortunately the conspiracy also extends into the Cabinet Office, so I expect a number of heads will roll when the full extent of it is revealed.'

'What are the chances that you may be wrong?'

'Less than zero.'

'Well, uh, thank you, Jeremy. I'm uh… I'm going to leave now. Listen, I'll make sure that the Chief of Staff allows BID to do its full vetting when I appoint another Head of Security.'

'If you'll permit me, top of my list for the job would be Chief Superintendent Bruce Lochart from the Met's SO14 unit.'

'Thank you, I'll bear that in mind,' the Prime Minister rose shakily still clutching the edge of his desk, indicating that the meeting was over.

# CHAPTER 19

The freezing cold night seemed endless to Gunn as he fought to preserve the fire and keep Doyle warm. Fortunately he'd found that one of the trucks was stacked with wood, which looked as though it might have been ransacked from one of the dilapidated wooden shacks back in Ash Shabakah. Doyle's pulse was steady, but he was either unconscious or in a deep, morphine-induced sleep. On more than one occasion Gunn had nodded off, only to awake with a jerk as his head fell forward, like an exhausted commuter. He smiled wryly at the thought; if only.

At last dawn crept over the eastern horizon and light spilled out over the desert. Gunn's first priority was to find the satcom radio. Luckily it was in the jeep with all the rest of the equipment they'd stripped from Doyle when they captured him, and it seemed as though it was untouched. Gunn unfolded the dish aerial, plugged it into the radio and switched it on. All the LEDs blinked to life while Gunn tuned the radio to their allocated frequency for day five of Op Raptor.

'Zero, this is Raptor One, radio check, over.' He repeated the signals contact procedure three times, adjusting the dish to get the maximum reading from the greatest number of satellites.

'Zero, OK, send over.'

'Thank Christ for that,' Gunn muttered, and then

he pressed the transmit button: 'Raptor One, Raptor Two seriously injured and in urgent need of medical treatment, roger so far, over.'

'Zero, roger, over.'

'My location - latitude 30° 47.26' longitude 44° 23.15'. Can you do a casevac from this location? Casevac only needed for Raptor Two as I can reach you within 24 to 48 hours, over.'

'Zero, roger – wait, out.'

While Gunn waited for the return transmission, he delved into the back of the jeep and retrieved all of Doyle's equipment. Clearly, the jeep was the property of the self-styled leader of the gang, who considered that the booty was his alone.

'Raptor One, this is Zero, over.'

'Raptor One, send, over.'

'Zero, all helicopters in use for major operation except one Lynx from HMS Ark Royal. Endurance is a maximum of 90 minutes. I estimate your position to be 220 miles from here. Helicopter available if you can get 50 miles closer, which will put you in range, over.'

'Raptor One, roger. It'll take me three hours to cover that distance, starting in ten minutes. Suggest you get the Lynx airborne to RV with me at.......wait....zero 900 hours, after I've sent you another GPS position. This will minimise delay in getting Raptor Two proper medical treatment, over.'

'Zero roger, wilco to your last. What are Raptor Two's injuries?'

'Raptor One, Iraqi army deserters tried to beat him to death. The injuries are to his back and soles of his feet. I'll contact you again when 50 miles closer, out.'

Gunn closed down the radio and examined the

jeep. It was a Toyota - always reliable - and looked newer than the one he'd arrived in so he transferred his kit across. He briefly switched on the ignition and was amazed to find that the petrol gauge registered half full. A last thorough search of the other vehicles turned up Doyle's water container and two more jerrycans of petrol.

Now all that remained was to transfer Doyle and his mattress into the back of the Toyota. Gunn moved the makeshift mattress first, piling the blankets up into rectangular heap, leaving Doyle cushioned by the rapidly warming sand. Then he carried his friend across his shoulders and laid him back out on the mattress. He stirred and groaned, showing signs of regaining consciousness, so Gunn quickly dug out another ampoule of morphine. He'd injected the first nearly twelve hours ago; the instructions stated that a minimum of six hours should elapse between injections. He jabbed a second ampoule into Doyle's arm, then fastened the jeep's canvas across the back to keep the sun off him. He arranged a light keffiyah over his face so that he wouldn't get burnt.

Moving quickly now, Gunn drove all three trucks close together and heaved the bodies of the Iraqis into one truck, followed by their AK47s, ammunition and RPG 7 grenade launchers. Then he placed a Semtex charge in each of the trucks, with the timer pencils snapped off at the five minute delay mark. He shut the jeep's tailgate and set off, driving it through the shallow river at the fording point and up the other side of the wadi. The first of the charges exploded as he reached the top of the wadi, followed quickly by the other two; the Iraqis and their trucks were burning fiercely in their own funeral pyre as Gunn lost sight of them in his rear-view mirror.

*

Gripping the Colt in both hands, Claudine stepped silently out of the gory bathroom and crept across the bedroom to the door leading into the lounge. Whoever had come into the apartment had gone into the kitchen and was making no effort to move about silently, which meant that it was either Mike Soames or...or...perhaps housekeeping? They were serviced apartments; it was possible… Oh God… Miles had specifically told her not to confront Soames, and with good reason. The gun started to slip in her damp palms, and her breath came in short gasps, barely able to keep up with her runaway heartbeat. If she blew this, like the records vault, she wouldn't just get a rap on the knuckles; it'd be game over. Had she become a liability? Oh Jesus… And yet she couldn't kill him; BID needed to use him to trace the embezzled funds and any other conspirators. She heard the sound of a kettle coming to the boil, then a cupboard being opened and the clink of crockery. Ordinary, domestic sounds; they seemed out of place. Was he making a cup of coffee? Claudine peeped round the edge of the door into the lounge; the room was empty. Her legs barely supporting her, she walked quickly across the lounge on the polished wooden floor, Colt still extended in front of her. Suddenly there was a crash from the kitchen as something fell and shattered on the tiled floor. Claudine froze.

'Oh shit!…' she breathed, steadying the Colt,

finger stroking the trigger, expecting Soames to appear at any second.

'Mierda!' It was a woman's voice.

Claudine blinked; a woman! It wasn't Soames! She swayed, suddenly feeling sick as the flash flood of adrenaline drained away. She swallowed hard and moved quickly and silently across the lounge into the hallway. In only a few minutes the woman would go into the main bedroom and discover the body in the bath and the very last thing that Claudine needed was to be caught up in a Brazilian police investigation. The door from the hallway into the kitchen was open. She peered round the edge of it; the woman had her back to her and was picking up pieces of broken china from the floor. Claudine took two quick paces to the front door, opened it and slipped through, leaving it ajar so that the latch wouldn't click shut. She hurried down the corridor until she was out of sight of the apartment door, than sat for a few minutes with her head between her legs, willing her heartbeat back to normal. Feeling better, she slipped her heels back on, walked down the stairs to the floor below to catch the lift - God forbid she'd escaped the apartment only to meet Soames on his way up - and hurried out of the building, pleased to be engulfed by the anonymous heave and bustle of the streets.

*

Through smiling and sign language, Quiller found a bus that was going south out of Beijing. It would take him to a town called Zhuo Zhuo, which was 40 miles to the south of Beijing and located right beside the

Motorway 107, which eventually ended up in Hong Kong. The bus was packed with people, their bags and parcels wedged into every available space, some with coups containing livestock. Three hours later, Quiller gratefully got off, leaving the stink of guano and curious stares to trundle off on their journey.

The map indicated that there was a petrol station somewhere nearby with a restaurant and parking space, which, he'd guessed, would be a stop-off point for truck drivers. It was now 3.30pm and Quiller was cripplingly hungry. He made his way along a minor road out of Zhou Zhou towards the autoroute. To his ashamed delight, he saw the golden arches of McDonald's looming over the squat building beside the petrol station; it was a small, familiar comfort in a lonely predicament. Half an hour later, hunger greasily sated, he walked out towards a row of trucks in the car park to negotiate a lift south towards Hong Kong. After three futile attempts to make the drivers understand what he wanted, he finally spotted a truck that had English as well as Chinese characters stencilled on its side. Even better, it had 'Hong Kong' written on its tailboard and a different number plate from the other trucks around it. The driver and his co-driver were standing by the front of the truck eating, using chopsticks to scoop rice out of small bowls. Quiller approached them.

'You go to Hong Kong?' he asked.

'Yes, go Hong Kong,' answered one of the drivers. Quiller had prepared a fee of 1,000 yuan equivalent of about £100, which he'd judged might be acceptable – He held out the 1,000 RMB made up of five 200 yuan notes.

'This for you,' he said, but the Chinese driver shook his head and held up the forefingers of both hands to indicate two. Quiller hadn't expected to have to negotiate the terms of his lift, but wisely, Quiller had some notes in reserve in his pocket; he wasn't going to show them what was in his wallet. He added a 500 yuan note.

'Okay now?' but a shake of the head indicated that it was not okay. Quiller added a 200 yuan note. When the driver shook his head again, he put all the notes back in his pocket and started to walk away.

'Is okay, is okay!'

'Shit,' Quiller muttered, 'I should have walked sooner.' He handed over the money and the three of them climbed into the front of the truck.

The two drivers took it in turns to drive and sleep; like everything in China, time was money and the 1,000 miles south needed to be covered as quickly as possible, with bonuses paid for making good time. It took three days to reach Guangzhou and another whole day before the truck finally arrived in Kowloon. Quiller handed over another 500 note to the drivers when the truck pulled into the huge container port enveloping Stonecutters' Island - once a separate island from Kowloon. By now he had four days' growth of beard, barely recognising himself when he booked into the YMCA in Kowloon and looked in the mirror, which could only be an advantage.

*

'How did it go?' Miles Thompson asked as he walked into Sir Jeremy's office.

'Predictable.'

'Er, initially, ridicule, followed by it all being someone else's fault?'

'How did you guess? Anyway he's now been told and, of course, once he'd recovered from the shock, started worrying about what might come out if Quiller is brought to trial. I warned him that it might well affect a number of people in the Cabinet Office, which didn't improve his day. Is there any more news from Iraq and Rio?'

'Yes; unfortunately Gunn and Doyle ran into a gang of Iraqi army deserters. They split up in the hope that they'd follow one and not the other, but although Gunn dealt with the smaller bunch that followed him, Doyle was captured. He was severely beaten and the prognosis isn't good. Gunn has asked Alan for a casevac; there was a Royal Navy Lynx from Ark Royal available so it's on its way. With the medical crew on board and operating at maximum range from Basrah, it can only pick up Barnes. Gunn will have to continue on his own, but he'll hand over the samples and camera to the chopper crew.'

'Isn't there any way we can get Gunn out?'

'Not at the moment - certainly no choppers and the British force defending Basrah airport just doesn't have the resources. Alan's view was that John possibly has a better chance on his own - he's in a jeep now, which he took from the bandits.'

'I hope he's right. OK, so what's happening in Rio?'

'Mary Panter's dead.'

'Dead...?'

'Claudine found her in the bath at Soames'

apartment.'

'Who killed her?'

'Probably Soames; my guess is that three's a crowd and two's too much company so survivor takes all. I went to see the Governor of the Bank of England; the account at the Banco de Brazil, which at one stage held nearly £200 million, has been cleaned out.'

'Any idea where it's gone?'

'None........at the moment.'

'Are you bringing Claudine back?'

'Not just yet. I want her to keep an eye out for Soames. A cleaner at the apartment block found Mary's body and the Brazilian police are crawling all over the building so it's highly unlikely that he'll return to the apartment, but I'd like to give it another 48 hours before redirecting her. She's made contact with Esmeralda Sanchez so she has help now.'

'Fine; when are you off to Basrah?'

'The flight leaves at 8.45 this evening. Malcolm's taking me and David Morris in the Gazelle, leaving here at 5.30.'

'And have we heard anything from Hong Bo?'

'He sent a very short message that the Chinese police had identified the hotel where Quiller was staying. They found all his formal clothes, so he must have had another set ready for his disappearing act, but obviously it all happened sooner than he expected.'

'Hmmm... Okay, thanks, Miles. Make sure we take good care of Doyle Barnes.'

'Of course.'

'And try and get some sleep...'

*

Gunn's GPS indicated that the bearing to Basrah was now exactly 90°, which meant that instead of travelling across the grain of the desert, searching for ways to cross wadis and gorges, he was now able to make better progress travelling along them. Anxious as he was to get Doyle flown out as soon as possible, he was determined not to bump into any other bands of Iraqi deserters, so he took it slowly. It was the right thing to do, as he had to backtrack twice to avoid small groups of Bedouin with their camels.

After two hours of driving, the odometer on the Toyota, which was working, registered 55 miles covered, while the GPS told Gunn that he was only thirty miles closer to Basrah, consistent with the backtracking. He stopped the jeep in the shade of a rock outcrop, set up the satcom radio, checked communications with Basrah and then sent his location: latitude 30° 27.12′ longitude 44° 52.03′. They acknowledged it and said the Lynx would be airborne in five minutes with a medical team.

Gunn placed all the samples and the camera into an empty cardboard box of what had been 5.56 ammunition and placed it on the front seat beside him, ready to hand over to the helicopter crew. He emptied one of the jerrycans into the Toyota's tank, walked out in front of the jeep for ten yards, looked through his hand-bearing compass and identified a landmark on the horizon to keep him on the 90° bearing. He pulled out his watch; the Lynx should have been airborne for about five minutes. Maximum speed was about 160mph and it was about 160 miles to Basrah so, with any luck, he reasoned, getting back into the truck and grinding into first gear, it would be about an hour before he met up with the chopper.

In the event it turned out to be no more than fifty minutes before Gunn heard the thob-thob-thob of the Lynx's rotors. He stopped the jeep in the open, got out and, holding one of the keffiyahs he'd taken from the bandits, waved it over his head. The Lynx landed some fifty yards away; a soldier immediately jumped out and covered Gunn with his SA80 assault rifle.

'Op Raptor; I have a casualty for you to take back to Basrah,' Gunn shouted to make himself heard above the noise of the Lynx's twin turbines. The soldier lowered his assault rifle, signalled behind him; two more men jumped out of the Lynx and hurried over to the jeep. They were all highly suspicious of Gunn and he could hardly blame them, having seen himself in the jeep's wing mirror. His clothes were torn and filthy, hanging in rags as though he was some sort of desert wraith; his face was caked with sweat-mingled dust and he had several weeks' worth of beard. Doyle was lifted onto a stretcher and carried into the Lynx. Gunn walked to the front of the helicopter on the observer's side and held his hand out with the thumb up. The signal was returned, so he walked forward and handed over the box with the samples and camera, the young Royal Navy Petty Officer wrinkling his nose as Gunn drew near. Gunn smiled at him, backed away and returned to the jeep as the Lynx lifted off.

As Gunn drove on, the parched wasteland gradually gave way to patches of scrubby flora. Ahead of him was another desert town, called Jalibah, and beyond that was the main road between Baghdad and Basrah. Now all he could do was hope that he met a

British or American patrol and not the Iraqi army. He reached Jalibah at 2pm, stopping about two miles short and studying it through his binoculars. Determined not to draw any unwanted attention that could lead to capture, Gunn decided to stop where he was until it was dark and do the rest of the drive under cover of night. The previous night, when he'd stayed awake looking after Doyle, Gunn had noted it was a three-quarter moon, which would provide more than adequate light for a night drive, particularly as the terrain was becoming less treacherous. He reversed the Toyota back into the wadi through which he had just driven and settled down to wait for nightfall.

The moon rose at 8.15pm. Gunn had cat-napped through the afternoon and early evening to try and get some sleep, having had none the night before. Before setting off on what he hoped was the final leg of his drive, he set up the satcom radio and spoke to Alan Paxton. Doyle had arrived safely on HMS Ark Royal and was receiving treatment. The box of evidence had already gone back to London on the evening air-trooping flight. Relieved, Gunn drove to the top of the wadi, stopped and got out of the jeep to take a reading with the hand-bearing compass, its figures lit by a minute radioactive source. The night sky was crystal clear and because there was no light pollution, the stars shone brilliantly. Venus languised low down in the eastern night sky and, on his left, high in the heavens to the north, the Pole Star flickered grandly above the Plough. Making sure the jeep's lights were switched off, Gunn let in the clutch and moved off, leaving the distant lights of Jalibah behind him.

Every thirty minutes, Gunn stopped the jeep and

checked the GPS, which told him whether he was erring left or right of his intended route. Slowly, slowly the miles went by until, finally, he could see an orange glow in the eastern sky, which had to be Basrah.

'Aaah!' Sudden, brilliant white light blinded him. Gunn's hands flew up to protect his face and he slammed on the brakes. He heard a voice speaking in Arabic, magnified by an electronic loud hailer. God, no! Gunn thought; so close and he'd been caught. He didn't even bother trying to reach for his Armalite.

'Get out of the jeep and keep your hands above your head!' the voice barked, seeming painfully loud. He did as ordered, standing clear of the jeep with his hands above his head. 'Do you speak English?' Gunn nodded his head. 'Give me your password,' the voice suddenly switched to English.

'Raptor,' Gunn croaked, hardly recognising his own voice. The lights went out, but Gunn could see nothing, having completely lost his night vision.

'Come on mate, you must be knackered.' It could only be a British squaddie. 'Jesus, you don't half fucking stink.' By now Gunn could just make out the four Warriors and the soldiers who had found him. 'Anything in the jeep you want, mate?' the Sergeant's jarring south London accent sounded like a chorus of angels to Gunn, as he allowed himself to be lead to the back of the nearest Warrior.

'Just the two backpacks and weapons; the rest you can get rid of,' Gunn mumbled. He looked up to find a young Lieutenant scrutinising him intently.

'Are you John Gunn?' he asked.

'Yes,' was all he could manage.

'Come on, sir; we'd better get you back to base.' Gunn climbed into the back of the Warrior and instantly fell asleep.

'Did you see the state of the other bugger they brought in by chopper this morning?' the Sergeant asked his patrol commander as he resumed his position behind the 30mm cannon.

'No, how bad was he?' the Lieutenant asked, climbing back into the command hatch

'Beaten to a pulp, someone in Two Platoon told me; you could even see bone through the torn flesh on his back and feet.'

'What the hell have they been doing out there on their own? OK, let's go!'

'Someone said they're spooks...'

But the rest of the conversation was smothered by the roar of the Warrior's diesel engine.

*

Claudine read her orders from BID, sent via text. She was to remain in Rio and, with the help of Esmeralda Sanchez, find out if Soames was still in there or had gone. She dialled Esmeralda's number and they arranged to meet in the coffee shop at Claudine's hotel. Esmeralda was a small, shrewd-looking woman in her late thirties, her short dark hair tucked boyishly behind her ears. She looked capable, thought Claudine, watching her approach, knowing who she was by the calm efficiency of her walk; that and the way her eyes roved over every face she passed, swallowing information greedily. Eventually they settled on Claudine, and she saw the flicker of recognition.

'Hello, Claudine, I'm Esmeralda Sanchez; Esme,' she offered a small, neat hand, which Claudine shook, enjoying the assured firmness, and the two women went into the café.

Esme told her that she'd seen Mike Soames enter the apartment building on the same day that she'd received the email from Peter Stone with photos of both him and Mary, and one of Claudine with dark hair. She had also followed Mary from the airport and had seen her go into the apartment building the previous evening.

'These bastards; they're all out to get each other now. Quiller imagines himself as 'Mr Big' in all this, but he's cunning more than intelligent. This is Mike's part of the world - he speaks the language - I'd wager he's been planning this from the start. Mary was small fry; they just used her to get inside BID - the bugs, the information in the secure records vault they used to blackmail...' Claudine's stopped, seeing the expression on Esme's face. She was staring hard at the hotel foyer, which Claudine had her back to.

'He's just walked into the foyer,' she whispered.

'Soames?'

'Yes.'

'Sure it's him?'

'Absolutely... He's walked over to the reception. What name have you booked under?'

'Clara Morales.'

'Could he have known that you were staying here?'

'No, no way; not even anyone at BID knew where I was staying. I made the reservation and haven't told anyone except you. Has he ever met you?' Claudine asked, but Esme held up her hand.

'Wait...wait...he's booking a room. He obviously can't stay at the apartment so he's come to stay at this hotel - mierda, of all the places! But I don't believe in sod's law; there are at least three other hotels in the Rua Farme Amoedo, between the apartment building and this hotel, which he could have chosen…'

'Has he…'

'No, he's never met me, though he's had access to the list of BID's in-country agents. But this doesn't make any sense; I've never had anything to do with this hotel.'

'We should go.'

'Yes. Okay, he's not looking in this direction. Go over to that table by the far window. He can't see you there.'

'What about you?'

'I'll keep an eye on him and then join you.'

'Okay,' Claudine picked up her food and moved across to the window table, releasing the safety catch on the Colt in her bag as she sat down. After a couple of minutes, Esme followed.

'He went up in the lift; it stopped at the tenth floor. Which floor are you on?'

'Fourth.'

'How long would it take you to pack?'

'Five minutes, max.'

'Right, I'll come up with you.' Claudine signed the bill and they hurried towards the lifts, Esme leading. She selected the lift furthest away from the one Mike had used. It stopped at the fourth floor, and Esme checked the corridor first before they ran to Claudine's room. True to her word, Claudine took five minutes to pack and then, with Esme leading again, they headed for the fire escape stairs, which brought them to the ground floor via swing doors off to one side of the foyer. Esme was half way through them when she pushed Claudine back with such force that she stumbled.

'He's there at the reception counter talking to the receptionist. I can't hear… those tourists…' A group of Japanese tourists moved out of the foyer, talking animatedly about something that had upset them.

'Can you hear anything?'

'Shhhh........the bastard; he's just told the receptionist that he's looking for his sister. He's shown him a photo - would he have one of you?'

'Quite possible....I suppose........Mary would have told him that I had been checking the files and so it would be a reasonable guess that I had followed her to Rio.'

'I'll bet he's been to a handful of other hotels asking the same question. He's clearing his back before moving on. He'll know that BID will be looking for him and he's now going through the standard procedure of ensuring there are no leads to his next destination…oh wait! He's learnt something because he's heading for the lifts. Come on, time to go, no...wait! OK, now!' they sprinted through the foyer and out onto the road where they launched themselves into a waiting taxi and breathlessly directed it into the maze of streets that zig-zagged up the hill overlooking Copacabana Beach.

# CHAPTER 20

When Gunn awoke it took a few moments for him to realise where he was. What was he doing in a bed inside a tent? All his Bedouin clothing had gone, and so had his underwear. A young medical orderly appeared by his bedside.

'Have a good sleep, sir?'

'Fantastic thanks; where am I?'

'This is 205 Field Hospital at the British base in Basrah. You were brought in just before midnight last night. Sorry about your clothes, sir, we've had to burn them.'

'That doesn't surprise me,' Gunn noticed the two chevrons on the man's shirt sleeve. 'What's your name, Corporal?'

'Morrison, sir.'

'And your first name?'

'Darren, sir.'

'What's the time, Darren?'

'Eleven in the morning, sir.'

'Call me John,' Gunn said, sitting up in his bed. 'Can you get me some clothes, please?'

'Yes, uh, there're some clothes on that chair over there…' he pointed to a chair on the other side of the large tent, '…and I think this is your watch,' and L/Cpl Morrison handed him his Omega Seamaster watch.'

'Thanks very much,' Gunn got out of the bed and walked over to the pile of clothes. It was only when he was half way across the tent that he realised there were female medical orderlies in the tent. 'Oh... Sorry,' Gunn laughed and grabbed a pair of pants from the top of the pile.

'Don't worry, we've seen it all before,' and as if to prove it, a female sergeant walked over and coolly held out her hand as he struggled to get the pants over his knees. 'Sergeant Tricia Carter; how're you feeling Mr Gunn?'

'Uh, very well rested, thanks to all of you,' Gunn eventually took the offered hand, then asked: 'Do you have any idea how my colleague is, who was brought in by chopper yesterday?'

'Yes, I was on the chopper; we did the best we could for Agent Barnes, but he's now on HMS Ark Royal and from there he'll be casevacked to the UK. He'll recover, but his back will have some pretty terrible scarring.'

'Hm. Well, thank you.' Gunn finished dressing in the military combat clothing they'd provided.

'We'd all love to know what the two of you were doing out there on your own, but we've been told it's all hush-hush and we mustn't ask you,' Tricia continued.

'Didn't work though, did it?'

'I had to give it a try.'

'I can probably tell you enough to satisfy your curiosity; it's the least I can do anyway. It goes back seventeen years to Operation Granby and the '91 Gulf War. Some soldiers were killed and incorrect identification was recovered at the time. We were sent to find the bodies, bring back samples for accurate DNA analysis and then re-inter them,' Gunn was silent for a moment, the pitiful sight of the skeletons' rags, riddled with bullet holes, replaying itself in his mind.

'What happened to Agent Barnes?'

'Uh, bandits; deserters and Bedouins...' Gunn winced at the thought of what Doyle must have been through. It was clear he didn't want to say any more.

'I think that's our lot, guys,' Tricia grinned over her shoulder at everyone else in the room, all concertedly eavesdropping. 'Come with me, Mr Gunn, your boss is waiting for you with the CO.' Tricia escorted him over to the tactical headquarters, where he found Alan Paxton, David Morris and Miles talking to Brigadier Monk, the officer in command of the base.

'John! I was just about to come and wake you,' Miles shook his hand warmly. 'How are you feeling?'

'Much better thanks, especially now that people can come within five feet of me.'

'Good, that's great. Er, this is Brigadier Graham Monk, the Commander of British Forces in Iraq.'

'Sir; my thanks to your guys who brought me in last night,' Gunn said as they shook hands.

'All part of the service, John.' He turned to Miles. 'Please, use this room and I'll make sure you're not disturbed.'

'John, I'm so sorry about Doyle,' said Miles once the Brigadier had left the room, anticipating what was on Gunn's mind.

'Is there any more news?'

'He's off the SI list, but it'll be some time before he takes on another assignment. He'll be flown to Qatar in the next 48 hours and from there back to London and then on to the USA. We'll make sure…'

'I know you will, Miles, thank you,' Gunn put a hand on his superior's shoulder, grateful for his obvious concern, which was etched onto his face by deeper lines than had been there a month ago.

'How are *you* feeling?' Miles asked again, surveying John's thinner frame.

'I really do feel fine. I just needed all that sleep.'

'And your head?'

'My head…?' It seemed like an age ago that he'd been recovering from a gunshot wound to the head. 'Uh, fine, apart from the sunburn.'

'I'm glad to hear it.' The Army medic hadn't reported anything unusual either; Miles had asked him to run a few tests while Gunn slept. 'John, what if I said I want to send you directly to Beijing to find Quiller? Are you fit for that?'

'So he's left already ahead of the PM's visit? Yes; a couple of proper meals and I'll be fine. I'd guessed that was what you had in mind when I saw that you had David with you.'

'Right……..if you're certain?'

'I am. I want to get this guy. Those poor bastards out in the desert…' Gunn trailed off; he didn't need to finish.

'I know. Okay; you'll be leaving here for Doha International Airport in Qatar at 1800 hours and then getting a direct flight with Saudi Arabian Airlines on to Beijing. I'll hand you over to David for the briefing in a minute…' At a nod from Miles, David Morris excused himself from the room, leaving Miles and Alan alone with Gunn. '…but is there any more we need to know about Doyle's capture?' Miles asked, switching on a small tape recorder.

'No; it really was just bad luck. It could easily have been me. When we bumped them, I made the decision to separate. We each had a set of all the samples and pictures, so my plan was to lead the Iraqis away from Doyle so he could get to Basrah and deliver them. Unfortunately it was only partially successful. I was followed by three jeeps, but managed to take care of them. The other three trucks and a jeep ambushed Doyle and, well, you've seen what they did. I found him just before they burnt him alive. I killed all his captors - there were 11 of them - found all Doyle's kit intact and then blew everything up - all the bodies too. Then I set up the satcom radio and made that call to you here. I think that's it.'

'Any questions from you?' Miles asked Alan.

'Uh, just for the tape: John, do you have any doubt that Quiller, acting alongside Soames, murdered all six of those SAS soldiers?'

'None whatsoever; firstly, their Landrover wasn't blown up by a mine. We found it in near perfect condition, so Quiller's report was false. Secondly, both Harker and Miller, who were supposedly blown up, were in fact murdered with a bullet to the back of the head. Thirdly, if Soames wasn't injured by a mine blast, again, as stated in Quiller's report, he must have been deliberately beaten by Quiller to authenticate the report that he'd been injured by the mine blast, but he was made to look much worse than he really was; I think his concussion was a fabrication..........probably morphine-induced. Fourthly, all four soldiers in the other patrol had been murdered, too.'

'Thank you, J...'

'I believe...' John continued, talking at the recorder, '...that Quiller and Soames planned this the moment the composition of the patrols was announced at their mounting base back at Al Jawf. Quiller would be on his own with his lookalike, Harker, and would have Soames to help him. That was phase one, if you like. Phase two came much later, after Quiller landed his senior advisory appointment in the Cabinet Office. That gave him access to the personal records of senior Civil Servants who were vulnerable to blackmail. Between the two of them, including the murder of Nina and my attempted murder, the two Cuban guys and the Miami chopper pilot, they're responsible for some twenty or more murders.'

'Thank you, John; you really have done a great job on this. I have nothing further to add, Miles.'

'I'll second that; well done. Perhaps you could tell David we're ready for him?' Miles asked Alan, who was gathering his things to leave.

'Will do,' Alan left the room to be replaced a minute later by David Morris.

'Four days ago,' David began, 'Quiller was confronted in the British Embassy by Major General Pennyfeather, the Defence Attaché and Quiller's former Troop Commander in Bravo Squadron of 22 SAS. He wasn't taken in by Quiller's pretence of being Harker and called in the Embassy security guys. Realising that his disguise was compromised, Quiller took a young Chinese girl hostage and made a run for it. During his escape, he broke the girl's arm, which mean's Sir Martin Bannerman, the Ambassador, has had a summons to the Ministry for Foreign Affairs to explain this assault on a Chinese national.'

'They didn't stop him?' Gunn was incredulous.

'Unfortunately not; took them all by surprise. Anyway, Quiller was staying at the St Regis Hotel. His room has been searched and from what was left behind we've assumed that he had a change of clothing for his planned disappearance from Beijing. His confrontation with the DA merely made him bring forward his plans, albeit suddenly. We have to assume that he now has a new identity; they found a torn up passport under the name of Harker and a first class ticket for Cathy Pacific to Hong Kong in a rubbish bin just outside the front entrance of the hotel.'

'Shit...'

'Quiller has never been to Hong Kong before, as far as we know - certainly not during his appointment as Head of Security at Number 10. The Chinese Government has put a watch on all ports, rail stations and airports, so his only escape route to Hong Kong is by road. Once he's there, he'll be amongst a lot of other Caucasians and not nearly as noticeable as he must have been in Beijing. What he'll do in, or from, Hong Kong is anybody's guess, but he has to meet up with Soames in order to get his hands on the embezzled funds, which, until recently, were deposited in the Banco de Brazil in Rio. If Soames or Quiller doesn't transfer the money into a country where we can get our hands on it, we'll have to rely on the Governor of the Bank of England, Sir Marcus Lord, to help us return those funds to the rightful owner - the British taxpayer. But there's just no way of knowing what'll happen now as it looks like our conspirators are turning on each other. Mary Panter has been killed - Claudine found her...'

'Claudine?'

'Yes, she's in Rio watching them but she found Mary's body at an apartment they'd bought with the funds. We're assuming it was Soames. Claudine's trying to find out if he's still in Rio or has left. Don't worry,' he added quickly, 'she's working with our in-country agent, Esme Sanchez, so she's not on her own on this one; Soames is just too dangerous. At any rate, the Caribbean is where he prefers to operate, so my guess is he'll be heading up there. And that's everything. As Miles said, you'll leave for Beijing via Qatar at 1800 hours. Wu Hong Bo will meet you and bring you up-to-date with anything else he's discovered. Bob Chang in Hong Kong has been fully briefed and will take care of anything you need. I suggest that you keep your beard. Quiller still thinks that you're dead, as does Soames...'

'That's good.'

'...so you'll continue under the name of Mark Knight. I've brought you some clothes to change into. Anything else you need you can buy at the airport in Qatar.'

*

Hong Kong was as alien to Quiller as Beijing had been; the only difference was that many more people spoke English. In preparation for his departure from the job at Number 10, Quiller had prepared three aliases for himself of which David Morgan was the first. He had passports and credit cards in different bank accounts for all three aliases so finance was no worry, but there was still no answer from either Mike

Soames' or Mary Panter's mobiles. He needed to find a way of getting out of Hong Kong without alerting the Chinese authorities, who would be watching the airport and harbour.

He walked down to the Star Ferry Terminal in Kowloon and by following the crowds, bought a ticket and crossed over to Hong Kong Island. Once again he attached himself to a group of people, which included three Caucasian men; as he got closer to them, he picked up the unmistakeable Australian accents. From the Star Ferry, they took the escalator up to a raised walkway that encircled Central District of Hong Kong through atrium cafés, shops, restaurants, barber shops and bars. Finally he found himself back at street level outside the 'Bull and Bear,' in Hutchinson House; the interior design, aping an English country pub, was instantly familiar.

Quiller went up to the bar and was told that if he took a seat he would be served by one of the waitresses. He sat down at the next door table to the three young Australian men and studied the menu. Eavesdropping on their conversation, he realised they were talking about boats - something that Quiller knew very little about. Having been born and brought up in Nottingham and raised by foster parents who had never taken him anywhere near the sea, sailing was something that had passed him by - even during his time in the Army. In the SAS he had specialised in Landrover-borne desert operations. It soon became clear that the three men had a boat and, at 52 feet in length, it was a big boat. They were discussing their indifferent performance in that year's China Sea Race from Hong Kong to Subic Bay in the Philippines and their intention to sail the boat, by stages, back to Perth in Australia. At the last comment Quiller, leaned back and turned his head slightly so he could hear them better. Here was a ready-made opportunity to get out of China, avoiding the police and immigration authorities. He'd also be among other Caucasians, making him considerably less conspicuous. The men ordered another round of Fosters and a large bowl of chips from one of the waitresses, and their conversation turned to finances and crew; it transpired that they were short of both. This gave Quiller the opportunity for which he'd been waiting. He waved to the waitress and ordered another beer and then turned to the man nearest to him.

'Hi mate, sorry to butt in, but I heard you might be looking for crew for your boat?' The three men turned towards Quiller. They saw a large, well-built man in his forties, with an oddly thin face, given his bulk.

'Yeah...you interested?' the man nearest to him said.

'I am if you plan to leave soon. I'd go with you as far as the Philippines and I can help out with the finance - if that's a problem.' He now had their full attention.

'Sounds good to me, mate; here, come and join us. I'm Mike, that's Aaron and this is Stuart - he's a Kiwi, but we talk to him because he knows a lot about boats!'

'Dave Morgan. I'm on holiday; I retired early, so I'm taking a sort of year out, to decide what to do next....'

'Too right!'

'...I don't know much about boats, but I could help you with money and muscle, if there's space for me.'

'There's plenty of that, mate. The three of us share the ownership of the boat; she's a Farr 52, mean anything to you?' Quiller shook his head. 'Thought not; she's designed by a Kiwi called Bruce Farr who's had a lot of racing success. There's room for twelve aboard her, but in bloody Spartan conditions - no cabins, carpets or fancy heads...'

'Heads?'

'Dunnies.......toilets. How much money would you be prepared to put up for your passage to Manila?'

'If you go soon, a thousand quid, up front, and I pay my share of anything else.'

'You're on, mate - let's drink to that,' and they ordered another round.

*

'How long have you been in your flat?' Claudine asked, as the taxi turned into Rua Conrado Niemeyer, stopping in front of a house that had been converted into flats.

'At this one you mean?'

'Yes.'

'Nearly five years. The deal I struck was for BID to pay the rent, but no annual retainer. I then sub-let the flat, which provides me with an income. This area is popular for holiday lets, but it's expensive.'

'That means Mike Soames knows about you and this address. If he's clearing his back - and I think you're right about that - then this is the next place he'll come, if he hasn't already. He must've found out that a young woman claiming to be a friend was in his apartment building. That must be why he's searching all the hotels in the proximity. How long do you think it'll take him to find that a woman has left the Ipanema Plaza Hotel without paying her bill? You know, he's very sharp and I reckon he'll be paying this address a visit tonight. We'd better stay somewhere else and just watch…'

'No need. I own the flat below this one myself. We'll be staying there. '

'Oh, well that's a perfect solution…'

'Besides, this flat has one or two surprises for intruders, or for people that BID has asked me to detain until they find a way of extraditing them.'

'OK……bearing in mind that BID has asked me to let him run so that the money can be traced, it's nothing lethal is it? '

'No. There are also tiny cameras in every room…' Esme pointed out their hiding places, '…so I can monitor what is going on from downstairs. '

'But what about clients on a holiday let?'

'No problem; I just disconnect everything. OK, let's make it look as though you are staying with me here.'

'Here,' Claudine took out some toiletries, underwear, a change of clothes and some shoes and positioned them around the smaller second bedroom.

'Perfeito! Vamos.'

*

By the time the preparation for the assignment was complete and Gunn was fed, showered and dressed in his new clothes, it was time for him to leave. David Morris had also given him a small backpack with everything he would need for the next 48 hours, including his wallet with credit cards in the name of Mark Knight. David himself would fly direct to Hong Kong and act as Gunn's controller from there.

At 10:00 am local time in Beijing, Gunn walked out into arrivals and Wu Hong Bo appeared beside him, beaming. They'd met in Hong Kong on two previous assignments, and Gunn had warmed to his affability, a rarity in their line of work. They chatted in Mandarin, which Gunn had been fluent in since his childhood on Hong Kong, as they headed out to the multi-storey car park.

'I like your beard; it's a good look for you.' The ability to grow facial hair was a racial trait that the Chinese envied most of Caucasians.

'It's itchy.'

'You look like an American scientist!' Hong Bo chuckled, as they settled into the 16-mile drive into Beijing

'Maybe you should focus on driving…'

'Ha! OK, John. I've booked you into the St Regis Hotel – the same one that Mr Quiller was in. I thought you might like to retrace his exact movements in case that was any help in finding him. But I personally think he's long since left this city for Hong Kong.'

'That makes sense. Thanks for the lift; I'll give a shout if I need any help.' Having dropped his backpack in his room, Gunn went straight around the corner to the British Embassy and asked to see the Defence Attaché. He had to wait for five or six minutes before the doors from the secure side of the embassy opened and David Pennyfeather walked out.

David had left 22 SAS five years before Gunn had attended his selection course and David's parent regiment was the Coldstream Guards, while Gunn had served in the Royal Artillery, so their paths had never crossed.

'Mark Knight, General; I believe the office in London told you that I'd be coming.'

'They did, I've been expecting you. Come up to the office,' David led the way back through the double doors into the secure area and then up the stairs to the first floor and through another set of secure doors.

'Take a seat,' more as an order than an offer, so Gunn did as bidden and sat in a comfortably upholstered rattan-framed chair while the DA sat at his desk.

'I understand from Miles that you've just spent a week in the Iraqi desert gathering proof of what really happened to that Bravo patrol. I left the Regiment some months before the Gulf War, but it was my Squadron Commander who had the unenviable task of visiting the families of those six soldiers. I'd be grateful to know the truth; I knew all those soldiers – and their families - really well.'

For the next half hour, Gunn explained in detail what he and Doyle had discovered. As he went on, David's face darkened and a vein started to throb in his right temple. When Gunn had finished, he nodded his head slowly.

'Well, I just hope this isn't made public when he's caught and tried. It would put those families through the misery of grieving all over again. Better for them to think they died heroically, doing what they loved.'

'It won't go to trial, but not for the right reasons. His conspiracy involved some senior members of the Cabinet Office, who were being blackmailed. That wouldn't reflect very well on the PM…'

'Shuh!' David snorted derisively, but didn't say anything.

'Uh, I'd like to hear from you exactly what happened when Quiller turned up here.'

'Right; well, he didn't do his research, did he? It would only have taken a few moments to check the names of the staff at this embassy for him to realise that he might well come face-to-face with his former Troop Commander. That's typical of the soldier that I knew for nearly three years. That may be of use to you in your search for him; if someone else did the prep, then Quiller was capable of executing it, but he was pretty bloody hopeless if left to do his own planning. His embezzlement of the Sergeants' mess funds is a classic example. Had he thought through what he was about to do it would have been abundantly clear that the finger of suspicion would immediately point at him. That's his trademark; act in haste and repent at leisure.'

'How do you think he got away with assuming Harker's identity for so long then?'

'Because of the fragmentation of the regiment between Saudi Arabia and Hereford at the close of the Gulf War and the fact that his due date to leave the Army coincided with his return to the UK. That and the apparent ease with which he managed to destroy all the requisite records and medical documents. And he must've got away with his Midlands accent because most of his colleagues were on leave in the aftermath of the Gulf War.'

'Miles mentioned it was the accent you picked up on?' Gunn nudged him on to the actual events of

Quiller's visit a few days earlier.

'Yes - as soon as he opened his mouth. Harker had a pronounced Scouse accent; totally different. As luck would have it, I caught him completely off guard; had he prepared himself carefully he would, firstly, have made sure he never had to meet me and secondly, if he did have to meet me he would have his cover story prepared. When I challenged him and called for the security staff, in typical Quiller fashion, he panicked and ran. That's about it.'

Gunn thanked David and was escorted down to reception by his PA. He walked back to the St Regis Hotel, where he spoke with the hotel manager and some of the staff. Everything they told him pointed to Hong Kong, so he called at the hotel's travel desk and booked himself on a 17.30 flight that evening.

# CHAPTER 21

Esme and Claudine locked the third floor BID apartment and went down to the one below it. Esme switched on a wide-screen desk-top computer in her study. A list of the rooms in the BID flat appeared, with a tick against each of them.

'All the cameras are working,' Esme flicked through the views of each room.

'Did you set all of this up yourself?' Claudine asked, impressed.

'Yes. All Brazilian men have to do twelve months' military service from the age of eighteen; women can volunteer. I volunteered. Afterwards I was sent to the Instituto Militar de Engenharia, where I studied electronic engineering, before doing five years' military service. Then when I left, I got a job with the Vera Cruz Film Company as a consultant for special effects and stunts. I still do it, actually.'

'I can see why BID approached you.'

'Are you ready?'

'Ready.' Claudine wasn't sure what she was supposed to be ready for.

'Okay, so Soames comes to the front door of the flat,' and the scene on the wide computer screen changed to a view of the front door. Then, as Esme touched the keyboard, the view changed to give a close-up of whoever was standing in the doorway. 'You will agree that it is important to confirm the identity.'

'Of course,' Claudine agreed warily.

'So he will then pick the lock – it's not too difficult or too easy, which gives me an idea of how skilful he is at his profession. He then enters the flat,' and the scene changed to the small hallway where Claudine had recently been standing. 'Once he is through the door, which has its own closing mechanism, it will shut and I can then lock it, so...' she pressed another key. 'But if he is a professional, as soon as he realises that it is a self-closing door, he will put something to wedge it open – so that it doesn't make a noise closing and allows him a quick escape if he disturbs someone in the flat. That is when one of us has to go upstairs and remove the obstruction when he has left the hallway.'

Step by step, Esme showed Claudine the modifications she'd made to the apartment. She could divert the carbon monoxide fumes from the gas water heater from the outside exhaust to either or both of the bedrooms. The brass handles of the top drawers of the chest of drawers in the main bedroom would deliver a very painful, but not lethal, electric shock. A number of the steps on the metal fire escape were designed to give way when weight was applied, which might lead to the victim breaking his neck, Esme accepted, but more likely to result in a severe sprain or broken bone or two. She explained that the psychology behind the devices was to make the victim panic, run to the front door only to find it locked, then run to the back door, which led onto the fire escape, and suffer a disabling injury when the steps gave way. None of it was lethal except for the carbon monoxide and that, Esme explained, had only been used once, at a request from the Mossad; they asked for BID's assistance in rendering a person unconscious before extraditing him to Tel Aviv to stand trial for war crimes.

'So now we should eat!' Esme announced.

*

Ian Quiller had said from the outset that Mary could be a liability, but they'd agreed that having someone inside BID – and especially her technical ability to bug all the staff mobiles - was too useful to pass up. It had warned them that Gunn was suspicious of the deaths of both David Chesham and Paul Manton, and they'd been able to catch him unawares; it had been a crucial advantage, as of all the BID agents, Mike feared him most. But then Mary had told him that Claudine de Carteret had survived the attempt to kill her in the records vault, and her high speed chase through London with Marilyn Green was exactly the sort of attention they didn't need.

Outwardly calm, Mike had fumed silently at her stupidity and the mile-wide trail she'd left right to his doorstep in Rio. After a companionable dinner in the apartment the evening before, Soames waited until Mary was asleep and then suffocated her with the pillows from the bed. He then stripped off her clothes and dumped her in the bath, slashing her left wrist with a carpet knife, which he threw in with her. He slept the night in the spare bedroom, was up early the next morning, packed and out of the apartment by

7.30. He went directly to a pre-booked room in a nearby hotel, the Santa Clara Hotel. This was but one of five hotels where he'd reserved a room to confuse any pursuit from a BID agent. As soon as the banks opened, he visited the Banco de Brazil and transferred all the money to his account in Kingstown. Then he went back to the apartment to check for police activity or any form of BID surveillance.

When he arrived at the building it was crawling with police so he walked on past it and decided to do a spot check of the hotels in the vicinity of the apartment. The Ipanema Plaza was the third hotel he tried where he learned - after generous bribery and the story of the search for his sister - from the receptionist that a young British woman on her own had checked in the night before. A further bribe secured the room number. The Ipanema Plaza was one of the five hotels where he had reserved a room. He went up to his reserved room on the tenth floor, and then came back down to the fourth floor. The cleaning lady was in Claudine's room so he told her that his wife had sent him back to the room to get something. The cleaning lady shrugged and let him look around, but there was nothing. He returned to reception on the ground floor, but the receptionist was unable to help him, except to say that the woman had not checked out of the hotel. He would have to come back to the hotel that evening and then, if still no luck, he would have to pay a visit to Esmeralda Sanchez's flat.

*

'Where are you staying at the moment, Dave?'

Mike asked Quiller.

'I'm in a hotel on the other side of the harbour.' Quiller didn't want to admit that he was staying in the YMCA.

'You mean Kowloon side? Look, mate, we all doss down on the boat. She's in the yacht club marina just along the waterfront over there,' Mike indicated the direction with his thumb. 'It still calls itself the Royal Hong Kong Yacht Club even though the Poms handed it back. You're welcome to join us if you don't mind sleeping on a bunk - we use the club's showers and toilets. It'd make it easier for you to learn about the boat and how to sail her.

'That'd be great; thanks.'

'No worries; we're planning to leave at the end of the week anyway, extra crew or not. The four of us can sail the boat on short passages and we can pick up extra crew in Manila when you leave us. What'd you say to that?'

'Done; what's the name of the boat?' This couldn't be working out better.

'She's called 'Kwinana'; that's the name of a town just south of Perth where Aaron and I live - red hull and 'roo motif on the bow.'

'Roo?'

'Kangaroo, mate - we're gonna have to teach you how to speak Oz! Hope you don't have any large suitcases?'

'Just a backpack.'

'Good on ya' sport - we'll make you a yachty yet.'

'Well, I'll go and get my backpack and see you at the boat later,' Quiller finished his beer, shook everyone's hand and made his way back to the Star

Ferry. The more he thought about it, the better the whole idea of him disappearing amongst the yachting fraternity became. He had enough money to buy half-a-dozen 52-foot yachts if he wanted, and now he was going to learn how to sail one at the same time as getting away from China under the radar of immigration officials. He packed his things in less than two minutes, paid for his one night and headed back again to the ferry.

As he left the ferry terminal on Hong Kong Island, pushing aside a young boy begging for money, he hailed a taxi and asked for the yacht club. The taxi dropped him at the entrance and after he'd explained to the security guard on the gate which yacht he wanted, he was admitted; the Australians had left his name with the security guard at the gate. Making his way down on to the pontoon, he didn't see the young boy he'd pushed aside at the terminal get out of another taxi and watch him head towards Kwinana's berth.

The three young men were back on the boat and as soon as he had dumped his back-pack on a berth down below, noting with relief that it wasn't nearly as Spartan as he'd imagined, Stuart, who was the skipper, offered to take him to the yacht chandlery shop to get properly kitted out.

'Now, Dave,' Stuart began as they climbed off the boat back onto the pontoon, 'I'm taking you at your word. Back there in the pub you said you weren't short of cash. These bastards in the yacht shop are daylight robbers; it's the same everywhere. You can buy a good, warm sweater in Marks and Spencer for two hundred dollars - Hong Kong that is; the same sweater in a yacht shop will cost you double or treble that. So I hope you weren't bullshitting us back there in the pub!'

'No bullshit - you tell me what's needed and I'll settle it with my credit card. An hour later, he needed a trolley to take all his new gear back to the boat. As soon as he'd unpacked everything and stowed it away, Stuart showed him round the boat, starting below decks first.

'I'll use the yachting lingo,' Stuart explained, 'because the sooner you get used to it the better. You never know mate, you might even get to enjoy it!' He explained how to operate the flush system for the heads, identified the various storage compartments, packed with food and life jackets, and the emergency pack, which would be taken in the life-raft if they had to abandon ship, and then took him up on deck. Mike explained the two large pedestal winches, the reason for there being two wheels to steer the boat and the myriad of halyards, sheets and warps which, to Quiller, were nothing more than a jumble of ropes.

'Right mate, no better way for you to learn than to do it, so we're gonna take her out. Get changed into some of that new gear you've just bought and we'll go sailing.'

For the next three hours, the only time that Quiller had worked harder was when he was getting fit for his SAS selection. He was nearly brained by the huge boom, as it whipped across when they tacked through the harbour's shipping traffic; he ripped several layers of skin off his hands when he tried to hold onto a weight-loaded genoa sheet instead of wrapping it around a winch; he lost count of how many times he banged his shins on various winches and other unidentified fixings; and walking along a surface that was heeled at nearly 45° and heaving up and down was a skill he had yet to master. He loved every minute of it.

'Why the fuck didn't I do this years ago,' he gasped, utterly exhausted, but invigorated, as they returned under engine power to their berth, with Quiller at the wheel.

'Right mate, three more days of sail training and then we'll set sail for Manila on Saturday. It's 650 miles to Cochinos Point at the entrance to Manila Bay, which'll take us about three days, depending on the wind,' explained Mike, who was the navigator, as the four of them sat in the wide cockpit drinking beer. 'We all reckon you're okay, so how do you feel now about an open sea passage?'

'Great, the sooner the better; tomorrow I'll settle up with you and transfer that thousand quid from my bank.'

'Good on ya' sport; we'll drink to that.'

*

Gunn landed at Hong Kong's Chep Lap Kok International Airport at 21.30. He only had his backpack as cabin baggage, so was out into the arrivals hall within 20 minutes of the aircraft coming to a halt at its stand. He didn't spot Bob Chang at the meeting point, but that was not unusual as he knew that Bob was very cautious about letting anyone see him meet a BID employee. Just as Gunn reached the entrance to the Mass Transit Railway, which would take him to

Hong Kong Island, he heard a familiar voice behind him.

'It really is you, isn't it?' Bob said, laughing. The two men embraced, having known each other since childhood. 'Come on, I've got the car outside,' and Bob led the way to the car park. Once they were driving on the dual carriageway, which would take them under the harbour through the western tunnel onto the Island, Bob told Gunn what he'd discovered so far about Quiller.

'The Chinese Broadcasting Service has been showing Quiller's face on the TV and it's also been in the papers for the last 48 hours. If he'd come in via the airport, the station or any of the port or ferry terminals he would have been spotted – I'm certain. The Chinese authorities are incensed by his assault on the young girl at the embassy - she's only 18, you know - and have offered a substantial reward for any information that leads to his arrest.'

'Any results so far?'

'A few false starts, but one piece of information was worth following up. There's a suburb of Beijing called Zhou Zhou.....'

'Heard of it, but never been there.'

'I think it's like Hong Kong's equivalent of Surbiton in the UK; very suburban and everyone wants to know what everyone else is doing.'

'I know what you mean.'

'You will know how obsessed we Chinese are with the acquisition of wealth. We have a joke about someone who likes to pretend that he's wealthy and smart. We say, "No, he's not wealthy, he comes from Zhou Zhou".'

'That's a new one on me.'

'Anyway, this couple who were taking their dog for a walk spotted a 'long nose' climbing over the fence that separates a service station from the main 107 Southern Motorway. They told the local police that he looked like the man shown on TV, but you know as well as I do, John, that Chinese think all Caucasians look alike, so it could have been anyone. However, two things make this sighting worth pursuing: firstly, it's highly unlikely – even during the Olympics - that there would be a Caucasian in Zhou Zhou. And secondly, a truck driver who commutes regularly from Beijing to Kowloon saw the TV picture of Quiller in a shop window in Kowloon and reported it to the police. He said that he had dropped off a gweilo at the container port over on Stonecutters. I think that puts Quiller in Hong Kong. Does he know the city?'

'Not from what I was told at my briefing. He'll be trying to work out a way of getting away from China without alerting the police or immigration officials. And I'm pretty sure he'll have a new identity, with passport and documents to support it. Let's face it, he's had masses of time to prepare for this and, at the moment, he's not short of cash. Have you got all your resources on this?'

Bob Chang, through his support for Hong Kong youth organisations, had a network of what he called his 'Wanchai Regulars;' his eyes on the street. They were reminiscent of Sherlock Holmes' 'Baker Street Regulars' - the street urchins of Victorian London.

'Yes, they're all out looking right now, hanging around the places where most of the gweilos go. Here we are.' Bob drove into the small forecourt in front of the Mandarin Hotel.

'Let's meet here for breakfast tomorrow - 8am in the coffee shop - and I'll bring you up to date.'

'That'd be good, see you at eight; night,' Bob drove off to his apartment in the mid-levels.

*

Aware that the Brazilian police would have a description of him from the receptionist at the apartment building on Rua Berata Rubeiro, Mike Soames had spent the remainder of the day altering his appearance. He shaved off all his hair and, using Gum Arabic, attached a moustache to his upper lip; a pair of shoes with blocked heels added two inches to his height. It was shortly after 7.30 in the evening when he returned to the Hotel Ipanema Plaza. A glance into the foyer revealed that the staff at reception had changed from the day to the night shift. He walked in and selected a young woman to make his inquiry.

'I wonder if you can help me Señorita? A girl I met this morning told me she was staying at this hotel and suggested that we meet here this evening. '

'Of course, Señor; what is her name please?'

'Clara Molares.'

'Just one moment, Señor,' she disappeared into an office and soon reappeared with the night manager.

'Good evening Señor; you know Señorita Molares well?' the manager asked.

'No,' Mike answered, 'we met down by the beach this morning and she asked me to call by the hotel at this time. Why, is there something wrong?'

'Señorita Molares has left the hotel without paying.

Do you know where she is, Señor?'

'No, Señor, I'm sorry I can't help you. It seems you can't trust anyone these days.'

'If you see her, tell her that I have given her name to the police.'

'I will; goodnight, Señor,' Mike walked out into the humid night. 'Fuck!' he said aloud. He must've missed her by only seconds this morning. He flagged down a taxi and gave the driver the number of a house in the parallel street to Rua Conrado Niemeyer - Esme's street. When they arrived, he paid the driver and made a show of walking up to the front door of the house while he was still visible in the driver's rear-view mirror. As soon as the taxi was out of sight, Mike cut through an alleyway into Rua Conrado Niemeyer and headed for number 87. He stopped about a hundred yards away; there were lights showing on all three floors of the building.

'Are you here, Claudine?' he muttered. The only weapon he carried was a slim, finely balanced throwing knife, which fitted into the heel of his blocked shoe. It was mid-week and at 8.15 in the evening the Rua Conrado Niemeyer was virtually deserted. He checked to see if there were any CCTV cameras, but being a residential area it was highly unlikely to have any. The infra-red-operated porch light blinked on, conveniently showing the names beside the three bells: Lozano, Balderas and Sanchez. Mike took a lock pick from his pocket and opened the front door with little difficulty. He could hear the sound of a TV from 87A and, as he climbed the stairs, a melodramatic Brazilian pop song trilled from 87B. He paused outside 87B and listened; mingled with the music were the voices of two men discussing the merits of two Rio football clubs, Botafoga and Flumeneiso. Mike carried on up the stairs to 87C; there was light showing from under the door and the subdued sound of a wireless from inside the flat.

Once again he put the lock pick to work and quietly opened the front door. The sound of the wireless was coming from the direction of a room to the right of the hallway, which Mike guessed was the kitchen. As he gently nudged the door open, he noticed a gas-operated piston slowly closing it again, so he bent down and moved the small coir mat, which was outside the door, so that it prevented the door from closing. He walked slowly through the hallway until he reached the living room; no one there. It seemed as though the two women had gone out - probably to a restaurant for dinner - so he would give the place a thorough search and wait for their return.

He went quickly from room to room to confirm that he was alone in the flat. Then he went into the toilet to check the cistern, which was still a favourite place to hide weapons. He removed the ceramic lid; nothing unusual inside. He looked into the small room beside the toilet, which, with its desktop computer, must have been Esme's study, and then moved to the room on the opposite side of the hall. This had to be the spare bedroom, he reckoned, as it had a woman's clothes on the bed. He'd come back to that later. Next was the main bedroom; once again, there was female clothing scattered on the bed. He went over to the chest of drawers and opened the bottom drawer; nothing but clothes; next drawer up, nothing but clothes; so he opened both top drawers together.

'Ahhhhh!' White flashes erupted in Mike's head. Everything exploded into a searing spasm of pain. He felt himself lifted and thrust back across the room. Sprawled over the bed, his body throbbed from the electric shock. He'd been suckered. Heaving himself upright, he staggered back towards the front door. Somewhere in this building or close to it, he knew the two women would be watching him.

'What the fuck?' The front door was locked. He clearly remembered propping it open. For the first time, anxiety coiled itself tightly in Mike's stomach. There was no way he could open the front door without some tools so he went into the kitchen to see what he could find to force the door. Then he saw the back door. He abandoned the search for tools and tried the door handle, but only after he'd checked and seen that it was plastic. The door opened onto a steel platform. Mike jumped down the staircase two at a time, which saved him from the first of the rigged steps. He then swung round onto the second flight, went down two steps, but then, as soon as his right shoe touched the fourth step, it collapsed, hurling him down to the bottom of the flight. He split his head open on a metal pillar, twisted his right ankle and shattered his right wrist in an attempt to break his fall.

Had Claudine and Esme chosen to deal with him at that stage, Soames knew that there was nothing he could do about it. He had to find a hospital, get himself patched up and get the hell out of Rio. He hauled himself back to his feet, and, one arm hanging limply, he hobbled round to the front of the house and back onto the street. It took him nearly half-an-hour to get to a main thoroughfare, his skin slick with sweat from the effort, where he flagged down a taxi and asked to be taken to a hospital.

*

At 8am, Bob Chang walked into the coffee shop at the Mandarin Hotel and joined Gunn for breakfast. When they had both ordered, Bob leaned in towards Gunn and lowered his voice.

'I have some good news - actually, I'm not sure if it's good, but it's news - from my kids. They had been concentrating on the hotels, so it was just by chance, two days ago, that one of them decided to drop in on a pen-pal who'd told him that he was staying at the YMCA in Kowloon. He nearly walked straight into your man Quiller, who was rushing out of the place with a backpack. He told me that he followed him and took a really close look at him, at the Star Ferry terminal, where he pretended to be begging. On the Hong Kong Island side, he followed his taxi in another one to the Royal Hong Kong Yacht Club and watched him go to a large, red-hulled yacht…'

'What kind of yacht? How big?'

'A racing yacht; the boy didn't know how big, but he said bigger that most of the other yachts; it wasn't for cruising. Anyway, he met up with three other gweilos – all men - then went with one of them to the chandlery shop and bought a lot of equipment. Ten minutes later the boat left the marina and was away most of the day. It didn't return until nearly 5.30 in the evening. I think he's found a way of escaping Hong Kong without leaving any trace of his destination.'

'D'you have any idea who owns the boat?'

'Not yet, but the kid said it had a funny animal painted on the bow. After a bit of questioning, this turned out to be a kangaroo.'

'Right; you would have had quite a few Aussie and Kiwi boats up here for the South China Sea Race back in March. I remember that many of the boats stayed up here until after the typhoon season before they were collected or the crews that stayed here sailed them back. Where do you think he'll go, all the way to Australia? Philippines or Indonesia?'

'I'm not sure,' Bob confessed, 'but if he's thought this through he must realise that there's every chance of BID catching up with his movements, so to isolate himself on a boat on a long sea passage wouldn't make much sense. His main intention has to be to get away from here to another country from where he can fly to wherever it is he wants to fly....South America or the Caribbean, David Morris told me. I think I'd put my money on Manila; it's only a three or four day passage in that kind of yacht.'

'Well done your boy; I'll get down to the yacht club and make a few enquiries. Can you go and see David Morris? He should be arriving here this morning.'

'He gets in at 11.15 on the Saudi Air flight from Qatar.'

'I need to know how BID wants to deal with him; is it a question of dead or alive, or is it important that he stands trial? I have to say, for the sake of the families I hope they decide it's too embarrassing and leave him to us.'

'Um-hum. But there's something else. It's just possible that El Niño may do the job for us.'

'Why, is there a typhoon warning?'

'My cousin in the Met Office said the El Niño current off the coast of Chile is warmer than ever and we should be prepared for at least one close pass over the next few weeks.'

'Bad idea to plan a sea passage if that's the forecast. Do you have something for me in that plastic bag?'

'Oh; I nearly forgot, here,' Bob handed over a bag containing Gunn's two Glocks, holsters and ammunition. 'They came in the Diplomatic Bag yesterday.'

'Thanks; I'd better get moving. David's staying here so let's meet up at six this evening in the Chinnery Bar, unless either of us phones to change that. Oh, by the way, is Peter Wyngarde still the boss of Euro-Pacific Construction? And if he is, does he still have that large, very fast motor boat?'

'Yes and yes.'

## CHAPTER 22

In the A & E department of the Hospital de Ipanema, a young house doctor set and plastered Mike Soames' right wrist, put five stitches in the deep gash on his head and bound his left ankle tightly in a crepe bandage. He suggested that his patient take a few days off work to ensure that he had no residual concussion and to rest his severely sprained ankle, which had swollen so much that he couldn't put his shoe back on. Mike agreed to the doctor's advice, paid for the treatment, left the hospital on crutches and returned to the Santa Clara Hotel, where he asked the concierge to order a taxi and went up to his room. He reappeared five minutes later with a rucksack, paid for his room, got into the waiting taxi and gave the driver directions to Rio's international airport.

At the airport, there were photos of him on display both on placards and on TV screens, fortunately under the name of Jesus Garcia and with hair. There was a very obvious police presence and Mike felt a great deal calmer once he'd got through security and passport control without a hitch as Carlos Martinez. He only had to wait ten minutes until his flight was called, and as a disabled passenger, he was boarded first. The plane departed just before 11pm on its nine-hour journey to Caracas.

At 23.48, an American Airlines flight also left Rio for Miami with a last minute booking in Business Class. Claudine was on her way back to St Vincent.

*

Each day had been the same. Up at 5.15am - some 45 minutes before sunrise - shower and shave in the marina washroom, breakfast of fried eggs and bacon cooked on the gimballed stove in the yacht's galley and then ready to cast off from the finger pontoon as the sun rose a few minutes before 6 am. Gradually, Quiller found that everything became familiar; he didn't trip over the warps, sheets and halyards, which, like snakes, had seemed permanently poised to snare him; instead they became friends. Every chance he had, when he wasn't grinding away on the winches, trimming the sails or heaving the massive spinnaker pole into its cup on the mast, Quiller learnt how to navigate the yacht.

Mike explained the weather patterns in that part of the world; how to judge the arrival of a changing weather system; and how to use the GPS, computerised charts and the conventional charts, sextant and almanacs. His three new companions were pleasantly surprised by his enthusiasm and the alacrity with which he became a useful 'hand' on the yacht - and one with plenty of cash. Just how lucky can you get? they asked themselves, as they enjoyed a beer together on their last evening, while Quiller was in the marina showers, after a day of relentless sail changing, tacking, reaching and running through the choppy waters of the congested harbour.

That evening, Stuart asked for everyone's passports and announced that he was going to pay their mooring fees to the yacht club, inform the immigration official at the club of their departure - hence the need for the passports - and then meet up with the rest of the crew for their last meal ashore until they arrived in Manila. Quiller handed over David Morgan's passport – a name he'd become very used to over the last few days – quite prepared to bluff his way out of any query as to why the passport had no stamp for his entry to Hong Kong. He had an equally false forged stamp for his arrival in Beijing, some ten days previously, but his arrival by truck in Kowloon had avoided the usual immigration checks. Stuart returned to the yacht and handed back the passports; the only comment he made was that the Chinese immigration official was new and didn't seem to have a clue what he was doing. Someone up there likes me, Quiller thought, glancing up at the darkening sky.

None of them was in the mood for a late one that night, well aware of the early start demanded by their skipper. After dinner, they were back on the boat by 10.30pm. They rose at 5.30am the next morning and were under way by 6am, heading east towards the Lyemun Gap and the Tathong Channel leading to the open waters of the South China Sea.

*

Gunn gulped down his breakfast at the Mandarin, eager to be on the move, waved goodbye to Bob Chang and took a taxi to the Yacht Club. On the gate, he explained to the security guard that that he was there to visit a friend on his yacht and was given a pass. He spotted the hefty numbered pile and turned onto the finger pontoon it marked, looking for the red-hulled yacht. All the narrow berth pontoons were occupied except for one; Gunn returned to the marina office and asked if the red-hulled yacht would be back later.

'Kwinana', Mr Knight? They left yesterday morning, very early.'

'Oh. Did the skipper tell you where they were going?' Gunn asked.

'Perth, sir - via Manila, Kota Kinabalu, Jakarta and Christmas Island.'

'Isn't that a bit risky? I've heard there's been a typhoon warning?'

'Don't know, sir...'

'Very risky Mr...?' the harbour master, who'd been listening to the conversation, interrupted his clerk.

'Knight; a friend of mine who has a cousin in the met office said there's likely to be a close pass.'

'I'm Patrick Zhung, harbour master,' he announced, visibly puffing his chest. 'He's right.........I don't know if it's global warming or El Niño or something, but for last three years the typhoons have come suddenly, out of nowhere. We used to get a lot of warning as they develop out in the Pacific and then go north-west to Philippines, South China, Taiwan and Japan; now we already have two, which develop in the South China Sea and reach Category 3 by time they make landfall on south coast.'

'And you think there's one on the way now?'

'The skipper of that yacht, er...what was name, Pang Hua?'

'Kwinana'.'

'Kwinana', yes; Stuart was man's name........a Kiwi and very good yachtsman, did very well in the races here in March. I told him I thought it was bad idea to be going along usual path of typhoons, but he just said "we'll be right", paid fees and sail yesterday.'

'Maybe not such a good yachtsman after all…'

'Yes, maybe not. You have friend on the yacht?'

'Yes.'

'Oh…'

'Thank you Mr Zhung,' Gunn hurried out of the yacht club, once again feeling Hong Kong's suffocating humidity wrap itself around him as the early morning's freshness wore off.

*

More than 12 hours after leaving Rio, Claudine wearily checked into the Sunset Inn in Villa Bay. After a shower to wash off the cloying cabin air, she rang Toby.

'Ah! Claudine. A lot has happened here in the time that you've been away.'

'That doesn't surprise me. Could we meet to bring each other up to date?'

'Sure, no problem,' there was a pause and then Toby continued, 'don' know how tired you are, but Letitia has taken the children to stay with their grandma. You wan' to join me for dinner out somewhere?'

'Sure; where?'

'Basil's Bar on Bay Street, 'bout seven okay?'

'See you at seven.'

*

The first twenty-four hours aboard 'Kwinana' were magical for Quiller. The yacht was on a course of 150°; there was a south-westerly wind, which allowed them to hold their course on a fine reach, one of the fastest and most comfortable points of sailing for a yacht; the weather was clear and bright and, during his first night sail, Quiller was awed by the vast black vault of the night sky, which felt as thick as velvet around the gently gliding yacht. He was on watch with the skipper, Stuart, who had just been below deck to check the log; he emerged to announce that in the last 24 hours they had covered 250 nautical miles - an average of just over 11 knots.

'Is that good?' Quiller asked.

'Damn right it is; if we hold this wind we'll be in Manila the day after tomorrow. Want me to take a spell on the wheel?'

'Thanks, I'll make us some coffee,' Quiller handed over the wheel and went below to boil the kettle. The other two men were fast asleep in their bunks. Quiller looked around him. I can do this, he reckoned; there's a GPS to tell me where I am and where I need to go and, in a boat even larger than 'Kwinana,' a girl had sailed round the world single-handed in record time through the roughest seas imaginable. If she could do it, he was damn sure that someone as strong as him could manage it.

While he was waiting for the kettle to boil, Quiller went to the chart table. Underneath the passage chart of the South China Sea was the chart covering the majority of the Pacific Ocean. He pulled it out and opened it up on the table. Get rid of these guys, no one would know what had happened out in the middle of the ocean, just like the desert; and then he had his own boat to cross the Pacific and not a soul knew where he was. Quiller traced the rhum line across the Pacific, calling at various islands and then via Hawaii to the Panama Canal and the Caribbean. The whistling of the boiling kettle interrupted his thoughts, but as he poured the water into two mugs, hope unfurled inside him for the first time in days.

*

Outside the gates of the yacht club, Gunn dug out the scrap of paper with the phone number of Bob's cousin, Miss Lok Choi Ying. He dialled the number; the phone was answered in Mandarin.

'Observatory, can I help you?'

'Miss Lok? My name's Mark Knight, I'm a friend of your cousin, Bob; he told me to contact you to get more information about a possible typhoon.'

'I'll put you through to Mr Chan Chik Cheung, he's our scientific officer in charge of emergency planning for typhoons.' There was a short silence and then a click followed by a man's voice.

'This is Chan; can I help you Mr Knight?'

'I hope so; I hear there's the possibility of a typhoon.'

'Are you a journalist, Mr Knight?'

'No, I have a friend in a yacht sailing to Manila and I'm anxious to know whether he'll get there safely.'

'When did he leave?'

'Yesterday morning.'

'Then he's taken a great risk; there's a low-pressure system developing in the Sulu Sea between the Philippines and the Palawan Islands. The pressure is falling rapidly; at the moment it's generating storm force winds, but as it moves northwest it is very likely to increase in intensity. It won't be long before we have to raise the typhoon warning signal in the harbour. Your friend would be well advised to return to Hong Kong, Mr Knight.'

*

The phone in Claudine's bedroom rang; it was the receptionist at the Sunset Inn to tell her that the taxi had arrived to take her into Kingstown. Basil's Bar overlooked the Kingstown waterfront and although it called itself a 'Bar', it had a popular bistro, judging by the lack of free tables as Claudine arrived. Toby Charbonnier had been expecting a blonde, and his eyes initially looked through her as she approached.

'Hi, Toby,' she said, greeting him with a kiss.

'Oh man! That hair colour sure changes you,' he laughed his easy laugh as she took a seat at his table.

'Can I get you a drink?'

'Uh, rum and Coke, thanks.' Toby ordered their drinks and then they quickly ordered their food so they could talk uninterrupted.

'You'll remember that I told you and John that our Prime Minister had ordered an inquiry into the award of contracts to golfing friends of the Commissioner?'

'Sure.'

'Well, the inquiry has opened such a can of worms that the PM has had no alternative but to suspend the Commissioner until the inquiry's complete. Malcolm Slater has been promoted to Assistant Commissioner and promoted over the head of the Deputy Commissioner as Acting Commissioner until the inquiry either clears Sir Leo Hugues or he's sacked.'

'So what's the can of worms?'

'At the moment this is all rumour...'

'Go on; it may fit with something that we know.'

Toby paused, and glanced around to see if anyone was taking an undue interest in the two of them or their conversation, but the hubbub of chatter and laughter all around them would easily camouflage their own conversation.

'Followin' the death of that arms dealer...'

'Hassan Hussein?'

'Yeah...an' the clean-up of his operatin' base on that island by the CIA, it seems that there was a link to a senior official here in Kingstown; that's how Hussein avoided any security checks and things like that when he flew in and out of this island.'

'And the rumour is that the contact on this Island was your Police Commissioner?'

'Yeah, that's about it; someone was payin' him a whole bundle of money. He has a house like a palace in the hills behind the city and explains it away by tellin' everyone its inherited money. But all Vincentians know that his ol' French family was broke

- hadn' two beans - which was why he joined the police.'

'Wow.'

'Uh-huh. So what's your news?'

'I think that Mike Soames is on his way back to St Vincent. He's in a bad way with a broken wrist, sprained ankle and quite a deep gash to his head. He got patched up at a hospital in Rio and then disappeared.'

'How'd he get hurt? Must've been some fight.'

'No,' Claudine giggled at the memory of what had happened at Esme's apartment, 'as it turns out, our girl in Rio has an interesting sideline in stunts and rigged up a hell of a trap involving a collapsing fire escape.'

'I'd like to have seen that. Why's he coming back here?'

'He's moved the money they stole from Rio to here - we think. The funds were in the Banco de Brazil, but the UK has no extradition treaty with Brazil and although we discovered where the funds were, there was nothing we could do about it.'

'Did he do this all on his own?'

'No,' Claudine explained the origins of the conspiracy during the Gulf War, the mole in BID and that John Gunn was in China looking for the chief architect; her assignment was to keep Soames under surveillance.

'My God...'

'Yeah.'

'Look, there's something else. You remember that John told us that he thought there were three men in the kitchen when he was shot?'

'Yes...'

'And I told him that we knew that there had been two men – the two Cubans - and suggested that he might have imagined the third man.'

'Yes.'

'Well, I went back to talk with the Rastas. When they're not pretendin' to be anti-social, anti-washin' and anti-establishment, they can be okay.'

'If you say so.'

'Yeah.....but they're frightened. They got orders and a payment, supposedly from this hood known as the 'Shark'...'

'Yes, that's Quiller, a.k.a. Steven Harker; when he signs his name it looks like 'Shark'.'

'......to cover the arrival of the Cubans at the airport. They thought this was to bring in drugs, not to murder someone.'

'Do you believe them?'

'I think so. When they read about the murders, that it was Nina Ramone, who was real popular, and all the shoutin' it caused in the St Vincent media, they realised that they could be charged with conspiracy to murder. They're all terrified of Soames, but they're more terrified of life in a St Vincent prison, so they were talkin'. They told me that although the orders came from this Shark guy, the call itself was a local call from within St Vincent, not from London. It was made to one of their cell phones; they gave me the phone and we were able to trace the call to a phone box in Bay Street.......just over there,' Toby pointed to the phone booth by a bus shelter on the quay.

'Oh my God; which ties in with what John said about three men in the kitchen.'

'Exactly.'

'So the murderer is still at large.'
'And here in Kingstown.'

*

It seemed to Quiller as though he'd only been asleep for ten minutes. Aaron shook him awake, dripping cold seawater on to his face, and told him to get into his foul-weather sailing gear and boots and get up on deck. He squinted at his watch through the fog of exhaustion; he'd been asleep for two hours. As he climbed wearily out of his sleeping bag, he felt the violent heaving of the boat, the waves pounding the carbon-fibre hull, and heard the wind screaming through the rigging, which clattered metallically against the mast. He struggled into his sailing gear and boots, the boat's motion slamming him backwards against one of the heads, then pitching him forward again. Holding tightly to anything that was bolted down, he headed for the hatch to the deck, but was sent back by Aaron to put on his life jacket and safety line. When he eventually emerged from the hatch into the wide cockpit, he blinked at the flailing, crashing chaos, the horizon - almost at right angles to the yacht's stern - obscured every few seconds by a granite mountain of sea.

Quiller forced himself out into the sodden cockpit and immediately clipped his safety line onto the nearest ring bolt as the wind crashed into him like a freezing freight train. He looked around, trying to take in everything. The headsail at the bow had been reduced to what seemed like nothing more than an oversized handkerchief and the mainsail, which had been billowing from the mast last time he saw it, had disappeared, replaced by a minute tri-s'l slotted into a separate track on the mast.

'Now mate, you're about to discover the really exciting side of sailing,' Mike shouted through gritted teeth over the rising turmoil of the waves.

'Where........where did this weather come from?' Quiller stammered, clutching the port pedestal winch grinder so tightly his knuckles turned white.

'Bit of bad timing on our part, mate; pressure was dropping like a stone, but thought we might just make it past the typhoon track!' Mike threw over his shoulder as he disappeared below to fill in the log and make a position check with the GPS. He reappeared 30 seconds later, cupped his hands like a loud-hailer and shouted to Stuart, who was on the starboard wheel.

'Pressure still dropping. Your decision, mate, as skipper, but I reckon we'll have to either lie to the seas or run before them - either way, we'll need a sea anchor!'

'What's the forecast?' Stuart shouted back, barely audible above the howling wind and stinging spray.

'Typhoon has formed.....name of 'Tina'......it's a cat 3 - moving north-west from the Palawan Islands!'

'Where's the eye?'

'About 150 miles north-west of the Palawan Islands, between us and Manila, travelling at 25 mph towards Hainan Island!' There was no response from Stuart as he weighed up the options. Quiller had never felt terror like it; his heart was battering his ribs like a caged animal and all his thoughts about getting rid of the other men and sailing the boat to South America now came back, mocking him, in his petrified funk in the cockpit.

'Right guys,' Stuart shouted, having made his decision, 'Tina's going to China so we'll go with her! We'll run before the seas! Strap on tight guys before you do anything! Take off all sails and we'll run under bare poles! I want every warp made up on the winch pedestals and then taken out in a loop over the stern! Aaron, grab Dave and get him fucking working............we need everyone working!'

Stuart, Aaron and Mike had all competed in the Sydney-Hobart Race, which was notorious for its foul weather, but all were well aware of the effect of severe weather on a newcomer to offshore sailing. All had exchanged glances in the last few minutes, realising that Quiller had gone from asset to liability in a matter of minutes.

The headsail was rolled up tight and the tri-sail was removed from the mast track. Mike and Aaron had to do all the work because Quiller had frozen; his fear had drained all the strength from his muscles and the wet cold had sent them into the first stages of hypothermia. The two Australians dragged out the heavy warps from the deep lockers in the cockpit, fastened them on to the winches and through the cleats and then fed them around the stern, so that 'Kwinana' had a long loop of water-logged ropes dragging behind her to slow her down. Now, the huge seas would lift the hull and run under it rather than turn it into a surfboard or, worse, pitch-pole the yacht 'arse over tit,' as Stuart explained to a wide-eyed and terrified Quiller.

Once the yacht's sea anchor was made up, Stuart chose his moment and then carefully steered the yacht onto a run, the wind now directly behind them, the standing rigging providing more than enough windage to drive the yacht ahead of the seas. The waves grew and grew in size until there was sixty feet between cavernous trough and wind-whipped crest. Aaron took over the wheel from Stuart, who went forward, unclipped Quiller from his ring bolt and guided him through the hatch and below deck.

'Not as much fun when the weather does this to you, eh?' Stuart grinned. 'Hot drink?' but there was no answer. Years of sailing in rough antipodean seas had taught him to recognise the trauma induced by a combination of terror and hypothermia. Treating Quiller like an invalid, Stuart helped him onto his bunk, fully clothed in his foul-weather gear, and tied him in with the lee sheet and straps. 'There you go mate; get some sleep and we'll wake you when it's all over.'

*

Gunn waved down a taxi and gave directions to the Maritime Rescue Coordination Centre in the Harbour Building in Hong Kong Island's Central District. In reception there was a board with the names and appointments of the key personnel in Search and Rescue. Mr Fung Ching Biu was the head of the department for co-ordinating commercial maritime shipping and the aircraft of the Government Air Services. The latter had taken over the responsibility for SAR after the British had handed over the territory to China and the Royal Air Force had left. The aircraft of the Government Air Services were based in one corner of the international airport at Chep Lap Kok. Gunn was shown to an open plan office, where he met Mr Fung and repeated his story, that he had a friend 36 hours out on a passage to Manila and likely to be in need of help after the sudden arrival of Typhoon Tina.

'Can you tell me what resources you have if they send a May Day?'

'We have Puma helicopters with winches, but they have a maximum operating range of 350 miles, so any boat further away than 100 miles would have to rely on its distress call being answered by commercial shipping. The winds generated by Tina are gusting up to 130 mph and no helicopter can operate in those conditions anyway. What's the name of the yacht?'

'Kwinana', Gunn replied.

'OK Mr Knight; thank you for alerting us. How far do you think he will be from Hong Kong?'

'It's a fast yacht and he's been out for 36 hours - about 150 to 200 miles on a south-east course to Manila.'

'OK........we will call you as soon as we hear anything.'

# CHAPTER 23

Jogging back into the lobby of the Mandarin Hotel, John ran straight into David Morris.

'Hello, Mark,' he said loudly for the benefit of everyone in the vicinity. Then, lowering his voice, he said, 'Look, I won't be more than a few minutes checking-in and dropping off my bag in the room. I'm meeting Andrew Smeaton, the Consul General, in twenty minutes and would like you to come with me. Can we meet down here in......ten minutes?'

Twenty minutes later, they arrived at the Consulate General in Supreme Court Road and were shown into his office. Andrew Smeaton was new to Gunn, but it was evident that David Morris, BID's Controller for SE Asia, and he had known each other for some time. After the introductions, they both looked to Gunn for an update on Quiller's movements.

'So that's about it for now,' Gunn concluded. 'He's in a very seaworthy yacht with an experienced skipper and crew, about 200 miles to the south-east of Hong Kong, facing winds of 130 mph and rising. Should the yacht - called 'Kwinana' - transmit a distress call, there's not a hope in hell of getting a chopper there in these conditions so they'd have to rely on assistance from commercial shipping.'

'It's not quite as bleak as that, John,' Andrew remarked, twisting a silver propelling pencil in his fingers. 'As luck would have it, Hong Kong has just completed its annual search and rescue exercise in conjunction with the forward elements of the US Seventh Fleet; SAREX 2008 finished last week. The aircraft carrier USS George Washington is not very far away, currently avoiding Typhoon Tina, as they've named it, I expect, and within that carrier group there are two fast attack nuclear submarines - USS Dallas and USS Los Angeles. All these ships have taken part in SAREX 2008 and I believe that as your assignment has been a joint one with the CIA, our friends in the US Consulate would be prepared to consider some form of assistance, should we ask for it.'

*

The three yachtsmen had endured severe storm conditions before, but nothing like the fury of the wind and sea generated by Typhoon Tina, which now seemed to be doing everything in its power to destroy Kwinana. Following their second knockdown after being hurled beam on to the seas, Stuart handed over the wheel to Mike and clawed his way down below. The scene below decks was chaotic. The fore'ard hatch had been split by the weight of the seas breaking over it, letting in the sea. Stores, equipment, food and clothing had broken out of lockers and stowage and now swilled around in seawater on the cabin sole. Stuart undid the lee sheet holding Quiller into his bunk, explaining that he had to come up on deck in case they needed to abandon ship. But Quiller wasn't going anywhere; he punched Stuart and re-tied the lee sheets.

Stuart heaved himself back on deck and shouted in Aaron's ear that he needed help to drag Dave up on deck. The two men went below and together tried to get Quiller out of his bunk, but found they were up against someone who had either temporarily or permanently lost his mind and fought with the strength of a madman. Both men retreated back on deck. Aaron suggested trying to talk to Dave and opened the hatch once again, but only just recoiled in time as Quiller lunged at him with one of the sharp galley knives.

'Where's the emergency pack of supplies to go in the life-raft?' Stuart shouted into Aaron's ear. Aaron pointed at the companionway hatch.

'Down there!......just inside the hatch in the locker on the port side!'

'We've gotta get it up on deck! She won't take much more of this!' They opened the hatch once again to be met by a frenzied Quiller who lashed out with his knife. Stuart aimed a well-placed kick at Quiller's head, which knocked him back into the water on the cabin sole; Stuart noted it was now nearly a foot in depth. Aaron leant into the cabin and grabbed the waterproof container of emergency supplies, but as he pulled back holding the container, Quiller struggled to his feet and lashed out again with his knife, slicing his right arm. Again, Stuart kicked Quiller back into the cabin as he pulled Aaron clear of the hatch. Both men fell back into the cockpit, gasping for breath as wave after wave broke over them from the stern. Stuart examined the gash in Aaron's arm. It was deep, but thankfully hadn't hit a major vessel. Stuart hauled himself back to Mike, who was fighting with the wheel to try and keep the yacht stern-on to the seas.

'There's over a foot of water in the cabin!' Stuart shouted. Mike nodded to indicate he'd heard. 'Twenty minutes max before she goes down, Mike!'

'What do we do about Dave?'

'I'll try and knock him out so we can drag him out of there.'

'Don't risk getting yourself hurt, Stu! We need you!'

'Don't worry, if the worse comes to the worse we'll have to leave him to fend for himself!'

Once again, Stuart crawled forward, and removed the largest of the winch handles from the locker by the hatch and held it behind his back. Aaron helped him open the hatch. Quiller swung round like a caged animal, thrusting with the knife, but both men kept out of his reach. Aaron made as though to go down the hatch. Quiller rushed towards the hatch with every apparent intention of driving the long galley knife into his chest, but as he reached out of the hatch, Stuart swung the heavy winch handle down on the back of his head with a crack that both of them heard in spite of the typhoon. Quiller slumped unconscious over the companionway sill.

The two men dragged his limp body out through the hatch into the cockpit. They clipped his safety line onto a ring bolt and then, using a light spinnaker sheet, they tied him to the port winch pedestal, immobilising his arms. Stuart glanced below decks. The water was now two feet deep and rising. He jumped down into the cabin and tried the radio. It was dead; the batteries had shorted out. He closed the hatch and crawled back to Mike.

'Cabin's two-thirds full, mate!'

'Time to go?'

'Reckon s...' but Stuart stopped when he saw the expression on Mike's face. He spun round to see Aaron lying on the cockpit floor and Quiller coming for him with another knife, which he must have had concealed in one of the large side pockets of his sailing oilskins.

'Oh shit!' Stuart turned to defend himself, but Quiller suddenly froze, staring over his shoulder. Stuart risked a glance and saw the biggest wave he'd ever seen looming higher and higher astern, like some great grey wall. The yacht was now low in the water and sluggish. It heaved itself up once more to try and let the wave pass under it and nearly succeeded, but the curling crest lifted the stern and flipped the yacht over in the pitch-pole they'd dreaded.

For thirty seconds the world was a roaring surge of sea, debris, ropes and rigging; and then relative calm returned as the yacht righted itself, jerking arthritically. Kwinana was sinking; the mast had snapped off a third of the way along its length and the top portion had driven through the cabin roof like a lance, smashing it wide open, letting the sea pour greedily in. The next trough the yacht plunged into would be its last. Stuart looked around dumbly; partially stunned by something that had hit him as the boat cartwheeled down the face of the wave. Mike had pulled the life raft out and thrown it over the side of the yacht. Aaron was crawling back towards him, dragging the emergency container. The fourth member of their crew had gone. Stuart started to move towards the hatch but Mike's hand stopped him. He turned round. Mike shook his head.

*

Gunn's mobile phone buzzed suddenly in his pocket. He apologised to the Consul General and David Morris, but took the call. It was the SAR co-ordination centre. He listened silently, the others watching him intently, then thanked the caller and hung up.

'The emergency beacon on Kwinana's life-raft has started transmitting a May-Day with a GPS fix of its position. The SAR centre has just told me that the nearest ship is a container carrier called Tokyo Star, which has estimated two hours to reach them. The centre has warned me that getting the crew from the life-raft to the ship in the current conditions will be virtually impossible.'

'Do we know how many of the crew are in the life-raft?' Andrew Smeaton asked.

'No; it's the Emergency Position Indicating Radio Beacon that's transmitting. It's activated automatically when the raft inflates.' Gunn explained.

'I think we can maybe do better than that,' Andrew said, picking up his phone and dialling a number. 'Gerry, it's Andrew; you were expecting my call? Oh, that's great news! You'll tell the Maritime Rescue Coordination Centre? Excellent. Thank you...thanks again,' he replaced the phone in its cradle with a triumphant flourish. 'That was Gerry Hornbeam, my opposite number in the US Consulate up the road. They've picked up the signal - the US Navy's picked it up - and will be at the position in a matter of minutes.

He said they have the necessary equipment to rescue the crew in these conditions. He said that one good turn deserved another; apparently you saved the life of a CIA agent a few days ago, John?'

*

'You go first!' Stuart shouted at Mike, 'then you can help Aaron into the raft!' There were only seconds remaining for the gallant Kwinana before she disappeared below the broiling surface. Stuart held the painter of the life raft while Mike struggled over the side and dived through the entrance in the raft's inflated canopy. Stuart grabbed the emergency container and passed it through after him, only letting go when he felt Mike grab it from inside the raft. But Mike grabbed his arm and pointed frantically over his shoulder. Kwinana was going down with both the life raft and Aaron still attached. Stuart pulled out the knife from its sheath in his oilskin trousers and slashed through Aaron's nylon safety line. Then he cut the life-raft painter and tied it and the safety line together as the seas finally enveloped the cockpit, eager to drag the yacht to the ocean depths.

In desperation Mike pulled on the painter, heaving Aaron closer to the raft. All the while he kept his eyes fixed on Stuart, knowing that if he lost sight if his friend he probably wouldn't see him again. But another wave tumbled into them, sweeping him away and out of reach. Though Mike strained desperately to keep him in sight, in the turmoil of mountainous seas, it was impossible to see even another ship, let alone a person in the water. In spite of the icy rain slapping into his face, Mike felt warm tears burn his salt-stung eyes before they were washed away. His closest friend had sacrificed his life to save his crew, and now he was drifting away into oblivion. Mike finally heaved Aaron through the aperture in the canopy into the well of the inflatable. Together they stared out into the heaving crags all around as the raft sank down into the trough.

To his astonishment, Mike suddenly spotted the dayglo orange of Stuart's jacket hurtling towards them as he bodysurfed down the face of an oncoming wave. He crashed into the raft as he reached the bottom of the trough. Mike grabbed the hood of the jacket and clung to it with a ferocity borne of desperation. As he felt the raft lifting for the next wave, he heaved with every ounce of strength left in his body and pulled Stuart over the side. All three of them collapsed exhausted into the bottom of the raft.

'Can't think what kept you, mate,' Mike gasped when he had enough. 'Please let's have no more heroics you dumb bastard!' and they clung to each other, cold and exhausted.

Stuart was the first of the three to stir. He pulled the emergency container towards him and unzipped the waterproof cover. Mike had grabbed a torch from the locker by the wheel before he'd abandoned Kwinana and now shone it on the container, an improvement on the dim light cast by the automatic light that had illuminated as soon as the raft self-inflated. Stuart found the first aid pack and then, with Mike's help, removed Aaron's jacket. Fortunately, the knife had gone through the fleshy part of his upper arm and the wound had stopped bleeding. Stuart unwrapped a bandage and bound it tightly, swearing as the little raft roller-coasted up and down huge waves.

'Wishful thinking,' Mike shouted, 'or is this fucking typhoon moving away?'

'No, I think you're right. Either that or we're getting used to it.' There had been no word from Aaron; Stuart checked his pulse and squeezed his hands. 'Very weak and his hands are stiff – think it's a combination of shock and hypothermia,' they pressed themselves closer against Aaron to try and keep him warm. 'What in sweet heaven happened to Dave? He turned psycho! I've never seen sea terrors like that!'

'Forget it; if he hadn't been in such a hurry to leave and so up-front with the cash we needed to pay off our debts in Hong Kong, we wouldn't have taken the risk of trying to outrun Tina!'

'Certain amount of truth there, but we didn't have to go! Final decision was mine and I got it wrong!'

'As I said, forget it. We tried to...' but whatever Mike was about to say stopped dead, as both of them clearly heard, cutting through the white noise of the storm, a voice hailing them.

"Ahoy there! ahoy there! Kwinana life raft!' Mike crawled across the heaving rubber sole of their craft and unclipped the flap covering the entrance while Stuart clung on to his safety line. Mike stuck his head out into the cold chaos again, squinting against the stinging rain-laden wind. His view was blocked by a huge black metal wall that rose out of the sea a few metres away. Craning his neck upwards, he made out the figures SSN 668 painted in white on the side.

'Jesus Christ!' He dipped his head back inside the

raft. 'There's a fucking submarine sitting right next to us!' At that moment a powerful spotlight beamed through the darkness, lighting them up like principal actors on a giant stage.

'Stay where you are! Stay where you are! Someone will come to you!' Moments later a figure in an immersion suit and lifejacket jumped over the side of the hull on the end of a safety line and grabbed hold of the raft.

'...the weakest...first!' their rescuer shouted, spitting out mouthfuls of seawater, his words drowned out by the thunderous noise. He unclipped something from his waist and passed them a second safety line attached to a circular halter. 'Put...the...line on from behind....' Stuart and Mike heard, but it was enough. They heaved Aaron across to the gap in the canopy, put the flexible halter around him and then eased him on his back over the side of the raft. They could see more men dropping down beside the hull of the huge submarine, which had positioned itself to act as a partial barrier between the waves and the raft. The sub's crew were all attached to safety lines, looking like spiders in a row. They took up the tension on Aaron's safety line and then, with precise timing, as both raft and submarine rose on a wave, they all pulled together. Aaron slipped over the side of the raft and up onto the sub, hardly getting his boots wet.

'This time you go first!' Mike put the halter over Stuart's head and helped him out of the life-raft. He made it safely onto the sub and then it was Mike's turn. He put the halter over his head and then with the help of the crewman who had been in the water throughout the rescue, was hauled aboard. Before he was pulled to safety himself, their rescuer slashed the rubber skin of the raft so that it would sink, then signalled and felt himself lifted out of the water, gratefully touching the slick-wet black skin of the fast attack nuclear submarine, USS Los Angeles.

*

Bob Chang had offered to drive Gunn over to the airport to meet the crew of Kwinana. The message of the rescue of three of the four-man crew had reached Gunn at the Mandarin Hotel via the Consul General. They had been winched from the sub onto a Sea Stallion helicopter and taken to the aircraft carrier USS George Washington. One of the yacht's crew had been suffering from mild hypothermia and a flesh wound to the right arm, but had been pronounced fit for the one hour flight to Hong Kong.

Bob Chang handed Gunn a small tape recorder, but chose to stay in the car while an official drove Gunn across the airport to the Hong Kong Government Air Services SAR Hangar.

'Mr Knight? Tony Field, Head of Air Services. I was told to expect you. You have an interest in the three men on their way to us from the Seventh Fleet?'

'Yes, just a routine matter; I won't keep them more than a couple of minutes.'

'No problem. The Australian Consulate General is sending a car for them and arranging medical treatment. Here's the helicopter now.' As he spoke the dark blue Sea Stallion with US Navy markings flared out and landed at the SAR enclave. The three yachtsmen were helped out of the helicopter and escorted into the hangar, where Tony introduced them to Gunn.

'This won't take more than a few minutes. I'm from the British Consul General's office here in Hong Kong. This concerns the fourth member of your crew, a British national.'

'You mean Dave Morgan?' Stuart asked.

'Stuart isn't it? Are you Kwinana's skipper?'

'Was mate; she's at the bottom of the Pacific.'

'Dave Morgan's real name was Ian Quiller. He's a serial murderer and blackmailer. You're all lucky to be alive. I need you to tell me what happened to him, then you can go on your way,' and Gunn switched on the small recorder.

'Christ, that explains a lot,' Stuart said. Then he and Mike told Gunn about how they had met up with Quiller in the Bull and Bear, taught him the rudiments of offshore sailing, accepted his payment, which enabled them to clear their debts in Hong Kong, and then briefly recounted the sequence of events from the time they were hit by Typhoon Tina to the moment Quiller was washed overboard.

'We tried to save him but...' Mike shrugged and trailed off, looking anxiously at Gunn.

'Look, don't worry,' he reassured them, smiling. 'The main thing is that you're okay. And you've probably saved the UK taxpayer an expensive trial. You're free to go now, thanks guys.' Gunn shook hands with them and returned with his airport official to the car park where Bob was waiting.

'Okay?' Bob asked.

'.....and then there was one. He's dead. That just leaves Soames, who we think is on his way back to St

Vincent. I need to speak to BID.'

*

Just after six Claudine's mobile rang while she was having supper on the veranda at the Sunset Inn. She got up from the table and went out to the courtyard at the front to take the call.

'He's just come into the arrival hall.'

'Thanks Toby; keep me updated.' Claudine ended the call and returned to her meal, but her phone rang again ten minutes later as she was gulping down some coffee.

'He's been picked up by a car. I have a car and scooter followin' him.'

Claudine signed the bill, returned to her room and changed into jeans, trainers and T-shirt. She put her hair up and covered it with a baseball cap. Her mobile rang again.

'I'm on my way to pick you up on my bike. I'll be about five minutes.' In less than five minutes, Toby pulled up on his motorbike and handed Claudine a spare helmet. Before leaving the Sunset Inn, Toby made a call, listened quietly for a few moments, then hung up. 'The car's headin' down Plantation Road.' He dialled another number. 'I just need to pass this on to Ashling; she's keepin' a log of what's happenin' in case somethin' happens to us.'

'That's good to know,' Claudine muttered truthfully as she replaced her cap with the helmet.

'Okay, let's go,' Toby let in the clutch and the powerful bike sprang off in pursuit of Mike Soames. They followed Plantation Road, driving past the church where Claudine had turned off to the clinic. It switch-backed round the steep sides of Soufrière Volcano before straightening out into a valley, lit by the early rising moon, with fields full of maize, bananas and sugar cane. Toby pulled the bike over to the side of the road to make a call.

'Uh, the car's turned into Sir Leo Hugues estate,' he told Ashling, glancing round at Claudine. She shrugged quizzically. He hung up, 'Jus' a short way from here, there's a track that goes roun' to the back of his estate. The ground's higher there so we may be able to see somethin'...'

'Let's do it.' Before moving off, they both removed their helmets and tied them to the bike's side panniers. Toby switched off the lights and after a couple of hundred yards, turned off the road onto the track. There was more than enough light from the moon to see where they were going. The track curved around above and behind the Hugues estate, a palatial white building with pillared colonnades and stately, manicured grounds; it reeked of corruption and backhanders.

Toby stopped the bike when they were directly behind the house, which was about a hundred yards away, and they both dismounted. Toby pushed the bike off the track into the undergrowth, pulled the thick foliage over it and then set off along the track for about fifty yards before stopping abruptly. He pointed to a pathway between the crops leading down from the left side of the track towards the house. He held his finger to his lips and then whispered with his head close to Claudine's.

'This leads down to the outhouses at the back of

the main house. The Commissioner has some local groundsmen who occasionally walk roun' the property.'

'How do you know all this?'

'When I was a kid we came here to steal the bananas and maize.'

'Look,' Claudine stopped him just as he was heading off down the path. 'Just remember I don't have my gun as I had to leave it in Rio.'

'Don' worry, I'll take care of you.'

'Gallantry is one thing, but up against someone like Soames - even disable...........I'd feel better with a bit of firepower.'

'Shhhhhh...' Toby pushed Claudine down. They both crouched in the thick undergrowth on the side of the path. The sweet, earthy aroma of burning cannabis resin reached them first, followed by muted voices and then the sound of footfalls on the path. Two men emerged out of the darkness, each carrying a nightstick in one hand and a joint in the other, chuckling amicably.

'Won't they find your bike?' Claudine whispered. Toby shook his head.

'Too stoned; come on,' Toby led the way down the path until they reached the outhouses. They waited for a few minutes in the shadows, watching and listening, before creeping off again. As they reached the house itself, cooking smells and clinking of utensils against crockery indicated that they were at the rear of the kitchen.

Toby paused as someone emerged from the scullery area and emptied something into a bin. Once the door had closed, they moved on round to the right side of the house towards the main reception rooms, from which light spilled out onto the gravelled path. Toby stopped and leaned towards Claudine.

'These two windows are the Commissioner's private study. All the other windows on this side are the lounge. The dining room is on the other side of the house.' He tapped in a text message to Ashling. There was no problem getting a signal this far from the city as the Commissioner had installed a powerful aerial in the grounds of his property. Once Ashling confirmed that she'd received his message, he put the phone away and edged along the side of the building to the study windows. He crouched down onto his hands and knees so that only his eyes would show above the windowsill and risked a furtive peek. He ducked down again and motioned to Claudine to follow him on hands and knees. She crawled under the window and then stood up beside Toby once they were past it.

'Soames is in there with the Commissioner,' he whispered.

'Send a message to Ashling confirming this - say you've got visual. It implicates Hugues in the conspiracy with Quiller and the murders on this island and elsewhere. Then we should get the hell....' but she was interrupted by a sudden movement from the front of the house and they were both illuminated by a powerful torch.

'Sergeant Charbonnier! How nice of you to take an interest in my security. Who's your friend?'

## CHAPTER 24

Gunn and his controller, David Morris, caught a Cathy Pacific flight back to London, which arrived at 6.10 in the morning. They cleared customs by 7am and then caught the Heathrow Express to Paddington. The two men walked into Kingsroad House just before eight and headed straight to Miles Thompson's office. For the first time in over two weeks, or so it seemed, Miles smiled broadly, pushing his glasses up the bridge of his nose as he poured them each a coffee with more flourish than usual.

'Well, Typhoon Tina has done all of us a favour, not least the PM. He almost fainted with relief when I told him that Quiller's dead,' said Miles. 'Thanks for your email David. Now we must deal with Soames. Don't bother unpacking, John, as you're booked on a flight to St Vincent in two-and-a-half-hours.'

'Good. It won't be easy catching him so the less of a head start he has…'

'Maybe, but someone's done you a favour. Our agent in Rio sent Soames on his way with a broken right wrist, severely sprained ankle and a deep gash in his head. But still, don't underestimate him.'

'Impressive…'

'Yes, I wouldn't want to get on the wrong side of her, she's a brilliant engineer. Well anyway, Tony Taylor has already sent your hardware ahead of you in the diplomatic bag, which will be picked up by the British Consul, Ben Myers. His office is on Bay Street on the waterfront, but all of that's in a brief Jason has prepared for you. You can read it on the flight. We've warned Malcolm Slater that you'll arrive as Mark Knight. Chopper's ready to fly you to Gatwick. John, we need this to be wrapped up. Do you have any questions?'

'Yes. Claudine?'

'She's already in St Vincent, with Toby Charbonnier. They're keeping an eye on Soames, but I've told them not to go anywhere near him.'

'Good,' Gunn said again, knocking back his coffee and standing to leave.

'Uh, John?'

'Yes, Miles?'

'That was good job you did in Iraq. Gained us some serious points with the Americans; thank you.'

Gunn smiled and nodded then made his way quickly down to Jason Wolstenholme's office to get his brief, before getting into the Gazelle helicopter standing by on the roof to fly him to Gatwick. He was eager to keep the momentum up, aware that before too long his body would find some way of forcing him to get the rest he should have taken after his surgery.

During the flight, Gunn read the brief, which explained the suspension of the Police Commissioner in St Vincent, Malcolm Slater's promotion and the events that had occurred in Rio. He read the report a second time, set his watch to Eastern Caribbean local time and then fell fast asleep.

He arrived at Joshua Airport at 17.15 local time and forty minutes later was in a taxi on his way to Bay Street in Kingstown, having phoned ahead to check the British Consul would be in his office. His call was expected and he was told that he could pick up his package from the duty receptionist at the Consulate. Having collected his two Glocks, he went over to Police Headquarters and asked the Desk Sergeant if he could see the Acting Commissioner.

'Who shall I say is askin' for him, sir?'

'Mark Knight.'

'Wait here a minute, sir, an' I'll check if he's free.'

'Thanks,' Gunn put his backpack down and paced around the reception area, stretching his legs after the long flight. His eyes scanned the framed photographic portraits of St Vincent's Police Commissioners, arranged from earliest to most recent in a single row around the walls. At the last framed photograph in the sequence he stopped dead. Staring back at him was a face he'd seen over and over again in his nightmares. The last time Gunn had seen the face of the man in the photograph in front of him was in Nina's kitchen, just before he felt the crashing blow of a bullet bursting into his skull.

'You okay, sir?' the old Desk Sergeant asked with genuine concern.

'I'm fine.' Gunn took one last look at the picture of Sir Leo Hugues.

'The Commissioner will see you now, sir. Constable Thomas, here, will take you to his office.'

Gunn followed the constable up the stairs to the Commissioner's office. Malcolm Slater got up from his desk and greeted Gunn warmly once they were alone.

'You look like a young Castro with that,' he chuckled, pointing at his chin.

'That's a new one!'

'Miles told me some of what you've been up to.

You're a glutton for punishment, sir! Now, we've got Toby and Claudine keepin' an eye on Mr Soames. Jus' let me check what's happenin',' Malcolm dialled a number. 'Ashling, any new...right...okay...right, thank you,' he put the phone down. 'Soames arrived at the airport twenty minutes ago and was met by a car. Toby has two men followin' him. We should have an idea any moment where he's goin'.'

'I'm pretty sure I can tell you where he's going.'

'How?'

'There were three men in Nina's kitchen when I was shot. The two Cubans who Soames killed in Miami and a third man. You have a photograph of him downstairs.'

'What? Where? In our rogues' gallery?'

'No, on the wall; it was Sir Leo Hugues; that's a face I'll never forget.'

'Are you sure?'

'Sure as I'm standing here talking to you.'

'Then we need to get Toby and Claudine away...' but Malcolm was interrupted by his phone. He picked it up, 'please call lat...oh sorry, Ashling........he's gone to the Commissioner's house?...Toby's followin' on his bike with Claudine...' Malcolm looked at Gunn, was shaking his head frantically. 'Right Ashling, listen. Get my car an' driver an' our armed response unit an' tell them to be ready to go in five minutes, okay?' Malcolm slammed down the receiver and started strapping on his holster and gun. 'John, I believe you, which means Toby and Claudine are in trouble. They are focusing on Soames as the main danger; they have no idea about Sir Leo. Are you armed?'

'Yes.'

'Okay, let's go.' By the time they reached the courtyard at the rear of the building, the Commissioner's Landcruiser was humming its impatience, already in gear, and six armed police were standing in two ranks next to a black minibus. Malcolm spoke briefly to the squad's Sergeant then dialled Ashling's number on the front desk as he joined Gunn in the Landcruiser.

'Ashling, it's me. Listen. It looks like the Sir Leo Hugues could be involved with the shooting.........yes, Nina Ramone and Mr Gunn. Please make sure no one is told where we're goin'. If anybody asks, we're headin' for the airport - say there's been a security alert... Okay, good. If you need to call me, use my cell-phone, not the radio. If you see any suspicious behaviour by anyone at HQ, I want to know about it.' He turned to Gunn. 'When we get to the house, you go roun' to the back and make your way into the house. Call my cell-phone when you're ready for us to move in from the front.'

*

'Since you both seem so interested in lookin' aroun' my house, why don't you come inside.......no, Sergeant Charbonnier, don' even think about runnin' away,' Sir Leo added as Toby turned to see if they could get back to his motorbike the way they had come. But as he turned he saw one of Hugues security guards blocking the way, cradling a pump-action shotgun. Both of them were searched before they were escorted into the house. They found themselves face-to-face with Mike Soames, who was still unable to move without the aid of a crutch.

'Come to apologise for the party pranks you pulled on me in Rio?' Soames muttered softly to Claudine, the ghost of a smile twitching the corners of his lips, though his eyes bored into her, unblinking, with a chilling ferocity. Claudine shivered despite the humidity. It was a look that revealed he was already planning exactly what he'd do to her, and in what order. Fear yanked at her gut, and she found her legs shaking uncontrollably. She tried to take a few deep breaths, but her abdominal muscles were clenched tightly by adrenalin, forcing the air out in a shallow gasps. In the years that she'd worked for BID, no one had frightened her as much as Mike Soames. She and Toby were prodded into the living room by the end of a shotgun barrel. Neither said anything.

'Michel' - Hugues insisted on using the French pronunciation of any name - 'and I have been watchin' you both on VDUs in my study ever since you turned off the road. I updated my estate with security cameras last year. Now the problem I have is what to do with you both. Tomorrow I will be payin' a visit to our revered Prime Minister, with a few of my friends, and I will then take over as Prime Minister. The two of you would be an embarrassment. Luckily, Monsieur Soames has a solution.' He smiled a smile that made the skin tighten on Toby's scalp.

'Sir…I...listen…'

'What, Sergeant?'

'I warn you not to do this…' Toby didn't know what, but he had to try and buy them some time - enough time for Ashling to realise something's wrong. It was their only chance.

'He's right,' Claudine said suddenly, grasping Toby's intention. Anything to delay being alone with Soames. 'BID…' she began, but was cut off.

'Shut the fuck up,' Soames hissed, then added to Sir Leo, 'I'm taking them.' Sir Leo simply nodded and smiled again, but in the next second it was wiped away by the squeal and static splutter of a loud hailer. Their heads whipped towards the front of the house.

'Sir Leo Hugues, this is the Acting Commissioner and armed response squad of the Royal St Vincent Police! You are under arrest for alleged crimes of murder, conspiracy to murder and conspiracy to armed insurrection against the Government of St Vincent! Mr Soames is under arrest for alleged crimes of murder and conspiracy to murder. You have five seconds to release Sergeant Charbonnier and Miss de Cartaret and come out of the front of the house!'

*

As soon as the Landcruiser reached the Hugues estate, Gunn jumped out and, keeping to the deep shadow, made his way round to the rear of the house. The clatter of pots and pans and the aroma of meat cooking guided him to the kitchen door. He removed the Glock 17 from his shoulder holster and pushed open the kitchen door. There were three kitchen staff, a woman and two men, who stared open mouthed at Gunn. He held up a St Vincent Police badge Malcolm had given him and held a finger to his lips, as he silently moved through into the dining room. He could hear voices coming from the other side of the hallway. He edged through the doorway into the hall and across to a door beyond the one from where the voices were coming. The room he entered looked like a study and had another door leading into what had to be some sort of reception room. He took out his phone and dialled Malcolm's number.

'Go,' he murmured, and before he hung up he heard clicking and rustling as the gunmen cocked their weapons and got into position.

He eased open the door from the study into the next room just a fraction. The man who was doing the talking had his back to Gunn. In front of him were Claudine and Toby, covered by Hugues security guards armed with shotguns. The gap in the door wasn't quite wide enough to see who was standing on Claudine's left; he assumed it was Mike Soames. Suddenly everyone jumped as Malcolm's booming voice cut through the cicadas evening overture. There was a split second of silence, and then Sir Leo darted towards the window, followed by one of his henchmen. Gunn heard the front door burst open before the full five seconds was up, then the living room filled with armed police in protective vests. Malcolm Slater strode in after them.

'Tell your men to leave the house at once or we'll kill Sergeant Charbonnier and Miss de Carteret,' Hugues shouted, giving up on the window and turning to face his accusers.

'I repeat, Hugues' - Gunn noticed the Commissioner's title had been dropped - 'you and Mr Soames are bein' arrested for murder and conspiracy to murder.'

'Don't be ridiculous, Malcolm. What proof do you have?'

'Very reliable; from the man you tried to murder with Nina Ramone.'

'What man?' the Commissioner snorted indignantly.

'The man standin' behind you.'

The Commissioner, who had drawn his large frame up to its full height, was about to make some remark about 'not falling for that old trick' when he saw the expression of horror on Soames' face. He whipped around and saw Gunn standing in the study doorway.

'You…' Sir Leo's mouth tried to articulate words but no sound came out. For a man of his size, he moved very quickly. He suddenly dived for an automatic, which had been on the table beside him, grabbed it and turned it on Gunn. But his body jerked as two shots reverberated around the room; one from Malcolm Slater's automatic and the other from the pump-action gun of the sergeant commanding the police squad. The gun fell from his hands and the Commissioner slumped to the floor, groaning and writhing. Soames chose this moment and grabbed Claudine.

'Let me leave or I'll break her fucking neck!' he snarled. He hobbled backwards towards one of the doors, swinging his automatic back and forth in front of him as he went. It was a desperate and pointless gesture, as both Hugues' security guards had dropped their weapons. Claudine kicked back hard with her heel at Soames' sprained ankle, bending forward at the same time. Two bullets from Gunn's Glock hit Soames in the head, hurling him back in a spray of blood and bone chips which embedded themselves in the expensive carpet.

There was a moment of stunned silence, then professionalism took over as all Hugues' security guards were cautioned and police radios crackled, alerting Police HQ to incoming prisoners. The sergeant, who was kneeling by Hugues' body, called over to Malcolm, who was speaking to Toby and Claudine.

'He's still alive, sir......mutterin' about 'wreckin'...or somethin'.' Claudine bent down by the dying Commissioner.

'It's French.........it's "requin" - it means the same as "tiburon".........that's what that Cuban gunman was trying to say in Miami before he died. They both mean 'shark'!

## OTHER BOOKS FEATURING JOHN GUNN BY BRIAN NICHOLSON

### GWEILO

The theft of a birthright has been the motive for murder since Jacob usurped it from his elder brother, Esau. The birthright to the immense riches of Hong Kong will be stolen at midnight on 30th June 1997 from the descendants of the first settlers on that inhospitable, fever-ridden island of decaying granite, as a result of the signing of the Anglo-Sino Joint Declaration in 1984. Not only the New Territories will be handed back to China - acquired by Great Britain in the 1898 treaty - but also Hong Kong Island which was ceded to Great Britain in perpetuity after the first Opium war in 1842, thus forming the birthright of the descendants of those intrepid traders and settlers who had arrived in Hong Kong - 'a place of sweet water' - under the straining canvas of the triangular sky and moonraker topsails of their lean-hulled trading clippers.

In 1986, two years after the signing of the Joint Declaration, the reactor at the Chernobyl nuclear power station exploded. The subsequent meltdown and escape of radioactive material turned the surrounding area for hundreds of square miles into a deserted wasteland of mutant plants and animals and humans riddled with cancer. The world reeled in horror and condemned the corrupt and decaying Soviet Union for its crass incompetence. But one man in Hong Kong, whose ancestor had disembarked from the first of the clippers to anchor in Victoria Harbour and whose father had died for Hong Kong, tortured to death by the Japanese occupation force in 1943, saw the Chernobyl disaster in a different light. It offered the solution to his all-consuming fury at being dispossessed of his inheritance and betrayed by his own country. If he and his descendants couldn't have Hong Kong, then no one would have it - least of all the Chinese.

## AL SAMAK

.......is about intrigue, treachery, conspiracy, revenge and violence. It's a story of the flawed and bungled political manoeuvring in the UN before the invasion of Iraq by coalition forces in March 2003. It's the story of Russia's fight to protect its embryo democracy against plotting by die-hard communists. It's the story of Iraq's struggle to achieve a WMD capability to prevent the invasion. It's the story of the desperate measures taken by the intelligence agencies of the coalition to prevent a nuclear holocaust in the Middle East.

It's John Gunn's second assignment with the British Intelligence Directorate, but above all, it's a story.... a story of 21st Century political intrigue and weapons of mass destruction, but this story started as long ago as the 7th Century, as a storm-lashed papyrus raft broke up in the Arabian Sea......but is it a story?....you decide.

## ASHANTI GOLD

An investigation into the disappearance of an ineffective agent, from the now-defunct Secret Intelligence Service at the British High Commission in Accra, reveals a conspiracy to overthrow the governments of West African countries by subversion, terrorism and tribal civil war.

The cruelty and corruption of the 18th century Portugese, Dutch and British slave-traders who raped West Africa of its human and mineral resources, is easily surpassed by that of 21st Century, power-hungry, West African exiles, ruthless arms dealers, diplomats and politicians on both sides of the Atlantic who are involved in the conspiracy.

Governments can be brought down by subversion, terrorism and civil war. Terrorists need weapons which must be bought with money....lots of it. Gold is money......and in Ghana is the priceless horde of Ashanti Gold ingots in the vaults of the Bank of Ghana and the richest gold mine in the world is at Sawaba in the Ashanti Region where nuggets as big as walnuts can be illegally panned from the Ofin River and then sold to dealers abroad......just as was done during the 18th Century slave trade.

## FIRE DRAGON

The slaughter of half a million Communists by Indonesia's President in the 1950s is a weeping sore for Arief Sulitsono (Alias Dr Ramano Rusman) the illegitimate son of Aidit- the Communist leader - who is determined to return Indonesia to a Communist

Dictatorship. He realises that he can do nothing against the power of the USA unless he and other developing countries of NAM possess nuclear weapons. He therefore enters into a conspiracy with the North Koreans to help them avoid US interference with their nuclear weapons programme.

Fortuitously, he stumbles on the enormous treasure amassed by Admiral Yamamoto and hidden in the islands off Irian Jaya and uses this unlimited funding to build a rocket launch site on Waigeo Island on the Equator. From this rocket launch site he plans to place the North Korean nuclear warheads in geo-stationary orbit out of reach of IAEA inspection and US satellite surveillance and available to any country resisting US interference.

Rusman's plan unravels because there are other clues to Yamamoto's treasure and his launch site is being built on the most likely epi-centre of a cataclysmic earthquake. This is John Gunn's fourth assignment for the British Intelligence Directorate where he is confronted by man-eating dragons in 'the ring of fire'.

## CALYPSO

The secret of what happened to the weapons of mass destruction - if they ever existed, died with Saddam Hussein on the gallows. Or did it? The United Nations teams of nuclear, biological and chemical scientists who searched for the WMDs were on a hiding to nothing, looking for something that Saddam Hussein had had ten years to hide in a landmass the same size as the United Kingdom. All of those involved in the hiding of those weapons had been murdered - some by Saddam Hussein himself, so we are told - or had they? One man who knew a great deal about the research and production of biological and chemical weapons had been sent to the USA just prior to the destruction of the World Trade Centre's twin towers in September 2001. In the 9/11 aftermath of mass arrests by the CIA, living under an alias, that man was incarcerated, along with some 600 other suspected terrorists, in Camp X-ray at Guantanamo Bay. He was a relative of 'Chemical Ali' and had been the instrument of the mass gassing of the Kurdish enclave in Northern Iraq in 1988.

His real identity and his location in Camp Delta - to which all 'illegal combatants' were moved in Guantanamo Bay in April 2004 - were known by two parties - one wanted to achieve his release to kill him very slowly to ensure he suffered as much as the thousands of Kurds he gassed with Lewisite and Sarin. The other wanted him released because of his knowledge of where Saddam Hussein had hidden his store of biological and chemical weapons so that they could carry out the postponed atrocity in the UK which had been planned to coincide with 9/11 in the USA.

But how is all this connected to the disappearance of charter yachts in the Caribbean, a British warship which disappears like the Marie Celeste and a Queen's ransom of jewels and gold buried on a remote Caribbean island by Blackbeard the Pirate in the 18th Century? To answer those questions, John Gunn is sent to the Caribbean by the British Intelligence Directorate and this assignment leads to a terrifying race against time to prevent a catastrophic terrorist atrocity in London.

## BRIAN NICHOLSON

Excitement started at an early age for the author; returning from India with his parents and sister in June 1945, aged 3, the ship in which the family was embarked was chased by a Japanese submarine which fortunately had run out of torpedoes. Brian Nicholson had an equally exciting career in the army for 35 years of which the last 10 were spent working with the Secret Intelligence Service in various overseas appointments in Hong Kong, Ghana and Indonesia. He was made an OBE in 1985 and received a Commendation from the Commander British Forces Hong Kong in 1987 for his success in the negotiations with the Chinese Government on the handover of Hong Kong. At the request of the Royal Navy Funeral Department, while he was Defence Attaché in Jakarta, he solved the mystery of what happened to Sub-Lieutenant Gregor Riggs, the last of the 23 Commandoes on the ill-fated Australian Commando raid, Operation Rimau, on Japanese shipping in Singapore Harbour in World War 2. The author discovered the remains of the young officer on a remote island in the Indonesian Archipelago and returned them to the family for burial with full military honours at the Changi Military Cemetery in Singapore. In 1990, as Military Advisor to Jerry Rawlings, Ghana's President, he was directed to plan the successful West African military intervention in Liberia after the horrific videoed torture and assassination of the country's despotic dictator, Master

Sergeant Samuel Doe. These are but a few of the exciting experiences in a colourful career which formed the backdrop to the six books which he has written. He is currently researching his seventh book. Brian Nicholson is married with two adult daughters and lives in Richmond where his time is taken up with writing, golf, shooting, sailing, travel and caring for his classic British sports car.

THE AUTHOR

BRIAN NICHOLSON